The Water's Dead

Catherine Lea

First published in New Zealand by Brakelight Press in 2022.

This is a work of fiction. Names, characters, places, and incidents either are the product of the author's imagination or are used fictitiously. Any resemblance to actual persons, living or dead, events, or locales is entirely coincidental.

Copyright © 2022 by Catherine Lea All rights reserved.

No part of this book may be reproduced or used in any manner without written permission of the copyright owner except for the use of quotations in a book review.

A catalogue record for this book is available from the National Library of New Zealand.

ISBN (TPB) 978-0-473-59474-9
ISBN (POD) 979-8-419-46597-8

Printed and bound by YourBooks, Grenada, Wellington, New Zealand

Moko kauae—a physical embodiment of spirit woven back through ancient ancestral ties by the artist's hand. It is a symbol of identity, of belonging, of spiritual entitlement. It is only worn by Māori women.

PROLOGUE

It was dark outside. Way past bedtime. Lily had always gone to bed when her mummy told her to.

Not tonight.

Tonight she was outside in the dark bush. All on her own. No mummy to tell her everything would be alright. No Huia to look after her. Only Bun-Buns, her toy rabbit to cuddle.

Lily wanted to cry. But Huia had told her not to. She said Lily had to be a brave little girl. She had to be very quiet or the horrible man who'd locked them in the shed would come back. Huia had kicked out a board away from the back wall. The shed was smelly, the wood soft in places. Huia said it was rotten. But she could only make a hole big enough for Lily.

Lily had peered out. It was cold and scary out there. She'd told Huia she didn't want to go; that Kevin at school had told her all about the taniwha, horrible monsters that lived in the river.

But Huia had said, "You have to go. But don't make any noise. You have to be as quiet as a little mouse."

Crouching there and peering wide-eyed into the dark outside, Lily felt her chin crumple.

Then Huia gave her a little push. "Hurry. Go before he comes back."

Lily didn't want to go out there. But she didn't want the horrible man to come back, either. So, she got down on her hands and knees and crawled through.

Then she got up and started running.

But she was only six years old. She didn't know where to go. Huia had told her that if she ran along the river bank, she'd find a house. "Go to the first house you find," she'd told her. "Knock on the door and keep knocking until someone answers. Tell them where I am. And hurry."

But now, after running and running and finding nothing, she crouched in the black of the night with cold wet leaves brushing against her and mud all over her My Little Pony pajamas, and Lily wanted to curl up in a ball and cry. All she wanted was to be in mummy's arms, with mummy telling her it was okay.

Then, a sound.

Lily stopped crying. She wiped her nose on her sleeve and looked all around. Over by the rocks, something rustled in the bushes—the horrible man's dog.

Lily made a tiny squeak, then remembered she had to be very quiet, so she clapped both muddy hands over her mouth just in case another noise came out.

The rustling came nearer. The man whistled the dog but it was getting closer and closer. Now it was crashing around, back and forth through the bush just a few feet away, its big feet thudding through the undergrowth, its nose sniffing.

Lily curled herself up into the tiniest ball and squeezed her eyes closed.

Suddenly, bushes rustled, branches broke and there it was, standing over her, inches away, snarling and barking. When she peeked up all she could see was all those sharp white teeth as it barked and barked. All she could feel was its hot breath in her face. Then it lunged.

And Lily screamed.

CHAPTER 1

Detective Inspector Nyree Bradshaw
Whangārei North CIB

Detective Inspector Nyree Bradshaw had been on the road for forty-five minutes with Detective Sergeant Jack Callaghan at the wheel.

A suspected homicide, the boss had told her—female, young. The call had come in at 8:39 p.m. Now after 10 p.m. officers had already been assigned for the body, evidence, scene preservation. They'd probably been working the area for the best part of two hours already.

When the first few fat drops hit the windscreen, Nyree looked up into the dead-black sky and pulled a face.

"Look at the bloody weather, will you?" Outside the oily black landscape, cratered and jagged by long past volcanic activity, was awash. "I've never seen a place rain like this, y'know? Look at it. Two weeks, and the place is a friggin' swimming pool." She made a dismissive noise at the deep green of the rolling hills, now smudged gray by blanketing rain, water cascading down jagged roadsides and splashing over the potholed road. "Keeps this up, I'm moving to Aussie—you just watch me."

Despite her words, she loved the north. Loved the people, the place, the long summer days when the red flower-drop of the pohutakawa trees spread a scarlet shawl around the edges of the white sand beaches. The colors in sharp contrast to the sparkling white foam of the breakers and the deep blue of the sea. She had moved into her 1920s character cottage twelve years ago after her marriage break-up, and sworn that's where she'd die.

"You heard Sean Clemmons got parole," Callaghan said conversationally. Like he didn't know how she'd feel. Like she'd just brush it off.

At the very sound of Sean Clemmons's name, the fizz of rage flared in Nyree's gut. She kept her voice neutral, eyes on the scenery. "I did. How that bastard got out is anyone's guess." That's all she was going to say about it. She'd just let it go, get on with the job. Let her blood pressure drop.

"Apparently, he got out on exemplary behavior." Callaghan snorted, clearly amused.

Nyree felt a muscle in her neck spasm. "Exemplary behavior, my foot. He stuffed that girl's mouth so full of paper she nearly choked to death, then he beat her to a bloody pulp. She's still traumatized." She clamped her mouth shut and took a long, slow breath. No good getting pissed now. She'd already given her Superintendent, Brett Nolan, a piece of her mind, told him she was ready to quit. And she'd meant it. Until this came up.

"They reckon it was a drug deal gone wrong," Callaghan said in the same dry tone, eyes still on the road.

"Does that make it better?" she snapped.

"No, but he still got out three days ago. What was the grandmother's name? The old girl that ID'd him, then faced him down in court?"

"Emere Grady. He told her she'd be next." She dropped her voice and turned her gaze to the rain-spattered window. "That little shit goes near her, he'll be back inside before his feet touch the ground."

"You'd have to catch him first."

A second surge of acid flared in her stomach. *Let it go. What's done is done.*

Corner of her mouth twitching, Nyree forced it from her mind and opened the file. "Let's concentrate on this case, shall we?"

Perhaps sensing her rising rage, he soberly replied, "Yes, Ma'am," and drove on.

They wound their way along narrow roads, twisting across rugged hill ranges until the land flattened out. When Callaghan hit the gas again and the car fishtailed on a greasy corner, Nyree stiffened in her seat and stamped her foot where the brake would be.

"Oy, slow down, will you? You'll get us both bloody killed before we get there."

Callaghan gave her a sideways glance and the car slowed to the speed limit.

"So, what've we got?" he asked.

Nyree relaxed and flicked on the light on her phone, shining it over the file on her lap. "Young female, European." She flipped the page back and forth. "That's all they've given us. Looks like she was bludgeoned and thrown down the falls."

"Did they say who found her?"

Nyree flipped the page. "A couple of tourists. They were parked just down from the river. They went up the track towards Mason's Rock to swim, saw her floating downstream."

"That'd be a tourist attraction they hadn't expected. What'd they do with her?"

"Says here they tried to pull her out of the water. Realized she was dead and left her on the bank while they went back to their camper van to call 111."

"Anyone else around when they found her?"

Nyree checked the notes again. "Apparently not," she said and looked up to check the road. "Whoa, slow down. This is it." She pointed up ahead where a road block had been set up at a short, narrow bridge, and an officer in high-viz vest and baton waved them down to a stop. Further on, they could see a sign next to a bridge indicating a parking lot and boat ramp within the cordoned off area.

Callaghan swung the car into an empty space with a brief slide of gravel and killed the engine. Parked immediately in front was a single police unit angled in behind a grey Lexus Nyree recognized as Whangārei Base forensic pathologist Christine Healey's. Seven other vehicles were lined up either side of the street.

Nyree squared up the file on her knee and tucked it into her briefcase. Up ahead, a second officer in a high-viz, police-issue raincoat approached, sweeping a flashlight across their car.

He ducked next to her, looking in. Nyree took out her ID, lowered the window and held it up.

"DI Nyree Bradshaw, Far North CIB. This is Detective Sergeant Callaghan," she added, tipping her head in his direction.

The officer nodded across at Callaghan, then addressed her. "Detective Henare's waiting for you, Ma'am."

He stepped back while Nyree unclipped her seatbelt, shoved the door open and got out, staggering a little where the loose gravel dipped away from the edge of the road.

He immediately stepped forward to offer an arm which she shook away as she shut her door. Perhaps a little taken aback, the officer stepped away, gesturing to where a tall, Māori man wearing a white plastic coverall and rubber boots was walking toward them, his black hair slicked stylishly back over his head.

"Henare, Ma'am," he said by way of introduction.

She rounded the car and introduced herself and Callaghan. "What have we got so far?"

"A young woman—early twenties, I'd say, hands tied behind her back with cable ties, bare feet, back of her head pretty smashed in. Probably came down the waterfall."

"With some help, by the sound of it."

They followed him back down the street and to the line of crime scene tape that had been stretched across the road. She lifted her collar against the rising breeze, and scanned the scene. On the far right and standing just outside the cordoned-off area and dressed in white paper scrubs, blue hair cover and white rubber boots, was the forensic pathologist, hugging herself against the chill of the night as she spoke with one of the uniforms.

"So, where is she?"

"Up the track there." He pointed to a dark gap in the bushes into which a narrow dirt trail disappeared. "And that's the tourists' van." He indicated the white camper van in the parking lot opposite.

"And they're the ones who found her?"

"That's them. We've already taken separate statements."

"Good, keep them here. I want to talk to them."

"Yes, Ma'am. Scene's ready, if you'd like to follow me."

Nyree and Callaghan pulled on white plastic coveralls and boots, signed in to the scene log, then followed Henare down the track past a sign pointing to Mason's Rock.

"Mind your footing," Henare said, shining his flashlight along the muddy path made rugged with rock-tips and tree roots.

Nyree angled her own flashlight a little further along the path and sighed. The trail led off into a black slash in the undergrowth hugged close by dense forest.

"Couldn't have got a better site for a murder scene." Annoyance rippled under the sarcasm. She staggered along the uneven ground, rubber boots slipping on the mud-slickened path, one hand out ready to catch herself. With every step, the roar of the waterfall grew louder. "How long ago did you guys get here?"

He kept walking, speaking over his shoulder. "About two hours ago. We froze the area and the SOCO's got here shortly after. They've been waiting for you."

"That was quick."

"They'd just left a shooting up in the Waipoua Forest so they headed straight down here."

Nyree paused to take in the surrounding bush. "It's black as the inside of a cow along here. How long since it rained?"

"It's been threatening for the last hour or so. We've got a tent ready in case it starts again."

"Let's hope we don't need it." She started after him again.

"There it is." Henare shone his flashlight thirty meters or so ahead to where a clutch of officers garbed in white plastic suits had taken up their places. Under the harsh, white lights they'd set up, the scene looked like something out of the X-Files.

Crouching on a mat of watercress edging the pool, Nyree recognized Constable Jodie Clarkson. Slim, auburn curls forming a soft halo around her face, nose and cheeks spattered with freckles, Clarkson had a strong work-ethic and an eye for detail. Keen to make her way up the ladder, she had requested a place on several cases that Nyree had worked. It wasn't lost on Nyree that she'd stayed in the office long after everyone else had gone, hung on every word from the CIB team. Perhaps recognizing Clarkson as a younger version of herself, Nyree had warmed to her from day one.

On seeing her, Clarkson straightened, gloved hands dangling at her sides as they approached. "Evening, Ma'am. You got here quick," she called with a smile.

"You can thank my driver for that," Nyree said as she sloshed her way toward her. "No such thing as taking bloody corners with him. You just about drive in one straight line." She paused to take in the scene in its entirety. High walls of volcanic rock surrounded the pool into which torrents of water thundered. Directly opposite, the overflow funneled into a bulrush-edged stream leading to the sea. All around, bloated drops of water fell from tall, ghostly pale gum trees and splattered on the sodden ground or plopped into the swollen pool. She shivered. Already she could feel the damp chill of the night air soaking through her clothes and stinging her skin.

"Who caught it?"

"Officer Preston over there." Clarkson nodded towards a uniformed officer making notes a few feet away.

At the mention of his name, Preston looked up. "Ma'am," he said with a nod. "The area's secured."

To Nyree, he looked about sixteen though now at forty-nine, her short hair mostly gray, crow's feet spreading under her eyes, she'd long since conceded that everyone looked like a kid these days.

"Right, then. Let's get a proper look at her." Nyree stepped gingerly down until icy water lapped over the top of her boot, causing her a sharp intake of breath. "Jesus, that's cold." She gave herself a second, then inched forward and bent over to view the body.

Under the harsh glare of the floodlights, the girl's skin resembled blue-tinged alabaster, her long brown hair strewn about her head and stuck to her face like seaweed after a heavy swell. A thin sleeveless top clinging to her body had lifted, revealing an upper torso dappled grey with the telltale signs of death, her water-logged jeans weighing her lower body down.

"You poor little bugger," Nyree muttered, grief and sorrow tightening in her chest. An image of her own son sprang into her mind, consuming her, almost overwhelming her.

Three years ago, now. It still felt like yesterday. That shame clung to her like a ragged coat. But this wasn't the time or place. So, she shook it away and pressed on.

She clenched her teeth and shook it away. That was done and past. She had this child's killer to find.

"She's Māori, then?" she said, her gaze pausing on the blue/black swirls of a moko kauae running from the edge of her lower lip to her chin.

"It would appear so."

"Well, that'll make life interesting," she muttered.

Clarkson spoke, echoing Nyree's exact thoughts. "Whānau will want the body back pretty damn fast. Last Māori vic's body got hijacked on the way to the morgue. No one knew where he was until he was six feet under."

"Yeah, and that's only the beginning. Any ID? Anything to tell us who she is?"

"None that we've found, Ma'am. Just the wee koru. It's got a date engraved on the back, so that could be something." Clarkson indicated a small, oval greenstone pendant on a thin leather tie around the girl's neck. "Joe here reckons she's been in the water for about two hours. Hands bound behind her back with cable ties. He reckons she was tied up after death."

Nyree passed a look on him, brow creased. "After she was dead?"

"Uh-huh."

"Well, that's a new one on me. Is that common practice around these parts?"

"Not that we've heard," replied Clarkson. "She's got scars, too, Ma'am. Someone's tortured her over the past few years."

"That wouldn't be a first."

"By a long shot," Henare sighed.

"What about more recent injuries?"

Clarkson returned her attention to the girl. "Ah, yeah, there's obvious lacerations and cuts. There's one deep injury to the skull here." She pointed, then tipped her head. "She could have got that coming over the falls."

Nyree lifted her eyes to where a torrent of dirty brown water gushed over the rocks above and into the pool.

"Is the river usually running this heavy?"

Clarkson surveyed the falls. "We've had a lot of rain up here lately—like I said, flash floods, heaps of surface water. The river's broken its banks in a few places further up. A couple of towns have been cut off."

"Right." Eager to get moving, Nyree called over the forensic photographer who was standing off to one side. "I want photographs of the body—all angles, then either side of the riverbank up there," she said, pointing to the crest of the waterfall. "Get some from further upstream, as well. Oy!" She shouted to one of the uniforms. "Get some more lighting in here. We need snaps of the entire area. And do it quick," she said, casting a dubious look up at the ever-darkening sky. "Before it rains again and we lose everything."

"Yes, Ma'am." With a small nod, he stepped away to begin.

Nyree took one more look at the girl, and sighed. "Right. Let's see what these tourists have got to say for themselves, shall we?"

CHAPTER 2

According to the notes the uniforms took when they arrived, the tourists were a couple in their twenties, doing a road trip the length of New Zealand in a camper van just big enough to accommodate sleeping facilities and nothing more. It was parked in an otherwise empty lot adjacent to the one-lane bridge Nyree and Callaghan had parked beside, with the track directly opposite. The entire area had been taped off.

As Nyree passed the van, she peeked through the side window. Even in the thin gloom of the street lights, the interior looked like a bomb had gone off in a drycleaner. She rechecked the statements they'd given, passed them to Callaghan, then rounded the van looking it over while the uniform trailed behind her.

"And these are the two who found her?"

"Yes, Ma'am."

"Any discrepancies with their stories?"

He glanced back at where they both sat huddled in tartan rugs, and dropped his voice.

"Nope. Both said they got here, found her in the water and tried to pull her out. Same as reported."

"Has the van been searched?"

"Nope. They refused to allow us."

"Oh, did they?" Nyree lifted her eyebrows back at Callaghan whose eyes widened in skepticism.

"That wouldn't be suspicious in any way, would it?" he chuckled.

"Get a search warrant," she told the uniform. "I don't care who you have to call. I want that van searched, and I want to know what's in there they don't want us to find."

"Yes, Ma'am," the uniform said with a hint of a smile.

"Right, let's see what they've got to say."

The couple sat in camp chairs next to the van, a portable gas stove set up on a table just off to one side. Both stared gloomily into steaming cups of tea, each caught in their own thoughts.

As Nyree approached, the young man looked up, then stood from his chair. Swapping his cup from his right to left, he extended an open hand to her.

Ignoring it, Nyree took out her ID, opened it, and held it for him to read. "Mr. Barrett. I'm Detective Inspector Bradshaw with Northland CIB."

The extended hand dropped. "CIB?"

"Criminal Investigation Bureau." Nyree refolded her ID wallet and tucked it away.

Barrett nodded to his left where the girl sat still huddled in her rug. "This is my partner, Gabby."

She also nodded. Now both of them were gaping at Nyree, the dim light from their hurricane lamp deepening the worry lines etched into their faces.

"I know you've already given statements, but do you mind if I ask you a few questions?"

Barrett looked to the girl who shrugged agreement. "No, go ahead." He sat back down.

When a drop of rain hit her nose, Nyree dashed it away and glanced up at the sky. Overhead, thunderous clouds loomed, threatening another downpour. She pulled her jacket collar up around her neck, turned to Barrett and asked what time they got there.

"We've already told the cop over there," Gabby complained.

Nyree gave her a wide, forced smile. "Well, now you're telling me."

They shared an irritated look, then, swapping the narrative back and forth between them, Barrett and Gabby reaffirmed that they had arrived at about seven, set up for dinner and gone for a swim.

"A swim?" Nyree interrupted. "A bit cold for swimming, isn't it?" She turned a doubtful frown on Callaghan whose eyebrows went up in response.

"We heard about this waterfall from one of the guys in my poetry class. He said we had to go swimming there."

Nyree wasn't convinced but let it go while they ran through the events of the night like a laundry list. According to the pair, they'd cooked a couple of steaks and finished around eight before heading up the track."

"And that's when you found her?" Callaghan asked.

Barrett nodded. "Yep. About ten minutes before we called the police. We thought it was a dead sheep. Gabby said she wasn't swimming with dead sheep, and I kind of pushed her."

"You shoved me," Gabby said. Scowling now, she sipped her tea.

"It was a joke," he insisted. "Jesus, get a grip. Anyway, she kind of stumbled over to the water's edge and stopped. I said, 'What is it?' And she said, 'I don't think it's a sheep.' We just about shit ourselves…sorry," he added. "But it was a shock, y'know?"

Nyree noted down the times. "Did you see any other cars around?"

"Just that blue Holden Commodore across the river there." Barrett pointed.

"Was it there when you arrived?"

"Dunno," Barrett said and turned to Gabby.

"Don't ask me," she said.

In the gloom of a single streetlight, Nyree could just see the distant outline of the cars parked on the street over the narrow bridge—part of the crime scene. Presumably both accounted for.

"Anyone else around when you got here?"

"I didn't see anyone," Gabby said, aiming the comment at Barrett.

"Me neither." Barrett's worried gaze cut from Callaghan to Nyree. "We're not under suspicion here, are we?"

"Not unless we find anything connecting you to the girl's death." Nyree lifted a questioning eye on each of them.

"We don't even know her," Barrett said.

"Is that all?" Gabby asked and hugged the rug in. Her features had grown tight, her brow a little furrowed.

"Is there any reason you don't want us to search your van?" Nyree asked.

"It's private," Gabby said immediately.

Barrett followed up, saying, "What's this got to do with anything? We didn't kill that girl."

"Why would we?" Gabby demanded. "We're the ones that found her. Now you're treating us like *we've* done something."

"I'm sorry you feel that way. But I'm afraid we're going to search your van, with or without your permission. With it would be better for everyone."

"You'll have to get a warrant," Gabby told her bluntly.

"Then I will."

"Can we go now?"

"I'd like you to stay put for a while. The officer here will escort you back to the station in River Falls."

This time, Barrett got lippy. "What for? What have we done?"

Nyree turned a slow look on him, quietly saying, "Until the van's searched and you're fully cleared, I'm afraid you're our guests. Henare," she snapped her fingers at the grinning detective, "get a uniform to assist our guests down to the station. Then first thing in the morning, get yourself up to the local marae. If they don't know her, we need to figure out who does."

CHAPTER 3

From the moment Nyree's head went down, the dreams started. The icy air of the prison cell. The empty seat opposite her. That sense of loss echoing.

Nyree casting a desperate look all around, her heart aching. The air cut by the sound of her own voice echoing. "I'll find you … "

She jolted awake to find herself sitting at her desk with the phone ringing.

Five in the morning, according to her watch.

She stretch-blinked the film from her eyes, shook herself awake, and grabbed the receiver.

"DI Bradshaw."

It was Constable Jodie Clarkson. "Sorry to disturb you, Ma'am. We're just bringing the body in."

"Thanks, I'll be there as soon as I can."

And with the all-too-familiar hollowness of too little sleep echoing through her brain, she headed to the Whangārei Base Hospital mortuary.

Christine Healey was already there. Early forties, she was slim, with close-cropped blonde hair with pink tinges front and sides. Heavy pouches under each eye and the sallow complexion indicated she hadn't slept properly in weeks.

"They're just wheeling her in," she told Nyree. "You're looking pretty chipper for someone who was at a crime scene until after twelve last night."

"Living the dream. What's your excuse?" she joked, knowing full well the pair of them worked the most ungodly hours.

Christine heaved out a long, weary breath. "Two days ago, I had a kid up in Tikipunga. Eleven months old. Bloody drugged-up step-father beat him to death. It's been a rotten week."

Nyree felt any sense of optimism punched out of her. "Good God. Who caught that one?"

"Terry McFarlane."

"Oh, right," she murmured noncommittally. She knew McFarlane; worked a three-month stint with him a couple of years ago when he'd been seconded up from Hamilton to help out with an unusually heavy caseload. His reputation as a brilliant detective with a solid work record went before him. He was worshipped by his peers, admired by his seniors, feared by the criminal fraternity. Nobody mentioned how often he crossed the line. He got results. That's what mattered.

McFarlane was typical of the boys' club culture rampant when Nyree had joined the force twenty-six years ago. Since then, the powers that be had made efforts to stamp it out. In many ways they'd succeeded. So, there she was thinking all that was in the past. Then he turned up.

He'd gotten up Nyree's nose from the word *Go*. Every day, listening to all his self-glorification and tales of derring-do to a rapt audience of his peers. She'd made pitiful excuses and left the room as soon as she could.

The following year, she and McFarlane both went for the role of DI. She got it. McFarlane had let it be known far and wide that she'd only been given the role because she was a woman. Those barbs stuck. She said she didn't care. But in her heart of hearts, Nyree had always feared he was right, that her appointment had been political rather than based on merit. So, she'd stayed off his radar —no love lost either side.

Christine snapped her back to the present, saying, "Yesterday I had a teen go over a cliff and hit the rocks. Rescue helicopter got there but he died on the way here."

"Bloody hell. What have they been putting in the water up there?"

"Meth, if the local sewage tox reports are anything to go by."

"And we keep fooling ourselves that we're winning." Nyree sighed.

Their amiable chat was cut short when the double doors hissed open and a hospital attendant in blue scrubs wheeled in a steel gurney, the body draped in blue sheeting. Clarkson followed them in along with a police photographer.

Christine signed the paperwork which the orderly folded and tucked away, then waited until he'd gone before peeling back the sheet exposing the head and shoulders. Then looked up. "Moko. Māori, then."

"Looks like. She'd be pretty stupid getting a moko if she's not."

"Has the family been notified?" Christine asked.

"Haven't got an ID yet. I've sent Henare up to the local marae to ask around."

"The one up by River Falls?"

"Yep."

Christine's expression fell. "If she's from there, it doesn't give me much time."

Nyree gave her a flick of the eyebrows. "I know what you mean. You'll have the entire whānau parked out on your doorstep, demanding her body back before you can blink. Okay if I give permission for one of the family to come and sit with her?"

"Sure. I'll sort a refrigerated room. Let me know when they're coming so I can make her look good."

"Will do."

Christine picked up her trusty old-fashioned Dictaphone, and the photographer immediately leaned in, snapping shots at various angles.

Nyree ignored him and turned a sorrowful look on the girl.

She looked different, somehow—younger. Probably in her early twenties, her knotted brown hair had been drawn back to reveal fine features, wide bloodless lips, high cheekbones, and a clear complexion. Sadness ached in her expression. Even now in the harsh lights of the morgue she looked beautiful, were it not for the mangle of flesh and bone peeping out just above her right ear.

Snapping her observations into the Dictaphone, Christine tilted the head, exposing a dark crevice surrounded by shattered bone, the grey of battered brain matter clearly visible. Again, the photographer leaned in, capturing everything.

At the sight of the injuries Nyree felt her chest tighten. She sucked in her lips and turned her head away. Memories bubbled up of her own son. Of him being taken away.

All that loss.

The sideways looks from her fellow officers. They'd said they understood. Said they felt for her. What did they know?

Christine looked up, gauging Nyree's reaction to the injury. "You okay?"

Nyree turned back. "Yeah, sure."

"Blunt force trauma to the skull. I'll take an x-ray, make sure there's nothing else, but I'd say one king-hit could easily have done this."

Nyree nodded. "Male assailant?"

"Probably. Or maybe a very strong female." She shrugged. "Load some of the young girls around here up on meth, they'd be in the picture." Once again, she checked Nyree. "You sure you're okay?"

"Just a little tired. I'm good."

Giving her a skeptical glance, Christine rolled the sheet down, then pressed on.

"Marks around the neck probably made by the leather cord she was wearing; shoulder showing abrasions consistent with a fall, maybe hitting the rockface as she fell. But I'd say that's post-mortem, so she was probably dead long before she hit the water. I'll check for water in the lungs."

"Question: If the blow to the head killed her, why tie her hands?"

Christine regarded the body for a second. "She could have had post-mortem muscle movement. Maybe she twitched and they tied her hands in case she came back to life. Or," she said grimly, "maybe it just made it easier to carry her."

"Any idea of time?"

Christine shook her head and heaved a deep breath. "This time of year, submerged in water, time of death is tough. She's slim, poorly dressed, it's mid-winter and it's rained cats and dogs up there for the past two days. Looking at the condition of her skin, I'd say she's been in the water for at least an hour. Possibly three. No lividity, so that confirms she hadn't lain in one position for long before she was found. Rigor's set in, but that could be secondary. Once the body's moved it's like it starts all over again."

"So, if she was washed down the river, that could account for the initial lack of rigor?"

"Absolutely. So, assuming she was dead when she was dumped, and taking the water temp into account..." she tucked one corner of her mouth back and swayed her head while considering. "I'd say death occurred two to six hours before she was found."

"Two to six?"

"Don't quote me on that yet. There are a lot of factors to take into account." Christine smiled and rolled down the sheet a little more and frowned. "Hang on." She moved her fingers down the girl's abdomen, palpating the flesh.

"What is it?" Nyree leaned in.

"I'm pretty sure she was pregnant."

"Oh, shit."

"Yep, make that a positive." Christine pressed her fingers in just above the pubic bone.

"How long?"

"Hard to say. Feels like around three months. But like I said, once I open her up, I might get a better idea."

CHAPTER 4

As instructed, Detective Joe Henare had driven the gravel road up to the marae. He crested the last hill with stones clattering on the underside of the car, to meet a solid wooden fence, an open gate, and a thickset Māori bloke who stood with crossed arms, eyeing his arrival.

Henare got out of the car with the guy still watching and approached the gate with his ID, casting a quick look to where the wharenui—or meeting house—stood at the top of the hill.

The heart of the local Māori community, the wharenui stood central on the marae—a broad wooden structure, pitched roof topped by a fierce-looking carved figure brandishing a spear; elaborately carved bargeboards angling down to similarly carved pillars, all in rust red with inlays of bright, white shell that told tales of the occupants' past.

Henare gave the guy a quick head-toss in greeting. "Gidday, mate."

In response, the guy cast the ID a sour glance, then lifted a no-bullshit gaze on Henare. "Bro'."

Taking a casual look around, Henare put the ID away. "We're trying to ID a body that's come in."

"Yeah, nothin' to do with us, Cuzz."

"Just trying to ID her, mate. Nothing else."

The guy dashed a hand across his nose and shifted his weight while he considered his reply. "You got a photo or somethin'?"

Henare cast his eye up to where a few of the locals were clearly preparing for a celebration, and took out the photograph. "You know most of the whānau round here?"

A quick shoulder lift. "Yeah, most."

Henare held the photo up. "How about her?"

"Shit. That's Huia Coburn."

"You know her, then?"

"Rawiri Cooper's kid. She dead?"

"Afraid so."

"Aw, man," he said and cast a worried look back over his shoulder. "Rawiri'll be gutted."

"Can I speak with him, Bro'?"

"He's not here."

"Anyone else I can talk to?"

"Yeah, this way."

The guy introduced himself as Wiremu Hanson, and led Henare around the back of the marae, and up the short hill to where several elders sat in a semi-circle in front of the wharenui entrance. Only now, Henare could see the sweep of the land behind—green hills arcing down to a broad, white sand bay overlooked by a small community of fibrolite houses surrounded by lush community gardens of kumara and pumpkin. All Māori land.

Henare paused in front of the three men dressed in suits, and two elderly women, one of whom wore an intricately patterned feather cloak. They'd obviously been in serious conversation when Henare arrived, and were now watching with suspicion as he approached. Henare paused, standing back while Wiremu went to a grey-haired man with faded blue traces of a long-worn facial tattoo, speaking in hushed tones. Both looked back to Henare and the older man rose to his feet.

"Officer," he said. Henare leaned in and each man placed a hand on the other's shoulder, leaning in to press forehead and nose together in traditional greeting known as hongi. "Kingi Hanson," he said by way of introduction. "I'm the kaumatua here."

Kingi Hanson took his seat again, and Wiremu hustled another seat over for Henare.

"Thank you for seeing me," Henare said.

"What's this about a girl?"

Once again, the photograph came out. "We've got the body of a young woman come in. She's got no ID on her, except a moko. Wiremu thinks it could be Huia Coburn."

He handed the photo over. Kingi dug a pair of eyeglasses from his pocket and put them on, the corners of his mouth turned down in silent concentration while he squinted over the image. "Yeah, that's her."

"Rawiri Cooper's daughter?"

"Yep. What happened?" He passed the photograph to the feather-cloaked woman sitting next to him, who took in a sharp breath, sadness creasing her features.

"I believe Mr. Cooper's away?"

When he looked to the old woman next to him, she said, "He went down the line a few days ago. I'll see if I can get a hold of him."

"Do you have a phone number for him?"

"Not on me. I'll ask around." Kingi Hanson's brow was still crumpled in concern. "What happened? Was Huia in an accident or something?"

Henare hesitated a moment, considering the situation. "We believe her death was suspicious. She was only found last night and if it's her, we need to formally ID her as soon as possible."

"When do we get her back?" the woman asked immediately.

Exactly what Henare had expected. "Soon as we can."

"We'd like her sooner than that," Hanson said without pause. "And we want her back in one piece. You tell your boss; we don't want our whānau butchered—chopped up like a piece of meat. We want every bit of her back. Just like she left here. And until we get her, we want our whānau with her. You tell your boss that."

Also, what Henare had expected. It was going to be a long day.

***

Desk Sergeant Gary Hooper was on duty when the woman entered River Falls station.

Medium height, shoulder-length blonde hair, dark rings under her green eyes, a small tattoo on her left wrist, he noted. Mud stains down the front of her short-sleeved shirt, tatty jeans over mud-slicked sneakers.

Her haunted gaze ran across the six steel waiting chairs, over the posters decrying the use of drugs and numerous illegal activities on the wood-paneled wall adjacent to the desk, then across to Hooper.

A meth addict, he figured. She had all the classic signs—thin, unkempt hair, sallow complexion, dirty clothing—although why she'd walk into a police station at 11 a.m. was anybody's guess.

"What can I help you with, love?"

She blinked herself into the moment, as if having woken from a nightmare to find herself in an even worse hell. She turned a panic-stricken gaze on him. "I need to speak to a cop."

"Can I ask what it's about?"

"I want to report a missing child."

Hooper instantly snapped out of his cynical evaluation.

"How old?"

She took a shuddering breath and pressed the knuckles of one hand to her mouth as if stifling a sob. "Six. She's only six," she whimpered. Then she buckled over at the waist, eyes squeezed shut, keening like a wounded animal.

Hooper quickly rounded the desk and bent with one hand on her shoulder. "Hey, hey, calm down, okay? Let's get you over here. Come and tell me all about it."

When she straightened, the words seemed caught in her throat, grief and shock and disbelief cutting them off. She nodded stiffly then followed him to an adjacent chair.

As soon as she sat, he crouched in front of her. "Now, how long has she been missing?"

Breath held, tears spilling and splashing onto her lap, the woman shook her head once. No.

"You don't know?"

Another headshake.

She gathered herself, pulling in a breath, desperate to speak. "The thing is," she began in a hiccupping voice, "I went out last night." She swiped away a couple of tears. "I left her at home with my babysitter—Huia. I thought maybe they'd gone back to her boyfriend's place—Huia's boyfriend's place, that is." She sucked in a faltering breath and held her red, swollen eyes on him. When she spoke this time, it gushed out all on one long breath. "But when I went there this morning, there was no one home. Now I can't find either of them. I don't know where they are."

He handed her a tissue box. She tore two off and dragged them across her face and nose.

Recognizing the name from Henare's outing, Hooper said, "I see. Listen, we've got an officer here who I think you'd be best to talk to."

She clamped her hands between her knees, stiffened visibly, and nodded once. As he straightened, she lifted a terrified gaze on him, desperate, beseeching. "Please, just tell him to find my baby. Just tell him to find her. She hasn't had her insulin."

"Stay here. She'll be right over." And he snatched up the phone.

CHAPTER 5

The girl was sitting in the reception area clutching an untouched cup of weak-looking tea when Nyree and Callaghan walked in. Hooper shuffled over and gave them a quick briefing, then gestured them towards her.

She looked up; eyes full of hope as Nyree went over to her.

"Hello. It's Kelly, is it?"

A nod. "Kelly Holmes. Have you found my little girl?" She put the cup aside.

"Kelly, I'm Detective Inspector Nyree Bradshaw, and this is Detective Sergeant Callaghan. I'm sorry, we haven't found her yet. But we're going to."

Kelly spread her hands wide. "I don't know where she'd take her. I've tried calling her, but there's no answer."

When a man entered the station through the front door and shot a questioning look from one to the next, Nyree glanced across at Hooper who jerked his head towards the back office.

Nyree touched Kelly gently on the shoulder. "Tell you what: why don't we go out back, get a fresh cup of tea, and you can tell me everything that happened before your little girl went missing."

In the rear office Kelly sank into a chair, lower lip clamped between her teeth, brow deeply furrowed. While Nyree positioned a chair opposite her, Kelly dropped her gaze to her jeans and shirt, suddenly aware of the mud stains.

"Omigod, look at me. I went right down the gully along the back of my place, looking for her. It's a swamp down there after all the rain." She brushed at them, then gave up, instead crossing her arms to hide them.

Nyree took out her phone and clicked the button to record the interview. "You don't mind if I record this, do you?"

When she shook her head, Nyree began.

"When did you last see your little girl?"

"Last night. I left her with my babysitter." Kelly switched position to clasp her hands on her lap, hands squeezed so tightly her fingers had turned white. "Well, when I say my babysitter, she's my cousin. She lives with me. See, I work nights," she said, lifting her gaze to Callaghan and back. "Nine till two. I restack the shelves at the supermarkets—you know, cleaning products and stuff," she said, and then shook her head, perhaps realizing that hardly mattered. "Anyway, Huia wasn't getting on with her mum, Annette. She said she was being overprotective—controlling, really. So, she came and lived with me."

"So, you work here in town?" Nyree asked softly.

"I work all over. River Falls, Paihia, right up to Kaitaia. I do all the supermarkets in the area. But you have to work nights—when there's no customers. Huia came and lived with me three months ago so she could babysit while I worked," she explained. "I mean, she gets cheap rent, and I get a free babysitter. And it has to be someone you trust, right? It's so bloody hard on your own, y'know? I just..." She dropped her head and bit her lip, visibly forcing back the tears.

"It's okay," Nyree said as encouragingly as she could. "No one's blaming you. You have to work, right? You had someone you could rely on to look after your daughter. Because you have to earn a living. I totally get that."

"Exactly." Kelly raised one palm at the injustice. "You're damned if you do, you're damned if you don't. You stay on welfare, everyone says you're lazy. You work, they say you neglect your kids. Nothing's good enough." Lips pressed tight she did a small headshake, clearly frustrated.

Nyree knew exactly what she meant. Hadn't she run that gauntlet of family versus job? And hadn't she suffered the consequences?

"And your cousin's name is Huia? Is that right?"

"That's right. Huia Coburn. If I'd thought for a minute—"

"It's okay, Kelly. Like I said, no one's blaming you."

"But where could they have gone?"

"That's what we have to figure out. Right?"

Kelly sighed out a weary breath and lifted her chin, eyes pinned on Nyree's tablet, watching as she noted down names and times.

"I'm going to show you a photograph. Can you tell me if it's Huia?"

"Sure." Her brow immediately crumpled with worry. "She hasn't done anything wrong, has she?"

"Not that we know of." Nyree smiled and slipped the photograph from the file and passed it to her.

Kelly sat up a little straighter. "That's her. Why? What's happened?"

"Thank you." Nyree put the photograph back in the file. "So, where have you looked?"

"I thought maybe they were down the back yard in the playhouse. I had one built for Lily last Christmas. That's my little girl's name—Lily."

"And Lily and Huia weren't there?" A statement of confirmation for the record, since they obviously weren't there.

Kelly shook her head again. "Like I said, I even searched the gully over the back."

"What about friends, neighbors?"

"Asked them all. I've been up and down the street all morning. No one saw them leave. I don't even know what time they left."

"And Huia was supposed to stay with your daughter all night?"

A nod.

But already things weren't adding up.

"Can you just confirm something for me, Kelly?"

Her thinly plucked eyebrows drew together to form an inverted V. "Yeah, sure."

"You said you start work at nine, right?"

The young woman's face blanched. "That's right."

"So, what time did you leave?"

Kelly blinked a couple of times, then dropped her gaze to her where she'd been picking at a badly chewed thumbnail. When she looked up again, her face was etched with guilt. The thumbnail went straight to her mouth.

"Um, about four. In the afternoon. Look, I'm not a bad mum," she insisted.

"Why four? What were you doing then?"

Knowing she'd been caught in something close to a lie, Kelly briefly squeezed her eyes closed, then rolled her eyes to the ceiling. "I went for a drink with a mate from work. But it was just one," she said, holding up one finger. "I promise. Then I switched to lemonade."

"Whereabouts was this?"

"Over in Paihia."

Nyree did some quick mental computations. "So, what time did you leave home?"

"Just after three-thirty. I never get to go out," she insisted. "You can't with a six-year-old. I hate asking Huia to do it every night. She's got her own life. But babysitters cost a fortune. And I don't drink and drive. I wouldn't do that. And I had to work."

Nyree raised a hand to calm the young mother. "That's okay. I'm not worried about that."

She leaned forward, adamant. "I totally trusted Huia. I'd never leave her with someone I didn't trust. But where could they be?"

Guilt and fear tightened the young mother's features. But Nyree had to move on.

"Were their beds slept in?"

Kelly froze, eyes riveted on Nyree's. Then she whispered, "I don't know." Her chin crumpled, worry lines deepening across her face, hands clasping and unclasping. She cut a glance at Callaghan, then said, "It's just...I don't make the beds. I don't get time. I'm too busy. It's just—"

Nyree placed a hand over the young mother's and squeezed it. "It's fine, Kelly. Like I said, we're not here to judge you. We're here to find Lily."

But as Kelly hunched over, shoulders squeezed tight, the self-recrimination and the guilt in the admission gave Nyree a clearer picture of Kelly Holmes—a young mum struggling to make ends meet, and to be a good mother. Nyree's heart went out to her. After all, Kelly Holmes wasn't exactly the first to leave the housework undone. Nyree couldn't remember the last time she hadn't come home to an unmade bed. Her own house looked as if the Drug Squad had done a number on it. What time did Nyree have for organization when everything went into the job?

Aware of how time was slipping away, she pressed on.

"Does Huia drive a car?"

"Yeah. An old Toyota. It's green, with a scrape on the driver's door."

"You've got a good eye for detail. That really helps. Does Huia have a boyfriend?"

A nod this time. "Brodie. Brodie Skinner. But he never came over to the house. I told her I didn't want him there."

"And she wouldn't have had him over while you were gone?"

"Never. I told Huia I wouldn't have anyone else there while she was babysitting. She promised me she wouldn't."

"And does Brodie have a car?"

Another nod. "I don't know what kind though. Huia spoke about him a few times but just from what she said, I didn't want him around."

"He wasn't the sort you'd like in your house?"

Kelly made an anguished face and shrugged. "I don't like to be judgmental, you know? But it was the things she told me."

"What like?"

"Oh, y'know, the way he spoke to her. He always ran her down, told her she didn't do things right, told her she was stupid. That kind of stuff. Plus, he was into drugs. At one point, Huia said she was going to dob him in to the cops—have him put back in prison. She'd have been better off if she had."

"How long had she been seeing Brodie Skinner?"

Kelly's eyes went to the ceiling in thought. "Um…I think she'd been seeing him about six months before she moved up here. Her mother hated him. Told her she couldn't see him. That's why she moved out, came to live with me. You don't think he had something to do with this, do you?"

Nyree noted down Brodie Skinner's name. "I can't say, Kelly. But I have to check everyone who might have been in contact with Huia or Lily."

"Thank you." She dropped her head and the first sob racked her chest. For a moment, she sat weeping the tears she'd been holding back. When she looked up, her eyes were red and swimming with tears, nose streaming. "I'm so bloody tired. I've been at work all night. Then I come home to this." After a moment, she sniffed hard, wiped the heel of her hand under her nose and looked up. Straight into Nyree's eyes. Suddenly, something in Kelly's expression registered. "Nothing's happened to Huia, has it?"

For a second Nyree hesitated. Telling her would panic the young mother. But she had the right to know.

"I'm afraid a young woman was found dead last night, up by Mason's Rock."

Kelly's mouth dropped open but no words came out.

"We think it might be Huia."

She leapt up in terror, face blanched of all color, eyes wide. "So, where's Lily? What's happened to her?"

"That's what we need to find out. Please, just sit down, Kelly. We're doing everything we can."

For a moment, Kelly looked ready to run from the room, blind panic driving her to find her child. Nyree reached out and softly touched her arm. "Kelly, sit down. We'll find her."

The young mother sank into the chair again, eyes pleading. "Tell me she's not dead. Please tell me she's not dead!"

"Kelly, we've got no reason to think anything's happened to Lily. But we need to find her quickly. And we need your help. Are you okay to do that?"

A quick nod as she wiped the tears away on her sleeve. "Yeah, go ahead."

So Nyree began.

CHAPTER 6

"Can you tell me her full name?"

Squeezing both hands between her knees, Kelly marshalled all her strength and replied. "Lily Marie Holmes."

"We'll need a good description of Lily. Can you do that for me?"

Kelly blinked away the last of the tears from her wet lashes as she reached into her rear jeans pocket and took out a creased school photograph. She drew her sleeve under her nose, wiping hard as she held the picture out. "I brought a photograph with me. That's her school photo. It's the most recent one I've got. Last night she had on her pink My-Little-Pony pajamas."

"And they're not at home? The pajamas?"

She squeezed her face in thought while she tried to recall the memory. Then a quick headshake. "I didn't see them."

Nyree took the photograph, offering her a box of tissues and letting Kelly tear several tissues off and blow her nose while she turned her attention to the photograph.

The child had bright green eyes like her mother, skin so pale it looked translucent, hair a wild auburn. Her smile radiated sweetness and innocence, one lower baby tooth missing in the front.

The very sight brought back all those memories. Nyree holding her own child. Nursing him. That infinite, all-encompassing love a mother feels.

She swallowed back those images and pulled herself back to the present. "This is great. You did good bringing this. It'll speed up finding her."

The young mother crumpled the handful of tissues into a knot in her lap. "Please, find her. She's only six and she's diabetic. She hasn't had her insulin shot since last night."

A shot of alarm zipped through Nyree.

"Okay. I'm going to get this into our system, put out an alert, and get a search underway. But first, can you tell me anywhere Huia has taken her in the past?"

Kelly rolled the tissues between her fingers. "Only her mum's. She lives in Whangārei. I'll spell the road for you," which she did, watching Nyree tap it into her tablet, correcting the spelling when she accidentally brought up the wrong address.

"Could she have taken her there?"

Kelly shook her head. "I called first thing this morning but they hadn't seen her. Oh, and she goes up to the local marae near River Falls."

"Just off Matai Road?" Nyree asked in a deadpan voice. The one she'd sent Henare to. After the kaumatua had made the ID, a couple of the local boys had taken exception to police presence. They'd cut up rough—accused Henare of turning on his own people, voicing their resentment of police picking on anyone with brown faces. Tempers had flared and they'd made threats, eventually sending Henare packing.

Which, as a Northlander, she might have expected. But as a cop, it made Nyree wonder if they had an alternative agenda—like harboring the guilty party. Or holding Lily.

"That's the place," Kelly was saying. "I never went up there. It's a pretty tight-knit marae. They don't really trust outsiders."

Nyree pressed on. "Does she have a phone number?"

"Yeah." She dictated the number she obviously knew by heart and watched as Nyree noted it down.

Suddenly, she looked up, worry crinkling her forehead. "How long do I have to be here?"

"Is there a problem?"

"What if Lily comes home and I'm not there? I should be there for her."

"Kelly, I'm sorry but I can't let you go home just yet. Someone will be at your house. If Lily comes home, they'll call us straight away."

Her voice rose in panic. "Where am I supposed to go?"

"I'll have one of our officers take you to one of our interview rooms. Have you had anything to eat?"

The young mother's shoulders dropped. "Why? I haven't done anything. Why can't I go home?"

"It's a precaution. I'm going to have a team go through your house and search for any evidence of anyone coming to the house. Believe me, if someone took Lily from your home, that's the best way to help us find her. Do we have your permission to search your house?"

"Oh God, it's a pigsty," she groaned.

"We're not doing a photoshoot for Good Housekeeping. We're only interested in anything that could lead to finding Lily."

Kelly shrugged. "Then, yeah, sure. Whatever you have to."

CHAPTER 7

As soon as Hooper had escorted Kelly Holmes to Interview One with a cup of tea, Nyree headed back to the car, snapping out orders to Callaghan.

"Get on the phone. I want forensics over at Kelly Holmes's address. I want every area checked, especially the child's bedroom, and the living area. Check for prints on the front door, the windows, anywhere he may have gained access. If someone came over there last night, I want to know how he got in, and how he left. Treat this as if it's a primary scene."

"Right on it."

"And tell them to bring something of Lily's clothing—preferably not washed. And a hairbrush and toothbrush if they can find them. Then get onto the search and rescue team. Get them to bring dogs."

He shot her a look.

She noticed. "Cadaver dogs," she confirmed. "As much as we want to find this kiddie alive, we have to assume she may not be."

"Will do." He looked as if the wind had been punched out of him, but noted it down.

"Right. Now let's get a search warrant for the marae. Send Hicks up there. I don't want to sully Henare's rep with the community any more than it has been. And tell Hicks I want every inch of that community gone over with a fine-toothed comb."

"I'll see who we've got available."

"Get a good team. Like I said, every inch of that place."

"Will do. You think Lily's there?" asked Callaghan.

She made a doubtful face. "I don't know. If she is, chances are she went there with Huia, and she could still be alive. A community like that, everyone knows everyone else and what they're doing. Whatever grievances they might have with the police, I can't see anybody being happy with one of their own murdering Rawiri Cooper's daughter—then murdering an innocent child."

"And harboring that murderer wouldn't go down well."

"Exactly. But if she is there, someone could be taking care of her."

He scribbled it into his notes.

"Then get onto the telcos. All of them. I want all the communications to and from Huia's phone for the last forty-eight hours in particular. We need to put together a picture of the last hours of her life to find out who she messaged, who she spoke to, and who she met."

"Got it."

They both got in the car where Nyree pulled her computer onto her knee, frantically entering notes into the nationwide database while Callaghan made the calls.

"Done," he told her and hung up. It had taken him some time, raking his hand through his thinning hair while wrangling with this department and that to get all the different teams together. Nyree had been listening, making suggestions every now and then. When he hit a brick wall and couldn't make further progress, she'd snatched the phone off him.

"Who is this?" she demanded.

"It's Auckland Central."

"Well, this is DI Bradshaw. I've got a missing child and I need feet on the ground right now. Today. You hear?"

"We don't have—"

"I don't care what you have and haven't got. I want every single available uniform sent up here for a search. Do you understand?"

"Yes, Ma'am."

She handed the phone back to Callaghan who could barely restrain the tiny smile of admiration as he started the car. "I've got the boys up in River Falls getting a warrant for the marae, and they're assembling a team for the house search."

"Good. And tread carefully. I don't want to wind up front-page news for all the wrong reasons. If she's there, I want her found without a fight."

"Where to now?"

"Let's head up to the marae, see if we can pour some oil on troubled waters. What?" she said when she noted his expression.

"Nothing. Just wondering if we should let them cool down a bit."

"We need their co-operation with the house-to-house on Māori land. Like I said, I don't need a national incident. And from what Henare said, the kaumatua is open to working with us. Let's foster that relationship. After that, I want to speak to Brodie Skinner, Huia's boyfriend. See what he has to say."

"That'll make for an interesting conversation," Callaghan said.

CHAPTER 8

Callaghan slowed the car next to the sign for the marae: the name carved into a sun-bleached wooden sign and adorned with colorful pāua shell.

They started up the stony road, following the same route Henare had taken just an hour or so earlier, and twisted their way up a rugged hill range, snaking around roads of loose gravel until the marae came into sight. A broad cast of rolling hills topped with the wharenui, a high, wooden fence around the perimeter. They parked at the end of a row of cars in the bumper-to-bumper carpark and got out.

As people trailed from their cars, waited in line to be called onto sacred ground, then filed in through the front gate and up toward the wharenui, Nyree and Callaghan fell in line with them. Men wearing their best shirts and pants, women in solemn black dresses, hand-in-hand with children trotting alongside who twisted around, eyeing Nyree and Callaghan with caution.

Nyree leaned in to Callaghan, whispering, "Wedding, I'd say. Bloody awful timing."

They stopped at the gate where each family member paused to press forehead and nose with the guy on the gate—a hongi, the traditional greeting. As Nyree and Callaghan approached, the guy straightened and looked them over.

"You guys here about Huia Coburn?"

Nyree replied, saying, "That's right. If it's convenient, we'd like to speak to your kaumatua, Kingi Hanson."

"Yeah, yeah, no worries," the guy said, beckoning them in. "He told me you'd be here. I'm Wiremu Hanson." He placed a hand on Nyree's shoulder and drew her into a hongi, did the same with Callaghan, and thumbed back over his shoulder. "Sorry about earlier with the other cop. Couple 'a hotheads got the wrong end of the stick," he explained, referring to Henare's recent send-off. He paused to greet a couple of passing families, then gestured them up to the wharenui. "We got a wedding going on. Sorry, you gotta go round the tradesmen's entrance. I'll get someone to escort you up there. My grandfather's probably sitting out front with the elders."

"Tēnā koe," Nyree replied, thanking him.

A heavily tattooed young man led them to a small semi-circle of elders who looked up with interest as they approached.

"Mr. Kingi, DI Nyree Bradshaw, and this is DS Callaghan," Nyree said by way of introduction, gesturing to her left where Callaghan nodded affirmation and ran a self-conscious hand over his balding head to tamp down the flyaway strands. "Is it convenient to speak?"

He gestured her to a chair and as both she and Callaghan sat, the elderly woman leaned forward. "You found who killed our Huia yet?"

"I'm sorry, not yet."

"Won't be any of us." Her tone held a note of belligerence; defiance.

Hanson cut the tension, saying, "So, how can we help?"

"Can I ask you to identify this koru?"

Nyree passed over a plastic bag containing the necklace. He studied the engraving on the back and passed it back to her.

"That's hers. We don't engrave them like that, but she did."

"Same with the ring," the woman added with contempt.

"The ring?"

"Greenstone. To match the koru. Put the date she met up with her father on them."

"And she always wore it?"

"Always wore both," Hanson replied. "Rawiri gave them to her. They were precious. High quality greenstone."

"Like this one," the woman said, holding out one hand on which she wore a simple, band of dark green jade.

"She wasn't wearing her ring?" Hanson asked immediately.

"We haven't found it."

"Maybe she was robbed," the woman said and made a noise of disgust.

"That's something we'll consider," Nyree said as she dug out the photo of Lily Holmes. "Also, can I ask if you know this child? Huia was last seen with her." She handed it over.

Hanson studied the photograph at arm's length, then handed it across to the woman who blinked down at it, clearly moved. "That's her cousin's child—Lily."

Noting the sympathy, Nyree added, "Lily's type-1 diabetic. She hasn't been seen since she was in Huia's care. She hasn't had any medication for the past two days. We need to find her quickly."

"How can we help?" the woman asked.

"We'd like your permission to do a door-knock…" Nyree tipped her head. "…maybe a house-to-house search if necessary."

"On Māori land?" the woman asked. Probably fully conversant with the fact that if under a life-or-death threat, police didn't need permission.

Hanson jumped in. "When did you have in mind?"

"I have a search team ready now," Nyree said firmly. "I'm sorry, I know the timing's bad," Nyree said and glanced around at the gathering crowds.

"I don't want anyone upset."

"You have my word; they'll be respectful and careful. But I need to find this child."

The woman nodded in thought while the corners of Hanson's mouth turned down in deliberation. They shared a moment of silent communication, then Hanson said, "You have my consent. I hope you find her."

"Thank you."

Nyree rose to leave when the woman said, "Have you questioned Sean Clemmons about Huia's death?"

On hearing his name, Nyree sat down again. "No, we haven't."

"You know what he did to Emere Grady's mokopuna. She's one of ours." The belligerence was back. Gaze flinty, tattooed lips curled down hard at the corners, finger stabbing in Nyree's direction. "He nearly killed her. Now he's out on parole. Tell me how that happens?"

"I'd like to know the same thing," Nyree replied. Which she did. Particularly since she was the one who'd put him away. "But I don't make the rules."

"Then you should start looking in that direction in my opinion."

The tense atmosphere was cut when a child—maybe nine or so—appeared from around the back of the meeting house where preparations for the wedding feast were underway, judging by the aroma wafting through the air. Milk chocolate skin, short brown curls, big brown eyes, she sidled up to the old woman, pressed into her side, and cupped a hand to whisper into her ear. The woman circled an arm around the child, drawing her in and smiling for the first time as she listened.

"You're a good girl, Marama," she told the child in Māori as she released her. "You go and tell them we'll be there soon."

While Marama flicked Nyree a shy glance, then scooted away, Hanson smiled. "One of my mokopuna. I've got six now. All trouble except that one. She's a good girl." The smile grew, then faded into concern. "Did you know Huia was pregnant?"

"I did. I'm so sorry for your loss. I believe Rawiri Cooper also knew."

The old woman grunted. "That's all we heard about. Anyone would have thought he was the only grandfather in the world." Sadness suddenly filled her eyes. "And now that child is gone."

"Then you'll understand how important it is to find Lily. For her whānau—for her family."

She nodded, long and slow. Then said, "Let me know when your officers are due. I'll be there to meet them and get them some assistance."

"Thank you," Nyree said. And really meant it.

CHAPTER 9

"Thank God for that," Nyree muttered when they got back to the car. "I thought for a second we were next to be seen off."

"Me, too."

"When is Hicks's search team due?"

He checked his watch. "Within the hour. You think it's worth checking out Clemmons?"

"There's a connection there, but I'm not convinced. Leave that to me. I'll see what I can dig out. Meantime, get the team to ask around. See who Huia knew there, what the connections were, family conflicts, that sort of stuff." She frowned across at the buildings. A figure appeared in the distance—a young male, heavyset, facial tattoos. He gave them a long, hard stare, then melted back into the gathering crowds.

"And pull any records on the two blokes who took exception to Henare being up here. See if you can find out what that was about," she said. She pulled down her seatbelt and buckled it. "Soon as the team gets here, tell them to find out when Huia was last here. Give them the photo of Huia's missing ring and clothing."

"Yes, Ma'am."

"Then, when they get a chance, see if you can get someone to question that girl Marama—the granddaughter. See if we can get anything out of her. Kids like her hear the gossip, know what's going on in these places. Check and see if anyone wasn't as welcoming to Huia as Rawiri Cooper was."

"Got it." Callaghan was still frantically writing.

"Then get onto the local high schools around Whangārei. Find out which ones are doing literacy courses. I want to know which course she was doing and what they know about her."

"Will do, Ma'am."

"Then get onto the local boys. See if they've got any updates on this marae. Sounds to me like they've had a visit from the local police. I'd like to know why."

"Got it, Ma'am." He hit the ignition and headed the car back down the driveway.

"Have we had contact with the parents yet?"

"Not yet."

"I'll get down there soon as we've seen the boyfriend. It's nearly eleven already. That child's been missing fifteen hours already. How long before her insulin wears off?"

"I wouldn't know, Ma'am."

Nyree opened her computer on the growing file as they drove out of the parking lot and headed back to the main street. She read off the address, then searched his name for prior offenses. "Surprise, surprise—database shows our Mr. Skinner's got form."

"That is a shock, Ma'am. What's he got?"

"Couple of B and Es. Drugs—long-time dealing, habitual user. Past connection with gangs, one assault on a female."

"Nice guy."

Nyree checked her watch. "He should be at work by now. Let's pay him an early visit, shake the bugger up a bit." She gave Callaghan the address for Crane Miller, a timber yard on the outskirts of River Falls. Callaghan tapped the address into the GPS and put his foot down.

They drove for some time, each lost in their own thoughts.

Then Callaghan said, "The thing I don't get is why dump Huia Coburn in the river? If you'd murdered someone, you'd want to get rid of the body where no one would find her. Why not bury her?"

Nyree slipped him a sideways look and snorted. "Are you kidding? You'd need two weeks' notice and a Bobcat to dig anything worth putting a body in. It's all volcanic, full of rocks. Even if you got a decent hole, you'd be spotted in two minutes flat in that area. Anyway," she said, and turned a thoughtful look out the passenger's window, "the way she was smashed over the back of the head, I don't think this was premeditated. Looks to me like she went to walk away and her killer lashed out. That indicates they acted out of fear or rage. Maybe she told him to stick it and walked away. I reckon he instinctively lashed out and killed her."

"To kill her outright with one blow like that would take one mighty whack."

"Yeah." She switched to the report. "Christine said the shape of the wound suggests we're searching for a blunt weapon with squared off edges—narrower at one end. Something like the back of an axe or a squared-off mallet or something. My guess is he already had it in his hand. Or very close at hand. The first thing he grabbed, maybe."

"Suggests we're looking somewhere near a workshop."

"Or a farm shed," she mused.

"So, he strikes Huia down, realizes she's dead...what about Lily? Why take her? Why not just drop her on the street somewhere?"

Elbow on the windowsill, Nyree put the knuckle of her forefinger to her lip, smoothing it back and forth in thought, her gaze directed to the passing fields. "Because she witnessed the whole thing. Probably saw him kill Huia. And at six years old, she'd be able to identify him. He can't let her do that. So, he takes her, maybe leaves her in the car while he dumps Huia's body, then takes her somewhere else."

Callaghan cut her a pained glance. "Huia's car hasn't been found. Maybe she's still in it."

Nyree heaved out a sigh. "Yeah, and that could be anywhere." Her eyes narrowed on the map. "There are two gas stations through town. Get one of the team to check their cameras in the hours before she was dumped. It's a long shot but maybe she stopped for gas before she left."

"Have we got anything from the ligatures on her wrists yet?"

"Not yet. Christine confirmed he tied her up post-mortem. I'm hoping we'll get some good prints off them."

"If Lily's still alive, how long's he going to keep her? And what's he going to do with a six-year-old whose mother's looking for her?"

"That's the sixty-four-thousand-dollar question. It depends on how desperate he is. And the closer we get, the more desperate he'll get. I don't want any details of our investigation leaked to the media. I want vanilla-flavored statements—'on-going investigation, no further leads, helping with enquiries, blah, blah' that sort of stuff."

"I'll caution the media center."

"Good."

"But get Kelly in. We need to get her desperation out on the television. Tug at some heartstrings. Right now, don't mention the connection between Huia and Lily."

"The press is bound to get it."

"We'll just have to fudge it. And don't let Kelly mention Huia. Just get her to make an appeal to whoever's got Lily. Ask them to drop her somewhere. Push the point that she's insulin dependent."

She turned to the window and grimaced. "What's not sitting right with me is the timing. If the tourists found her just before nine, and she'd been in the water for, what? Two, three hours? He'd have been dumping her seven o'clock. It's still light then. Anyone could have seen him carrying her up the track."

"Are we sure he used that track?" Callaghan asked.

"It's the shortest route. Even carrying a dead body that far over that kind of terrain would take some effort. And there's nowhere along that track he could have easily put her down to take a breather."

"Then I guess that rules out a female attacker?"

"Or it means there's two of them. So," she said and closed the laptop and tucked it down at her feet. "Let's see if her boyfriend, Brodie Skinner, was one of them."

CHAPTER 10

Crane Miller Timber was situated six kilometers north of River Falls just off the main road. A vast corrugated iron building painted moss green, it sat square on to a driveway broad enough to accommodate lorries, the wide entrance allowing full view of the inside where forklifts zipped back and forth between stacks of neatly-sawn timber stained pink with preservatives.

Down the left-hand side of the building, several men labored on wide work benches, nailing frames and trusses, their nail-guns popping repeatedly against the squeal of enormous band-saws.

A tall, thin man wearing khaki coveralls and carrying a clipboard looked up as they got out of the car, then ambled towards them waving a hand to shoo them off.

"Sorry, you can't park there. We've got a truck arriving in about five minutes."

Nyree held up her ID as she approached. "Police. I'm DI Bradshaw, this is DS Callaghan. Do you have a Brodie Skinner working here?"

The guy looked from Nyree to Callaghan. "Why? What's he done?"

"We just need to talk to him."

He tucked the clipboard under his arm and his pen into his coveralls pocket. "Sure, I'll go and get him. Could you just—"

"And we'll move the car," she assured him.

Brodie Skinner slipped a leather glove from one hand then the other as he sauntered out to meet them. He wore a red plaid shirt, scuffed steel-capped boots and a look of defiance plastered across his face.

His faded jeans, Nyree noted, were held up using a broken leather belt repaired using a black cable tie. His pale ginger hair was razored almost to the scalp, a jagged scar just above his left ear clearly visible through the stubble, another just under the right eye. The open vee of his shirt revealed an intricate tattoo that ran around to the back of his neck and up to his hairline, and on his right arm, a tattoo of a snake disappeared up the sleeve. Everything about him suggested he'd spent time inside. From Kelly Holmes's description, he was exactly what Nyree had expected.

He stopped in front of Nyree with his big, square head tilted, his expression sour.

"Brodie Skinner?"

"Yeah? What do you lot want?"

Callaghan cut Nyree a look, then excused himself and went to move the car.

Skinner's scathing glare remained on the departing Callaghan while Nyree slipped the photograph of Huia Coburn from the file tucked in the crook of her arm, and held it up. Right in his face.

"Do you know this girl?"

Skinner narrowed his flinty gaze on the picture, then shifted it to Nyree. "Why? What's she done?"

Same question the foreman asked about him.

Nyree ignored it. "Can you confirm her name for me?"

"You didn't tell me why."

Nyree wanted to tell him it didn't matter why. When a DI asks you a question, you answer. Instead, she said, "Can you just confirm her identity for me, Mr. Skinner?"

He shifted his weight, smoothing out the gloves, mouth still in the sneer. "It's Huia. Coburn. Why? What's this about?"

Again, Nyree ignored the question and pressed on. "Can I ask what your relationship is with her?"

"She's my girlfriend." He switched his attention to Callaghan who was walking up behind Nyree. "Well...kind of girlfriend," he added with a snide, one-sided grin.

"When was the last time you saw her?" she asked.

The frown deepened, eyes remaining on Callaghan who walked back to join them. His attention came back to Nyree. "Yesterday. Why?"

"When yesterday?"

He huffed and hiked his jeans up as he cut a look back at the factory. "Look, I just got this job. I'm already on parole. If they think I'm in trouble with the cops again, I'll get the boot and they'll chuck me back inside. So, just get on with it, will you?"

Callaghan said, "You can't lose your job just because you're helping with a police inquiry."

Skinner's eyebrows shot up. "You reckon? And what perfect universe do you live in?"

Nyree glanced across to where the foreman stood watching while the other men continued their work, occasionally glancing up at them and making comments among themselves.

"I'll have a word with your boss. Now, can you just answer the question? Or," she offered with a shrug, "we could do this back at River Falls police station."

Perhaps realizing she could make life much worse for him, Skinner dropped his shoulders, head cocked. "Yesterday morning. She'd stayed the night."

"What time did she leave?"

He focused his attention on folding the gloves into one hand, and made a doubtful face. "Six? Six-thirty? I dunno. I start here at seven."

"What time do you finish?" Callaghan asked.

"Four, why? Are you going to tell me what this is about?" he asked.

"Four o'clock exactly?"

The scowl deepened. "Yeah, why?"

"And you were here the whole time from seven in the morning until four o'clock yesterday afternoon?"

He dashed a knuckle under his nose then folded his arms. "Yes." Irritation rose in his tone.

"And where did you go after work?"

"To the supermarket then straight home. This bloody leg bracelet doesn't let me go anywhere else." He lifted his pants leg to reveal the electronic bracelet.

"Which supermarket did you go to?"

"Why?"

"Just answer the question," said Callaghan.

"The one in town." His eyes narrowed. "Why are you asking all this? Is Huia dead or something?"

The question hit Nyree like a slap in the face. "Why would you ask if she's dead?"

"Because she looks dead in that picture," he said and jerked his chin at the file she'd slipped the photograph back into. "You go around asking questions about her, you wanna try trying something she looks alive in, mate."

He stuck his hands on his hips. Like he had the upper hand now.

"You don't seem surprised that she's dead." *Or upset,* Nyree thought but didn't say so.

A bark of grim laughter. "Surprised? Have you seen that bullshit lot she hangs out with at that marae?" He thumbed off into the distance. "That bloke up there is seriously weird on her."

"Which bloke?" Callaghan asked before Nyree could.

"Some Māori bloke, I dunno. He works in the gardens up there. Told Huia he'd teach her to read. Yeah, right," he scoffed and briefly looked away. Skinner's expression morphed into an ugly grin. "He'd teach her stuff, alright, but it wouldn't be about books."

"What did she say about him?"

He leaned in. "She said he was *nice* to her. Gave her a ring. Next thing, she's got a moko and she's into that 'te reo' shit—speaking Māori and learning stupid fairy tales. I said to her, 'You're about as Māori as I am.' I said, 'You keep this up, you're gonna piss someone off and wind up dead.' And big surprise," he said, spreading his hands like an introduction, "here we are."

"You don't think she was just trying to connect with her roots?"

Skinner's eyebrows went up in the middle. "She's pakeha –white as you and me. Or has that escaped everyone's notice? She goes wandering up there making out she's Māori, doing hakas and getting tatts. Some around here take exception to that kind of shit. So, no, I'm not surprised she's dead."

Nyree let that lie for the moment.

"Do you know a child named Lily Holmes?"

For the first time Skinner looked confused. A deep frown crumpled his brow as his head jerked back. "Well…yeah. She's the kid Huia looks after. Why? What's she got to do with anything?"

"Lily was with Huia the last time she was seen alive."

Skinner's eyes switched from Nyree to Callaghan and back. He wrapped his arms tightly across his chest. "So where is she now?"

"We don't know, Mr. Skinner. That's what we're trying to find out."

Before leaving, Nyree confirmed his presence at work until 4p.m. the previous day, took down his address, parole officer's name, and car registration.

"I feel like I need a shower after talking to him," Nyree said as they drove out of the yard.

"Yeah, but he's right, we really have to get a better photo of her."

They stopped at the intersection with the main road where Callaghan leaned forward, searching the main highway each way before pulling out and heading back to River Falls.

"You notice the cable tie holding his belt together?"

Nyree drew back one corner of her mouth and gave a flick of the eyebrows as she rechecked her notes. "I certainly did. And the times fit. If Huia had been in the water for three hours when she was found at nine, he would have had time to kill her then dispose of the body."

"The leg bracelet puts him out of the picture, though."

"Not if she was at his place when she died. Give his parole officer a call and confirm the times match with his bracelet. Then get onto the supermarket. See if they've got any CCTV footage that might show him entering and leaving. I don't like him," she said, although that made no difference to whether he'd murdered Huia or not.

"Trouble is, if he'd gone to the river to dump her, the bracelet would have activated. And he'd know that."

"Yes, but what if someone else dumped her? He could have picked them up, killed Huia, then gotten someone else to get rid of her. I want his car brought in for evidence of Lily being in it, and I want a search of his house. Just in case," she added.

"Will do." Callaghan massaged his chin. "He did look shocked that Lily was missing, though."

"Yeah, I noticed that. Take the car in and do the search anyway. Did we get an address for her family?"

"Came through while you were talking to Skinner."

She checked the time. "Good. I'll pay them a visit soon as I get back to Whangārei. They could know of anyone Huia might have left Lily with—somebody she could have dropped her with before she met with her killer."

"Let's just pray that's the case."

"We'll find her. We just have to hope it's soon. If whoever's got her doesn't kill her, she could fall into a diabetic coma. It won't matter what we do. She'll still be dead."

"We've got the search teams in place, the house-to-house, police divers at the river, everything we can do to find her."

"I know. Now it's the waiting game with time we don't have. Meanwhile, I've got the unenviable job of telling a mother that her daughter is dead, and that her niece's child is missing."

"Rather you than me," Callaghan said.

CHAPTER 11

Annette Coburn opened the door after the first knock. A thin, pale woman in her early forties, she peered out at Nyree and immediately clutched her bathrobe in at the chest. Eyes filmy, hair ruffled, she'd clearly been in bed.

"I'm sorry to disturb you, Mrs. Coburn. I'm Detective Inspector Nyree Bradshaw." She flipped open the ID wallet and held it up for Annette Coburn to see.

"What's this about?"

"It's about your daughter, Huia. May I come in?"

For a second Annette Coburn looked somewhat bewildered. Then she said, "Um, yeah, come in." She gestured to somewhere behind her and stood back for Nyree to enter.

The house was typical of government housing built in the 1960s—weatherboard, wooden window frames, tile roof. Nyree stepped into a narrow hallway lined with religious pictures—Jesus on the cross, the garden of Gethsemane, the Last Supper. A threadbare length of carpet ran down the well-worn wood floor leading to the kitchen beyond. To her left, she noted a small living room, large-screen TV, new leather sofa strewn with multicolored cushions. To the right was a small bedroom, one single bed with a purple throw, exercise bike that looked unused, curtains closed.

Walking ahead, Annette Coburn said, "What's happened? What's she done now?"

Nyree waited until they'd entered the tiny kitchen at the rear of the house.

"Would you like to sit down, Mrs. Coburn?"

Annette slowly rounded the table, suspicion-filled eyes pinned on Nyree. Then she sank onto one of the plastic-seated, chrome dining chairs.

Nyree sat opposite her and leaned in, her voice gentle. "I'm afraid I have some bad news. The body of a young woman was discovered up in River Falls. We believe it's your daughter, Huia."

Annette Coburn's hand went straight to her mouth and her eyes widened in horror. "What? It can't be."

"When did you last see her, Mrs. Coburn?"

She shook her head, vehement. "It can't be her. She can't be dead. She's my only child. She's all I've got."

Nyree reached out a hand and gently covered hers. She could feel it tremble, the skin cold and dry.

"Mrs. Coburn, listen to me..." When she lifted her gaze, Nyree gently said, "Can you just tell me when you last saw her."

Clearly fighting back a wash of emotions, Annette Coburn turned her head away before gathering herself. "Um, last Saturday. About twelve. She looked terrible. Was it that boyfriend of hers?" she demanded suddenly. "Was it that little shit that got her pregnant? Did he do this? Did he kill her?"

"Why would you think he had something to do with it?"

She huffed and rolled her eyes to the ceiling. "Oh, come on. I know what he's like. He's a nasty little piece of work. I told her to stop seeing him. I knew this would happen. I *knew* it."

"Did he ever strike her?"

The very suggestion seemed to ignite a vat of long-held resentment. "Oh, he did way worse than that. He burned her with cigarettes and said it was an accident. An accident? Not likely. I told her this would happen. And what does she do? Keeps on seeing him, the stupid girl. And now this happens. I warned her. And would she listen?" She twisted away, her upper lip curled in abject hatred. When her gaze returned to Nyree again, her eyes were narrowed, calculating. "So, are you going to arrest him?"

The sudden change hit a sour note with Nyree. "We're still conducting our inquiries."

"I'll save you the time. Just go and pick him up right now. He did it. It'll be written all over his face."

"Mrs. Coburn, we've already spoken to Mr. Skinner, and he said he hadn't seen Huia since earlier that day."

"Oh, and you believe him?"

Nyree had always felt for every victim. She'd stepped into their shoes and felt their sense of loss. After all, wasn't that the reason for her hands-on approach? Right from her early days on the force, she knew that the role of Detective Inspector was more like a ringmaster, directing the flow of information gleaned by the investigation team, stepping back and taking a clinical, helicopter view of the case. Even Nolan, her Superintendent, had told her she got too involved.

But this was an approach that worked for Nyree. She needed to see the victims, to connect with the family and whānau of the dead, to know that her search for the guilty brought some kind of closure for those affected. Nolan had told her it could cloud her judgement.

She begged to differ. It sharpened her resolve.

But already Annette Coburn's reaction to the death of her daughter had set a cold stone of doubt in the pit of her stomach.

Nyree clasped her hands loosely in front of her. "Mr. Skinner's employer has confirmed he was at his place of work the whole day, Mrs. Coburn."

"Then he did it before work. Or the night before. Or that crowd he works for is covering for him. It's him, you mark my words."

Annette Coburn wrapped her arms around herself, seething.

Nyree let a silence fall between them.

Let the scene play out. Don't push it.

"So, what happens now?" Not so much a question as a demand.

"I'm afraid I'm going to have to ask if you or one of your family can identify the body."

"To see if it's her, you mean? Because it might not be, right?"

"To confirm that it is her, yes. I'm so sorry."

For the longest moment, Annette Coburn stared at a point somewhere mid-distance in front of her. Not a word. Not a breath.

The silence was broken when the back door opened and a man stepped in. Brown hair thinning on top, watery blue eyes, pale pudgy skin, slight paunch under the blue checked shirt and grey wool jacket, he was clutching a Dunkin Donuts bag. "I got the chocolate one but…" he said, and looked up, stopping short at the sight of the two of them. "What's happened?"

Annette Coburn's face crumpled and her thin body seemed to collapse in on itself. Releasing a guttural howl like a trapped animal, she threw back her head, wailing, "She's dead, Pete. Our Huia's dead."

For one long moment, he blinked, as if unsure what to do. Then, tossing the donut bag on the table, he went to her. She rose to meet his embrace as he pulled her in and held her, patting her back with the flat of his hand. "It's all right, it's all right. Come 'ere, come on." As his wife calmed, he held her back to meet her eyes. "What's happened?" He cut an accusing look back at Nyree. "Who are you?"

She rose from the chair. "Detective Inspector Nyree Bradshaw, Whangārei Base CIB, sir." She dug out her ID and lifted it for him.

"She told me Huia's dead." Annette collapsed into his arms again, her face nestling into his neck. "She can't be, Pete. Our little Huia can't be dead."

He altered his stance, wrapping his arms further around her, stroking her hair. "Sh-sh-sh, calm down. What makes you think this dead girl is Huia?" he asked Nyree.

"The body of a young woman was found up in River Falls. We have reason to believe it could be your daughter. I'm sorry but we can't confirm it until someone—preferably a family member—can identify her."

"I'll do it," he said. "Hey, shush. It's okay," he told his wife as he held her. "I'm here now. It's all going to be okay."

"Thank you," Nyree said. "I'm sorry, I know this is a hard time for you, but Huia was last seen with a small child—Lily Holmes." She plucked a photograph from her pocket. "She's still missing and we need to find her. Is there any chance you've seen her?"

He glanced down at the photo and made a doubtful face. "Huia babysat for her but I wouldn't know the last time she did that."

Annette Coburn pulled out of the embrace to look at the photograph, dashing away non-existent tears. "We only saw her on Saturday, didn't we, Pete? Huia, I mean," she told Nyree. "She didn't have Lily with her then."

"So, where is she?" Peter asked.

"That's what we're trying to find out."

"Did you ask Skinner?" Annette asked urgently. "He'll have taken her."

Peter shrugged. "Why would he take Lily?"

Nyree put the photograph away, determined not to be led down the path of accusing Brodie Skinner again. "Would you both mind answering a few questions for me?"

"Yeah, sure," he replied.

"Did Huia call either of you anytime yesterday?"

A headshake from both parents.

Nyree knew that if they had no involvement in Huia's disappearance, she was pressing them at a tough time. But she needed as much information as she could get, and she needed it now.

"I believe Huia had a literacy problem. Can you tell me how that affected her?"

"Well, she couldn't read too well," Peter Coburn offered. "But she wasn't stupid. She could read text messages and stuff. Didn't stop her on Facebook, did it, love?"

Annette shot him a steely glance, then turned away with a reluctant headshake.

"Do you know her username on Facebook?"

"Nope," Peter Coburn replied and looked to his wife.

"Not a clue," she added without any offer to find it. "I don't have anything to do with that sort of stuff."

"We'll see what we can do," Nyree told her and made a note on her phone. "Did she ever stay here?"

"Sometimes." Again, Annette looked to her husband. "Why?"

"Do you mind if we search her room? Just in case she left anything there that might give us a clue who she was last with."

"I doubt there's anything there," Annette said bluntly.

"If you have to," Peter said. "It might help," he told his wife.

"When was the last time you had any communication with her?"

The parents shared a questioning look. Then Annette said, "Last Saturday. She texted me to say she was on her way here. She wanted to use our computer."

"May I see that text?"

"I deleted it," she said immediately. "I delete all my texts."

Annette Coburn stood at the living room window and watched the cop return to her car, hop in, and get straight on the phone. Rattled as she was, Annette had kept her cool, watched every word she said, deliberately answering every question without giving anything away. The trick was to tell the truth without telling all of it. She'd done well.

But that wouldn't be the end of it. She stood hugging herself, gazing out, watching the cop in case she came back.

Finally, the cop hung up the phone, buckled up her seatbelt and drove off. About bloody time. But, just as Annette went to turn back to the kitchen, her attention snagged on movement from the house across the street. In the front bedroom window, that interfering cow was standing behind the glass, staring at her. The bile in Annette's throat rose. Nic Robson, the slut. Interfering in Annette's family. Ever since they moved in across the street, she and that rotten daughter of hers had turned Huia against her own family; planted seeds of rebellion in her head.

The two women stood there, staring each other down from the relative safety of their respective homes, a matter of thirty meters apart due to the proximity of their properties. Neither looked away. Even from this distance, Annette could see the scowl carved into Nic Robson's features. The standoff broke when Peter entered the room behind her.

"What are you doing?" He glanced toward the window. As if he didn't know.

"Nothing. Out of my way, I've got to get dressed."

Peter stepped aside and let her pass. Without another word she made straight for the kitchen and began cutting up carrots. The sooner they were in the clear, the better. As long as everyone kept their gobs shut, everything would pass. They'd arrest Brodie Skinner and everyone else could get on with their lives.

But first, they'd need evidence. And that, Annette realized, was something she could provide.

Back in the car, Nyree's phone rang.

Checking the rear-view mirror and the street ahead, she snatched it up, answered it, and spoke with it shouldered against her ear. "DI Bradshaw."

It was Christine, the pathologist. "Nyree, I just wanted to let you know something I found."

"Go on," she said.

"Right in the back of Huia's throat, I found some shreds of paper."

"Paper? What kind of paper."

"I don't know. There was also a matching wad in her pocket."

"And what's on it?"

"Don't know. I can see there's writing but it's pretty delicate. I'm sending it away to the lab to see if they can get anything off it."

"Sean Clemmons stuffed his last victim's mouth full of paper to shut her up while he tried to kill her."

"I remember."

"Do you remember the grandmother? Emere Grady?"

"She was very vocal at Clemmons's trial."

"She's the one who ID'd him; stood up to him in court. He threatened she'd be next. Said he'd kill her. I wouldn't put that past him."

"What'll you do?" Christine asked.

"I'm going to visit her, see if I can shoehorn her out of her house until he's back inside. Last thing I need is another death on my hands."

CHAPTER 12

Everything that could be done to find little Lily Holmes, was being done. Search teams were scouring the area, neighborhoods canvassed, search and cadaver dogs brought in, though Nyree didn't even want to think about that possibility.

All the way back to Whangārei, her heart broke for Kelly Holmes. Losing her child would be the end of her world. Nyree was no stranger to the loss of a child, but this would be so much worse.

The sun had set over the hills cloaking the horizon in silken gold streaked with red wisps. By the time she hit the backstreets heading to Emere's house, streetlights flickered on and the city fell into shadow.

Lights showed at the windows of Emere's old villa, and as she pulled into the driveway, the flicker of the television danced across the uncovered windows. A flash of alarm went through her. Emere always drew her curtains at night. This was unusual.

Nyree got out of the car, hurried to the front door, and she hammered on the wood panel with the side of her fist.

"Emere! It's me, Nyree Bradshaw. Open the door."

A second blast of alarm. This time sharper.

She left the porch and stepped into the garden to peer in through the front window. Inside the fire was lit and the television on.

No Emere.

So, she went back to the porch, reaching for her phone…

…when the door opened and Emere peered out.

"Nyree," she said in surprise. "What are you doing here?"

Nyree's heart thrashed once against her ribs, then returned to a slow gallop. "I was worried. You didn't answer the door."

"I was out back making a cup of tea."

Nyree pressed a hand to her still thumping heart. "Oh, thank God."

"Well? Are you coming in, or are you rushing off again?"

Nyree sat in the warm living room with the china teacup in her hands, checking her watch every couple of seconds and searching for the best way to approach this.

"Emere, this isn't just a social call."

Emere sat in her old easy chair, facing her. "I guessed that. You're here because he's out, aren't you?" She took a sip of her tea, then put the cup down. "Victim Support called me this afternoon. I've got all the doors locked. He won't get in."

The confidence in her voice tugged at Nyree's heartstrings. She'd seen what the worst of humanity could do, and a locked door or window wouldn't stop them.

She nodded to the uncovered window. "Your curtains are open. Why didn't you close them?"

"So I could see if he came here. He thinks he can scare me? To hell with him. I'm ready for anything he can bring on," she replied.

Nyree sighed. "I want you to leave, Emere. Sean Clemmons will come here, there's nothing more certain. And locked doors won't keep him out. I don't want to frighten you, but if we could just put you somewhere…"

Already she was shaking her head. "You saw what he did to my beautiful Hana. Left her terrified of her own shadow. And I'm buggered if I'll let him drive me out of my own home."

"I understand. But…"

She put her cup down. "No. I'm staying here. If he turns up, I'll call the police and he'll go straight back to prison." She gave one sharp nod to indicate her mind was made up.

If only it were that easy.

"And what happens if he breaks a window and gets into the house? What if you can't call the police in time?"

The confidence leached from her face. "But he can't. He's got that non-molesting order on him. He's not allowed to come near any of us."

Nyree sat forward and reached out, her hand gently covering Emere's.

"Then, how about if I stay here a while? Would you mind?"

The old woman's face brightened. "Well, of course you can. Let me make up a bed." She went to get up but Nyree stopped her.

"Don't worry about the bed," she said. "I doubt I'll be sleeping."

The faintest sound jolted Nyree awake. Like a gentle knock on wood.

She sat up instantly alert, pulse throbbing.

Her mouth felt parched, and the flesh down her spine prickled.

She must have fallen straight into a deep sleep the moment the old lady had gone to bed. According to her watch it was now 11:15 p.m. Much later than she'd intended staying.

The fire had burned down to a mound of smoldering ashes. The chill of the night air had begun seeping in.

Silence radiated around the room.

So, what had woken her?

Rising soundlessly from her chair, ears straining, she switched off the light, moved to the curtains, and parted them an inch to peek out.

The streetlight threw a dull, yellow shroud of light across the front garden. Beyond, the street and house directly opposite were all silently bathed in in that same yellow mixed with a hint of moonlight. A light coating of frost sparkled over the roof of her car. To the left, the same three cars from the night before.

Not a squeak of sound.

Had she dreamt it?

Then, she heard it again.

From the rear of the house.

With her heart pounding she made her way down the darkened hallway to the kitchen. Tiptoeing quietly through the shadows, she ducked down and crept along through the galley kitchen, pausing next to the stove. Outside she could see the outline of an enormous tree at the rear of the property. When she raised her head, moonlight picked out the path running down the back to the vegetable garden.

No sign of movement.

Then, a *thump!* This time from the side of the house.

On the wooden weatherboards. Like the flat of a hand slamming against them.

Nyree raced back down the hallway to the spare bedroom where the sound seemed to have emanated from. Outside the bushes formed deep pools of shadow. Staring into the darkness she held her breath and waited.

Everything remained icily still. Not a twig, not a leaf moved.

Another thump. This time from right outside. Next to the window.

"You bastard," she whispered as she reached for the window catches. They were old, painted over and stuck fast.

Abandoning the window, she hurried out into the hallway and straight to the front door. Hands trembling, she fumbled with the lock and yanked it open to the sound of a car starting up. Outside, exhaust clouded in the chill of the night air, and the tail lights of a car went to the end of the street and disappeared around the corner.

"I'll get you, you little shit," she growled. "Just you wait."

But he'd already gone.

CHAPTER 13

"I want an urgent alert put out on Sean Clemmons's car."

She was sitting in the living room, Emere handing her a hot cup of tea.

"Thank you," she mouthed to the old woman, then returned to her phone call.

"No, I didn't see him," she replied to the Comms receiver's question. She hadn't been able to raise anyone from the station. So, she'd resorted to booking it through 111. Now she was wishing she hadn't bothered.

"Can you give us a description of the car?"

Nyree threw out a hand. "I didn't see the car. Look, I know it was him. Who else would it be?" In frustration, she dropped her head to cradle her forehead in her hand. It wasn't the call-taker's fault. Nyree knew the procedures as well as anyone.

"Listen, don't worry about it," she said, interrupting the call-taker mid-sentence. "I'll deal with it my end."

And she hung up.

"What do you think he'll do now?" Emere asked in a worried voice.

"I have no idea. But I need you to agree to move from here. Just until Clemmons is back behind bars."

"Will they arrest him again?"

"He'd have to cut off his bracelet to get here. That'll be enough to get his parole revoked."

"But how will you find him? Where would he go?"

"I don't know," Nyree told her in a tight voice. "But there's one person who might."

Nyree had waited for a police woman to take Emere to a motel, then gone straight back to her office in Whangārei, writing reports and making calls, hounding the teams to find out what they'd discovered.

All she'd gotten back was the same statement—no news. They'd let her know as soon as they found something.

Little Lily Holmes had been missing now for almost twenty hours. And as much as she wanted to get back to River Falls, Nyree headed back to the place she dreaded most.

Thirty-two minutes later, she crested the last hill. The sight of the razor-wire fences and guard tower bathed in the spotlights of Northland's Bankhill prison all dredged up memories that sat in her chest like a rock. The second private high-security facility to be built in the north, Bankhill had already met its capacity of inmates.

What the hell is going on with this country? she wondered for the millionth time as she drew the car in through the security gates and turned into the parking lot in front.

At this time of night there was no hint of activity from the outside. She'd called ahead on her way there and the prison warden had agreed to meet her out front.

After inspecting her ID, the officer on the door had admitted her in through the front entrance, past those same all-too-familiar metal detectors, through the security gates, moving from one area to the next, deeper and deeper into the bowels of the prison.

How many times had she been here? Just the sight of these barred windows and the same familiar smell of the corridors made her skin itch.

"You're here to see Tony Vericich?" the young security officer confirmed. He obviously didn't know.

"I'll take it from here," said a familiar voice.

She turned to find Henry Patton entering the room.

"Henry," she said with a grateful smile. "How are you?"

"Better than you by the looks of it. Here to see him?" he asked gently as the young officer made his exit.

Nerves jangling, she felt herself swallow involuntarily. "How is he?"

Henry signed her in and gave a grim chuckle. "Doesn't change."

"That's a shame," was all she could say.

Sure enough, after completing the formalities, she entered the visitation room to find Tony slouching back in a pale blue plastic chair, an officer standing alongside him.

Maintaining a calm façade, keeping her voice moderate lest her emotions give her away, Nyree casually crossed the room and sat before making eye contact. First time in months. And all those feelings surprised her once again as they bubbled up like a pool of boiling mud.

She sat bolt upright, business-like, voice calm, her nerves radiating shockwaves beneath the surface. "Thank you for agreeing to see me."

He gave her a one-sided smirk. "Like I had a choice."

Even the familiar sound of his voice raised needles under her skin. Like the prickle of extreme high-frequency vibrations.

She swallowed involuntarily and fought to keep her voice steady. "You're looking well."

When he snorted and folded his arms, she noted the amateur tattoo on his arm, the broken front tooth. Both recent. Certainly not there when she last saw him.

She sat forward, appealing to him. "Look, I just—"

"Why don't you just tell me what you want and get out?" he interrupted her. He knew her only too well. Knew the chinks in her armor. Knew how to hurt her.

Releasing a long breath as if she'd been caught in a lie, she simply said, "Sean Clemmons."

He chuckled and shifted position. "And what makes you think I know anything?"

"You were great mates at school. I hear you've been pretty good mates in here."

"So?"

When he just glared at her, she continued. "Come off it, Tony. You know what I'm asking you."

"And you think I'm just going to spew it all out, tell you what you want cos you asked nicely?" This time he laughed. Like it was the greatest joke he'd heard all year.

"If not for me, then do it for the girl he beat to a pulp. He's going back after her grandmother, Emere Grady. She's the one who got him put away. He'll kill her. I don't care what you think of me. But I care what happens to her."

Tony leaned forward, concentrating on scratching his dirty thumbnail back and forth across a gouge etched into the table between them. As if deliberating. Then he looked up. Withdrew the hand and met her gaze. Those dark eyes boring into hers.

"Well, I s'pose I can tell you one thing you obviously don't know."

"Which is?"

"Sean isn't going after the old lady." He refolded his arms, clearly relishing the hold he had over her.

Ramrod still in her seat, desperate to remain calm, she said, "He was at her house last night. I was there."

The one-sided smirk broke into a wide grin, exposing the broken tooth again. "Yeah. He was there. But he's not after her. He's after you. He said he's gonna get you for putting him inside."

Nyree stared at him in disbelief.

Containing her shock, she kept her tone even. "Well, thank you for letting me know."

"And don't ask me where he is now. Even if I knew, I still wouldn't tell you."

She nodded sharply and threw up an internal wall, fighting to hold back the tears.

How could he? The cruelty was almost too much.

In her mind's eye all she could see was that tiny baby she'd once held, the sweet little boy who'd held her hand, who'd cried when she'd left him on his first day at school. Image after image assailed her—that angelic smile as he transformed into a handsome young man. Then the angry teen he morphed into. The fury he'd unleashed when she'd left his stepfather…

"Is there anything you can tell me? Where Sean would go? What he's got planned?"

"I wouldn't tell you the time of day," he said mildly and waited for her reaction.

That young man she'd loved with all her heart. The memories of how he'd fallen in with that awful crowd, the parties, the crime, the violence. She should have been there.

All my fault.

Then the murder. A life snuffed out in a moment.

The police on Nyree's doorstep.

"Your son," they'd said.

Realizing she'd been sitting in stony silence for some moments, she looked up to find Tony studying her.

"Was there something else?" he asked.

"No."

Was he waiting for her to apologize? To atone for her failures?

"Then I'll go back to my cell." He got up and turned for the door, the officer at his side. But just before he disappeared through the open door, he paused to turn back to her. "And don't come back, Mum," he said. "I never want to see you again."

Out in the car, the sobs racked her chest and squeezed her heart until it broke into a million pieces all over again. Through the physical pain, through the tears and self-recrimination, those images re-emerged over and over: the tiny baby, her beautiful son, the anger in his eyes, his decision to live with his father, to keep his father's name.

The murder of that boy.

Another woman's child.

His total and utter rejection of her.

When the sobs eventually abated, she wiped up her tears, dried her face, and switched on the car engine.

The last thing she could do was sit here feeling sorry for herself.

She had another woman's child to find. And the key to finding her lay in the final moments of her dead babysitter.

She had just hit the ignition when her phone rang.

"Ma'am, it's Henare here. We finally got the search warrant on the tourists' van. It came through this morning."

"And...?"

"You're never going to believe what we found."

CHAPTER 14

It took Nyree fifty-one minutes to get back to River Falls, beating Callaghan's whirlwind trip the previous day by an even six minutes. All the way, the sun had stayed hidden behind the watery rainclouds, mere threats for most of the journey. By the time she pulled into the police station parking lot, heavy rainclouds had draped the town and thunderous drops were now hammering down on the car roof.

Nyree grimaced out through the misty window at the gloom as she cut the engine. Shoving the door open, she tented her raincoat over her head, and hopscotched between puddles to the front door. Inside, she swept the coat to one side and shook the water off.

"Where did that come from?" she asked the desk sergeant as she patted down the sleeve of her jacket to find it sodden.

"Welcome to the winterless north, Ma'am," he said with a grin. "Here, let me take your coat. I gather you're here to see our intrepid tourists?"

She passed across her coat and glanced down the hallway to the interview rooms. "They all settled in?"

He nodded in the direction she was looking. "Interview rooms one and three. They've been well fed and watered. DS Callaghan's in there with them. Oh, and I've assigned him our one and only pool car."

"Cheers. Then let's see what they've got to say, shall we?"

The couple had been separated for interviewing. Nyree entered to find Callaghan sitting in silence, glaring at Barrett who sat with his arms folded, pouting towards the only window like a grounded teen.

Callaghan immediately straightened in his seat. "Ma'am."

She gave him a curt nod and placed the now inch-thick file on the table between her and Barrett, avoiding his gaze while she sat and read the notes made by the warrant search team. Next to her Callaghan settled down in his chair and folded his arms, smugness radiating like the underdog's trainer at a prize-fight, where he knew the opponent didn't stand a chance.

Without a word, she took several minutes to look over the report in front of her. Then looked up to regard Barrett. The sullen demeanor did nothing to ease her contempt of him. Elbows on the table, she clasped her hands at her chin and looked him straight in the eye.

"As you're aware, Mr. Barrett, we received that search warrant for your rental van, registration number..." She broke away to find the report and recited off the details. Hands clasped again, she continued. "And yesterday evening, my team did a thorough search of the contents of the vehicle."

"Where is it now?" he demanded. "If it doesn't go back to the rental outfit tomorrow, we pay penalties. If that happens, I'm taking you lot to court."

Nyree's eyebrows rose mildly. "I think at the moment the van rental is the least of your worries, Mr. Barrett." She slid the photographs from the file, twisted them on the table and pushed them towards him. "A hundred-and-forty-two-point-six kilograms of kiwifruit."

A questioning shrug. "So?"

"You stole those kiwifruit, Mr. Barrett."

His eyes searched the room before coming back to her. "What's that got to do with anything? We didn't kill that girl. We're the ones that called the cops. You can check your own records, if you like."

"Oh, I know what our records say. But the theft from the kiwifruit orchard overlooking the river had *everything* to do with the *murder* of *Huia Coburn*. Would you like me to tell you why?"

He drew in an irritated breath while his eyes went to a point just above her head. Sullen, sulky.

Nyree stabbed an accusing finger on the table between them. "You left a dead girl floating in the river while you and your girlfriend went stealing fruit."

"It was only a few minutes."

"A few minutes? Seriously? You tell me you picked a hundred-and-forty-two kilos of fruit in a few minutes. And yet, two experienced pickers would take a minimum of a few hours. You missed your forte in life, Mr. Barrett. With that kind of speed, you're wasting your time at university. You'd make a fortune picking fruit."

He huffed out a breath. "I still don't see what difference it makes."

A flash of anger burst in the back of Nyree's brain. "It makes a lot of difference. That girl you so callously disregarded while you went on your thieving jaunt, was last known to be looking after a six-year-old child. That child is now missing. Would you like to see her? Would you like to see a photo of the child whose life is now in jeopardy?" Nyree savagely pulled the photograph of Lily Holmes from the file and shoved it across the table at him.

Barrett's Adam's apple bobbed.

"And what about this?" She drew a small greenstone ring from a paper bag also tucked in the file and held it up. The distinctive inscription the kaumatua had told them about, the date confirming it.

After laying it on the photograph between them, Nyree leaned in and stabbed her finger on the tabletop, punctuating her words. "So, let me tell you what difference it makes, Mr. Barrett: We've been searching every entranceway to the river to find the route our killer had taken her. We've spent hundreds of manpower hours that we could have deployed in the kiwifruit orchard searching the area where you found this ring. You have wasted my time and put a type-one diabetic child's life at even more risk than it already was. I hope it was worth it." She got up, addressing Callaghan.

"Lock him up and charge him."

Barrett also leapt up, aghast. "You're charging me with theft of a few kiwifruit? Are you serious?"

Nyree spun around. "I'm charging you with attempting to pervert the course of justice, Mr. Barrett. You deliberately misled the police in a murder investigation. You withheld key evidence in a possible double-homicide and put your own selfish needs in front of those of an innocent child. That charge carries a minimum seven years in prison. Believe me, by the time we've finished with you, you'll wish we'd only charged you with theft."

And she walked out leaving Barrett gaping after her.

CHAPTER 15

Henare and Willis had spent the best part of the last two days tracing the river, knocking on doors, then backtracking to revisit houses where there'd been no answer. Where there was no reply, they'd followed paths to the rear of the property, scanning the area for tool sheds or chicken coops where a child might be held, calling Lily's name and giving the outbuildings a cursory search before moving to the next house. They were almost at the last property overlooking the carpark, ready with the same questions:

Where were you on this night?
Did you see anyone at this time?
Have you seen this child?

Each time someone had answered, getting the same response:

Why? What's happened?
No, I haven't seen anyone.
Oh, that poor child. Do you need more searchers?

The last of which had tugged at Henare's heartstrings. He and Willis had taken a moment's silent communication and, depending on the age and agility of the homeowner, either gratefully refused the offer, or given a phone number where they could volunteer their services.

"Every bit helps," Henare had said each time.

They had worked their way around all streets surrounding the river, moving south to a point where they could see the police divers in the pond below the waterfall. Swollen with flood waters and muddied by the pounding waters, Henare hadn't envied that job. Searching for a small body in the silt thickened waters near the bottom would be grim at best.

But the two detectives had their own job to do, so they'd made a few noises of gratitude for their own roles, and moved on.

They were making their way towards the final property up a long private driveway at the southernmost end of the river when Henare's phone rang—DI Bradshaw.

"Yes, Ma'am."

"How's the house-to-house going?"

"Ah, not too good. No one's seen anything unusual. Not really surprising. It's pretty dark along here at night. We've picked up a few extra potential searchers, though."

"That's good." After a moment's hesitation, she said, "I hate to be the bearer of bad news, but the tourists found a ring we think belonged to Huia Coburn. It was up in the kiwifruit orchard about half a kilometer north of Mason's Rock."

"Shit!" Henare said. Then remembered himself. "Sorry, Ma'am. That means we've spent all this time searching in the wrong place."

"Exactly. Not only that, the tourists lied about the time. We're now looking at a timeframe between six and eight instead of seven to nine."

"So, Lily Holmes has been missing longer than we thought."

"By at least an hour, maybe two." Both knew for an insulin-dependent kiddie, that could mean the difference between life and death.

Henare threw an exasperated look skywards. "Shit. Where do you need us now?"

A deep sigh of frustration echoed down the line. "Get back up the river. There's a road into the campground two hundred meters to the east of the river. It's likely that's where he came in. On the positive side, there's only a few houses along that side of the river and there's lighting along the path."

"We've only got one house to go here. You want us to finish off?"

"May as well. Don't spend too long on it, though. We've got a hell of a workload ahead." And she hung up.

Henare turned to Willis. "You're never going to bloody believe it."

"I heard," he said grimly. "Shall we, then?" He gestured toward the house that now sat at the very end of the street overlooking the harbor.

"Lead the way."

They both walked up the gravel path to a glass enclosed porch where a green glass panel door with flaking paint looked like the only entrance. While Henare knocked, Willis intuitively moved to the glass panel of the porch that overlooked the small jetty below and the bridge next to the carpark.

Inside, a figure appeared on the other side of the mullioned glass and approached the door.

"Who is it?"

"Police, sir. Can we speak to you a minute?"

The door opened and an elderly man wearing black-framed eyeglasses peered out.

"Yes? What do you want?" he asked abruptly.

Henare raised his ID. "I'm Detective Joe Henare. This is Detective Greg Willis, sir." He gestured to his colleague.

The man's eyes blinked incomprehension behind the glasses. He took them off and looked them over. "What's this about?" He put the eyeglasses back on.

Automatically, Henare fell into the same rhetoric he'd used over and over for the last two days.

"The body of a young woman was found up in the pool below Mason's Rock. She had a little girl with her who is now missing. We're wondering if you saw anyone early Wednesday night between the hours of five and nine."

The man turned a bewildered look on Willis. "I didn't see any *one*."

His tone begged the question:

"But you saw some*thing*?"

"You better come in." He gestured them in then led them down a scruffy hallway to a cluttered living room. Here, an expansive window looked out over the harbor to the opposite coast peeling out to the right, the bridge and river on the left. He moved to a dining table directly below the window and leaned over to tap the glass. "See there?" he said. "In the street across the river there?"

Henare moved across next to him and peered out to where that same blue Holden Commodore still sat, and his heart dropped into his shoes. *Shit!*

The man turned to him. "I saw that car park there the other night. Just after that white camper van turned up. Next thing I know, the car park's full of police. I thought the Commodore was another police car. But it's still there."

Henare and Willis shared a look. Clearly both thinking the same thing, if the look on Willis's face was anything to go by.

"You don't know whose it is?" Henare asked.

"Nope."

"And you didn't see who parked it there?"

He shook his head again. "Nope. I heard the engine because it was one of those loud, rumbling jobs, you know, like a V8 or something. Like the young yobbos round here drive."

"So, what happened next?"

"I looked out that window there," he said, pointing. "But whoever left it there must have already gone. I didn't see anyone else all night."

Henare could have kicked himself at his own oversight. He'd been the officer in charge of the scene. He'd noted the vehicle but after discovering the car wasn't reported stolen, he'd failed to follow up.

Too late now. All he could do was fall on his sword and pray for mercy.

The moment they were outside, he called the DI.

"Ma'am, I think we've found something."

After an uncomfortably terse conversation with the DI, the two detectives quickly retraced their steps back down the driveway, down the road and across the bridge to where the blue Holden Commodore sat.

Henare approached the car from the left while Willis gave the vehicle a wide berth, taking down the registration before moving to the driver's window. Each officer bent with hands cupped at the glass, ensuring zero contact, and peered inside.

Several parking receipts lay on the front passenger's seat, a McDonald's drink cup, and, from what Henare could make out, a gas station receipt.

Willis looked up hopefully. "Well, he's left us plenty of evidence."

Henare was less optimistic. "A little too much if he's got any brains."

Bunched up in the rear seat was a plaid car rug.

"Perfect for wrapping a body," Henare said. "Specially a small one. Call it in. See if we can locate the owner and get forensics to see if we can get anything off the rug."

While Willis stalked back and forth with the phone to his ear, waiting for the responder to come back with the ownership details, Henare slipped on a vinyl glove and used one finger to draw back the door handle. When it clicked open, he paused and shot Willis a look.

"It's unlocked."

Willis froze, eyes riveted on the car. He hung up from his call and joined Henare at the open door. Henare leaned in, turning over the receipts and rubbish with gloved hands, checking dates and locations.

"Gas station receipt in Whangārei. Big Mac and fries in River Falls."

"What a genius," said Willis.

"Get everything you can into bags. What did Central say about ownership?"

Willis circled the car to the driver's side, drawing out a pair of gloves and an envelope to collect the castoff rubbish, relaying the conversation as he did so. "The car belongs to a Philip Wright in Whangārei. Didn't even know it was missing until he was called."

Henare did a face shrug. "Hardly surprising it's unlocked, then. Looks to me like our killer stole the car, met Huia somewhere, then killed her and drove her up here to get rid of her."

"And then what? He took Lily and walked off somewhere?"

"Or he had help."

"Or…" Willis did a head-tip toward the car.

A meaningful silence hung between the two officers. Both cut a chilled look to the car boot. Henare was the first to speak. "Or he left her in the car."

The silence from the car wasn't encouraging.

Henare snicked one finger under the release and lifted. Both detectives held their breath as the boot popped. Using the side of his index finger, Henare lifted it and they both peered in.

The boot was empty. They both heaved out a breath and their shoulders fell.

Then back to business. Tension rapidly dissipating, Henare spoke. "Get on the phone, get forensics up here. I'll call the boss." He plucked out his phone again, dialing once more.

It wasn't a conversation he was looking forward to.

CHAPTER 16

"How the hell did that car get overlooked?" Nyree demanded of Callaghan as she stormed into the office.

It was the first question she'd asked Henare, and in the same tone.

Callaghan looked up from his computer. He'd spent the last hour arresting the tourists and reading them their rights. After locking them away in the small holding cells in the rear of River Falls police station awaiting transportation to Whangārei, he was at his desk transferring all the information on the case into the national database, then catching up on his emails. He watched her stalk around her desk and sit, opening up a thick file and flicking through the pages before speaking.

"Henare said they'd made a note of the car when he first got there. At the time they checked the database it hadn't been reported stolen and the owner couldn't be contacted."

"That's unforgiveable," she growled. "It's sloppy work."

"Yes, Ma'am."

"If it's any consolation, Henare sounded totally gutted about it," he offered.

She eyed him. But he was right. Bollocking team members would only bring down morale.

"Then I guess there's no point in chasing our tails now. But, from now on, I need everyone working to their best."

"Yes, Ma'am." Perhaps a little relieved, he returned his attention to his computer.

"We got word back from Huia's school. She was enrolled in a literacy class after school, but she never showed up. The only teacher who might have known anything about her is on holiday. They're trying to locate her."

"How'd you get on with the parents? If you don't mind my asking."

"I didn't like them. They've made the A-list of suspects." She hoisted her briefcase onto the desk, fishing out more paperwork to add to it, instantly guilty over the admission.

He looked up in surprise. "Because?"

She frowned, recalling the moments of her telling Annette and Peter Coburn their only daughter had been murdered. Then broke herself from the moment and opened the file. "Something felt off."

Callaghan stopped typing. "In what way?"

She shifted in her chair while she recalled that moment. "The mother immediately pointed the finger at Skinner, the boyfriend. Told me he'd gotten her pregnant. Said he was abusive."

"Which is what Kelly Holmes told us."

"Yeah, but it was when the husband got home her whole attitude changed. She got ugly. Almost every death-knock, the mum, or dad or whoever, reacts in a different way, right? I mean, I get that."

"Shock," Callaghan agreed.

"I've had people tell me we're wrong, that their mother, father, daughter, son, whatever, isn't dead; that we've made a mistake. I've had them fall on their knees in front of me. I've even had a door slammed in my face." A brief series of images of Annette and Peter Coburn slid through her brain. "Huia's parents seemed to go through all the right emotions, but…" She paused, searching for that tiny needle that had prickled her senses. "I got the feeling they already knew. When she spoke about Skinner, I felt like it was practiced. She had all the information about Skinner ready at hand. You know?" She momentarily massaged her forehead. "Or maybe I shouldn't have gone right then. Maybe I was just in the wrong mental state."

He straightened, directing his attention to anywhere but her, clearly feeling as if he were in unknown territory.

She felt his discomfort and leaned to brush a speck of unseen dust from the desk. "I'd just been out to see Tony."

Callaghan's features blanched. "Oh," was all he said. He'd worked with her long enough to know the story surrounding Nyree's relationship with her estranged son. His sympathies lay with her.

"Listen, I know it's not my place, but you're professional enough not to let that overshadow your investigation." He dipped his head, leaning to catch her eye.

She met it. "Tony told me not to come back. He told me he never wanted to see me again." Once again, her heart squeezed with that old familiar pain. She broke eye contact and looked away, too mortified to face him directly. "Maybe that colored my reaction to Huia's parents. Maybe I missed some vital signs. Or maybe I just came out with the wrong impression. I should have sent someone else."

Callaghan scraped his lower teeth along his upper lip before speaking. "Ma'am, I trust your instincts. You say something didn't feel right, I'd say you're on the money. You want us to focus on the parents?"

She gave it a long moment, gathered herself, and got to her feet, facing him. "Yeah. Pick up their phone records and have someone tail them for a few days. Annette Coburn said she deletes all her text messages. I don't know anyone that does that. Then canvass the neighbors. See if they knew Huia's car and see if anyone saw it there in the past few days. We still haven't located that."

"I'll get right on it."

"And don't let the parents know they've made the suspect list. If they murdered Huia, they could be holding Lily. She could be still alive. But if they feel under threat, that situation could change."

Letting the thread run, Nyree continued on. "If the blue Commodore wasn't there when the tourists arrived, then the killer could have dumped Huia's body minutes before they turned up. Then, while they're off stealing kiwifruit, the killer ditches the car and takes off. I want a background check on the car's owner. That could nail down the time the killer was here. I want to know why that car wasn't reported missing, and if there's any relationship between this Mr. Wright and Huia. Wright lives a few doors from Huia's parents. As Henare said, that's some coincidence. Check whether Wright has any connection with Huia's family."

"On it," Callaghan said and began tapping keys on his computer.

Just then, her phone rang. "DI Bradshaw."

"Nyree." It was Christine. "I've got some information you might want. We found tiny fragments of paint in the head wound. They're almost bound to have been transferred from the weapon."

"Any idea what kind of weapon?"

"The shape of the wound means that when we find the weapon, you'll know it. I'll send you a sketch."

"Fantastic." At last, something concrete. Nyree switched on her PC and went straight to her email. "Right, send it straight over. I'll get the team to keep an eye out."

"Also, there were minute traces of dirt. And when we matched up the samples under the microscope, we found the dirt in the wound has a different composition to the soil where she was found."

"In what way?"

"The samples are tiny but there's a higher concentration of phosphates and organic material. Which could be consistent with garden soil."

"You think she was hit with a gardening implement?"

"I'd almost put money on it. But then," Christine admitted, "I can only go on what I find."

"And the paint—what color was it?"

"Rescue orange."

"So, we're looking for an orange-painted garden tool?"

"Correct. Most likely steel with a squared end narrowing slightly at the base. I've assumed that from the position of the indentation."

Nyree opened the email. "Got it. Thank you."

"Plus, I flushed her nasal passages for pollen. Looks like we've got a couple of varieties so I've sent the samples off to a specialist I know at Auckland Uni. That might help us narrow down the location she took her last breath in. We're doing some further analysis on the dirt under her nails, but she had a couple of splinters of wood under her index finger nail."

"You know what I'm going to ask next," she said and left it hanging.

Christine sighed as though she now regretted mentioning it. "I doubt I'll get the results back for a few days. Sorry," she added, and sounded it.

"Can you put a rush on it? I've got a six-year-old child's life depending on finding where Huia died."

"I'll do what I can but some of the processes simply can't be done any faster."

Nyree's heart fell. Every tick of the clock brought Lily Holmes another second closer to kidney failure, or blindness, or liver failure.

Or death.

"What about time of death?" Nyree asked.

"I've got it down to death three hours before she was found by the tourists. I'd say she was in the water for less than an hour."

"So, you think she was killed at, what? Seven o'clock?"

"Pretty close to that."

Nyree did a quick mental calculation. "That indicates she would have been dumped a matter of minutes before the tourists found her."

"That's what I get."

"I've added her parents to the list of suspects so expect some analyses from their car and house."

"I guess I'm stating the obvious here, but it's an hour's drive from Whangārei," Christine reminded her. "To have murdered her, changed her clothes and driven her up to River Falls, then carried her to the dumping spot, they'd have to have moved pretty damn fast."

"Correct. But it doesn't mean they were in Whangārei when it happened. Now all I need is something tying at least one of our suspects to the scene."

"Good luck with that," Christine said.

"I think I'm going to need it," Nyree admitted.

CHAPTER 17

The morning team update had been scheduled for 10 am. Thirty-eight hours after the tourists had first called police to report Huia's body being found.

Forty-two hours since little Lily Holmes had gone missing.

Fifty plus hours since her last insulin injection.

Hopes of finding her alive were fading.

Nyree and Callaghan were on their way to the briefing room when the desk sergeant stopped them.

"Excuse me, Ma'am, we've got Kelly Holmes in Interview One and the television crew setting up in the comms room."

"How is she?"

"Looks dreadful. Said she needs to speak to you, Ma'am. Says it's urgent."

"Did she say what it was about?"

"She won't talk to anyone but you."

"That's fine. I'll be right with her." She checked her watch. "Tell the team to grab a coffee," she told Callaghan. "I'll be there in ten."

Kelly jumped up from her chair, talking nineteen to the dozen before Nyree was even in the room.

"Whoa, whoa, whoa. Come and sit down and tell me."

"I remembered something." Despite the eagerness in her voice, she looked as if she hadn't slept for days. Eyes were bloodshot from crying, her blonde hair matted into a tangle of knots at the back where she obviously hadn't brushed it. She wore the same mud-stained clothing as on the previous day.

"Now, tell me what's happened." Nyree guided her back to her chair and sat opposite, arms folded on the small table between them.

Kelly also leaned in, urgency animating her features. "I remembered something. She'd have her Bun-Buns with her."

"Her what?"

Kelly flapped a hand in frustration, desperate to get the information out. "Her *Bun-Buns*. It's a toy rabbit thing. Like a floppy, grey bunny with a red ribbon tied around its neck. She's had it since she was a baby. She wouldn't go anywhere without it." She heaved out a relieved breath, as though the information had been burning a hole inside her. "She'll have it with her. I know she will."

"Do you remember seeing it at home?"

"No. I'm sure I'd have noticed if it was there because she takes it everywhere with her. Here's a photo of her with it."

Kelly scrabbled through her pockets and drew out her phone, then scrolled through to a photograph of the child. That same auburn hair, the happy smile, although obviously a year or so younger, she was snapped clutching a grey toy rabbit, the soft body squished in against her cheek.

"Like I said, she takes it everywhere with her."

"Thank you. Can you email this to me?"

Nyree gave her the email address. But as soon as she'd hit send, all hope in Kelly's expression drained, as if she'd suddenly realized that the information wouldn't instantly bring her child back, and that she was as far from her as she'd ever been.

Desperate to keep her from falling into a black hole of despair, Nyree reached across the table, cupping a hand over Kelly's and ducking her head to speak to her.

"Listen, this is fantastic information. Anyone who might have seen her would remember Bun-Buns."

Kelly nodded but said nothing.

"Kelly, listen to me."

She looked up.

"You're obviously starting to remember things, right?"

"Well, I remembered this."

"And that's good. Now, think hard: can you remember if there was anything else she might have had on her? Ribbons in her hair, hairclips...anything?"

She blinked at a point somewhere in front of her for a moment, then her features squeezed up in self-recrimination as she shook her head. "My brain's a mess. I only remembered not seeing Bun-Buns. Soon as I realized, I came here. But there's nothing else."

Kelly drew the phone toward her, gazing longingly at the child smiling out at her. In that moment, every ounce of her energy seemed to dissipate, leaving her a withered remnant of the person she'd been only seconds before. Then a wall of emotion. Clutching the phone close to her heart, she folded forward, her face squeezed tight in pain, her voice just a tiny squeak.

"Where is she? Please find her," she begged. Her first breath rasped in and the resultant sob rocked her from the inside out.

"Kelly, we're doing our best. And this will be a huge help. Listen, we need to do a television appeal. Do you think you're up to it?" If they were going to get it aired in the next hour, they had to move fast. Nyree left her chair, crouched beside Kelly, and slid an arm around her shoulders. "Oh, sweetheart, I know this is hard, but somewhere out there, someone may know something. And the quicker we find that person, the quicker we'll find Lily."

Kelly gently moved out of her grasp and nodded.

Nyree straightened. "Right. Let's see if we can find you some clean clothes, eh? By the time we're done here, the search team should be finished at your place. Then you'll be able to go home."

Kelly shoved the chair back, the legs groaning against the linoleum floor. "I don't want to go home," she whimpered as she held the phone to her heart, like a lifeline to her child. "I want my baby back. I want my Lily back home." And she let out a wail of abject loss, the sobs heaving her shoulders so hard that Nyree took her in her arms, holding her, rocking her like a child, and stroking her hair.

"We're going to find her, Kelly. I promise you we'll move heaven and earth, and we'll find her."

She deliberately avoided the word, "alive."

CHAPTER 18

"I'm going to keep this brief," Nyree told the crowded room.

Sleep-weary officers rubbed tired eyes and blinked back at her, though each was just as eager to get back out and start looking for the child again, each praying this would be the day they found her.

"We have three areas of interest." She pointed at the board where the photographs of each individual had been pinned along with their relationships to both Huia and Lily.

"First up, the North team carried out a search of the community up by the marae. Anything else to report there?" She lifted her head, directing the question to Hicks.

"We made a pretty thorough search and no one stood in our way."

"How was the atmosphere?"

"They were accommodating. A few mentioned that Huia had been up there a couple of days ago but he couldn't remember which day. Said they hadn't seen her since."

"Okay, but keep in touch with them. You never know what might come out of the woodwork after a bit of thought." She turned back to the board. "Next on the list is the boyfriend, Brodie Skinner. By all accounts, he's a little too handy with his fists. According to her parents, he's been abusive in the past. Huia's mother is convinced he was the father of the Huia's unborn baby. We'll know that when the DNA tests come back."

Suddenly realizing that that unborn child was also a victim in this ugly saga, Nyree faltered a moment. An unbidden image of a tiny form wrapped in her mother's womb swept into her mind's eye. She mentally dashed it aside, but when she went to speak, her voice caught. She cleared her throat, pushed it aside, and continued on.

"Christine thinks Huia was murdered around seven, so that means Skinner's also still in the frame."

"What about the ankle bracelet? Have we checked his curfew times from that?" This from Detective in Training, Alana Bowman. Late twenties, short blonde hair with severe bangs, Bowman's father had been a Superintendent down south. Determined to follow in big footsteps, Bowman was ever eager to make her mark—though, maybe a little too eager, at times. She still had a lot to learn.

Nyree signaled to her in reply. "Good point. He's got a certain number of hours during which he can attend work. Callaghan, check with his parole officer. See if he broke curfew anytime during that day. In the meantime, I've impounded his car pending a forensic search for any sign of Lily."

"He'll be thrilled," someone chuckled.

"Tough," said Nyree. "This child is our priority. I don't care who we upset trying to find her." To which a few around the room nodded approval.

She tapped the picture of the third suspect in the list. "Next on the list is Huia's father—Rawiri Cooper. He's been conveniently missing and out of any communication ever since Huia's death, although from what we have so far, I'm not convinced he's our man. By all accounts, he was excited about the birth of his first grandchild. Let's see what he's got to say when we do finally catch up with him."

"He does have access to gardening equipment, though," someone called.

"You did a search on the gardening tools, didn't you, Hicks?" she asked and searched the room for him.

Hicks put up a hand. "Yes, Ma'am. First place we looked. Nothing orange, nothing that shape. No blood spatter in the tool shed or any of the other buildings. Or none that we saw, anyway."

Exactly what she'd read in the report, so she moved on.

"Next are the parents. I interviewed them briefly yesterday, but I felt like something was off. I've got three uniforms canvassing the neighbors to find out if they remember any cars in the area and showing pictures of Huia's car and Lily Holmes, just in case they called in there."

Bowman raised a hand. "Do we know what Huia was wearing when she was last seen?"

"Kelly couldn't remember exactly, but she thinks she had on jeans, a green top of some kind, and her puffer jacket. The green top and jacket are still missing. Lily was wearing pink My-Little-Pony pajamas and pink knitted slippers."

She gave the team a moment to take notes, then pressed on.

"We have one definite vehicle of interest—the blue Holden Commodore parked down by the bridge. It was stolen in Whangārei two streets from the parents' place. If that isn't a coincidence, I don't know what is."

She could see everyone wanting to know the unasked question.

"Okay, you're probably wondering how the car slipped through the cracks on the first scene investigation." She noticed a few heads tilt in interest. "The officer in charge of the scene noted the car and ran a search on it. It turned out to belong to a resident in Whangārei who hadn't reported it stolen. It wasn't until we contacted him this morning that he even knew it was missing. Unfortunately, he's going to have to go without it for a few more days. It's over at Central and forensics are doing a priority search for anything that might link it with either Huia or Lily."

Deciding that had probably quelled the speculation for the moment, she turned back to the board and ran through the details of her chats with Christine, although each of the officers would have received the reports by now.

"Timeline-wise, we've got Huia at Kelly Holmes's house at four, then murdered at seven. Her car is missing so we're assuming she left to meet someone, probably her killer. Henare," she said, and jerked her chin to where he stood at the back of the room, dressed in a dark grey suit, crisp white shirt and dark blue tie.

He lifted his chin. "Yes, Ma'am."

"Get around the local gas stations. Take a look at the footage an hour each side of the time we now know Huia was murdered. See if Huia's car went through there. Or Brodie Skinner's," she added, tapping the photograph to the far right of the suspect list. "And while you're at it, look out for the blue Holden Commodore from across the river. You never know, one of them might have been low on gas and called in."

Turning back to the room, she let her gaze range across the team. "Right, back to it, guys. We need to work hard and smart. Anything comes up, let me know. We're on the clock and the clock is ticking. If we don't find Lily Holmes today … "

The room fell deathly silent. All eyes riveted on her. No one moved a muscle.

"…well, let's just hope we do."

CHAPTER 19

The comms room wasn't much bigger than Interview One. Kelly sat like a frightened mouse behind a small desk, hands clutched between her knees, tension oozing as she watched the cameraman peer down into the camera viewer, adjusting knobs to get better angle, then twiddling more knobs to adjust the lens. Off to one side, his offsider scanned the lights across the ceiling, yanking on the cord to tilt and raise and lower the blinds for the best lighting.

The moment Nyree gave the door a quick knuckle-tap, Kelly cut her a look so aching with hope that it chiseled another notch deep into Nyree's heart. Someone had obviously rustled up the clothes. Perhaps from a policewoman's locker. The cream and lace blouse, a couple of sizes too big, had been cinched in at her back using a couple of bulldog clips. Her hair, while still lank and dirty, had been pinned back from her face.

Noting Nyree's sympathetic smile, Kelly reached a hand behind her to touch one of the clips. "I know, gorgeous, eh?"

"They do the job. How's it going?"

Kelly turned her focus on the guy still fiddling with the blinds. "They gave me some things to say. I hope I get it right."

"We can do it as many times as we need to. Just relax. The people you're talking to want to help. Just remember, they're on your side." She gave her a brief smile that she hoped would offer encouragement.

The cameraman stepped forward and planted both hands on his hips like it was a wedding shoot. "Right, we all ready?"

Kelly pressed her lips hard together, shoulders tensing up. She visibly swallowed back her fear, then nodded quickly.

"Just follow the cues up here on top of the camera if you get stuck, okay? You'll do great."

Another nod.

"And remember what we said, just speak like you're talking to someone who doesn't know what happened. Just tell them when Lily went missing, what she looks like, and ask if anyone's seen her."

Kelly hunched her shoulders a little higher, took a deep, shuddering breath, and, at his sign, they began.

"Hi," she said in a trembling voice. "My name is Kelly Holmes. Two days ago, my little girl went missing. Her name is Lily Holmes and she's only six years old." For a second, she blinked as if she'd lost her way. The cameraman pointed to the cue card and she rallied. "She's wearing pink My-Little-Pony pajamas, and a pink pair of... pink pair of knitted slippers. This is a picture of her." She lifted an A4 glossy photograph of the child. Kelly turned the photograph to gaze at it briefly, then clutched it to her heart and continued on.

"She'll also have her bunny rabbit with her. It's a floppy, grey, toy bunny she calls Bun-Buns. She carries it everywhere with her. I know she's got it with her and it'll probably be in her My-Little-Pony backpack."

The information hit Nyree like a bucket of ice-water. She crossed her left arm in front of her, resting her elbow on her forearm, forefinger pressed her mouth to prevent a gasp bursting from her lips.

Clearly unaware of her own revelation, Kelly soldiered on. "The thing is, Lily's diabetic. She was born with type-1 diabetes and she needs her medication. If she doesn't get it, she could..." Her chin wobbled. "Well, she could get really ill."

She steadied herself, pulling in a couple of jagged breaths before proceeding. "Please, please, if you've seen her, or even if you just *think* you've seen her, please call your local police station. She's my little angel, she's my b.... baby." Kelly's face crumpled on the last word, her voice trailing up into a squeak. She drew a couple quick, hiccupping breaths and a series of sobs carried her next words. "I don't know what I'd do without her."

Nyree scratched at a tear forming at the corner of her eye and swallowed back the wash of emotion.

A couple of heavy intakes of breath racked Kelly's tiny frame, but the cameraman, eager to get on with it, lifted his head and gave her a rolling gesture, easing her on.

Kelly visibly wrestled back her grief, sniffed hard and blinked hard at the ceiling to clear the tears from her eyes. Looking straight down the barrel of the camera now, her demeanor solidified. "Please, *please*, if you know where she is, or if you've got my baby, if you've got Lily, I don't care who you are or what you've done. Please just take her to a police station. Or leave her somewhere we'll find her. Please, I'm begging you," she squeaked out on a long, desperate breath, "please don't hurt her. She's just a little girl. She's my little angel," she managed to get out before folding onto the desk, sobbing violently.

"And cut."

Nyree dashed to crouch at Kelly's side, her arm around the young mother's shoulders, pulling her close. "That was perfect. You did great."

"Yeah, that was really good," the cameraman said without conviction as his offsider handed her a box of tissues. Nyree gave him a cool stare, ripped three tissues from the box and passed them to Kelly who pressed them to each eye, then blew her nose.

"Listen, ah...do we have time to redo the last bit?" the cameraman asked Nyree.

"No," she told him bluntly. "Just do what you can with what you've got. Now," she said, turning back to Kelly, "tell me about this backpack you mentioned?"

CHAPTER 20

Kelly told them that Huia regularly used the backpack if they were going anywhere for more than a couple of hours. She used it to carry Lily's insulin and sugary snacks, just in case they got waylaid.

Nyree had filled Callaghan in on everything she'd discovered and was heading back to the incident room, speaking over her shoulder to him as he followed her down the hallway.

"Get a picture of that backpack circulated to every station, and get it out on the news."

"Already on it, Ma'am.

"What about the house?"

"I called the team out at Kelly's place. They had a good look around. No sign of the backpack."

"And the fridge?"

"They looked. There were a couple of vials of insulin, but no insulin pen."

Nyree stopped and chewed her lip while the information sank in. Then shoved her way into the incident room. "So, wherever they are, Huia must have expected to be there long enough that they might need Lily's insulin." She turned to face him. "Get someone to check with the local pharmacy. See when the last prescription was filled for Lily's insulin and her daily usage. That might give us a clue how much Huia took with her."

"Yes, Ma'am." He noted it down.

She stacked her notes, tucking all the pages back into the file, then paused.

"In fact, better still, get all prescriptions dating back to day one. Get in touch with the diabetes team at Whangārei Hospital and find out what dosages Lily's had over her lifetime, and get them to correlate the scripts and quantities with Lily's probable usage over the years. Let's see if there's any slight possibility that the killer took extra meds." She noted the doubtful look on his face. "Yeah, I know. It's a shot in the dark. But I have to know what her chances of still being alive are."

"Right away, Ma'am. I'll see who we've got." He noted it down.

"Have the Scene of Crime boys come up with anything else at the house yet?"

He shook his head. "No unusual fingerprints on either the front door, or around the windows. Looks like Huia packed her up, insulin, insulin pen, and toy rabbit in the backpack, and they left of their own accord."

"Still no sign of the car?"

"No, Ma'am."

"And, where the hell are the telco printouts? What are they doing? Handwriting them?"

Callaghan sucked in a defensive breath. He'd been tasked with following up all calls and texts to Huia's phone.

"Haven't heard from them, Ma'am. I'll get right on it."

Shaking her head and sighing, she tucked the file into the crook of her arm and headed for the hallway. "Well, if we've got any chance of tracking her car, we need all the cell sites Huia's phone registered on. Tell them to get their acts together and get us those reports."

"On it," he said.

She shouldered open the door to her makeshift River Falls office, slipped into her chair and clicked on her computer. Callaghan waited at the door.

"Anything else, Ma'am?"

"No, that's it." He was about to leave when she said, "Oh, by the way, has anything interesting show up on the Occurrence List yet?"

He opened the top file on the heap he was carrying, and flicked back a few pages. "A woman five properties back from the river had three charges of child abuse against her. Had two of her kids taken off her. Still hasn't got them back. She blames us."

"Nice," Nyree said flatly. "What else did she say?"

"When the uniform asked her if she'd seen any unusual activity in the area, she told him to, and I quote, 'Mind your own bloody business and get off my property.'"

Nyree's eyebrows lifted. "Model citizen, then."

"Yes, Ma'am. Also told him that if the pigs keep knocking on her door every time someone sneezes in this bloody town, she'd lodge a complaint of police harassment."

"Good. Tell her to lodge it with all the rest. Anything else?"

He flicked to the next page. "There was a forty-two-year-old male living in the camping grounds just upriver from the murder scene," he read off, as if reciting it by rote. "Record of fencing stolen property, possession of cannabis. Said he didn't see anything. According to the uniform who interviewed him, the guy suffers from chronic back pain and never leaves his caravan. Admits to self-medicating on cannabis on the odd occasion. Unfortunately, this was one of those occasions."

"Right. How about the search of Brodie Skinner's place?"

Callaghan drew back one side of his mouth in apprehension. "Won't get it done until the team's finished at Kelly Holmes's place, I'm afraid. But they'll get right over there soon as they can."

"Well, tell them to get on with it. A child's life is at stake, in case they've forgotten."

He waited while she huffed and tsked as she consulted her list of tasks, checking them off one by one. Then she looked up, eyes narrowed. "Any word on Sean Clemmons? Or is that too much to ask?"

He focused briefly on a point just above her head, obviously not relishing telling her. "Um, yes…and no. No sign of him. But on the upside, I spoke to Comms and they said they're pulling in another detective specifically to help track him down."

"About bloody time," she muttered. She was keeping her suspicions of Clemmons on hold for the moment. No point in adding him to the mix right now. Nolan would have her guts for garters—'harassing an ex-con who'd served his time,' he'd say. 'Keep off Clemmons's back or we'd have Human

Rights or some other bloody do-gooder outfit giving them a serve.'

No one needed that—especially now. But at the vaguest hint that Clemmons had anything to do with Huia Coburn's death, she'd track him to the ends of the earth and see him back inside for the rest of his life.

Perhaps not noticing her silence, Callaghan carried on speaking. "Yeah, that's what I said—about bloody time. What with a threat to a police officer and all, there wasn't a lot of choice, really, was there?"

"Sooner the better," she said idly, turning her attention back to her computer and rolling the mouse along the mousepad. Then glanced up, caught his gaze and did a double take. Suspicion darkened her expression. "Who are they sending?"

He looked away momentarily to deliver the news. "Um, Terry McFarlane, Ma'am."

Her shoulders dropped. "Oh, for crying…" she groaned. "Couldn't they find someone else? *Anyone* else?"

"No, Ma'am. Apparently not."

"Jesus wept."

If there was anyone in the world whose help she'd turn away, it was McFarlane. That irritating boys' club attitude and senior-rank brown-nosing turned her stomach.

"Anyway, he's on his way here. Should be here…" Callaghan consulted his watch. "In an hour or so."

"Fine. He can hunt down Sean Clemmons and let us get on with the job of finding Lily Holmes. Just tell him to stay out of our way."

Callaghan turned to leave, but almost ran into the duty sergeant who appeared behind him.

Speaking across Callaghan, who stepped back, he said, "Ma'am, sorry to bother you."

"Yes, what is it?"

"A, um…gentleman is at the front desk. He says he wants to talk to you."

"Did you ask him what it's regarding?"

The duty sergeant cut Callaghan a telling look, then turned it on Nyree. "He says his name is Cooper, Rawiri Cooper. He's demanding to know what we've done to find his daughter's killer, and says he wants her body back. Like *now*."

Nyree put her pen down while her mind scrolled through the long list of cultural rites and sensitivities around the dead. "Shit. Right. Invite him in, make him comfortable, make him a coffee or whatever he wants, and tell him I'll be with him shortly."

"Can I tell him how shortly, Ma'am?"

"However long it takes me to contact Christine down in Whangārei and find out how the hell long I need to stall him for."

CHAPTER 21

Henare pulled into the gas station and crossed into the second of five vacant parking slots on the far side of the forecourt.

Both he and Bowman twisted in their seats, surveying the place. Directly across the street was a supermarket, the number of cars present at this time-of-day testimony to the number of retirees who had fled Auckland housing price rises and washed up in the winterless north.

Henare ducked his head to view the front of the gas station, noting the yellow For Sale sign in the window. "You ready?"

"Yep," Bowman replied and got out. She waited until Henare rounded the car and joined her before heading for the sliding glass front door.

Inside, a young man with fair dreadlocks and wearing a crumpled shirt with the gas station logo switched his attention from the customer he'd just served to the two officers. Judging by his guarded demeanor, he picked them as cops before they opened their mouths.

He tucked a couple of twenties into the till and slammed it shut. "Hi. You here about the drive-offs?"

Henare and Bowman shared a quick glance. "Ah, nope."

The kid's shoulders slumped. "Oh, okay. We thought you guys would have sent someone out by now. We called you, like, four days ago." Perhaps realizing that bitching wasn't getting him anywhere, he asked, "So, what can I do for you?"

"We'd like to speak to the manager."

"I am the manager," said the kid. "Danny Yelavich. What's it about, then?"

Cutting to the chase, Henare slipped his ID from his breast pocket. "Detective Joe Henare, and this is CIT Bowman." He gestured toward her, then put his ID away while casually scanning the place for security cameras. "You wouldn't have any security footage for Wednesday night, would you, Danny?"

"What? Last Wednesday?"

Henare cocked his head briefly in assent. "That's the one."

"Hey, mate." Danny Yelavich signaled over a teenage kid who ambled across. "Take over here for me, will you?" Danny slipped off his stool and tucked the magazine he'd been reading below the countertop. "You're lucky," he told Henare as he switched places with the kid. "We usually delete the video the next day, but we had a couple of drive-offs last week. We're still waiting for your lot to come out and do something about it."

"Sorry, you'll need to follow up with River Falls station," Henare told him flatly.

"Again," Danny complained with a huff, then jerked his head toward the rear office. "This way."

He led them into a cramped office with a Formica table that served as a lunch table, and a wooden desk which held an aging computer. Along the rear wall sat three black file cabinets under a window with a shriveled pot plant on the sill. Beyond, through the security bars in the only window, Henare could see an unsealed area in which two cars were parked. The passenger door of a grey Ford Falcon was open.

"They your cars?"

Danny Yelavich's eyes flicked defensively to the window. "Warrants and Rego's are all current if you want to check."

"You always leave the door open?"

Danny shot another look out the window followed by Bowman. "Oh. I'll close it when we're done here."

Henare returned his attention to the computer where Yelavich wriggled the mouse and the screen jumped into life. From the lower toolbar, he clicked across to the relevant video feed.

"We've got four cameras. One at the entrance to the forecourt, one at the other side, one on the front door, and one on the counter." The screen flickered onto a grid of four images, one in each quadrant. In the top left, cars entered the station from the main street, while in the top right, cars departed onto the same street. In the lower left, the front doors glided open and shut as customers came and went, and in the lower right, three customers stood in a line as the kid in the shop served them.

"Okay, so here are all the feeds. What's the date today?" Yelavich asked.

Bowman checked her watch and told him.

"So, we're looking at the day before yesterday, right?" He rolled the mouse and the video feed began rolling backward, the time counter snapping into reverse next to the toolbar. "About what time?"

"Between four and six?" Bowman asked Henare.

"About that." Henare leaned over, one hand on the back of the chair, eyes narrowed on the screen as the images whizzed back in a series of freeze-frames, then slowed and paused on three-fifty-six.

Now the images ran in normal time. In the lower image, a girl, probably in her late teens, deeply tanned skin, and brown hair with sun-bleached ends wound into a messy knot at the back of her head. She hurried to the door with her backpack slung over one shoulder, passing an older man who leered after her as she hurried out and disappeared.

"Who's the girl?" asked Bowman.

"Kiri Perrett. She works here part time. Who are you looking for?" Yelavich asked.

Henare replied. "A guy by the name of Skinner. Drives an orange ute."

"You mean Brodie Skinner?"

"You know him?"

Yelavich snorted. "I went to school with him. The guy's a douche. Keeps hitting on Kiri. She said he gives her the creeps. Hang on, I'll speed it up a bit."

They watched in silence as the images snapped into silent-movie mode, cars zooming into the forecourt and drivers leaping out to fill up, then scurrying to the front door passing others going out again.

"Hold on. I think that's him." Yelavich pointed to the upper left image where an orange ute swerved in off the street and into the first bay. He rolled the mouse to click on the image and the feed slowed.

Bowman leaned in, checking the time on the toolbar. "That's him. What's he doing there at six o'clock? I thought his curfew ends at five."

"Is the time on this accurate?" asked Henare.

"Yep. Even takes daylight saving into account. I can zoom in, if you want. Hang on." With a couple of mouse clicks, Yelavich brought the image to full screen and zeroed in on the figure. A pixelated image of Brodie Skinner filled the space. The tattoos, ginger razor-cut and bulldog face were slightly blurred, but fully recognizable as he twisted around and moved out of the frame.

"That's him, alright." This from Bowman.

The screen cut back to the four quadrants from the video feeds to show Brodie Skinner positioning the nozzle in the tank, and setting it to fill before wandering up the row of cars, searching.

Yelavich made a derisive noise. "He's looking for Kiri, the prick."

After searching each bay, Skinner returned to the ute, hung up the nozzle and walked casually toward the door where the store camera picked him up paying for the gas. All the while, his gaze ranged out searching the store. After tucking his card back into his wallet, he returned to the ute once more. But instead of going to the driver's door, he went to the covered tray, lifted the lid a couple of inches and peered in through the dark gap.

Eyes widening, Bowman shifted position and leaned further in. "What's he doing?"

Yelavich clicked on the image and zoomed in.

Not one of them blinked.

"He's got something in the back there. Can you see what it is?" Bowman said at last.

They watched as Skinner reached one arm into the tray, speaking to whatever was in there.

Then he hiked the lid of the tray, lifting it.

A dark shape moved within, and a large black dog leapt out.

Bowman let out a breath and her shoulders dropped in relief. "It's a dog."

On the computer, Skinner guided the dog around to the front of the truck, opened the door and commanded it in.

"Hang on a minute, what's that? You recognize him?" Henare tapped a finger on the top right image where a white BMW had pulled into the forecourt. The figure ducked in and out of the frame while he filled the tank, but finally came clearly into view as he crossed to the front doors.

"Oh, my God." Bowman leaned in. "What's he doing there?"

"More to the point," said Henare. "When exactly did he leave town?"

After making notes of the times and requesting a copy of the video footage, Henare thanked Yelavich and they returned to the car.

Bowman fastened her seatbelt while Henare ran a cynical eye over the forecourt, then got in.

"What now?"

"We'll see what the boss wants."

Henare lifted his phone.

After two rings, DI Bradshaw answered.

"We've got some news, Ma'am."

Henare relayed what they'd discovered in the footage.

"Right. I'll get out there and see Skinner. Find out why he's at a gas station an hour past his curfew, and damn near exactly the time Huia Coburn's body was dumped at the riverside."

"Yes, Ma'am. Also, it seems Rawiri Cooper was in town on the night of Huia's murder. We copped him driving a BMW into the gas station at exactly the same time Skinner was there."

"Oh, he did, did he? Thank you."

Henare waited while she made a note.

"Something else," Henare said and slipped Bowman a knowing look, "there was definitely eye contact between Skinner and Cooper. Like an almost imperceptible nod."

"You get the feeling they knew each other?"

"Just from what we saw, I'd say they at least had a passing acquaintance."

"Good work." Another pause while he imagined her adding to the notes before speaking again. "Interestingly enough, we've had a bit of progress as well. The telcos finally got their act together and sent us the call records for Huia Coburn's phone. According to them, it's still switched on and we've located the cell site it's polling off. We've got Traffic searching all the streets in that vicinity."

When Henare gave Bowman a flick of the eyebrows, she whispered, "What?"

"That really is good news, Ma'am," he said.

"Right, you two get back here and get your paperwork sorted. Meantime, I've got a meeting with Rawiri Cooper. I'm dying to know why he was still in town at six o'clock that night when we were led to believe he'd left days before, and how he knows Skinner. I want to find out why we haven't heard from him until now, what he's been up to for the past forty-eight hours, and whether he'd kill his daughter."

CHAPTER 22

According to the desk sergeant, Rawiri Cooper's mood had taken a shift for the worse. As Nyree made her way to Interview Two, the desk sergeant had leaned in, whispering a few words of warning, telling her Cooper's demands to see Nyree had now taken on an edge of aggression.

"He's talking the Human Rights Commission and the Māori Affairs Select Committee."

"He can threaten whatever he wants. Did he mention why he's been mysteriously absent until now?"

"Apparently, he's been down the line on business. He said he didn't hear about Huia until he got back."

"And Annette Coburn? She didn't tell him his only child was dead?"

"He said they weren't in contact since Annette Coburn put a restraining order out against him."

"Because…?"

"Several years back, she laid a complaint of domestic violence against him." The sergeant flicked his eyebrows, his expression dubious.

"Oh, she did, did she? A man pretty handy with his fists? Then, let's not keep him waiting."

Cooper sat broad-shouldered in the chair facing the door, arms crossed firmly over a broad chest, defiance and indignation turning the corners of his mouth down. Probably somewhere in his mid-forties, his close-cropped black hair showed a dusting of grey at the edges; dark, intelligent eyes crinkled at the outer edges suggesting a life working in the sun, a glimpse of a tattoo at the open throat of his shirt. He lifted his chin at her arrival but didn't get up.

Nyree ignored the defiant posturing, dragged out a chair, and sat opposite him. "Mr. Cooper. Detective Inspector Nyree Bradshaw. I'm sorry to have kept you waiting."

He nodded slowly as if he wouldn't have expected less, but the pent-up aggression remained.

She consulted a sheet of paper from the file she'd brought with her and took a deep breath. "I believe Huia Coburn is your daughter."

"That's right."

Keeping her voice low, calm, she said, "Then, I'm so sorry for your loss."

The words seemed to take the wind out of him. For a second, he floundered for a response, then drew a hand roughly down his face and refolded his arms. "So, where is she? I'm taking her home. She needs to be home with her whānau—her family."

No surprises there. Still maintaining the soothing tones, she pressed on. "Mr. Cooper, I was aware that your daughter was of Māori descent, and I've made every effort to put procedures in place to keep the whānau informed."

"Yeah well, you did better than that bitch," he said, stabbing a finger off over Nyree's shoulder. "She wouldn't 'a told you."

"Who are you referring to, Mr. Cooper?"

His chin inched a little higher, his tone scathing. "Annette. Her old lady. She's shacked up with that arsehole Coburn. Calls herself his wife." A snort of scorn burst from his pursed lips. "Thinks she's too good for the rest of us. Thinks she can take my mana, take my child, cut off our blood." The scowl deepened as he sat forward and slapped both hands to his upper thighs, his gestures becoming more animated. A hair-trigger bomb ready to explode at the slightest touch. "The hell she can."

Gently steering the conversation back to Huia, Nyree lowered her voice, speaking in gentle tones. "So, tell me, when was the last time you saw Huia?"

His lower lip jutted and his gaze slipped sideways for a second. A quick headshake. "It'd be last…Saturday? Yeah, Saturday. About two." He sat back again. Cooling.

"And where did you meet with her?"

His face twisted briefly as he looked away and dashed a knuckle under his nose. Then refolded his arms. Still defensive. Still angry. But when he spoke this time, his voice had softened notably. "At the marae. She'd started coming up there. Not too often. Just a few times, you know. I was bloody proud. She'd come back to me, back to the people." He swallowed hard.

"Did she say why she'd started coming to the marae?"

"She found out I was her dad. Said she'd been looking for me. Wanted to find out about her roots, her iwi, her whānau. Where she came from." He beat his clenched fist twice to his chest as he spoke, pride and honor reflecting deeply in his expression. To anyone who didn't know, the sentiment seemed over-the-top. But the battle Māori had endured to retain their land, their heritage, their place in New Zealand, had been hard and long. Not just in recent years. Throughout their dealings with the Crown.

On many fronts, they were still fighting.

"She was searching to regain her mana—her honor. To be with her people. To be amongst us. Where she should be. Where she should be now."

"Did she tell you how she found you?"

"She found her birth certificate. Her mother hid it from her. But Huia found it." His eyes dropped to a point just in front of him as the emotions conjured a mental image. With finger and thumb, he savagely pressed the tears from his eyes and his demeanor softened. "Now she's gone. I hardly got to know her. Hardly got to see my own flesh. And now she's gone."

From beneath the exterior bluster and rage, grief and pain, and an overwhelming sense of despair erupted into the room. Like a living thing. A connection drawing them together in grief and sorrow.

"Did her mother know she was seeing you?"

His gaze snapped up; the compassion gone. As if someone had flicked a switch. "Doubt it. She would have stopped her." His head lifted in pride. "She never understood the culture. Didn't understand our ways. Didn't want anything to do with it."

"Did Huia ever bring a little girl up to the marae with her?"

The question threw him for a second. He blinked incomprehension. "You mean Lily? Yeah. We were teaching her the language. We got her into our language class. She was quick. Caught on fast." A flicker of a smile caught his mouth. "Nice kid. A good kid."

"Was she with Huia the last time you saw her?"

His head jerked back. Genuine confusion this time. "No, why?"

"She's missing. The last time she was seen, she was with Huia."

He spread his hands wide. "So, where is she now?"

"We don't know, Mr. Cooper. We're trying to find her. I believe if we find Huia's killer, we'll find Lily."

The corners of his mouth went down while he nodded solemn understanding.

"Anything I can do to help, let me know."

"Please understand that I intend to do everything in my power to find Huia's killer and bring him to justice. That means following police procedures. I can't have vigilante groups running around looking for their own justice. Are we clear on this?"

He met her gaze. He knew exactly what she was driving at.

"I'll talk to the kaumatua—our spiritual leader—"

"We've already met with your kaumatua, Mr. Cooper," she said. "He's giving us every assistance."

"Yeah, well. I'll let him know, too. Tell him we spoke. The people will listen to him."

"I'd appreciate that." She shifted uneasily. "We've already spoken to those on the marae who knew Huia and Lily." She showed him both palms to diffuse the situation before it flared up. "We're just trying to get a picture of their last whereabouts. See if anyone's seen them since their last visit. That's all."

Once again, he dashed a knuckle under his nose, his expression tensing for a second. "I'll ask around, too."

"Thank you." Nyree gave it a beat. "Did Huia ever share any secrets with you? Anything she might not have told anyone else? Maybe something she might not have told her mother?"

"Like that she was seeing me?"

Nyree tipped her head. "Like that."

He thought hard. "She told me she hated that Coburn bloke."

"Did she say why?"

His gaze hardened again. "Said he was always picking on her. I asked if he was doing stuff he shouldn't. Like touching her, abusing her. She said he wasn't." A soft snort.

"You didn't believe her?"

"She had scars. On her arms and legs." He touched his fingertips to his upper arm and thigh and the anger was back.

"She didn't say how she got them? Who put them there?"

"Nah. She made out they were accidents. I told her, I said, 'I'm not stupid. I know what they are. Tell me who did that to you.' She clammed up. Told me it was a long time ago and it didn't matter."

"Did she mention a boyfriend?"

"That Skinner kid? I told her not to hang around him. He's bad news. I said she could find herself a much better man. Someone that'd look after her." He made a dismissive face. "She was pregnant. Did you know that?"

"I did, Mr. Cooper."

His jaw trembled, pain radiating so deeply he dug his teeth into his lower lip to control it. "That was my mokopuna, my grandchild. My loss is two-fold." A tear formed at the corner of his eye. It swelled and burst forth, then ran down his left cheek unchecked. "He told her to get rid of it—to just throw away my grandchild. I told her, I said, 'If the father of your child won't look after you, I will.' I said, 'Come to me. You'll always be safe with your whānau. We will take care of you.' Tell him you want nothing from him."

"And what did she say?"

"She said she was going to break it off with him. But she had to do something first."

"Did she say what that was?"

He shook his head. "She wouldn't say." Suddenly, he sat forward, hands planted on broad thighs, his features transformed at the snap of the fingers into a mask of hate. "Did he do this to her? Did he kill my girl? I'll bloody kill 'im."

Nyree showed him both palms again, her voice low, but firm. "We're still investigating, Mr. Cooper. I promise you I'm going to find Huia's killer, but I need you to work with me. Please." The fury abated. For now. So Nyree continued. "I've contacted the pathologist and she's told me they've almost finished their investigation, and they'll send her straight to the undertaker…"

Rawiri jabbed a finger off into the distance, his voice raised. "I don't want her going to any undertaker. She comes home. Now!"

Nyree faltered. Cultural funeral rites included touching the body, stroking the hair, weeping over the loved one, addressing them with stories, expressions of love and respect. The belief that the spirit remained with the recently deceased for three days, and this was the whānau's last chance to address them, to honor them, to say their goodbyes. To bring peace to the departing spirit.

"We'll do what we can. It's my recommendation that if your whānau want to have contact with the body, it would be best to preserve Huia so they can do that."

"Nope. She comes back as she left. And I want every cell of my girl's body back. *Every. Cell.* I won't have my girl go to her grave incomplete."

"I fully understand. But as you can appreciate, I also have to contact Huia's mother so her wishes can be taken into account."

His shoulders went back, chest puffed as he sat tall in his seat. "And what's she gonna do? Send her off somewhere way down country? Bury her where she's miles from her people? Take her away from us for a second time? She can get stuffed." He drilled home the message stabbing a finger at the floor. "She comes home. She comes here. Now!"

"Mr. Cooper, Huia and her baby are not the only victims here. Lily Holmes is insulin-dependent and as far as we know, she hasn't had her medication for almost two days. We need to find her now, and I can't afford to have this investigation derailed by two families fighting over the body of their loved one. Now, I understand how you feel. Truly, I do. But I need you to work with me on this. For the sake of that child. Another woman's child. That's all I'm asking."

He nodded. There seemed to be an alternative narrative going on in his head. Nyree had a pretty good idea of what that narrative was.

"So, where's Huia now? Where's my girl?"

"She's at the Whangārei morgue, Mr. Cooper. And her body will be made available the instant I can make that happen." Nyree neglected to add that that would almost certainly be to her mother.

Feeling she'd gotten as much as she could at the moment, Nyree had just thanked Rawiri Cooper, when her phone bleeped, indicating she'd received a message.

It was from the front desk. Traffic had just called in with a description of an old green Toyota Corolla that had left the road and plunged down the bank. One of the uniforms had clambered down the bank and confirmed the registration plate matched that of Huia Coburn's.

It was the break she'd been waiting for.

CHAPTER 23

"I'm walking a bloody tightrope," she told Callaghan as they wound their way down Inlet Road to where Traffic had cordoned off the section of road where the car had been found.

"Annette Coburn didn't even mention Huia's father. Now, I can see why."

"Yeah, and if we're not careful we'll wind up with a bloody feud over Huia's body on our hands, and Lily long forgotten."

"Rawiri Cooper has promised full cooperation. He could break down some walls we can't. But, why didn't the mother mention all this when you spoke to her? Was she hoping he wouldn't find out? That she could get Huia buried before the whānau turned up demanding the body?"

"Believe me, that'll be the first thing I'll be asking her. According to Cooper, Annette Coburn took out a protection order on him. She says he's got a history of family violence. He says that's rubbish. And that's before you get into who gets first dibs on the body." Nyree puffed her cheeks at the enormity of the problem and turned her gaze to the passing landscape.

"We can only do what we can, Ma'am."

"Yeah. Speak softly and carry a big stick." Nyree lifted her chin and caught sight of a traffic unit on the road ahead. "Oy, slow down. This looks like it."

Up ahead, two Traffic units were angled in to the side of the road where an officer in a high-viz vest stepped out as they approached, waving them down.

Callaghan eased the car to the side of the road and stopped, looking around before killing the engine. "Bit of a slap-dash way of getting rid of it, isn't it?"

"Panic. Whoever dumped it here knew they couldn't be seen driving it. They obviously thought this was far enough out, but not too far." She undid her seatbelt and snatched up her notebook. "Also proves the killer knew the area. This is the only section of Inlet Road with this much bush coverage."

"Someone local, then?"

"Maybe."

As the officer approached her side of the car, Nyree lowered her window, lifting her ID to the officer. "DI Bradshaw. I believe your lot found the car."

He stepped back as Nyree got out and tucked her hands into her coat pockets, shoulders hunching against the unseasonably chilly wind as she surveyed the gorse and tussock covered riverbanks.

"Yes, Ma'am. Just over there." The officer pointed. A jagged gap opened amid a stand of straggly manuka trees into which a fresh churn of tire marks led, marking the spot where the car had left the road. Given the terrain and the density of the surrounding brush draped in a spread of creeping blue morning glory, it wouldn't have taken long before the car was swallowed right up.

"How long ago was it reported?"

The officer followed her line of sight to where a glimpse of the car roof could be seen several meters below.

"'Bout an hour ago. We just got here."

"Have you checked whether there's anyone in the car?"

"Yes, Ma'am. Officer Ricks went straight down to make sure there weren't any occupants trapped in there."

"What about the boot? Did you check the boot?"

"It's empty, Ma'am. The boot was open. Probably popped as it went over."

Determined to see the damage herself, she crossed into the knee-high grass lining the road, and almost lost balance as the gravel underfoot gave way and she skated a few feet down the bank before hitting solid ground. "Shit!"

She paused, one hand out to get her balance, then moved on. Shoes slipping, right hand snatching at the weeds for stability, she dropped at a semicontrolled run until she came to an ungainly halt at the bottom, steadying herself on the rear of the car.

"Ma'am! *Nyree!*" Callaghan called after her, then immediately followed, scrambling down the bank with the officer falling in behind.

"I'm alright." Nyree tore away a length of grass looped around her ankle and lurched across to the side of the car.

The Toyota had gone over the bank, the rear skewing to the right, before coming to rest in a thicket of mangroves at the water's edge. Nyree clambered along to the passenger's door, hands shielding against the light as she leaned to peer into both front seats and back. Opposite, the driver's door had fallen open, the key dangling from the ignition.

"Did you open the door?" she called back and pulled on latex gloves.

"Driver's door was open when we got here. So was the boot," a second officer called from the road.

"We haven't touched anything," the first officer told her. "It's still got half a tank of gas."

Nyree hooked one finger under the doorhandle and pulled. With the car on such an angle, the door weighed a ton. Callaghan reached over to take the weight, hauling it open then leaning his shoulder into it while she leaned in.

"Did you check the glovebox?" she called back to the first officer.

"No, Ma'am. We didn't touch a thing."

Using the tip of her gloved finger, she released the glovebox. It dropped open with a clunk to reveal a mess of old receipts, chocolate bar wrappers and an owner's manual heavily stained with oily fingerprints. Nothing else.

She ran her eyes across the dash to where the petrol gauge showed half a tank. "So, she didn't run out of gas, then." Nyree searched the footwells, then backed out. "A girl in Huia's position doesn't fill the tank. Price of fuel, she'd never fill it beyond half. Get onto all the gas stations in the area," she told Callaghan. "Get any CCTV footage you can. Then get someone to run through it and see if she filled up at any time that day, what time, and where?"

He let the door drop closed and noted it down, then immediately made the call while Nyree wrenched open the rear passenger's door, Callaghan reaching across, holding it while she leaned in.

A few receipts, a McDonald's bag in the rear passenger's footwell, a car rug and a pair of boots on the seat. No sign of the backpack.

"Shit." Nyree sighed as she backed out and gave the area a quick visual. There was no way out except for the bank both she and the car had slid down. Just a few skid marks in the muddy bank where someone had obviously climbed up.

"Were these marks here when you got here?"

The first officer leaned over to check where she was pointing.

"No, Ma'am. That's where we got up the bank. There were no marks there previously."

"So, there's nowhere else the driver could have gotten back up the bank?"

"No, Ma'am. Unless he waded out into the river and got out on the other side." He made a doubtful face. "That'd be risky, though. The mud's pretty thick in the middle there."

"That's what I thought." Nyree scanned the river bank opposite, then turned her attention back to the car. "I'd say he had the driver's door open at the top, stuck it in gear and shoved it over. I can't see how else he would have gotten up to the road."

Trudging around to the right rear door, she hooked one finger under the handle and tugged it. The door fell open, halted by hard-packed grass. First thing she spotted just under the driver's seat was a pink, knitted slipper.

"Bag," she said, snapping her fingers urgently at Callaghan. "C'mon, bag!"

Responding to the urgency, he scrambled around towards her, drew an evidence bag from his pocket and passed it to her, then peered over her shoulder to see what she'd found.

Gently lifting the slipper by one woolen tie, she dropped it into the bag. "It matches the description of Lily's slippers." Spurred on by the find, she dropped to one knee in the wet grass, peering up under the driver's seat. Finding nothing but a couple of screwed-up wrappers, she pressed down harder, searching.

"Where the hell's the other one?" She dug out her penlight and shone it into the dark recess under the front seat. Sure enough, a flash of pink, and the light picked out the other slipper caught up on the passenger's side. Nyree repositioned herself, ribs pressed painfully against the doorframe, and carefully tugged it out. Like the first, the sole of the slipper was engrained with dirt, the woolen tie knotted as though they'd been tugged off. She reached back and Callaghan added it to the bag.

Nyree held out a hand and Callaghan helped her to her feet. "So, wherever she is, the poor little kid's got bare feet." The inexplicable urge to hold those little feet swept over her, a need to warm them, to press them to her cheek. Like a mother would. She could almost feel the soft, chilled skin, the tiny bones; the icy little toes. A memory so distant, and yet so vivid.

"Are you all right?" Callaghan tipped his head, regarding her with concern.

"Yeah. Yeah, I'm fine. Lily was definitely in the car."

Then the faint plink sound of a low battery alert. Somewhere in the car. She cut a look back at Callaghan. "Did you hear that?"

Callaghan frowned. "No. What was it?"

"I think it's a phone. Could be Huia's. Have you got the number?"

"Hang on." He dug out his notebook, flicked through it, and keyed the number into his own phone.

From somewhere beneath the passenger's seat, a mobile phone lit up and rang.

"Is that you calling?"

He shrugged. "I assume so."

Nyree dropped to her knees again and leaned in, peering into the darkness under the seat. Lodged under the frame of the passenger's seat, she could just see the faint glow of the screen. Ducking down with one hand on the seat and her ribs once again pressed painfully to the door sill, she groped until her fingers found the phone and she dragged it out.

Six missed calls and five message alerts showed.

With the casing held between gloved finger and thumb, she clambered to her feet with Callaghan's help, and tapped the message icon. Five messages popped up. All five messages were from Huia's mother, Annette Coburn. All one minute apart. Each more urgent than the last.

On the final one, Nyree lifted one eyebrow and turned the screen to Callaghan. "Now, isn't that interesting?"

CHAPTER 24

The task of canvassing the Coburns' street was assigned to Detective Greg Willis and Constable Jodie Clarkson. Clarkson had changed out of her uniform into a black business suit and white blouse. Slim and standing just on five feet four in stockinged feet, she was a model of contrast to Willis who, in his mid-fifties, bore deep lines etched down each cheek, forehead furrowed like a newly ploughed field, shoulders and neck like a bull. As the day had warmed, Willis had removed the suit jacket from his thick shoulders and now walked from house to house with it folded over one arm, a ring of damp showing beneath each armpit.

From this angle Clarkson thought he looked like a waiter, but didn't say so. She'd been tasked with taking the opposite side of the street from Willis, moving from door to door with a pre-written script, asking about any unusual movements in the neighborhood over the past few days, citing a general inquiry as their point of interest.

So far, they'd done half the street and had no response at one out of every three houses. Jodie figured they would still be at work. Of the rest, none had heard or seen anything untoward, and most looked disappointed they'd missed out on the drama being played out on their own doorstop.

Now, directly opposite the Coburn's place, WPC Clarkson walked up a narrow, concreted path toward the front door, checking quickly across to gauge her progress with that of Willis.

She knocked twice and waited. Two doors back, Detective Willis stepped away from a closing door and returned to the street. He met her gaze and gave her a 'No luck' tip of the head, then turned toward the house immediately neighboring the Coburn's house. She'd just turned back to knock again when a lock clicked back and the door cracked open. One dark eye peered out, shadowed by a hank of dark hair.

"Yeah? What do you want?" A woman's voice. The husky sound of someone with a dose of 'flu.

"Hi, I'm WPC Jodie Clarkson." She dug out her ID and held it up. "I wonder if I can ask you a few questions."

The door widened. The woman was probably in her late forties, dark, unwashed hair shot with harsh red highlights, deeply-lined lips, eyes pinched in suspicion. She hiked a plaid shawl up over her shoulders, and leaned against the doorway, arms folded. "So, what's it about?"

"We're making some routine inquiries about cars that might have been seen in this street."

The woman made a face of incredulity and rolled her eyes away. "Cars? What would I know about cars? I work nine hours a day. You only caught me now because I'm sick."

Ignoring the comment, Jodie twisted her clipboard bearing a picture of the blue Holden Commodore, similar to Philip Wright's, the license plate blurred out.

"Can you tell me if you've seen a car like this in the street lately?"

Slumping in irritation against the doorframe, the woman adjusted the shawl and groaned aloud. Still avoiding the picture. "Look, I wouldn't know a Toyota from a quadbike. I don't know why you're asking me."

"Can you just look at the picture?"

Sighing deeply, she angled her head briefly to view the picture, then looked up, "Nah. Nothing like that." She stepped back, hand on the door.

"How about this one?" Jodie interrupted and flicked over the laminated print to a second photograph, this one of Huia's car. She thrust it in the woman's direction.

The woman paused, stepped back eyes narrowed on the photograph. "That looks like Huia Coburn's car. Heap of shit that it is." She refolded her arms, shrugging against the cold. "Needs a new exhaust pipe. You can hear it coming from the other side of Whangārei."

Jodie folded the pages back down and held it clutched to her chest. "So, when was the last time you saw Huia's car, Mrs...?"

"Robson. Nic Robson." Nic sniffed and shifted uneasily. "So, what's this about, anyway?"

"We're following up a homicide up north."

Nic Robson froze momentarily. "The girl they found at the waterfall? You're not saying that was Huia, are you?"

"We don't have a formal identification of the body yet."

"Oh, Jesus."

"Did you know her well?"

"Well enough. We were neighbors until her bitch mother chucked her out. What happened to her?"

"We're still gathering information at this stage." Jodie gave her a quick smile. "When was the last time you saw Huia Coburn's car?"

Nic twisted her mouth sideways as she thought, then screwed up her nose. "About a week ago? Yeah, last Saturday, I think. She pulled into the driveway at about one o'clock. I swear to God; the thing sounds like a bloody tractor. You'd think Peter Coburn could at least do something about it. They're never short of a dollar or two. Always got the latest doo-dads and gadgets. Not that they look after anything. That shed over there's full of crap. They buy shit, play with it for five minutes, and chuck it away. Worse than kids."

Steering the conversation back, Jodie said, "Do you remember seeing who was driving Huia's car last Saturday?"

"Well, I assumed it was Huia. Who else would it be?"

"But you never saw her?"

A shrug. "Well, who else would be driving it? Unless," she added with a meaningful shrug.

"Unless, what?"

"Well, that brother of hers uses it sometimes. Maybe it was him."

Clarkson blinked for a moment while she scoured her memory for any mention of a brother. "What brother is this?" she asked.

"Darrell Coburn. Well, he's her stepbrother. Same difference, though, isn't it?"

"So, you're saying he's Peter Coburn's son?"

"That's right. Useless article that he is. Couldn't hold down a job if it was glued to his hand. Why?" Nic asked in a guarded tone. She shifted her weight and gave Jodie a calculating look. "What's he in trouble for this time?"

After continuing to the end of the questions and thanking Nic Robson for her assistance, Jodie stepped away and called Willis. He was four doors down on the opposite side of the street when he answered.

"Sir? I think I've found something," she said.

CHAPTER 25

"Five messages Annette Coburn sent, all begging Huia to get in touch. 'This is bloody urgent,' the last one reads. 'I need you to call me right now.' That's followed by six unanswered phone calls, all made in quick succession. Send someone down there to pick up Annette's phone. Let's see what else she doesn't want anyone seeing." Nyree switched the phone in question off and replaced it in the plastic bag as they drove back along the twisting back roads to River Falls.

"So, what's so urgent? And how come she suddenly forgets sending five messages pleading with Huia to speak to her?"

Callaghan's eyebrows shot up. "What if the baby's father isn't Skinner? What if it's a little closer to home?"

"That's what I was wondering. But that leads to the next question: Was it, in fact, Annette Coburn who sent the texts? Could it have been someone with access to her phone?"

"Good point. What time was the first one?"

Nyree checked her notes again. "Wednesday, 9 a.m. It tells Huia to call. Says she needs to talk to her…or whoever the sender was."

"Would Huia read well enough to understand it?" Callaghan asked.

Lip jutting, Nyree slowly shook her head. "Maybe that's why the successive phone calls. Whatever it was about, Huia never replied."

"What if Huia couldn't get to her phone? Or, maybe she was driving when the messages arrived?"

"Could be. Or maybe she knew who sent the text and that's why she didn't respond."

Callaghan's mouth twisted while he thought. "I reckon the phone was under the seat before the car went over the bank. From the angle the car finished up, it should have been thrown forwards, not sideways."

"That's what I think. And I don't believe Huia or Lily were in the car when it went off the road. There were no tire marks on the road to suggest the car swerved suddenly. No blood to suggest there were any injuries, and all the shopping bags and miscellaneous crap in the boot was evenly distributed. Surely, if they swerved to avoid something on the road, you'd expect everything to have shifted to one side as the car spun around. And if it wasn't an accident, I can't think of a single reason why she'd deliberately drive down there with Lily in the car."

"What if someone was chasing them?"

She shook her head. "Nope. No sign of anyone climbing the bank. Besides, I'm sure she wouldn't deliberately risk her life and Lily's like that. And why would she be out there in the first place? There's nowhere to stop along that stretch of road so she wouldn't have been meeting someone. And the road comes to a dead end out at the peninsula, so why would she be headed out there?" She shook her head in frustration as they hit the main road and the *Welcome to River Falls* sign loomed into view, then whipped by.

"Unless that's where she met her killer."

"So, where the hell would she take Lily at that time of the day? What was so urgent that she couldn't wait until Kelly got home the next morning? She's made some arrangement to meet someone. And it's somewhere she thinks is safe enough to take Lily, but she'd be gone long enough that Lily could need the insulin. Then, whoever she met either had an accomplice with him, or that person took them somewhere else to meet the accomplice. That could have been a surprise to Huia."

"Unless the accomplice turned up after Huia was dead and the two of them disposed of the car and the body."

A chill ran down Nyree's spine. "So, what did they do with Lily?"

They drove on in silence for some minutes, each lost in their own dark thoughts as the outlying industries of River Falls began to dot the roadsides. Suddenly, Nyree's phone rang. She checked the screen and answered.

"Ma'am, it's Willis here. WPC Clarkson and I just finished canvassing the entire street. Last sign of Huia's car was last Saturday, late afternoon. Someone drove it into Coburn's driveway. One of the neighbors identified it but there was no sign of Lily with her."

"Good work, Willis. Ask around, see if any other neighbors remember that."

"One other thing, that same neighbor mentioned a brother."

Nyree snapped a look up at the street ahead. "A brother? What brother?"

"A stepbrother, Ma'am. Darrell Coburn. Said he was from Peter Coburn's previous marriage."

"That's interesting. I'd like to know why Annette Coburn conveniently forgot to mention him."

"I ran a check on him and it turns out he's twenty-two, last known address, the same as that of the parents. He's got prior for burglary, possession and distribution of Class B narcotics, the usual."

"Right, let's get onto him." Nyree made a note to follow up.

Willis continued. "Also, I did a routine check on Philip Wright. Turns out he also had some previous for objectionable content found on his computer three years ago."

"How objectionable?"

"Doesn't get much more objectionable, Ma'am." The revulsion in Willis's voice reverberated down the line. A dedicated family man with a wife and two small children, he'd previously been a part of the online investigations team, but the images he'd witnessed had left him permanently sick to the stomach, and he'd requested a transfer. Nyree's team was the first thing that had come up and he'd leapt on it.

She checked her watch, then her schedule. "Right. I've got an update briefing at six this afternoon, and a media conference first thing in the morning in Whangārei. Get out there and see Annette Coburn, find out how she and Peter conveniently forgot to mention he had a son. And if he's not living with them, get his current address."

"Yes, Ma'am."

"Then pay this Darrell Coburn a visit. Ask him where he was on the day Huia and Lily went missing. I want alibis and positive ID's. And see if he'll consent to a saliva test and get it to the lab asap. If he won't, doesn't matter. We'll have it on record. But it'll be interesting to see how he reacts. Then we'll see if his DNA matches up with anything we've already got."

"Will do, Ma'am."

"Meanwhile, I'll get Hicks to lean on our Mr. Wright. See if he can account for his whereabouts during the time of Huia's disappearance." She lifted her eyebrows to Callaghan who had obviously heard because he nodded and picked up his phone as he drove.

"Get back to me the minute you find anything out. If I'm in the briefing, have me called out," she told him.

The chances were high that Lily Holmes would now be dead. Nyree had to work as if she were alive. Every minute counted. Despite the fact that she'd been covering all bases with everything she knew, the sickening feeling that they were getting nowhere fast kept welling up.

A breakthrough—any breakthrough—would help to boost morale. Because now, there were signs it was wearing thin.

CHAPTER 26

The home of Annette and Peter Coburn was ten minutes away. All down the street, the late afternoon sun stretched the shadows of roadside trees, creating dark slashes of shade across the road and dropping the front porches of neighboring properties into gloom.

Willis pulled to the side of the street opposite and looked the house over while he undid his seatbelt. An unremarkable ex-state house typical of those constructed in the 40's and 50's, it was a single-level detached bungalow, its weatherboard outer walls painted a pale green that could have done with a fresh coat. Out front, a cracked driveway led to a double aluminum garage down the left-hand side of the property that had also seen better days. Despite what Nic Robson across the street had said, the house didn't reflect a family with plenty of cash.

Willis got out and crossed the street. No sign of any lights from inside the house, so he checked the street and went up the two steps to the front porch. Peering through the darkened glass, he could see no signs of life inside, but knocked anyway.

After waiting a few moments with no response, he made his way back down the steps and followed the narrow path around the side of the house to the garage where an overgrown lawn had all but swallowed up the remains of a vegetable garden. A rusting rotary clothes line stood center of the backyard, one side leaning as if someone had swung on it and wrecked it.

Cupping his hands to the darkened window in the rear of the garage, he took out his flashlight and peered inside. The beam picked up various shapes covered in tarpaulins, a small boat leaning against the opposite wall, a kayak resting at an odd angle in the corner, a variety of dressers and cabinets lining the walls, the bulk of some kind of vehicle occupying center stage.

"Lily? Are you in there, love?" Willis called, then gave the backyard a quick glance to make sure there was no one else around.

Nothing. So, he knocked on the glass. "Lily! Are you in there, sweetheart? Come to the window if you hear me. I'm a policeman. I'm going to take you home to your mummy."

No movement inside. Checking the surroundings again, he moved to the side of the garage to find a door with a square of glass set into the upper half.

Again, he knocked. "Lily? Can you hear me, love?"

He tried the handle. It turned and the door squeaked open to the stench of stale engine oil and rotting plywood. As he stepped inside, the old linoleum covered wooden floor creaked and flexed under his weight, as if the damp had seeped up from the ground below. Now inside, he could see the place was crammed wall-to-wall with junk. Dirt-encrusted tarpaulins partially covered what he now recognized as the carcass of a rusted-out 1971 Ford Mustang. The doors and engine had been removed as though someone had begun renovating it, then given up, consigning it to what had become a scrap-heap.

"Lily? Are you in here, sweetheart?" His heart fell. He knew the child wasn't there, knew she would have called out.

If she could.

A wash of light swept across the front of the garage, slicing through the gap around the garage door as a car pulled to stop in front of it. He quickly exited the way he'd come, closing the door, and retracing his steps to the front to find a silver Honda Accord. Both front doors opened and a couple got out—Peter and Annette Coburn.

They paused to give Willis a suspicious look as he approached and took his ID from his coat pocket.

"Mr. Coburn? Mrs. Coburn? I'm Detective Greg Willis, Whangārei CIB."

Annette Coburn hiked two grocery bags in her arms and elbowed her door closed. "What do you want now?" She passed Willis and headed toward the front door, scrabbling through her handbag for the key while Peter Coburn retrieved four bags of groceries from the back seat.

"I'd like to ask you a few more questions, if you don't mind," Willis called after her, just as she was about to step inside.

"I don't suppose I've got much choice, do I?" she muttered and disappeared inside.

Peter Coburn paused next to Willis who offered a hand with the groceries. Coburn handed two bags over, both, Willis noted, filled with pre-prepared salads and wafting with the aroma of roast chicken.

"Smells good," Willis said jovially as he followed Peter Coburn up the front steps and into a dim hallway lined with religious pictures and cluttered with boxes and cabinets that were strewn with a variety of cheap knick-knacks and ornaments. To his left, a tiny room, a sewing machine set up on a table and surrounded by boxes and fabric and more junk. Like the beginnings of one of those hoarder's houses Willis had seen on some reality show. Above the sewing table, a picture of the Savior stared forlornly out over the mess.

Neither of the Coburns appeared to notice as they wove their way around piles of newspapers and past rickety cabinets and headed for the kitchen.

"I see you do a bit of sewing, Mrs. Coburn?" Willis called after her.

"She does alterations. Brings in a few extra bucks. Mind yourself on the bookcase there," Peter told Willis as they passed a lop-sided bookcase. "She's a bit dodgy. I haven't gotten around to fixing it yet."

The thump of an apple hitting the floor emanated from the kitchen where Annette had dumped her grocery bags on a cluttered kitchen counter. By the time Willis got there, she'd retrieved it and was leaning against the counter, arms folded. "So, what's it about now?"

Willis positioned the bags next to hers. "Couple of things: can I ask when you'd be able to come in to identify the body?"

"When are we allowed to?"

"Right now, if you'd like," Willis replied gently.

Annette checked her watch. "Yeah, I can do that. What was the other thing?"

A little taken aback by the curt reply, Willis said, "You said Huia came to visit you last Saturday."

"What about it?"

"Was it to tell you about the baby? Or something else?"

"She wanted to use our computer. Printing out photos."

"And that was the last time you saw her?"

"That's right."

"And you didn't see her at all on Wednesday?"

"How could I? She's up in River Falls."

Willis frowned, considered her reply, then changed direction. "How long ago did Huia move out...I know this is hard, but we need to know."

Annette pushed off where she'd leaned against the bench and began putting away groceries, irritation clear in the rough handling of the items. "Couple of months ago. Said she wanted to be up north near her *real* father."

"And you were happy for her to go?"

She made a derisive sound. "No, I wasn't. After all the crap she put us through, she wants to go and be near him." She slowly shook her head. "That was a real kick in the guts. I mean, what's he ever done for her? I raised her. Peter here's been more of a father than he ever was. Rawiri turns up out of the blue, and next thing, he's the best thing since sliced bread. 'Well, she wants to go, let her go,' I said. 'Leopard doesn't change its spots. She'll find that out,' I said. 'She'll see what he's really like.'"

Peter, who had been standing in the doorway with his mouth turned down, nodded in agreement, but said nothing.

"So, it wasn't your idea for her to go?"

Annette's face morphed into an expression of disbelief. "Of course it wasn't. This was all her big idea, wasn't it? I don't know what was going on with her. All of a sudden, she was talking back to me and Peter, starting arguments, going out without telling me. When she left, I told her, 'Don't think you can just come swanning back.' You know what she said? She said, 'I won't.'"

Perhaps realizing how those words had come back to haunt her, a single tear formed in Annette's eye. She swiped it away, but the attitude returned.

Willis softened his tone. "And did you know she was pregnant?"

"*She* didn't know she was pregnant. How would I know? Mind you," she said, turning to shove a few items into the fridge, "Would she listen to me? Not on your life. I told her that Skinner kid was no good. And did she listen? Course not. She'd gotten far too full of herself—*that* was her problem. Ever since she moved in with Kelly." She paused for a second. "And now look."

"Mrs. Coburn, do you have your cell phone with you?"

She paused, baked bean can in hand, blinking total incomprehension at him. "Why? What do you want that for?"

"If I could see it...?" He held out a hand.

Her eyes flicked to Peter. He shrugged in response, so she clunked the can down on the counter and went to her handbag. After plucking out her phone, she shoved it at Willis. "Here. You won't find anything on it." She folded her arms, scowling at him.

He twisted it around, checking the screen. "Thank you."

"If that's all, you know where the door is."

"Just one more thing: I wonder if you can give me the address of your son. And a phone number, if you have it."

The Coburns exchanged a pointed look this time.

"Why? What's this got to do with him?" Annette demanded.

Peter Coburn stepped forward, speaking for the first time. "He hasn't done anything. What do you need him for?" Peter Coburn's demeanor had also shifted, and now both of them glared at Willis.

In turn, Willis lifted his rugby-cratered head, his bull-muscled shoulders back. "We'd just like to speak to him. Now, if you don't mind..."

Another pointed exchange crossed between the Coburns during which Peter nodded.

"He lost his phone," Annette said. "I don't know his new number."

"Then his address?"

"He's probably out," Annette said.

"I'll take my chances. His address?"

Annette hesitated. "Forty-two Karaka Street. Is that all you want?"

"For now," Willis replied as he wrote it down.

She jerked her head toward the hallway. "Then like I said, you know where the door is."

CHAPTER 27

Callaghan had just swung the car into the first parking spot outside the River Falls station to find a late model Ford Falcon at the end of the row.

"Whose is that?" Nyree asked, despite the dull thud of her heart hitting the bottom of her gut telling her she already knew.

"Dunno." He leaned to look it over. "It's one of ours."

"Yeah, I know." It was inevitable. Bound to happen sooner or later. She'd simply hoped she was wrong.

Inside the station, the desk sergeant handed her a stack of handwritten memos as she swept by. According to the notes, five sightings of Lily Holmes had been reported after the TV plea. One as far away as Dunedin. Each needing to be checked out. None likely.

How was Kelly Holmes feeling now? A mother's loss. Her child possibly dying, frightened and alone. She pushed it aside, and went to the next note.

The blood found in Brodie Skinner's car had turned out to be animal blood —possibly a dog. Huia's DNA was found in the car, but that was hardly surprising. Nothing from Lily.

"Bugger," Nyree whispered to herself and went to the next one.

All the tools confiscated from the marae had been run through the wringer, and came out clean —nothing but soil, vegetable matter, and rust spotting.

A tsk and a sigh of frustration.

Every inch of Kelly Holmes's house had been raked over. Plenty of fingerprints. Huia, Lily, and Kelly. Three unidentified on the front door, presumably the postman or door knockers or neighbors. None on the database, and none matching any of the suspects.

"Do you know what I see?" she asked Callaghan as they walked to her office. "I see a young woman who's been abused, who's been neglected, who's so downtrodden, she's at the very bottom looking up. Then I see that young woman suddenly fighting back, taking control over her own life, finding herself. And I don't think she had this great love of Brodie Skinner." Her lip curled, anger for yet another victim at the hands of a violent man. "You know what I think?"

His eyebrows lifted.

"I think Huia found an escape and took it. She told Rawiri she was going to dump Skinner. Maybe Skinner also knew that."

Right then, the desk sergeant stuck his head in through the door.

"Local press is waiting for a statement, Ma'am. They've been camped out here for the past two hours. Seems like they've put the numbers together and figured out the connection between Lily Holmes and Huia's murder."

"That was bound to happen. Where are they now?"

"We've stuck them in the communications room."

She glanced at her watch. "Give me a minute and I'll give them a thirty second statement."

After dropping her briefcase on her desk, Nyree checked her emails, then made her way through to the communications room in the rear of River Falls police station. Three bedraggled journos sat at the table. Each looked up as she walked in.

"I'm sorry, I can't tell you anything at the moment, guys. I've got a press conference in Whangārei at ten tomorrow morning. I suggest you make your way there."

"Can you just confirm that the death of Huia Coburn and the missing kid are connected."

The dead girl. The missing kid. A news item. A scoop. The words infuriated her. Not a courageous young woman and a sweet, innocent child both lost. Not a desperate mother facing her worst nightmare, or justice unserved. Just a storyline to be pounced on.

Nyree's voice hardened. "Like I said, there's a press conference tomorrow. I suggest you be there." And without another word, she walked out.

The clock in the hallway read ten past six. She was late for her own briefing. She flicked quickly through the raft of notes as she hurried to the briefing room, and entered to find Bowman, Hicks, and Jodie Clarkson all down the back, surrounding Terry McFarlane, who sat perched on the edge of a desk, arms folded, regaling them with some feat of brilliance he'd pulled off. The only one who refused to hang on his every word was Henare who stood leaning on the wall near the front. Once, many moons past when he was in uniform, McFarlane had called him a *wannabe Māori boy*. Henare had taken exception. He was not one to let such a slight go.

Everyone turned as she entered.

"Evening people...Detective," she added, jerking her chin at McFarlane. "Nice to see you again."

The slight tip of his head in greeting did nothing to convince her his lousy attitude had changed. His refusal to acknowledge her position, to acknowledge her work, her dedication, had grated from the day she'd been promoted over him.

The team rallied and scuttled back to their seats, expressions aching with guilt like a bunch of schoolkids caught smoking behind the bike sheds. A few heads dropped. The tension in the atmosphere cranked up a couple of notches. No one made immediate eye contact.

Lifting her chin in McFarlane's direction, she said, "It's good to have you with us, Terry, but since you're on the Sean Clemmons case, I doubt you'll get anything out of this briefing. I'll come and see you afterwards."

McFarlane scratched the side of his nose. "On the contrary. If our Mr. Clemmons is gunning for you, I think it's imperative that I know what's going on in your camp."

A battle of wills with McFarlane wasn't on her agenda. The team was already tired and red-eyed from sleep deprivation and excessive hours. She let it go.

For now.

"Right then, let's crack on." She turned to the board where the photographs of Annette and Peter Coburn had been added to the timeline, along with a snap of Huia's car and Lily's knitted slippers.

"Huia Coburn's car was sighted at her mother's house last Saturday evening. Up until then, everything seems fine. So, between last Saturday evening and the time of her death, something happened that made Huia the target of her killer. The evidence to date is leaning heavily towards that killer being one of her family."

She tapped the left-hand side of the time-line. "Then, between the hours of four and six on the following Wednesday, she left the house with Lily and one vial of Lily's insulin in the child's backpack. Where she was going, we don't know, but she'd received five messages and several phone calls from her mother's phone, begging her to meet. Considering her car was found in River Falls, I think we can assume she never made it out of town."

A hand shot up. Bowman. "Were there any other calls on Huia's phone?"

"A couple from Brodie Skinner, five from an unknown number. We're trying to find who that call was from."

"What if it wasn't the mother who called and left the messages?" Henare suggested.

Nyree tipped her head briefly and sat one hand on her hip while she glanced over the board again. "I considered that. Obviously, it's someone with access to the phone, but the mother is still in the frame." She drew a line in marker pen under Annette Coburn's photograph, then stepped back. "Neighbors didn't remember seeing the mother at all that day. But she's adamant she never left the house. Unless anyone comes forward to corroborate or discredit her story, we've nothing else to go on. Next," she said, moving on and pointing to the next photograph, "both Brodie Skinner and Rawiri Cooper happened to have been in the same gas station at around six pm on the night Huia was murdered. What's more, from the security feed we got, they seemed to be at least on nodding terms with one another."

"And what did they have to say about that?" called out McFarlane.

Nyree turned to him. "We're following up. This information's only just come to us. But so far, my money isn't on Cooper. He's devastated about his loss."

McFarlane chortled softly and dropped his gaze. As if he would have gotten better results.

Irritation needled at her. It was as if he were testing her, trying to find a weakness in her investigative skills. Well, there were two ways of playing this game: his, and hers. And as soon as the briefing was over, she'd put him straight that it was hers they were playing. So, she returned to the board and continued on.

"We think Huia and her killer had a meeting. Huia's car was found at Inlet Road but it's unlikely the meeting was there. The area's open and any passerby could have seen them. It's more likely the offender drove the car to Inlet Road where he was met by an accomplice who helped push it over the bank into the estuary, and they both left in the other vehicle."

"It's not far from River Falls, Ma'am," said Bowman. "Wouldn't they realize someone would see it eventually?"

"Exactly. Which makes me think they were in a hurry. It's late afternoon, and they either have Lily with them, or they've left her somewhere."

"Do we know if the car was disposed of before, or after Huia was killed?" This from Bowman again.

"Don't know. Could have been either. They'd have to be utterly stupid not to have worn gloves of some kind, but we've got the boys taking it back for fingerprinting. If they've left any trace, they'll find it."

This time Terry McFarlane spoke up. "The killer murdered the girl, then realized he had to do something with the kid. That's a given. So, what does he do?" he asked, now addressing the room. "He calls up a friend, father, brother...whatever. They lock the kid up while they get rid of Huia's body – somewhere quiet where no one will hear her, then ditch the car. Limit the connection. But they can't leave the kid for so long. So, with one of them driving Huia's car and the other following, they travel to Mason's Rock, dump the body, ditch both cars, and go home."

"Why just leave the body there, though?" asked Bowman, turning to the senior detective. "Why not attempt to hide it?"

McFarlane did a deep shrug. "They were disturbed. Someone nearby saw them. Probably your kiwifruit pickers. Or, at least, the killer thought they saw him. Maybe he panicked."

"Thank you, Terry." Irritated because that's exactly what she'd just said, she returned to the board. "So, if the killer thinks he's been seen…?" Nyree began.

McFarlane jumped in again.

"They bugger off. After all, by now they've got the ring and a van full of stolen fruit." Which brought a brief chuckle from the room. "You need to question them again. Lean on them hard," he added. "There's a connection somewhere. Then you need to find out who this accomplice is. A small town like this, everyone knows everyone else's business. Someone knows who he is. Find out if these tourists have any contacts in town."

Which was contrary to the line of enquiry Nyree was following. But she let it go.

"Thanks, Terry, I'll keep that in mind." Twisting the marker pen so firmly between taut fingers that it hurt, she stepped back to the board.

Another hand went up. Willis, this time. "So, is there any evidence the stolen blue Holden across the river was used for that purpose?"

"Well, that would seem obvious," McFarlane muttered loud enough for all to hear. "There's your connection right there."

Nyree's irritation cranked up another notch.

"There's nothing to suggest any association between Huia's family and Philip Wright, apart from the proximity of Wright's home to Huia's parents' place. And the car," she added begrudgingly.

"So, you've ruled it out?" McFarlane cocked his head, a look of semi-disbelief on his face. Still testing her.

"We haven't ruled it out. The investigation is still ongoing. And I'd like you to get me a report on your progress with Sean Clemmons, if you would, Terry."

The entire room turned to him, waiting for the response. He eased himself off the desk and stretched out his back.

"It's already on your desk. Ma'am," he told her.

"Then we'll meet in my office when I'm finished here. Give me ten minutes."

For the longest moment the entire room went still. McFarlane brushed down his suit pants, and nodded. "I'll see you there," he said as he sauntered toward the door and left the room without a backward look.

The atmosphere in the room lifted measurably.

Nyree returned to business, tapping a nail on the picture of the stolen car. "Okay, Willis, I want everything we can possibly find out on Philip Wright and his blue Holden. Where was he that night? When was the last time he used the car? Did the neighbors see him leave the house at any time on the day?"

"Yes, Ma'am."

"Bowman, go out and pay Brodie Skinner another visit. Find out how long Huia stayed with him, what time she left, and how he accounts for his fuel stop on Wednesday night when he was supposed to be in home-detention."

"Will do."

"I've got Willis out visiting Annette and Peter Coburn, then looking for Darrell Coburn, the son. I want to know where he was on the night Huia died and how he fits into all of this. Most of all, I want Lily Holmes found. And I want her found today. Let's go."

The scraping of chair legs on the linoleum and the murmur of tired voices filled the room, then faded as the team exited the room.

Nyree put down the marker, checked the board once more, and walked to her makeshift office. This was one meeting she wasn't looking forward to. One of them would come out victorious. The other would fall.

She had to stay strong.

CHAPTER 28

He was already there. Sitting. Didn't offer to stand as she entered.

"Terry." She faltered for a second, then rounded her desk and sat, avoiding eye contact as she shoved files and notebooks aside. "So, let's hear what you've got, and what you've got planned." She folded her arms, then unfolded them and laid them along the armrests, keenly aware of the rise in her own heart rate. Why did he make her so nervous? Why couldn't she just feel in charge?

"I ran some background checks before I got here."

Her eyebrows went up. "And...?"

McFarlane tucked a hand into his jacket breast pocket and dredged out a small red, leatherbound notebook. His own. Not police issue. It looked expensive. "Our Sean's latest girlfriend..." He flicked it open. "...Sherilyn Grant. Lives twenty klicks north of Kamo. She knew Sean from school." He snorted. "Hardly surprising. A right little rogue's gallery came out of that place." From what she could see of the page there was a lot more written than two names. All the same, he tucked the book away.

"I'm glad to see you found them so quickly."

He gave her a lop-sided grin. "Cops know every crim in the Far North and how to find them. 'Specially if they've got gang associations."

"And Clemmons? Does he have those same gang associations?"

The corners of McFarlane's mouth drew down. "Could be. But they wouldn't do anything unless there's something in it for them. I'm picking he's on his own."

Sean Clemmons was no mastermind. Nyree knew that. McFarlane was dragging his heels. Was he testing her? Taking her for a fool?

She spun on the chair to study the wall map of the upper North Island behind her. "Kamo. Okay. That's halfway between here and Whangārei. So yeah, it might pay to have a word with Sherilyn."

"Already did. She says she hasn't seen him. Says he called in but didn't stay. Said he had a job to do."

"Job? What kind of job?"

The smug grin pulled back one side of his mouth again. "Putting the shits up you, I reckon. Anyway, I got his car deets, put out an APB. We'll see what comes back. If it's anywhere on the road between here and Whangārei, I'll know."

"And what's the plan from here?"

"Ear to the ground. Make some enquiries. I'll find him."

Didn't sound like much of a plan to Nyree. "Good. Soon, I hope."

With nothing else to add, Terry McFarlane got up, told Nyree it was good to see her again, and left. If she didn't know better, she might have believed he'd changed. She could have thought for a moment there that he'd mellowed. Lost the attitude. The resentment.

If only.

Exhaustion prickled at the backs of her eyes. Her limbs felt like dead weights. All she wanted to do was sleep. But when her phone rang from her open briefcase, another shot of adrenaline blasted through her. She hooked it out, checked the screen and answered.

"It's Christine here."

Nyree clutched the phone even tighter and found herself preparing for the worst. "What have you got for me?"

"Well, quite a bit, actually. Annette Coburn came in half an hour ago and identified the body."

Nyree dropped her head into one hand. "Bugger it. I should have been there."

"Don't beat yourself up. You had other things on your mind."

That may have been true. And Nyree may not have liked the mother, but the woman had lost her only daughter. The least she could have done was be there to support her. But Christine was right, she had another woman's child to find. And the guilt of that already weighed heavy. "What was Annette's reaction?"

"Subdued."

"Shock, you think?"

"Could be. She came with her husband but he waited outside. I'm pretty sure they already knew it was her. She just took it in her stride, no statements of denial, if you know what I mean."

"Anything back on the samples and swabs?"

"Yep. Hang on." From the background came the click of a few keys. "I've already sent the full reports on to your office."

"Then give me the quick and dirty version."

"Right. First up, the pollen samples came back. They're Syzygium Maire, or Swamp maire."

"Uh-huh." It meant nothing to Nyree.

"That indicates her last breath was taken in a swampy area. Fragments of debris in her hair confirm that. These trees are found in swamp or wetlands. We found a wood splinter under one of her fingernails and three tiny feathers caught in the fabric of the tee. I've sent them off to an ornithologist to see if he can identify the bird."

"You think she was locked in an aviary? Or somewhere on a chicken farm?"

"Hon, believe me, if I could tell you that, I would. I'll find out more when the results come back."

"Cheers. Anything else? Something a little more definite would be good, right now."

"Well, you're in luck. We got the DNA back on the fetus."

"Hallelujah. Any matches?"

"A positive for the father."

"You're absolutely sure?"

"Can't get closer. Well, you could, but—"

"So, go on: who's the lucky man?"

"Brodie Skinner. His DNA's already registered on the police database. He was brought in for assault on a female last year but no charges were laid."

Was that assault on Huia? Had Skinner gone one step too far this time, and the injuries had come to someone's attention? Had he convinced her not to press charges? A deadening sense of pity washed through Nyree. The image of that poor girl simply discarded in the water. Her family only tolerating her as long as she brought in a buck or two. The family Rawiri Cooper entrusted her care to. Instead, they had robbed her of any confidence, stolen her dignity, then in her hour of need, abandoned her to go and live with Kelly Holmes, the only person who would take her in. Illiterate and struggling, she had clung to Brodie Skinner in the storm. Only to find that he too had abused her, then tossed her aside when it no longer suited him.

Nostrils flared, Nyree added his name to her notes, thanked Christine, then hung up. For the longest moment, she sat glaring at his name.

But why would Brodie Skinner murder Huia? Rawiri Cooper had said he'd take care of Huia and her baby. She was already living with Kelly Holmes. What would Skinner have to gain?

Or lose?

She immediately lifted the phone again, hit redial. As soon as Willis answered, she snapped out her orders.

"Have you found Darryl Coburn?"

"I'm on my way to see him."

"Bring him in to Whangārei and keep him there. If the press get wind, just say he's helping with our inquires. Don't let him out of your sight until I get there. He's got more explaining to do. But I've got one more interview to do before I get to him."

CHAPTER 29

Skinner was sitting in Interview One when Nyree walked in. The attending officer straightened from where he'd been leaning against the wall with his arms folded, then nodded. "Ma'am."

With a curt nod, she tossed the file on the table as she rounded it and pulled out the chair opposite Skinner and proceeded to open the file.

"Mr. Skinner," she said in a chatty tone. "You must have known your previous records were on our files. Let me see here: Assault on female, drugs, dealing. You have been busy."

His eyes went up to stare dully at a point just over her head while he spoke with forced patience. "What do you want now?"

Nyree studied the file as though doubting herself. "And by all accounts, you haven't changed much since school, have you?"

A withering glare dropped to meet her. That same sneer. The glint of loathing in his eyes. "So much for home detention so I can make a living. You're going to lose me my job."

She opened her file and checked her notes. "Are you still in touch with Sean Clemmons these days?"

Radiating exasperation, his gaze left hers. Then returned. "I've already told you everything I know. Huia left me around six-thirty in the morning and I went to work."

"Yes. You told us that Huia was your…what? Sometime girlfriend? Not really serious, though, were you?"

He frowned deeply. "Since just before she moved to River Falls. What's this got to do with anything?"

"And did you know she was planning on ending your relationship?"

"I don't know where this is going, but if you're asking if I murdered her, then I'll tell you again, I didn't."

"I'm simply trying to find out what terms you and Huia were on, on the final day of her life." She tipped her head and waited. "So, did you argue with her on that day, Mr. Skinner?"

"Oh, Jesus, you're trying to stitch me up for this."

"We're trying to find the truth. Was Huia the woman mentioned in your assault last year?"

His face puckered into utter frustration. "No."

"That's a coincidence because Huia had a number of old injuries—" She made a show of checking the notes, despite knowing then word-for-word. "Cigarette burns, a couple of fractures, a few scars. Do you know how they got there?"

"No idea."

"Well, we have no idea how else she could have got them, do we? Who was that woman in the assault, then, if it wasn't Huia?"

A short shake of the head. "I don't remember. She was a one-night stand."

"Lovely," Nyree said sarcastically. "Seems like you certainly have a way with women. But we'll come back to that. Tell me, what do you know about Crystal Robson?"

He shrugged, mouth briefly turning down at the corners. "Topped herself, didn't she? What's she got to do with anything?"

"You knew they were close, didn't you?"

He huffed out a breath. "So?"

"You knew both Huia and Crystal from school."

"So?" he said, more irritably this time.

"Then tell me, Mr. Skinner," she said and twisted a single frame photograph cut from the yearbook. "Of all the girls in the world you could hook up with, why would you pick Huia Coburn?"

He remained still for some moments, then looked up, that slimy grin back again. "Cos she was the easiest. Anyway, it wasn't me that wanted it. It was her. She caught up with me at the gas station. Told me we should get together. For old times' sakes. I thought, *Yeah, why not?*"

"And where was that?"

"In River Falls. We had a few drinks, talked. Then after a while she moved up to live with Kelly. Was all her idea. I didn't ask her to move. And the kid wasn't my idea, either. I told her to take precautions. You'd think she could remember to take a pill."

Nyree ignored the comment and settled onto her elbows. "And how well did you know Lily Holmes?"

"I didn't. Huia hardly mentioned her. Why?" For the first time, the faint whiff of fear fell between them.

"Because we have your part-time girlfriend who was about to leave you, dead; and the child she was caring for, missing, Mr. Skinner. And if I get one whiff of evidence that you had anything to do with Huia's death, or Lily's disappearance, you'll wish you had been charged with that assault and were currently rotting in prison."

CHAPTER 30

8 p.m. already. It was as though Nyree's world had been folded into a fire-damaged crucible and time was leaking away through the cracks. And with every moment that seeped away, so did little Lily Holmes's life.

Exhausted, and blinking against the glare of oncoming car lights, she drove at a sober pace, and hit the speed dial on her phone. It rang twice and Callaghan picked up.

"Ma'am, I was just about to call you. We've got more phone records back from the various providers. I'll run through them with you when you have a minute."

Despite herself, Nyree found herself leaning toward the microphone of the handsfree speaker and raising her voice. "Thanks for that. Email them to me. I'll be home in around half an hour. I'll look at them then."

"Make sure you get some sleep," he said.

Tired as she was, she smiled. "I will."

"How'd you get on with Skinner?"

She snorted softly. "He's a right Romeo. The assault was on some girl he picked up last year. Can't remember her name."

"What a guy."

"He knew she was pregnant. Says none of that was his idea."

"Course not."

"What I'm struggling with," she admitted, "is there's no motive. Okay, I like Brodie Skinner for it. He's in the right place, he's got the means, and he's the father of Huia's baby. But why kill her? Rawiri Cooper said he'd look after her and the baby."

"Goes back to the family, then."

"Yeah, that's what I keep coming up with," Nyree admitted in defeat. "But again, why? She's left home. Even if they don't want her back, they won't be financially responsible for her. She's over eighteen. She can get state assistance. The family have absolutely no legal responsibility for her."

"Not that they're skint. According to the neighbor, they travel a lot, buy up expensive toys."

Nyree mentally stepped back, taking an aerial view of the picture in her head. "We've got the messages on Huia's phone, and the stolen car. Someone in that family stole Philip Wright's car, and took off up to River Falls. Why?"

"Because they didn't want to be seen in their own car?" Callaghan ventured.

"Or because they didn't have access to their own car. Maybe they were following whoever was driving their car. They called Huia telling her to meet up with them. What do the phone records tell us?"

Callaghan fell silent for a moment. Then came back on the line. He sounded exhausted. "Three calls to her from Annette Coburn's phone. Then five calls from another phone. Prepay. Burner phone. Hasn't transmitted since the last call."

"What time was the first burner phone call?"

All Nyree could hear was Callaghan's breath and the odd click of a computer key as he searched back. "On the Saturday morning. The next is at three-oh-six on the Wednesday, then three more calls."

"Shit. We need to find that phone, link it to whoever was in the car. Put out a public plea for any sightings of Philip Wright's blue Holden."

"I'll get straight onto it."

"What happened on that day that set the whole thing off? The only thing I can think of is that Huia became a threat. What kind of threat? What did she have over them? Get Bowman to look into the family's financial situation. Find out exactly where their money comes from. Look for large, regular payments."

"Yes, Ma'am. Anything else?"

"Not right now. I feel like I've got rocks in my head," she admitted.

"Any news on Sean Clemmons?"

She let out a cynical noise. "Detective McFarlane says he's hot on his trail. Assures me that all the cops in Northland know the whereabouts of every crim on their patch...*except,* apparently, Sean Clemmons."

The atmosphere on the line cooled a couple of degrees. "I'm sure he's doing his best, Ma'am. He's a good cop."

Nolan's words, exactly. Nyree instantly regretted her words. Had Callaghan been present at the last briefing, he would have been one of those hanging off every one of Terry McFarlane's words. So deep-rooted had the Police Boys' Club been back in the 80's, the pale ghosts of misogyny and male ego still lay festering in darker corners of the organization. Stirring it back into the air would do no good to anyone. Sometimes you simply had to let it die naturally.

"Ignore me," she said. "I'm tired. Let me know when you've got what I need."

"Will do, Ma'am," he replied. "Drive carefully," he added. But the warmth in his voice had gone.

"I'm home now. I'll talk to you in a few hours." She hung up with a sick feeling of having betrayed herself lying in her stomach.

Nothing she could do now. Nyree hit the indicator and swung the car around the last corner and into her street. She couldn't remember the last time she'd slept in her own bed. Every bone in her body cried out for rest. But just as she was about to turn into the driveway, she stamped her foot on the brake and jerked forward as the car came to a sudden, jolting halt. A sharp intake of breath and any thoughts of sleep fled her mind.

"Holy. Bloody. Shit!" she said.

CHAPTER 31

Built in what was once a new-build area of low-cost housing to meet the growing population demands, Rearton Estate had mushroomed on the outskirts of Whangārei, high-density housing in the form of townhouses and terraced apartments. Dwellings sold at, allegedly, 'affordable rates' had been scooped up by slum landlords, then rented out over the subsequent years until the exteriors had faded, gardens overgrown, and paths cracked, leaving a less-than-desirable area in which the crime statistics grew and spread like the mold seeping through the leaky buildings.

Willis wound his way through the tangle of streets until he came to the two-story terraced house at the address and parked opposite. A single light bulb could be seen through the lower floor window of Forty-two Karaka Street, the two-story duplex where Darren Coburn lived.

Aware of the time, Willis checked the rear-view mirror, then got out and walked quickly across the street and up the front path. Music thudded from inside, pounding like a heartbeat into the night air as he approached. But it was a good sign that Darryl Coburn was not only in, but awake.

Willis banged on the door with the side of his fist to ensure he was heard over the din. After a few moments the volume of the music dropped and footsteps approached on the other side of the door.

"Who is it?"

"Police. Can you open the door?" Willis got out his ID, ready to flash it.

The door remained closed. "What do you want?"

"I need to speak to Darryl Coburn." He waited.

Finally, the lock clicked, the door cracked, and a face peeked out.

Willis didn't have to ask. Darryl Coburn was the spitting image of his father, the same pasty skin, thin blond hair, insipid blue eyes. Even the same scowl. The difference was that Darryl Coburn was markedly thinner, his skin and teeth showing the tell-tale breakdown prevalent in the habitual drug user. A dark purple bruise the shape of Stewart Island colored the left side of his jaw.

"Yeah? What's it about?"

"Is it okay if I come in?"

Darryl narrowed the gap while he shot a worried look behind him, then shrugged. "Can't we talk here?"

"I'd rather it was inside, if that's okay." Willis flicked a glance over his shoulder. "You don't want the neighbors nosing in, do you?"

Maybe considering the lesser of two evils, Coburn said, "You'll have to wait a minute."

Willis nodded his big, bull head amiably. "All good."

He closed the door. Inside, Willis could hear him scrambling hurriedly around the living room. Probably removing incriminating items, wafting the air in the hope Willis wouldn't pick up the stink of pot. Next thing, the door opened again.

"Come in. Place is a mess. I've got crap everywhere."

"I'm here about your sister, Huia," Willis assured him. "Nothing else."

"Oh." He visibly relaxed, though his demeanor remained nervous. He gestured to a small, scruffy living room furnished in mismatched and worn sofa and chairs. The Coburns' good fortune obviously hadn't extended to their son. Wearing tatty blue jeans, a faded Metallica concert tee-shirt, and bare feet, he walked ahead of Willis but remained standing, feet slightly apart, the fingers of one hand stroking his temple to hide the bruising. "So, what's this about?"

Willis hesitated for a second, then sat on the grubby sofa, and waited for Coburn to sit. When he remained standing, Willis finally said, "What happened to your face?"

He shook it away. "Uh, hit it on the cupboard."

Yeah, right, thought Willis. "When was the last time you saw Huia?"

Coburn shrugged, dismissive. "Dunno. Last week?"

"Saturday?"

Another shrug. "Could have been. Yeah, I think she came down to Mum and Dad's."

"Do you remember why?"

A huff of frustration. "Just a visit, I guess."

"Did she and your parents argue at all?"

"Argue? What about?"

"I don't know. If you were there, I thought you might have known if they'd raised their voices. Sounded angry with each other."

His attitude took a dive. "Well, how would I know? I was out in the garage."

"And what time did she leave?"

He folded his arms and gave a quick shrug. "Dunno. I left before she did. Why? What's this is about?"

"We're just trying to get her movements the days before she died."

Coburn said nothing, just scowled.

"Do you have a phone, Darryl?"

For a fleeting moment, Darryl Coburn's expression solidified. Willis could see what he'd be like when challenged. Darryl Coburn thought he could lie; thought he was a chameleon. That he could blend in between the lines of truth and lies. He was wrong.

He quickly gathered himself. "Why? What do you need that for?"

"Just routine. Ruling out numbers on Huia's phone records."

He scratched the side of his nose then refolded his arms. "She had a prepay. So, that wouldn't show up." He suddenly sounded less convinced.

"But the calls and texts are still on record." Willis gave him a fake smile.

Again, Darryl gathered himself. "I lost my phone a couple of days ago. I've got a new one."

"I see. What kind of phone was it—the one you lost?"

Darryl froze for a second. Deer in the headlights. "A Samsung. An old one."

"What model?"

"Dunno."

"Where did you lose it?"

"If I knew that, I wouldn't have lost it, would I?"

"What service provider do you use?"

"I don't remember."

"You don't remember who you pay for top-ups?"

A slow headshake.

"That's okay. We'll check the phone number and IMEI number through all the telcos. They'll be able to tell us," Willis offered with a smug grin.

"Sure. Go ahead."

"So, when you say you lost it a couple of days ago, can you remember what day? And when you got the new one?"

He gave the ceiling an irritated look, then shook his head. "No."

Guilty as sin, thought Willis, who simply smiled again. "Can you remember *where* you bought it?"

"In town somewhere. I can't remember where."

"Don't remember much, do you?" Willis said. "So, what was the number of the phone your lost?"

Darryl flicked his tongue over his thin, dry lips and shifted his weight.

"Dunno. Who remembers their own phone number? It's not like you call yourself, is it?" A snide grin slid across his mouth, then vanished.

Willis had dealt with bigger smartasses than Darryl Coburn. "So, tell me, Darryl, did you, at any time in the last few days, call Huia? Think hard. Because this is important."

Darryl's cheeks puffed out and his eyes rolled upward again while he made a show of pretending to think. Again, he shook his head. "Nope."

Willis pulled in a deep breath, huffed it out, then got up. "Okay, thanks for your help."

"Is that it?"

"Unless there's anything you *can* remember."

Darryl almost smiled. "I'd have told you if I did, wouldn't I?" He showed Willis to the door, waiting impatiently while Willis checked all his pockets for his car key before leaving.

Just as Darryl went to close the door behind him, Willis slapped a big meaty hand on the upper panel, stopping it.

"By the way, do you know a man named Philip Wright? Drives a blue Holden Commodore."

"No," Darryl replied immediately. "Never heard of him."

"Oh, that's odd. Because he only lives a few doors from your parents' house."

"Does he?" A wide-eyed shrug. "Still don't know him."

"Mr. Wright's car was stolen the night Huia was murdered."

Darryl Coburn's Adam's apple leapt. "So? What's that got to do with me?"

Again, Willis flashed him a wide grin. "Nothing, I guess. Thanks for your time."

"Yeah, sure," Darryl said, and leaned into the door, preparing to close it. "Is that it?"

"For now." Willis walked off down the path. "Guilty as bloody sin," he muttered to himself as he returned to his car.

Back in the driver's seat, he picked up his phone. "Sir, got something you might like," he told Callaghan.

He gave him the short version of the conversation and heard the satisfied determination in Callaghan's voice when he replied.

"Bring him in, Willis. Last thing we need now is for him to do a runner."

He glanced up to where Darryl Coburn was watching from the living room window. "Yes, sir. I'm sure he'll be delighted."

"By the way, I just got the forensics report back on the Holden. Darryl Coburn couldn't have left more evidence if he'd written us a note."

Willis grinned and ducked his head to view the front of Darryl Coburn's scummy rental property. "Sounds like we've got our guy."

"It does indeed," Callaghan replied.

Now all they had to do was prove it.

CHAPTER 32

Nyree's front door stood wide open. Even from here she could see black and red graffiti had been sprayed so thickly, it trailed down the inside walls like bars of a cage. Outside, windows were smashed, her front garden trampled. Leaving the door open, she stumbled from the car and, for the longest time, stood numb, surveying the damage. She couldn't read the words that had been sprayed across the hallway wallpaper, but had a fairly good idea. To the left, the living room lights shone dimly through the broken front windows where a curtain had hooked on a shard of the smashed glass and dangled hopelessly outside in the rain.

Nyree slowly walked up the front path. As if walking through a living nightmare. Feeling an unseen presence at her back, she spun around to check the street.

Not a soul in sight.

Had anyone witnessed this? Surely, someone had to have seen something. You didn't break the front windows of a house and have no one notice.

Not a hint of movement from the neighbors. In the thick silence of the night, she stepped up into the front porch and leaned through the front door into the hallway. A beautiful 1900's villa, she'd bought it when she first moved there, the knotted wood floor had been what had sold her on it. Beneath the broken crockery and stuffing from her red velvet lounge suit cushions it was obvious someone had taken time to score the planks. She was about to return for her phone when she spotted the corner of her photograph album lying open and askew amongst the wreckage.

Tony!

Ignoring all her instincts to preserve the scene, she dashed inside, flew down the hallway and scooped up the album. Turning page after page, every photograph she'd ever had of Tony when he was a child, as a youth, his past and hers, had been slashed or torn. As she turned to the front of the album where his baby photos had been stabbed and wrecked, a photograph fluttered to the floor. She picked it up. It showed her ex, Jack, Tony at about twelve, and herself in a tight group, happy and smiling into the camera. It was one that had been taken during a trip to Queenstown—God, how many years ago?

With a well of fury boiling up inside, she closed the book. Sean bloody Clemmons! She knew it. Who else would go to such trouble to destroy the things she loved?

Clutching the album to her chest, Nyree long-stepped into the kitchen at the end of the hallway to find the fridge door wide open, food scraps and mayonnaise and tomato ketchup smeared across the floor, the countertops, frozen foods from the upper freezer pulled out and left to thaw. A pack of frozen lambchops had been used to smash the glass panels of the antique hutch, and all the plates and keepsakes she'd gathered after the death of her mother had been wiped off, smashed and ground underfoot into the wood floor.

"You little bastard."

Exhaustion just a memory, fueled now by anger and loss, Nyree had gone back to the car and called it in. Twenty-six minutes later, she stood out front of her house with Superintendent Brett Nolan, both watching uniforms cordon off the front yard while paper-suited members of the forensics team entered and exited her home.

Still clutching the photo album, her mouth tight, she said, "I'm going to kill him."

Nolan's hands were driven deep into the pockets of his overcoat, a concerned frown cutting two deep lines between his brows. "Are you sure this is Clemmons? Could be coincidence, you know."

Even the suggestion irritated her. She cut him a highly dubious look. "Seriously? The guy is out for me. Even Terry McFarlane told me that. This is just him proving to me he can do anything he likes and think there's not a damn thing I can do about it."

"Terry'll be right on top of this. Just give him time. What's he got so far?"

She turned a deadpan expression back on the house. "According to him, Clemmons has suddenly gone ghost. Terry says he's followed the girlfriend line, and that's the extent of the investigation so far."

"McFarlane plays his cards pretty close to his chest. He'll have something up his sleeve. You wait and see."

"I'm sure he will." Her tone was flat.

A stiff silence hung between them. Then Nolan said, "Listen, I know you've had your issues, but Terry's a damn good cop. He's got good instincts. Trust him."

"What choice do I have?"

Ending the conversation, Brett laid a gentle hand on her shoulder. "Listen, you've got a motel booked in town. It's not the Ritz, but it's the best we could do this time of night. Get yourself off, get some rest."

"Yes, Sir. Fat lot of sleep I'll get." Now she felt as if she were moaning about her lot. Six-year-old Lily Holmes was still missing out there somewhere, perhaps dead or dying, her mother heartsick with worry. Then there was Huia Coburn lying alone in the morgue, her whānau desperate to be with her, to bring her home. And Emere Grady, torn from her only sanctuary, and taken away for her own protection.

Nyree swallowed back the anger and gave herself a mental slap-around. "Sorry, Sir, I'm just tired. And frustrated."

"I know. Try not to get too emotionally involved. Not easy, but it's all part of the job. And I need you fresh for the press tomorrow. By the way," he said in a voice that sent a wave of dread through her. His focus remained on the house. "We've downscaled the search."

Nyree's jaw dropped. "What?"

"We've searched the entire north-east sector, and all around the kiwifruit orchards in the area. We've found nothing, Nyree. There's no point in going over and over the same ground."

"But Lily's still missing. How can you...?" She bit off the end of the question.

"We've only got so much in the way of resources." It was the end of the conversation. Again, they stood in silence.

Then she spoke. "Where are the tourists?"

"Still in Whangārei."

"Have they been charged?"

He nodded. "Just waiting for space up in Bankhill."

"A waiting list to get into prison—it'd make you laugh, if it wasn't so sad. Do me a favor, keep them there until at least tomorrow morning. I'd like to talk to the girl—Gabby whatever-her-name-was."

"Johnson," Nolan supplied. "You think you've got a new lead?"

"We've got a possible suspect at the gas station, them at Mason's Rock, and Huia being murdered sometime either side of that. I need to get the timeline nailed down."

"Good work." This time he squeezed her shoulder. "Get off and get some rest. I'll see you in the morning."

And he left her with her only port of refuge in this world destroyed, Huia Coburn's killer yet to be found, and six-year-old Lily Holmes still missing and probably dead.

CHAPTER 33

Intrepid camper and one-time kiwifruit-picker Gabby Johnson was slumped over the table in Interview Two at Whangārei Police Station, her hair a tangle of knots, eyes swollen from long-shed tears and lack of sleep. She lifted her head momentarily as Nyree sat down opposite her, then laid her forehead back down on her crossed wrists.

"What now?" she groaned.

"I need to clarify a few points from your statement."

The girl sighed. Nyree ignored it and opened the transcribed copy of an earlier interview.

"Gabby, I hope you don't mind if I record our conversation."

Her head came up sharply. "Why? What are you going to try and charge us with next? Drug trafficking? Freedom camping? Sheep shagging?"

"Is that a yes, or a no?"

She heaved out a breath of despair. "Who cares?"

Nyree switched on the recorder and stated the time, and those present.

"I just need to confirm the times you were at the parking lot opposite the track to Mason's Rock, and the exact time when you first found Huia."

Gabby lifted her head and pressed the fingers of both hands to her eyes, then sat up arching her back as she raked her fingers through her hair. "We already told you this. Like a thousand times. What's the point if you don't listen to me?"

Nyree ignored the comment and consulted her notes. "In your original statement, you told us that you arrived at the car park at around seven."

Gabby gave her a dead-eyed look but said nothing.

"But in fact, you arrived at around six. Is that correct?"

Both hands dropped to the table with a thud. "I didn't check the time, so I don't know."

"But you must have had some idea because you built something like an hour into the timeframe for the fruit picking."

Gabby looked away and did a slow head shake before bringing her gaze back to Nyree.

"It would have been about six-thirty. We stopped, got dinner which would have taken about half an hour, then went up the track. It was just starting to get dark. But we could still see where we were going."

"So, it wasn't anywhere near eight-thirty?"

"Well..." Her eyes rolled across the room. "...you already know that."

Again, Nyree ignored the attitude.

"And you didn't see anyone there?"

"We already *told* you we didn't. Don't you think we'd have said the first thousand times you asked?"

"I want you to think carefully. Run back through exactly what happened."

Gabby huffed and slumped back in her seat. "We got there," she said, repeating it flatly. "We parked and got out the camp stove."

"Was the blue Holden parked across the river?"

Her tone was blunt. "I don't know. I don't remember."

"Okay, so what was the mood?"

"What do you mean?"

"Were you excited? Happy? Nervous? You were just about to go and steal some kiwifruit. It's not something you do every day. How did you feel?"

She tipped her head. "I guess it was kind of...exciting. I mean, we're students. Like you said, we don't do this kind of thing every day."

"So why this time?"

"We thought we'd sell them at one of the markets. Make a bit of extra cash."

"So, you were excited. Grab some fruit, make a little extra cash, nothing that would hurt anyone."

"I s'pose," Gabby conceded.

"And who cooked the steaks?"

"Justin. I hate cooking. Especially with that stupid stove. I'm always terrified it's going to blow up."

"And what did you do? While Justin was cooking?"

She made a face and shrugged. "Just, you know, looked around."

"Took photos?"

Gabby's eyes came back to her. Clearly coming to the same conclusion as Nyree. "I took a few, yeah. Where's my phone?"

"I'll have it brought in."

Seven minutes later, a uniform knocked at the door and handed Nyree a property bag. Inside was a Samsung phone in a blue case with a daisy motif on the cover.

"Is this your phone?" She held it up.

"Yep. Can I do it?" She put her hand out for it.

Nyree watched as Gabby switched on the phone and rapidly tapped her way through the menu to her photo album.

"Here we go. That's the first one. We'd just arrived." She swiveled the phone around on the table and pushed it toward Nyree.

The image was time-stamped at 6:21 p.m. and showed Justin Barrett opening the rear door of the van and smiling into the lens.

Nyree positioned her finger over the phone, ready to swipe. "May I?"

"Yeah, sure."

Several photos showing Justin preparing the meal followed, then several of the estuary and the surrounding scenery. It wasn't until Nyree had swiped through several more that she came to one photo that was angled around to the right where a sliver of blue caught her eye. She flicked through ten or so more until she came to the shot she'd been looking for. The rear of a Holden Commodore parked just across the river, to the right. Nyree spread her fingers on the screen to enlarge the image. It expanded to show a pixelated, but clear image of the car. The photograph was timestamped at 8:53 p.m. After they'd stolen the kiwifruit. Still just light enough to make out the details.

Gabby angled her head around to see the photograph. "Is that the car you're looking for?"

"It is. You didn't see who drove it?"

"We didn't see anyone at all."

"And you never saw anyone on the track to Mason's Rock?"

She shook her head.

"Or further up?"

Another head shake, lower lip jutting. "Only the dog."

The words hit Nyree like a circus performer's knife. "The dog? What dog?"

"A big black one. Like a Rottweiler or something. It just appeared out of the bush. Gave me a hell of a fright."

"And where did it come from? Which direction?" Nyree's heart rate picked up. This was one of those things that happens every now and then that breaks a case wide open. She could taste it.

Gabby shrugged. "I dunno. Up in the bush on the other side of the kiwifruit orchard, I guess. I told Justin, I said, 'I'm not going up there with that dog running around.' He said, 'It's fine. It'll only go for you if it knows you're scared.' I said, 'I *am* bloody scared.' He didn't care. He's such a dick, sometimes," she muttered.

Nyree leaned in. "And...what? The dog hung around while you were picking fruit? Went away? What did it do?"

She shook her head. "The guy whistled it back again."

Nyree's head jerked forward. "What guy? You never mentioned a guy."

"Well...we didn't actually *see* him. But the way he whistled, you know, I just assumed it was a guy. Especially with that kind of dog. Women don't have dogs like that, do they?"

Quelling the urge to reach over and shake her, Nyree lowered her voice. "Now, listen, I want you to think very carefully: was there anything, *anything* else out of the ordinary that you saw or heard. Think hard."

Two lines appeared between Gabby's eyes as she thought. Then her gaze came up to Nyree's.

"Does this help us get off the charge?"

A bolt of pure fury flashed down Nyree's spine. She gave it moment. "No. The charge stands. But I can put in a word with the judge. He can minimize the sentence. Make life a lot easier for you."

"But you can't get us off?"

"The charge stands."

Nyree felt the connection slipping away. Vital evidence just beyond her reach.

"But I'll see what I can do about where you're held."

"I don't want to go to prison."

"I said I'll see what I can do." When Gabby chewed her lip while she considered this, Nyree added, "Gabby, I have a lost child to find. Look at her." She groped feverishly in her pocket for the photograph of Lily. The little face smiling out. She shook it in Gabby's face. "Her name is Lily. She's six years old. She's been missing for *three* days. She's insulin-dependent. Do you want her to die?"

Gabby's focus hung on the photograph for the longest time. There was something. Nyree could feel it. The words seemed to well up behind Gabby's teeth. Like a deluge waiting to breach the dam the moment the first crack appeared. Her chin trembled for a moment and she bit hard into her lip, and her eyes came up to meet Nyree's.

"Justin took the ring."

The revelation took a moment to penetrate. Nyree blinked in disbelief. *Surely…surely not…*

"I told him not to," Gabby insisted.

Nyree sat back and felt herself breathe for what felt like the first time since she'd sat down. The horror of both the act and the repercussions crashed through her brain. It was as though Gabby's dammed-up words had burst forth bringing with it a tsunami of shifts in the landscape, shattering timelines, readjusting facts, changing everything they had come to believe.

Just to confirm, just to make absolutely sure, she said, "When you say, '…took the ring…?'"

"Off her finger," Gabby said. "He took it off her finger."

CHAPTER 34

The pharmacy was still closed when CIT Alana Bowman arrived. She peered in through the darkened front glass door, and when she saw a shadow pass across the rear of the service area, she knocked. A moment later, a young Asian woman approached the door and frowned out.

"I'm sorry, we're closed until nine. Can you come back in half an hour?"

Bowman, dressed in her customary navy skirt, low heels and cream blouse, took her ID from her jacket pocket and pressed it to the glass.

"Police. Can I have a word?"

"Oh! Sure, hang on a sec while I get the key."

Maria Tang looked to have been in her mid-twenties, although, Bowman figured, with that beautiful Asian skin the pharmacist could have easily passed for that and been ten years older.

"Come in," she told Bowman as she slid the door open, watching the street in case she wound up inviting more than just the one visitor onto the premises. The moment Bowman was inside the door, Tang quickly slid it closed and locked it.

"You never know," she explained as she jangled the keys back into her pocket. "It's store policy not to open the door if there's only one person here." Her eyes widened momentarily. "And the things these people do to get in would make you wonder. Now, how can I help you?"

Bowman drew the copy of the prescription they'd received from Kelly Holmes's doctor from her notebook. "Did you get a chance to look back at the prescription history for Lily Holmes?"

"Yes, I did. I made all the calculations the minute I got it. I sent it through to your office last night."

Bowman followed Tang through the store and around the dispensing counter to a small office area out the back. The computer jumped to life the instant Tang moved the mouse, and they waited until the pharmacist had brought up the file listing all prescriptions throughout the past four years since Lily Holmes had been diagnosed. Down the left-hand side ran a column with a series of computations allowing for dosage, each with a "+" or "-" showing each side.

"It's not an exact science," Tang said as she ran down the columns. "We have to assume that sometimes the dosage would be delivered later or earlier, and the following dosages could have been changed by the mother to take that into consideration."

"So, what did you come up with?"

"Well, if the mother is meticulous with the meds, then I'd say, apart from what she had with her, there's nothing missing. But interestingly," she added. "I checked when the last script was picked up."

Bowman's heart skipped a beat. "And...?"

"An emergency repeat was collected last Friday night just as we were closing. It's enough for a couple of days. I got one of the girls here to email the details through to River Falls police station late yesterday afternoon. I'm surprised you didn't get them."

"Do you know who picked up that script?"

"Apparently, our new assistant, Maddy, dealt with her. I called her this morning, and she said the woman identified herself as the mother, Kelly Holmes." Tang checked her watch. "Maddy's due in at nine. I can have her call you the minute she gets here."

Bowman also checked the clock. Nine was half an hour away. She glanced up, scanning the corners of the store. "What about the security cameras?"

"Yes, sure. It's not exactly up to the minute tech equipment, but it covers all angles of the store." Maria Tang clicked back through the computer files until she came to what she was searching for. Much like the footage at the gas station, six frames appeared on the screen with a date and time-stamp located in the lower left-hand side of the screen.

"Here we go. Let me run it back to the right date. Apparently, she came in just before we closed."

The date stamp rapidly rewound time as images flashed by. Maria Tang slowed the reel, and a distant shot of the store counter came into focus. She tapped the screen. "Five-twenty-two. There she is."

A grainy image froze on a figure at close enough range that it had caught a young woman from the waist up. Whoever she was, she wore a fur-trimmed puffer jacket, the hood pulled up over her head. As the video wound on, she moved up toward the counter where a white-smocked assistant stepped forward to speak to her. The figure glanced left and right, clearly nervous. Still no image of her face. Resolution hopeless.

"Do you have a camera over the counter? Facing her?"

"Let me look."

Again, the screen jumped from image to image until the time-stamp paused on 5:22 p.m. In the top right-hand screen, the image of the girl appeared. Head down and tugging the hood of her jacket forward, she hurried in through the front door and up the counter.

"You can't see her face," said Maria.

"It's not Kelly Holmes. Just give it a second."

Tension radiated from the girl's mannerisms—turning to check behind her, tugging the hood down, jamming her hands in her pockets. The assistant returned from behind the dispensing counter. All that was visible of the assistant was the back of her head and shoulders. She pushed something across the counter. The girl raked it in, stuffed it into a small blue backpack...

...and looked up. Straight into the camera.

"Pause it," said Bowman. "Is that the girl from the gas station?"

Maria Tang squinted and leaned in. "It's hard to say, but I think you're right. That's Kiri Perrett."

Bowman called it straight in.

CHAPTER 35

Nyree clapped both hands to her face and dragged them down. Blinking her eyes open again, she gathered herself, then clasped both hands at her chin, listening to Callaghan on speaker phone.

"Get someone straight out to the gas station. Find that girl."

"Yes, Ma'am. Already got Bowman headed there now." Callaghan sounded equally exhausted. "So, what do we do about the search? If he's taken the ring off her finger, that means he could have been anywhere. And here's us searching every inch of that bloody kiwifruit orchard for nothing."

Nyree could feel a dull ache sitting at the back of her skull and stretching down into her shoulders. She pressed her fingertips to the nape of her neck, massaging it. "Doesn't make a lot of difference. We'd have searched there anyway. We searched the whole bush area around there and didn't find anything. And let's face it, there was a lot of trampled grass in the orchard. He still could have brought her in that way."

"I said from the beginning, it's a long way to carry a dead body." Callaghan let out a long breath. "I'd like to strangle him."

"You mean Justin Barrett or the offender?"

"Both."

"You are not alone." She raked her fingers through her hair and sat back. "Never mind, Rawiri Cooper's got half the marae out searching. If Lily's anywhere up there, they'll find her."

"True that." After a moment, he added, "By the way, I got Willis to bring in Darryl Coburn. He felt he could be a flight risk."

"Good job. I'll get to him right after I've done this press conference. See what bloody lies he can come up with this time."

"Yes, Ma'am."

"For now, let's get back to what we've got. Gather everything together, build up the current timeline on the board. Check with Christine, see what she's got for us, then follow up the phone records. I want the team in for an update briefing at…" She checked the time. "I should have this press conference out of the way by ten-thirty. Then I'll head straight back up there, so let's say noon."

"Will do." Callaghan hung up.

She printed out her notes and made her way back to the front desk for the press update. This was something she wasn't looking forward to.

CHAPTER 36

The desk sergeant jerked his head in the direction of the elevator. "Press are waiting for you now, Ma'am."

"Already?" The clock on the wall next to him told her it wasn't yet nine o'clock.

He also glanced across at it. "They've been camped out here for the past two hours. Looks like they've put the numbers together, figured out the connection between Lily Holmes and Huia's murder, and come up with forty-six."

"That was bound to happen. Where are they now?"

"In the media room."

She glanced at her watch. "If they're already here, let's bring the press release forward."

"Yes, Ma'am."

"Give me a minute and I'll give them the thirty-second statement."

Nyree nipped into the restroom to check her looks in the mirror. She looked dreadful: grey-streaked hair sticking up in front, dark rings under bloodshot brown eyes, crow's feet like cracks in the pavement. She splashed water on her face and tried to stick her hair back down. It sprang back up so she gave up and made her way through to the media room on the second floor of Whangārei police station. The murmur of distant voices swelled to a rumble as she approached. From out here it sounded as if half the country's journos had turned out. She patted her hair down again, straightened her jacket, and opened the door.

The second she stepped inside, the room fell silent. Journos packed around the periphery of the room, turned her way. Then, as if a switch was flicked, the room suddenly burst into a cacophony of shouts and questions, phones held high to track her all the way to a table set with a line of microphones, trails of cables leading from each one.

She raised one hand in a stop sign, and the din died down to a few camera-clicks and the shuffle of feet, photographers trying to get a better angle. She positioned her notes on the table, adjusted the angle of the closest microphone, then looked to the media assistant, who nodded.

Hands set folded on the desk in front of her, she began. "Good morning. After a great deal of speculation regarding the events that have unfolded in the River Falls district lately, I can now confirm that the cases of the missing child, Lily Holmes, and the murder of Huia Coburn, are connected. We now know that Lily was with Huia on the day Huia was murdered. This is a dreadful situation for two mothers who have lost their daughters. Police want to hear from any witnesses on the night of Wednesday fifteenth of June – that's last Wednesday, if they remember seeing either Huia or Lily. They were last known to have been traveling in a dark green 1996 Toyota Corolla. Contact numbers will be at the bottom of your screens." This remark was made to the local news channel cameraman.

A hand went up. "Do you have any suspects yet?" This from a young reporter she knew was with the *Northland Gazette*.

"We have a number of people helping with our inquiries." She pointed to a twenty-something woman at the back who had her hand raised.

"I believe you've been speaking with the members of the marae. Can you make any comments on that?"

"Huia Coburn was of Māori descent. The Māori community is assisting with the search for Lily Holmes."

A guy shouted the next question: "You spoke to the boyfriend, Brodie Skinner, but you haven't brought him in for questioning. Is he a suspect in Huia Coburn's murder?"

"At this moment, he is not a suspect."

The woman again. "I believe you found the victim's ring. How close are you to making an arrest?"

He took the ring off Huia's finger.

A hollow pit opened up in Nyree's gut. "We've gathered a significant amount of evidence, and we're confident an arrest will be made in the not-too-distant future. Yes?" she said, pointing for the next question before she was grilled for further details.

The heavily-built man she'd picked out, shouted, "Do you have any idea whether Lily Holmes is alive or dead?"

The question reverberated through her like quake lines, shattering her known ground. She overrode the sensation and kept her voice level. "We've received nothing to indicate Lily has been harmed, so we're assuming she's still alive."

"Even though she's a type-1 diabetic who hasn't had insulin for almost three days?" This from the same man. He looked around as if seeking support. "You're running on a bit of a prayer, aren't you?"

The comment and the derisive snort sent a flare of irritation through her. "We're remaining positive. This is a child's life. We're doing everything we can to find her. We will make further comment when we have more information. Thank you." Guilt and betrayal remained wedged in her chest as she snatched up her notes, cutting off any further questions.

She was on her way to the door when her phone rang. She dug it out and checked the screen, exiting as quickly as she could.

Bowman. "Ma'am, we've got something."

Nyree hurried back to her office while Bowman ran through the events to date, then stopped short when she added, "I just called the gas station. Kiri Perrett hasn't shown up for work since that evening."

"That means Lily could still be alive." Nyree rocked her head back, then let out a shuddering breath. "Right, get out to Kiri Perrett's place, find out where she could be: friends, family, you name it."

"Yes, Ma'am."

Nyree's heart almost burst from her chest in relief. "Let me know immediately what you find," she said, and hung up.

Then she made her way to Interview One.

CHAPTER 37

Willis stood in the corner of Interview One, meaty arms folded, his big battle-scarred face bearing down on Darryl Coburn. By the look of it, Coburn had given Willis some lip, and Willis had set him straight about what he could and couldn't say and do.

Coburn now sat meekly awaiting the interview in silence.

A wise move, in Nyree's opinion. Uplifted and driven now by the message from Bowman, she sat opposite Darryl Coburn and opened her notes.

Darryl Coburn shifted in his seat and sat a little straighter as he watched her.

After studying the notes for long enough to make him nervous, she looked up. "Mr. Coburn, thank you for coming in."

"Yeah, sure. Anything I can do to help."

"I understand you lost your phone."

"Yeah. Why?"

"Because a call from that phone was the last Huia received on hers. And you don't remember that?"

"No." A quick headshake. "Maybe I didn't make that call. Maybe someone else found it and called her. How would I know?"

Nyree let him squirm for a moment. "We've received forensics' report back on Mr. Wright's car—the blue Holden Commodore."

Darryl's eyes flicked up to meet hers, then dropped back to where he began picking at a thumbnail.

She opened the file in front of her and flicked to a page. "Forensics found a few hairs in the car, and fingerprints on the steering wheel and gear lever."

This time, his gaze faltered as it lifted to her. He couldn't meet her eye.

"DNA analysis indicates the hair came from you, as did the fingerprints."

Still, he said nothing.

"Darryl," she said, leaning forward on her elbows. "Why did you take the car?"

"I didn't."

"Well, that's not going to fly, because all the evidence points to the fact that you were in that car." She gave him a second to think about it. "C'mon, Darryl. Don't make this any harder. We know you took the car. We know you drove up to River Falls because that's where the car was found with your prints all over the steering wheel and door. What happened?"

Darryl's face blanched white. "I think I'm going to be sick."

"Get him a bucket," Nyree told Willis who left the room like it was on fire.

Darryl sucked in a deep breath and blew it into the air through pursed lips. His color improved.

"How do you feel?"

"Sick," he said.

"Darryl, please understand that at the moment, you're only helping with our inquiries. You've been read your rights, but you're not under arrest."

A rapid nod. Far from assuring him, Nyree's words seemed to unsettle him. He dragged his upper teeth along his lip and swallowed hard. He blinked away the sweat beading on his forehead, then swiped it away with the back of his sleeve.

Willis returned with the bucket and offered it to him.

He pushed it away. "I don't need it."

Willis put it on the floor and stepped back against the wall again.

They had evidence he was in the car. It wasn't enough. They needed more.

"Tell me about your sister, Darryl. Huia Coburn."

"My *step*sister," he corrected, and leaned back, clasping both hands into his lap. His color had almost completely returned. Now he looked flushed.

"My apologies. Your *stepsister*." She laced her fingers under her chin, leaned on them, her tone relaxed. "Tell me about your relationship with her."

Fear flashed across his features again. "What about it?"

"Well, how did you get on? Were you close?"

"We got on good. She was my sister—you know, family." His leaned forward, hands curled on the table, his focus back to the split thumbnail.

"If you didn't kill her, we need to find who did. You understand?"

A nod.

"Do you have any idea who might have reason to hurt her?"

A headshake. Nyree let it go.

"Did your mum say she'd texted Huia that day?"

"No. Why would she?"

"I'm just wondering whether Huia would be able to read the messages. She had reading difficulties, didn't she?"

He gave the matter a moment's thought. "Well, she could read texts. Not books or anything. But she got by okay." Worry lines creased his brow.

"Did Annette tell you why she wanted to speak to Huia?"

A quick headshake. "No."

Nyree changed tack. She leaned forward and lowered her voice. "Tell me, did you notice any marks on Huia? On her arms?"

"Nope."

"None at all?"

"Nope."

The fact that he never asked what kind of marks was telling in itself.

"And exactly where were you at six o'clock last Wednesday night, Darryl? Think carefully, because this is important."

"I was at home," he said without hesitation.

"At your place?"

"Yes."

"Is there anyone who can verify that?"

"Nope."

"When was the last time you saw Huia?"

He swallowed hard and looked away to his left. "The Saturday before. At Mum and Dad's."

To use the computer—printing out photos. That's what Annette had said.

"Do you know why she visited?"

The worry lines deepened. He met her gaze straight on. "No."

"Do you have any pets?"

"What?"

"Pets. Do you have a cat or a dog?"

"No, what's that got to do with anything?"

She let the moment spool out, then said, "Do you have a girlfriend?"

Darryl Coburn's face creased in confusion. "Why would you want to know that?"

"I'm just asking."

"Then, no. I don't." Irritation edged his tone now.

"Any special girls you know as friends? Girls who might help you if you got into a scrape?"

"If I got in a scrape, I'd go and see my dad. I don't know what you're getting at."

"How well do you know a girl named Kiri Perrett?"

Both sides of his mouth drew down. His tone sharpened. Belligerent now. "I don't even know who she is."

"Are you sure?"

The anger swelled. "Yes, I'm sure."

For one echoingly silent moment, she studied him. "Thank you, Darryl. We'll be in touch."

CHAPTER 38

Nyree swung her car into the River Falls Police parking lot just after ten. The time she'd set for the press conference. That didn't matter. Anyone who'd missed it would get it from those that were there. Or make it up.

Callaghan was just getting out of his car two slots along. He veered in and joined her as she walked in the front door. "News in from Christine—the feathers caught up in Huia's tee-shirt were from ducks."

"Ducks? What kind of ducks?"

"Common or garden variety Muscovy. They're everywhere. She could have been in the local park and picked them up."

"Bugger it! So, what's happening with Kiri Perrett?"

She'd spent the last couple of minutes in the car, reading up on the latest notes.

"I've got Bowman following up on her. She called the gas station. Apparently, Kiri hasn't been seen since she collected that emergency insulin script for Lily."

The station doors swept aside and Nyree entered, speaking over her shoulder to Callaghan who was right behind. "The quicker we find her, the quicker we find Lily. Although, why she wouldn't just let her go home to her mother is anyone's guess."

They paused inside the door while Nyree picked up her messages.

Callaghan gave the area a quick scan. No one around. So, he asked, "How's Darryl Coburn looking?"

"Says he doesn't have a girlfriend, or a dog, and he doesn't know Kiri Perrett."

"Big surprise."

"He worries me," she told him as she took the messages from the desk sergeant. "Huia wasn't the only one being abused. Darryl shows all the signs." She flicked through the handwritten notes as she spoke. "He says he had a good relationship with Huia. Said they were family."

"That doesn't mean much. Not judging by half the families we see," Callaghan said.

"We've already got him inside the car. We need evidence of him driving it to River Falls on that day, at that time. To get that, we need his lost phone."

The desk sergeant leaned in to catch her attention. "Excuse me, Ma'am, you have a visitor."

"A visitor? Who?"

"Miss Holmes, Ma'am. She's in your office."

Nyree's heart fell. What new information did she have that Kelly didn't already know?

"I'll be right with her." She turned back to Callaghan. "Let me know the instant you hear anything from Bowman."

"Will do, Ma'am."

The instant Nyree appeared in the doorway, Kelly Holmes jumped to her feet. Already thin, the dark circles under her eyes and desperate expression reminded Nyree she was as much a victim as the dead.

"What's happening? They've stopped the search." Kelly angrily pointed off into the distance.

"They haven't stopped, they're concentrating in different areas," she said, then realized the girl had the right to know the truth. "Sit down. Let me get you some coffee and something to eat. Have you had breakfast?"

Before she could answer, Nyree twisted back to the door and leaned out, snagging the first officer who passed. "Nip out and grab some breakfast for me, will you?"

Dispatching him with a short order, she closed the door and sat opposite Kelly again.

Kelly's shoulders had slumped. "What's happening? Why haven't you found her? She has to be somewhere."

Nyree sat in the chair next to her, reached across and took her hand, squeezing it between both of hers. "We're going to find her, Kelly."

"You keep saying that, but when? She hasn't had her meds. She'll be..." Her shoulders hunched briefly. Then her head went down. Gathering herself, she withdrew her hand sharply and pressed her finger to her eyes. "Then how come you've stopped the search? You think she's dead, don't you? You've given up."

"Kelly, I know how this looks right now, but we have not given up. I *won't* give up. I will find her."

Kelly pressed a finger and thumb to her eyes. "I'm sorry. I'm just so bloody exhausted."

"I know you are." As the young mother's shoulders relaxed, she said, "Kelly, tell me why Huia came to live with you."

She blinked away the fug and refocused. "She needed somewhere to stay. She'd had arguments with her mother. She said everyone hated her and she had to get away." She lifted one shoulder. "So, when she started talking about moving somewhere up here, I told her I needed a babysitter while I worked, so she came to live with me." Kelly leaned to Nyree, beseeching. "Huia's a *good* person...or she was." She dug her lower teeth into her lip as the tears threatened. "Who would kill her? How could anyone be so horrible?"

"What was the problem that came up?"

Kelly looked up. Her eyes briefly met Nyree's, then dropped guiltily as she spoke. "What problem?"

Nyree gave her a moment, then said, "I believe there was some kind of trouble in the family."

Another one-shouldered shrug. "There was always trouble in the family. If they didn't have something to argue about, they'd have argued about that. Huia had had a gutful of it."

"I'm talking about something recent. Something the family didn't want anyone to know about." Nyree angled her head to meet Kelly's gaze. "And I think you know what that is."

Kelly let out a deep sigh and turned her head to the window. It was as if she'd fought to keep whatever it was at arm's length. She pressed her lips together briefly, then said, "I promised I wouldn't tell anyone."

"Who did you promise?"

She made a doubtful face. "It won't have anything to do with this."

"How about you tell me, and I'll know if it has...or if it hasn't." She gave her an encouraging smile.

Kelly dragged her teeth along her upper lip while she considered it.

Again, Nyree reached across, covering Kelly's hand with hers. "Huia's dead, Kelly. She would understand. And anything you can tell us could help us find Lily."

She shook her head slowly back and forth. "They wouldn't. They just wouldn't."

Nyree waited.

Kelly withdrew her hand and took a shuddering breath. "When Huia found out she was pregnant, she told her dad, Rawiri. He's was, like, over the moon. Like, totally stoked. Everyone at the marae got to hear about it. Huia thought it was hilarious. She said they'd kick him out if he didn't shut up about it." Kelly chuckled at the memory. The smile remained for a moment, then faded.

"And what happened?"

Kelly clenched her fists between her knees. Her tiny frame visibly tensed up. "Rawiri said he'd look after her. He said that everything he had was hers."

"Which meant...?"

"He was going to sell up the house Annette and Peter live in."

"But Annette would still get half. So, how is that such a problem?"

Kelly's voice dropped to a whisper. "Because they're up to their eyeballs in debt. They owe more than the whole house is worth. And they've got nowhere else to go."

Callaghan trailed behind Nyree as she entered her office. "We've got means, motive and opportunity. Someone in that house murdered Huia and took Lily. Where are those bank accounts? I want to know every cent they owe and where it went."

"The accounts should be here today."

Nyree sat behind her desk and opened up the spreadsheet she'd formulated. "All three of Huia's family had the opportunity and the means to kill Huia. We've got Peter and Annette at home with no one else to confirm it. Likewise, Darryl Coburn has no one to corroborate his story. Darryl took Philip Wright's car. Whether he went up there to meet Huia, or following whoever did.

"Put out a description of Darryl's phone and a plea for anyone who finds it to bring it in. Then put a call out for eye witnesses of Philip Wright's car anywhere between here and River Falls on that night. We're that close," she told Callaghan, measuring a tiny gap between her thumb and forefinger. "One of that bloody family is holding Lily Holmes. One of them has her life in their hands. Let's find out which one."

CHAPTER 39

The call came in thirty-five seconds after the television appeal went out. A girl who had called in on the televised number. Nyree sat with her hands cupped over her nose and mouth, intently listening to every word on the playback.

It started with the caller:

"Hi...um, you were looking for a phone up near River Falls, right?"

She sounded young. Around fifteen, maybe sixteen.

"That's correct," replied the Comms receiver. "Do you have information about it?"

"Well, I found *a* phone. I don't know if it's the one you're looking for. I thought maybe someone threw this one away. Cos it was just lying there by the river."

"Of course."

"But then I saw on the TV that the cops...I mean, the police, are looking for a phone, and I thought maybe this was it."

"Well, thank you for your call. Can you describe the phone for me?"

"Is there like, a reward or anything for finding it?"

A brief silence before the Comms officer replied. "I'm sorry there's no reward for it. But we'd be really grateful. And you might help solve a serious crime."

"Oh."

"So, can you tell me what kind of phone it is?"

"Yeah. It's a...lemme see, a Samsung Galaxy. It's in a crappy blue cover." It sounded as if the girl was turning it in her hand as she spoke.

"That's really great. Can I ask your name, please?" The Comms officer gave it a long moment, then said, "You don't have to."

"Yeaaah, nah. I won't, if that's okay."

"That's fine. I'm just really pleased you called us. So, can you tell me if you've made any calls on the phone?"

A long hesitation this time. "Yeah, well...I didn't know if it was lost or someone just threw it away, or if it was broken, or anything. So, y'know..."

"Of course. You had to know if it was working, right?"

"Exac'ly." The relief was palpable.

"And if you've made any calls on it, we're not worried about that. All we need to know is what calls you made. That's just so we can rule them out of the investigation. You're not in any trouble."

Good work, Nyree thought. *Reel her in gently.*

The sound of the girl sucking air in through her teeth. "Okay, well, I acshully made a couple of quick ones, y'know...to the UK. Cos, I got a auntie there."

"That doesn't matter. If you can just give us the numbers so we know which ones to ignore, that's fine."

"So, how do I get the phone to you?"

"First of all, can you tell me where you found it? And when?"

"Oh."

"Is that a problem?"

"No, I s'pose not. It's just...I found it the other night."

"Okay."

"And I don't want my mum finding out I was there. She'd go apeshit."

"We're not going to tell your mum."

"I found it by the camping ground, up near the Fairy Lights waterfall there in River Falls. There's a platform up there you can go up and stand on to see the waterfall."

A popular hangout for kids. The Comms officer was probably already Googling it. "I know the one. Was it on the platform, or under it?"

"Under it. It was like, a couple of meters from the track going up to the waterfall."

The Comms officer was obviously searching the area. "Oh, I see, you mean next to the pool there?"

"No, on the other side. Next to the acshul track, down at the bottom of the falls. Like someone had chucked it from the platform. That's why I made some calls on it. Cos, I thought someone had chucked it away or something."

Which didn't make sense. If you managed to make a call, it worked. You didn't need to make a second one. But calling the girl out on it wouldn't get the desired results. And besides, according to the report in front of Nyree, the Comms officer had already initiated a search for the caller's position, so she'd simply said, "No problem. Listen, I need you to bring the phone in."

"Where to? I'm not going to be arrested or anything, am I?"

"No. Whereabouts are you?" the Comms officer asked casually. "Maybe if you can tell me where you are, someone can come and pick the phone up from you."

"Oh, shit no! I mean...I don't want the cops around here," she said quickly. "Cos, I don't want my mum knowing, ay?"

"I totally get it. So, how about I direct you to the nearest police station. You can just drop it in there."

In the background, a second girl's voice. "What the fuck are you *doin*?"

The call muffled, as if she'd put her hand over the mic. "I'm callin' the cops to tell them about that phone."

The second girl. "Are you mental? The cops'll get you for killing that girl."

After a brief silence, the first girl was back on the line. Now she sounded worried.

"Um. I dunno. Now I'm thinking this isn't even the phone you're looking for."

The Comms officer jumped in. "How about we decide that?"

"Nah, I think I made a mistake—"

"Hang the fuckin' phone up! Just hang up, ya egg." The second girl again.

"Listen, wait a minute," the Comms officer urged.

"I gotta go," she said, and the line went dead and the Comms officer let out a deep, disappointed sigh.

Nyree's shoulders also dropped. Not that it mattered. The girl's location had immediately been pinpointed, and the call had gone out for Henare, who was closest, to go and pay her a quiet visit.

As long as the kid didn't dispose of it before he got there.

CHAPTER 40

Henare had ditched his usual crisp white shirt and police tie and expensive suit jacket in favor of a blue polo and smart chinos for the visit up at the marae. He'd been sitting in easy conversation with four of the elders, discussing what they'd heard, who Henare might speak to for information, and what they knew about Kiri Perrett. All the while in the background, food in the form of trailer-loads of potatoes, whole pig carcasses, and boxes of frozen chickens, was arriving for the tangi, the three-day wake preceding Huia Coburn's funeral.

If Annette Coburn thought she was going to whisk Huia's body off to some unknown location before the whānau got wind of it, she'd be badly mistaken. The entire community was gathering for the event. People were arriving, not only from all over the country, but from Australia. The living quarters were packed with guests, their sleeping mats lined up side-by-side like sardines. Enormous serving dishes were loaded with food and the hangi, the massive underground oven, had been prepared.

No doubt, the delegation on watch at the morgue had their ears pricked. The slightest change in the wind would be instantly reported back. Māori whānau had been known to spirit a body away and have it back on the marae before anyone knew it was missing. The quick and the dead, so to speak.

That wasn't Henare's problem. All he'd been tasked with was finding whatever information he could. Fortunately, the elders who'd been helping him were just wrapping up the conversation when his phone buzzed in his pocket and the message came in.

He'd politely excused himself, thanked the residing kaumatua for their cooperation, then left.

Now he was on his way to a tiny backstreet off the main drag in the small town of Hikurangi, just north of Whangārei. That was the location the girl who'd found the phone had been tracked down to. Little wonder she didn't want her mother knowing she was almost an hour's drive north of home the night before. Probably meeting boys.

Henare slowed his unmarked car at a 60km zone through a tiny settlement just north of the turnoff when he spotted a car he recognized, coming the other way. His gaze dipped briefly to the license plate then back to the driver. Everything confirmed his initial recognition—Terry McFarlane.

While Henare was traveling south, McFarlane was traveling north. They would have passed, but McFarlane's car slowed, and the left-hand indicator blinked on. Henare also slowed, checking his rear-view mirror before pulling over to the shoulder of the road. He stopped, watching McFarlane's car turn off toward the Whangārei suburb of Kamo, then speed off.

Henare also hit the indicator. He checked the street front and rear, and the instant a gap opened up in the traffic, he swerved across the street, and followed McFarlane.

Keeping his distance, Henare settled back into a relaxed cruise, elbow on the window ledge, eyes pinned on the car in front. Speeding up marginally when he thought he'd lost McFarlane, slowing when he caught him. Eventually, McFarlane indicated a right-hand turn and swung off at the next intersection. Henare indicated and also turned.

Up ahead the streets lined with 1960's bungalows and wire fences gave way to open fields, straggly grass lining the road, sheep dotting the landscape. Several kilometers along, the road narrowed and the traffic thinned. Henare eased back and watched McFarlane indicate once more, then turn into the driveway of the Northland Golf Course.

Outside the clubhouse, seven cars were lined up at varying points along the front parking area. McFarlane's was the eighth. For a second, Henare hesitated. McFarlane would see him pull in. Then again, where else was he going to go? So, he took the risk.

Gravel crunching under the wheels, he turned into the parking area and pulled into a space, three slots down, his back to McFarlane. If he'd been worried about McFarlane spotting him, he needn't have. Almost as soon as he cut the engine, the door of a silver Mitsubishi Lancer at the end of the line opened, and the driver got out.

Henare picked him up in the wing mirror and tracked his progress. Immediately recognizing the guy, he turned in his seat to confirm what he thought he'd seen. Sure enough, there was Sean Clemmons, walking purposefully toward McFarlane's car. Henare adjusted the rear-view mirror, shrugged down in his seat, and watched.

Clemmons gave the area a quick scan, jerked open the passenger door of McFarlane's car, and got in. From the instant he was in the seat, McFarlane was at him, finger-stabbing Clemmons in the face, Clemmons was clearly arguing back. Even from here, McFarlane looked fit to kill. After one long, heated exchange, McFarlane gave an exasperated, slow head-shake and leaned his elbow on the window ledge, massaging his temple while Sean went on, hands gesturing here and there, gob flapping.

If only Henare could hear what they were saying. Although, you wouldn't have to be Einstein—Clemmons on the loose, Detective Inspector's house torched, Special brought in to locate him. But why was McFarlane meeting with him? Why not just bring him in?

After a few minutes, McFarlane dropped his face into his hands, rubbed at his eyes (or at least, that's what Henare figured he was doing), then he sat up. By now, Sean had gone quiet, sitting with his head back against the car headrest, staring belligerently out the passenger window. McFarlane twisted in his seat, turning to him, said something. A couple more finger jabs in Clemmons's face, and the meeting came to an end. Sean got out of the car, leaning with one arm along the top of the door, the other on the roof to deliver his parting comments. After a barked response from McFarlane, he slammed the car door and stalked back to his own car.

McFarlane hit the ignition and pulled forward. It was the perfect time.

Henare started his engine and threw it into reverse. He eased back out of the slot, reversing left at exactly the same time McFarlane swung right. Like a choreographed dance, they each came to a halt. For one earth-shattering moment, the two drivers sat next to each other, one facing north, the other south.

Across the divide of no more than a few feet, their eyes met.

In that instant McFarlane knew.

In that instant, a wry smile curled across the lips of the wannabe Māori boy in the adjacent car.

The fury in McFarlane's expression was priceless.

Henare simply eased down on the accelerator and guided the car back out of the parking lot. The smile remained all the way down to the gate he'd driven in through only moments earlier.

There was a time to use an advantage for the best results, and this wasn't it.

That time would arise in the very near future. They both knew it.

He carried the certainty of that thought all the way to Hikurangi where a girl with a phone she'd found was about to get the shock of her life.

This, for one wannabe Māori boy, was a good day to be a cop.

CHAPTER 41

So small was the town center of River Falls, Bowman could have walked to the gas station from the pharmacy. She didn't have time. The minute she'd left the pharmacy, she'd leapt into the car, then realized it was in a one-way street. After negotiating the ridiculous loop circuit around the town, she'd gotten back around to the main street and headed for the gas station.

Danny Yelavich had looked up in surprise as she'd burst through the front door and marched straight to where he sat. Before he could even open his mouth, she'd demanded to know where Kiri Perrett was. To which he'd replied that she wasn't working that day, and hadn't been seen the last few.

Bowman had gotten her home address, home phone number and cell number before hurrying back to her car and reporting it in. Then she'd driven the twelve kilometers to the address Danny had given her.

Now, with her heart pounding, she had parked out front, jumped out of the car and was halfway up the front path before she even registered the *Beware of the Dog* notice she'd glimpsed on the front gate. That's when she heard the first howl. A big dog, by the guttural sound of it. Next thing, a black monster, all teeth and saliva streaming, ears pinned back and eyes wild, came charging from around the far side of the house and headed straight for her.

Bowman let out a yelp and threw her arms up across her face.

"Oscar! Get back here, ya big dope!" a woman's voice yelled from the front porch. "Don't worry about him," she called to Bowman. "He's a big wuss."

It was all very well telling her not to worry about him. She wasn't standing where Bowman was. When she lowered her arms and peered down at the dog, it was stopped two feet from her, leaping side to side, barking, strings of saliva yo-yoing.

"I said *shuddup!*" the woman yelled. "Get over here."

The dog gave Bowman one last, disappointed look, then skulked away with its hindquarters tucked under, tail between its legs. It crept up the steps to the porch where it circled in behind the woman's legs and dropped, still eyeing the newcomer.

The woman regarded the dog. "You stay there." Then she turned her attention back to Bowman. "What can I do for you?"

Keeping a respectable distance, one eye still on the dog, Bowman drew out her ID and held it high.

"Police, Ma'am."

The amiable demeanor snapped to the off position. "Yeah? What do you lot want?"

"I'm looking for a young woman by the name of Kiri Perrett."

Suspicion darkened in the woman's eyes. She angled her head and frowned. "What do you want her for?"

"I need to ask her a few questions."

"She's not here."

Bowman lowered the ID and tucked it away, approaching cautiously, one eye on the dog. "Can you tell me where she is?"

"Nope. Haven't seen her for the last three days."

"You're her mum, aren't you?"

"Yep."

"Is it unusual for her to be away for that long?"

The woman pursed her lips in thought, still scowling. "You didn't tell me why you're asking."

"We believe she may have some information leading to the location of a missing child."

"You mean Kelly Holmes's kid?"

"That's right. You know her?"

A dismissive sound burst from her lips. "Everyone knows everyone else around here. You can't fart without people three streets away knowing."

"Then can you tell me where I could find Kiri?"

"What's this about?"

Bowman wasn't sure how much to say. So, she went with, "She was last seen at the pharmacy, picking up a prescription on Friday afternoon. I needed to ask her who it was for."

"Who saw her?"

"Well, the pharmacist, for one."

"And what's this got to do with the Holmes kid?"

"It was her insulin script Kiri was collecting."

"Then it wasn't Kiri, was it?" she said without hesitation.

Bowman gave it a second, then said, "We have video footage of her, Mrs. Perrett."

"Is that so?"

"I have a frame taken from it, if you want to see it."

Mrs. Perrett nodded once. Bowman dug the printed image she'd lifted from the video footage out of her pocket and gingerly walked up the three steps, watching the dog every step of the way. When a deep, throaty growl rumbled from its throat, she figured she was close enough. She reached up and handed the photo up to Mrs. Perrett.

The mother unfolded the page, squinted at it from arm's length as if she needed eyeglasses, then made a face and handed it back. "That's not her."

Bowman's gaze snapped up. "I'm sorry?"

"I said, that's not her."

Bowman checked the image. As if something she'd missed might account for the response.

"Are you sure?"

"What'd I just say? It's not her. I'm her mother. I should know what my own kid looks like. Get your bloody facts right before you come around here accusing people of shit." She nudged the dog with her foot and both retreated inside the house, and the door slammed shut.

Bowman stood staring at the worn and dirty green door for some seconds, then went back to the car.

In retrospect, she should have asked Danny Yelavich to ID the photo. Maybe she could have saved herself some time. Now, as she picked up the phone and called it in, the expression, *falling on your sword*, sprang to mind. She was the one who'd reported the girl as Kiri Perrett. And that was based on the identification of a pharmacist from a single picture taken from a low-resolution video feed. Already, she could feel the blade slicing between her ribs as the burr of the ringing phone echoed down the line.

DI Bradshaw answered immediately. Bowman gave her the details, leaning a little on the fact that it was the pharmacist who had ID'd the girl. The DI asked her if there was any way the mother was lying. Bowman had reopened the image and studied it again, marrying it up with her memory of the girl at the gas station. Now that she looked, the image was really grainy, the features obscured by shadow. Maybe it wasn't her.

"I'm sorry, Ma'am," she told DI Bradshaw. "I should have gotten a positive ID from Danny Yelavich at the gas station."

"Follow it up. Check all the neighbors. See if they can ID her from the photo. Find out who the girl hangs around with, where she might be now. There's every chance the mother is lying to protect her. Then get back to me with what you find." The DI hung up, leaving Bowman feeling as if she'd been physically assaulted.

As she tucked the phone back into her pocket, her gaze cut to the house across the street where a forty-something woman in jeans, a black wife-beater singlet, and bare feet leaned inside her doorway, smoking a cigarette. Lip curled in distaste, she met Bowman's eye, defiant.

"Oh, shit," Bowman said, and headed towards her.

CHAPTER 42

Henare cruised down the backstreet and stopped outside the address he'd been given. A tiny town on the outskirts of Whangārei, Hikurangi was undergoing a long, slow resurgence as Aucklanders sold up and moved north. Villas and bungalows were being bought up and renovated, new roofs and timbers, gardens tended and lawns mowed regularly. Auckland fifty years ago.

The house in question wasn't one of the *nouveau riche*. The roofline along the front dipped where the guttering had clogged and given way. A downpour would probably result in a waterfall onto the front porch which looked rotten even from here. Peeling paint curled from the downpipe, and the entire place was in desperate need of some TLC.

Henare got out of the car, locked it, then adjusted his sports jacket as he approached the house.

The door was answered at the first knock. The girl looked more like fourteen years old, rather than sixteen, which was what the comms officer had guessed. Big brown eyes, dark brown hair bleached to rust on the ends from long days in the Northland sun, she stared up at Henare like he was the ghost of Christmas Past. Obviously knew who he was.

"Hi, I'm Detective Joe Henare from the Northland District Police," Henare began in a relaxed tone. "We got a phone call from this house, from someone who said they'd found a phone."

The kid gulped air, and her eyes widened.

"Was that you?" he asked gently.

She cast a panicked glance behind her. "Um..."

"All I need is the phone. I don't need to tell anyone where it came from."

Behind her, a woman approached the door and glared out over the kid's shoulder, frowning. "Who is it, Ana?"

"Um, I dunno."

"Police, Ma'am," Henare said and launched his ID. "We got a phone call from someone at this address, saying a phone had been found."

"What phone?" she demanded of the girl.

"I believe your daughter might have found a phone that'll help us solve a homicide case, Ma'am." His focus dropped to the girl who looked terrified. "We're very grateful for her help on this."

The woman scowled from Henare, to the girl. "Why didn't you tell me about this phone?"

Henare chipped in. "She called us straight away. Which we really appreciate. Like I said, this could help us solve a very serious crime."

The girl shrugged deeply. "I saw it on the TV. They said they were looking for a phone." She bit her lip briefly and lifted one shoulder at her mother. "And I found this one. I just called them."

"So where is it?"

With a skeptical glance at Henare, Ana disappeared back into the house. The woman looked Henare up and down, and the girl returned a minute later with the phone—a Samsung in a tatty blue cover with badly frayed edges and a black smudge down the spine. It looked as if someone had printed their name on the spine in black ink, then tried to scrub it off.

"Where'd you find it?" the woman asked bluntly.

"It doesn't matter," Henare cut in before the mother could go right off the deep end. "All we needed was the phone, and believe me, we really are grateful for all your daughter did. It must have been a bit scary calling the police about it."

Ana shuffled in place; eyes wide. "Yeah, was a bit."

"Do we get anything for it?" the mother asked.

"Just our gratitude."

The woman made a dismissive noise.

Holding the phone between finger and thumb, Henare gave them a wide smile and tipped his head briefly. "Well, I won't take up any more of your time. Thank you, Ma'am."

Back at the car, he slipped on a pair of gloves and switched the phone on. By now any latents on the casing would have been obliterated, but you never knew.

12% battery life remained. He figured the kid had charged it at some point. His heart just about burst out of his chest when he checked the number. It matched one of the phone numbers on Huia's phone records. Instead of calling it straight in, he made a quick call to Chris Dayson, one of his contacts at the telco, who had originally pulled all Huia's phone records.

"Yeah, gidday, Chris. It's Henare here."

"Gidday, mate. What can I do for you?"

"I think I've got the phone we were looking for. Can you do me a favor and run some polling on it?"

"Yeah, sure. Give me a sec."

In the background came a few clunking sounds as if he'd been in the middle of his lunch, but a moment later, he was back on the line.

After getting the details of the phone from Henare, Chris said, "Okay, just doing a quick check now. It'll take a few minutes."

"Yeah, sure."

"So, you think you guys have nailed the bastard that killed that girl?"

Henare scrunched one side of his face. "Dunno. We've got a few suspects on the go. It's a matter of drilling down on the evidence."

"Jesus, I don't even know where I'd start," Chris muttered, as if to himself.

"Yeah, it looks exciting from the outside. Most of it's grunt work. Checking details, following up dead-end leads. Dead boring, most of the time."

Chris mumbled a sympathetic reply because most of his job was dead boring, checking phone records after some dumb customer complained about the cost of a call they'd forgotten, or some dick who'd lost their latest iPhone at the pub and wanted to know if they could locate whoever had lifted it. At least this part was exciting, making a difference to whether a murderer was brought to justice, helping keep New Zealand safe from the arseholes of the world. Or at least, that's how he'd described it to Henare the last time they spoke.

"Okay, I think we've got something," he told Henare, who sat a little straighter in his car seat.

"What is it?"

"That's weird."

"What's weird? What have you got?"

"The number's showing several calls, alright. If you take out the ones to the US and the UK..." He chuckled. "It looks like that kid and her mate made a few prank calls, the little buggers."

"And the other calls?"

"Lemme see. Last Wednesday the account is showing it did a *Where's My Phone* search, late afternoon. Give me a sec while I do a bit of stalking."

Henare didn't ask. Whatever Chris was doing, he wasn't required to know.

A second later, he was back on the line. "Got it. That's weird, though. According to my data, the phone you found did a search to locate Huia Coburn's phone."

"And...?" Henare wanted to drive down to wherever the hell he was and shake him.

"The search located it about a kilometer north of a place called...shit, I don't know if I can even pronounce it."

"Spell it." Henare had his pen and notepad ready.

He spelled it out.

"Lightning Falls," Henare translated, then checked the GPS on his phone. "One klick north would be just outside the search area. What can you see?"

"Ahhh, nothing. It's registered opposite a dirt road just off State Highway one. But from the satellite..." The line went quiet while he narrowed down the search, probably on Google maps. "...I think there's a hut of some kind."

"What kind of hut?"

"It's near the river. Could be some kind of scrub maimai. You know, like duck shooters use."

The feathers. Duck feathers.

"Send me the co-ordinates," Henare replied immediately. "Do it now."

CHAPTER 43

Nyree broke out of a video conference with Brett Nolan the instant she got the message. A duck feather—okay, that wasn't much. But a duck hunter's maimai? Two minutes from the search periphery in River Falls? That had a little more grunt. So, she'd rung off, called Callaghan, and now they were in the car.

"These are the exact co-ordinates," she told Callaghan, who booted the station pool car full-throttle.

"Yep, got it."

"I've got a good feeling about this. We've found nothing so far that indicates the primary scene. It'd take less than a few minutes to drive to this place."

"But why not leave her there? It's in the middle of nowhere. God only knows how long it would be before she was found. Why take her to Mason's Rock?"

"Who knows? We don't even know why he killed her."

Now they were talking as if the place had been confirmed as the primary scene. For all they knew, it could be a wild goose chase. Or a wild duck chase, Nyree mused.

The landscape consisted of scrubby fields, the coarse kikuyu grass dotted with purple and black pūkeko birds, stalking between mounds of dead grass with their long, red legs, picking here and there with spindly claws. Poverty in the Far North had extended its reach into the farming community. Up here, there were few beautifully landscaped fields or newly-constructed barns. The city wealth hadn't found its way this far. Not yet.

"How far now?" Nyree asked.

"According to the GPS, just up here."

They stopped at the spot.

"This is where the last connection was made."

"Down there." Nyree pointed to a loose metal road opposite, newly-cut ruts carved deeply by the passage of vehicles. "Follow it."

Callaghan swung the car off the black, tar-sealed road with a clatter of loose stones hitting the underside of the car.

The car swayed and bumped as they descended into a swampy area surrounded by bush. At the end of the road, a ramshackle wooden hut came into view. With a sudden flutter of wings, a flock of ducks leapt from the surface of a nearby pond. They flew off in a northerly direction leaving the area choked in a suffocating silence.

They both turned in their seats, looking all around.

"Call in. See who owns this place."

While Callaghan lifted his phone, Nyree got out. Stillness stretched out all around them. Dense scrub surrounded the clearing, obscuring anything beyond from view except a line of scrappy gum trees towering in the background.

"No coverage. We're in a dead spot," Callaghan told her, then grabbed the car radio set and began calling it in.

Without waiting for him, Nyree pulled on gloves and went to the hut. She followed a well-trodden and muddy track past a rusting barbecue and around to the front where a wooden door hung open. Either side of the path, the grass was heavily trodden. On the left a patch of dark staining was obvious. Nyree leaned over. Despite the rain, it definitely looked like blood. Carefully avoiding contact, she stepped across to the open door of the shack and leaned in. Pushed up against the rear wall was a stretcher bed with a tumble of dirty blankets and a sleeping bag, a shaft of light wedging in from where the lower board had been broken out. The stink of stale blood was sharply evident

Nyree's face puckered. "I think this is it!"

Callaghan strode up behind her. He peered over her shoulder as she pointed.

"It stinks of blood in here. Hang on, what's that over there? In the corner?"

He tiptoed in and crouched next to the jagged break in the wallboard. "It's recent. Looks like someone's kicked out the loose planks in the wall." He kneeled and peered out. "And look at this." He pointed to a couple of blue threads caught on the splintered end of the wood.

Nyree also crouched, squinting. "Looks the same color as Lily's pajamas. This'll explain where Huia was between the times of four o'clock and six. She was locked in here. I'd put my bottom dollar on it. Get the CSO's to check the dirt under her nails and match it with dirt around the hole in the wall. I can just about guarantee they'll be a match. Right, out," she said and thumbed toward the door. "Try to step into my footprints. Let's not contaminate the area any more than we already have."

Outside, Callaghan peered around the side of the hut. "Look." It was a large, black, plastic garbage bin.

Nyree's heart sank into her shoes. "Shit." After a moment's pause, she gave a single nod. "Look inside."

Callaghan took three long strides to limit contamination, slipped on a latex glove, and parted the top between finger and thumb. "Looks like a plastic bag full of clothes."

The urge to dash in and open it up almost overwhelmed her. But the last thing she wanted was to destroy evidence.

"Huia's missing clothes, I'm guessing. When are SOCO going to be here?"

"They're on their way."

She stepped away from the hut and peered down a grass-trodden trail leading into the bush. Callaghan joined her.

"This is the prime murder scene. I'd bet my life on it. Let the Crime Scene boys know. I want every inch of this place gone over. I want every hair, every speck of dust identified. I want to know who's been sleeping rough here, I want to know what the hell Huia was doing here, and I want to know who kicked that hole in the wall." She met his eye. "Because every bit of evidence shows us this is where Huia's life ended, and Lily disappeared. And the sooner we find who killed Huia, the sooner we find Lily."

While he made a second call, she updated her notes, took photos, scanned the area, until he came back. "So, who's the owner? Did you find out?"

"I did. This whole area right back to the main road is owned by Rawiri Cooper."

"Huia's father?"

"That's the one."

"Well, there's a turn-up for the books. Let's get him in. See what he's got to say about it. See if he knows who the last person here was. Or if it was him."

CHAPTER 44

Rawiri Cooper wasn't hard to find. He was at the marae directing traffic for his daughter's funeral. Making sure the firepit was properly prepared, much to the irritation of the guy whose job it was. Henare had dropped the phone the kid found into Whangārei Central and was headed north when he'd gotten the call to go and bring Rawiri Cooper in. Sending him made sense. He was one of a very few with an open invitation onto the marae. He already had a relationship with the elders.

That didn't guarantee this would go well.

At the gate he had paused to speak briefly to one of the guys standing guard. He was a big bloke, standing like a tree trunk with his arms folded, offering a hongi to friends and family and mourners as they were called in; also keeping a jaundiced eye on the odd brave journo, or nosy bastard that came up the gravel road hoping for an eyeful.

Obviously thinking Henare just wanted a quiet word with the father, the guy had immediately obliged, ushering him onto the marae and pointing him around back to the 'tradesmen's' entrance. Cooper had meted out directions for those around him, then wordlessly accompanied Henare back to the River Falls Station.

Now, Cooper sat in Nyree's office once again, the corners of his mouth pulled hard down, knees wide, broad hands planted on his thighs, eyes like thunder.

"Thank you for coming in to speak with us," Nyree said, knowing he hardly had a choice.

"You could have just talked to me up at the marae. I dunno why you drag me all the way down here. My daughter is dead. You can't leave me to bury her in peace?"

Nyree ignored his outburst. "Mr. Cooper, I believe you own a cabin up near River Falls."

His face clouded. "So what?"

"What do you use the cabin for?"

"Hunting."

"So, you use it as a maimai? Something like that?"

"What the hell difference does it make?" His gaze cut to Callaghan and back. Fist pounding his chest, he said, "It's a cabin. On *my* land. That's Māori land. You got no right going there without my permission."

"Mr. Cooper, I don't need to remind you that this is a homicide enquiry. The police will go where they need to, Māori land or not."

His face crumpled in irritated disbelief as he leaned in. "Seriously? You're gonna pull that shit on me?" When he got no reply, he folded his arms tightly across his chest. "I told you everything you need to know. I don't need to tell you anything else."

"Mr. Cooper…Rawiri, I'm trying to find whoever murdered your daughter. Now please, just help me here."

He considered it. Dark, intelligent eyes burning into hers. "I use the hut for all kinds of things. Are you gonna tell me what this has got to do with anything, or do I have to guess?"

"When was the last time you visited the cabin?"

"How would I know? I don't keep a bloody diary."

"Is there anyone else who might use the cabin?"

"Anyone I say can."

"And who might that be?"

He shifted in his chair. "Let's just cut to the bloody chase here. You brought me in here earlier. I told you what I know. I got half my people out looking for Lily Holmes. I'm doing your bloody job for you. I'm grieving for my girl. I'm grieving for my mokopuna—my only grandchild. Now, you tell me why you're asking, or I'm walking out of here."

THE WATER'S DEAD

Which he could. Nyree had nothing to charge him with. She also needed him onside. So, she lowered her voice. "We have reason to believe that Huia was at that cabin when she died."

For the longest moment, Rawiri stared at her. Behind his dark eyes, the wheels were turning. Then the implication hit home. "Oh, this is bullshit." He leaned back, jabbing himself in the chest. "You think I killed my own girl? You think I took her up there and buried a bloody axe in her head? Is that what you think?"

Nyree cast the brutal image aside, one hand up. "Mr. Cooper, we're not accusing you. But we need to know who might have been at that cabin last Wednesday. Someone who knew about the cabin took Huia and Lily there. Whoever that was murdered Huia and took Lily. Now, I need the names of anyone that might have been. Anyone who regularly used the cabin. Or anyone who simply knows of its existence," she added to cover all her bases.

He made a sound of disgust. "That's about a thousand people." An exaggeration, but Nyree let it stand.

"Alright. What about anyone who used it regularly?"

No reply. He sat glaring at her, challenging her. Mouth clamped shut.

"Mr. Cooper, can you please answer the questions?"

He considered it. But the shift in his attitude was obvious. He'd clearly run that list through his head and come up with some possible names. Perhaps names he wanted to protect until he'd carried out his own investigation. "I haven't been there for about six months. Dunno who has." He swiped a knuckle under his nose, folded his arms again.

"But you have friends, acquaintances, who use the place?"

"Some."

"Can you give me their names?" Nyree twisted a notebook towards her, pen poised.

"No, I can't."

"Do you know whether Annette Coburn or her family knew about the hut?"

The cogs inside Rawiri Cooper's head spun again briefly. Then clunked into place. "You think that bastard Peter Coburn killed my girl? Is that what you think?"

"We don't think anything right now, Mr. Cooper. We're just finding the associations."

"Did you arks him?"

Arks. His intonation had changed. The timbre in his voice had deepened. That deep, warrior layer within Cooper's roots, boiling to the surface. The one that would demand retribution. *Utu*, revenge.

She kept her voice low. "Mr. Cooper, we have no reason to believe Peter Coburn had anything to do with your daughter's death. I have a forensics team going up there now. I need a list of anyone you know hasn't been there in the last week so we can rule them out."

He drove his finger down on the table between them. Pounding it with every word. "You tell me who you find that's been there. You tell me who's been on my land without my permission. And I'll tell you if they killed my daughter or not. And if it's that Coburn arsehole, you tell him he's mine."

Nyree's heart fell.

She had to get Peter and Darryl Coburn into protective custody. And she had to do it now.

CHAPTER 45

Nyree blazed past the front desk, files in hand, and headed for the incident room. "Sergeant, call Detective Willis for me, will you? Tell him to get back to Darryl Coburn's place. Tell him to bring him in and I don't care what for. Littering, if it'll hold him for the next twenty-four hours. Then tell him to do the same with Peter Coburn."

"Yes, Ma'am."

Just as she pushed open the door, Callaghan burst from the back office. "Ma'am, the records for the lost phone are back."

She stopped short. "And what do they tell us?"

"Take out the prank calls the kids made to the UK and the US, there were three other numbers dialed on it."

"Tell me one of those was Huia's."

"Spot on. And—no surprises—there are a number of calls to Brodie Skinner's number. Buying drugs, I'd bet."

"Well, I can hardly see Annette calling him. What about the other numbers?"

"We're just checking." He followed her into the incident room where they surveyed the wall now checkered with photographs following the timeline.

"So, this is what we've got: Huia visits Rawiri Cooper, tells him Skinner doesn't care about the baby, wants it gone. Rawiri is furious. He tells Huia he'll look after her. To do that, he'll sell the house Peter and Annette live in."

"And that kicks off a huge problem for Annette and Peter Coburn,"

Callaghan chipped in. "They're up to their necks in debt. So, even if Annette got half the proceeds from the house, and they sold all the crap in the garage, they'd still have a ton of debt to contend with. And that's without paying rent for somewhere else to live."

"Anything come out of the bank statements?"

He shook his head. "They've increased the mortgage three times over the past ten years. But, apart from wages, there's nothing to suggest they were getting income from anywhere else."

"So, Peter Coburn's income, and whatever Annette earned? What does she do, by the way?"

"Clothing alterations. Works from home. Willis said she had a sewing machine set up in a back room of the house."

"Huia was wearing a home-made top when she was found. A second blood-stained top she was probably wearing when she died was found in the bag of clothing. Get the house searched. See if you can match the fabric."

Nyree perched on the edge of a desk, looking over the photographs and the timeline. "Who told the Coburns that Rawiri Cooper was about to sell the house and kick them out? That's the key here. That's what set this whole thing in motion. Huia went to visit them on the previous Saturday. If *she* told them, why would they wait four days to do anything? What happened in that intervening time before one of them drove up to River Falls and she ended up dead?"

Callaghan shook his head slowly. "Practically anyone in the town could have told them about Huia's pregnancy. Kelly said it was common knowledge. Cooper was thrilled about being a grandfather. Everyone at the marae knew."

"Yes, but how many would he tell he was going to support Huia by selling up the house?"

"Kiri Perrett, the girl from the gas station? She's the obvious connection. We've got her picking up the prescription."

"I'm not convinced. We still haven't confirmed that was her. And what's she got to do with it, anyway? What's her connection with Cooper?"

He shrugged. "She's known at the marae. Maybe she's sweet on Danny Yelavich. Maybe he's spun her a sob story and she's covering for him."

"Any word on where she is?"

"Nothing yet."

"Bugger. If it is her, she could be the accomplice. She could have heard about Peter and Annette losing their house."

"And maybe she's the one who told the Coburns."

"But how does *she* know them? What's the connection?"

"Brodie Skinner. Remember Danny Yelavich saying he always went looking for Kiri at the gas station? So, what if we're looking in completely the wrong direction? What if Brodie Skinner is still in the frame? Plus, he has the dog."

She frowned deeply, scrubbed at her face and huffed. "It doesn't sit right. I can't see why Kiri Perrett would tell Skinner anything. She avoided him." She let it hang for a moment, thinking through the implications. There were just too many threads that led in the wrong direction. "Evidence. That's all we need. Eventually, everything will point to the guilty. That's how it works. If I'm right, that plastic bag in the garbage bin containing Huia's clothes will be the last nail in our killer's coffin. I want every scrap of DNA in that cabin ID'd. I want that fabric matched with the tee-shirt Huia was wearing. I want someone who saw Philip Wright's car in River Falls. I want to know who the hell was driving it. I want to know who's at the end of those other numbers on the phone that kid found. And I want Lily Holmes found. Is that too much to ask?"

And she walked off, leaving Callaghan still writing notes. He lifted his head in her wake.

He sighed. "Not too much at all," he muttered.

CHAPTER 46

It just so happened the same Comms officer picked up the call. This one was from a woman who gave her name as Julia. She said she was a neighbor of Kelly Holmes.

"Well, not a neighbor, exactly. I live across the road, about three doors down."

"Thank you for calling in, Julia. What can you tell us?"

"Well, I've been away for the last few days. I had to go down to Wellington to see my daughter. She's just had her third baby."

The Comms Officer sounded less than interested in Julia's familial associations. "That's nice. So, what information did you have for us?"

"Oh! Yes, sorry. It's about the car."

"The car? Which car?"

"The blue one. Well, it's quite obvious, isn't it? The color, I mean. I haven't seen a Holden Commodore that color before. It looks like a custom job. That's why I noticed it. My husband used to be a car nut. You have no friggin' idea how much money he spent doing up cars. And who gets to clean up all the grease and hear about the latest technology, and acceleration differentials, and torque ratios and crap? Moi."

The Comms Officer didn't give two hoots. "And when was it you saw this car?"

"Last Wednesday, about four-thirty-five in the afternoon. I remember because I was just taking my dog down to my neighbor's place a few doors down. She'd offered to look after him while I was away, and I was running five minutes later than I'd told her." Perhaps realizing she was rambling, Julia said, "Anyway, I remember the car because it came down the road from the direction of State Highway One, and it swerved in front of me into Kelly's driveway. I was right across the other side of the road, so I got a good look."

"And you're sure it was a Holden Commodore, Julia?" the Comms Officer asked, using her name to keep the connection.

"Positive. I know my cars."

"I see. So, can you describe the car for me? Like, whether it was a late model, or an earlier model?"

"Late model. Pretty new. Looking at the rear lights, I'd say it's last year's."

"Can you describe the color?"

"A kind of a bright mid-blue. Which is really unusual for a Holden. Particularly if it is last year's model. Most of the more recent models are grey, or black, or red. Actually, I'm pretty sure it would be an import. Like I said, you live with my husband long enough, you can't help but pick up all this rubbish."

"I see. And can you describe the driver for me?"

Julia drew a soft breath. As if she'd closed her eyes to conjure up the memory. "He was young. Had kind of shaggy blond hair. Looked a bit dirty, you know. Medium height, slim-ish. Pale skin. A few spots. Pale blue eyes. He looked straight at me. To be honest, I thought he looked like a druggie. You know, that kind of washed-out, putrid look. Which wouldn't have surprised me. Kelly had that cousin of hers living with her, and I don't think she made the best life choices. Not that I'm the judgmental type, you understand."

"No, of course not. Did you recognize this guy? The driver, I mean. Had you seen him before?"

"No, I'm sure I haven't. And I'd know. I've got a photographic memory."

"Well, that's helpful. So, can you remember what the guy was wearing?"

"Jeans, grey tee-shirt from a Metallica rock concert. It had all the dates of the concert down the back when he turned around. Dirty white sneakers. Like I said, he looked unwashed, like a druggie."

"Thank you, this is really helpful. Julia. Do you think you'd recognize him again from a photograph, if you saw one?"

"I'm pretty sure I would. Why? Are you going to send one to me?"

"Are you able to get to your local police station for a formal ID? If you can't," the Comms Officer offered before she could answer, "I'll have someone come by and show you some photographs."

"No, that's fine. I'll go over there today."

"Thank you, that would be really helpful. Listen, Julia, just one more thing: I don't suppose you took down the registration plate of the car, did you?"

"Didn't have to," Julia said with a hint of pride in her voice. "Like I said, I've got a photographic memory."

CHAPTER 47

Darryl Coburn was already in Interview One when Nyree and Callaghan arrived. He and his solicitor sat on one side of the table, lined up like two little ducks. Nyree introduced herself and Callaghan, and the two of them sat.

Nyree stated the time and those present for the record, and then opened the file she'd brought.

"Hello, Darryl."

"Campbell McCraw," the solicitor said by way of introduction with a nod of his head. "I've been asked to represent Mr. Coburn here."

Campbell McCraw had to be in his seventies. Gray bushy eyebrows sprang from above heavily hooded lids over watery blue eyes set a deeply lined face. His crumpled brown suit looked almost as old as he was. The smell of stale cigarettes wafted from one of them. Nyree wasn't sure which, but suspected it was McCraw.

"Darryl, I'd like to ask you a few questions about last Wednesday, the day Huia and Lily went missing."

Darryl looked to his solicitor who shrugged but said nothing.

"Yeah, what about it?"

Nyree regarded McCraw. He'd probably come out of retirement to pay the bills in a burgeoning Auckland housing market, and wound up doing the pro bono. His eyes narrowed on Nyree. As if he knew exactly what she was thinking. Maybe he had the chops after all.

She'd soon find out.

"Darryl, let me level with you. We have an eye witness who saw you on Wednesday afternoon, driving Philip Wright's car."

"Where?"

McCraw placed a cautioning hand on Darryl's forearm. "When you say an eye witness…?"

"This person has identified Darryl from a photograph. Plus," she said, returning her attention to Darryl, softening her voice, "we have a sizeable amount of forensic evidence that places you in that car."

"I didn't kill Huia," he said.

"Why were you there?"

"Can I see this forensic evidence?" McCraw asked.

"Certainly." Nyree pushed the file across to him.

He took a pair of eyeglasses from his top pocket and opened the file, leaning forward and squinting at each of the pages. Evidently satisfied that the evidence was, in fact, what Nyree had stated, he sat back.

"I'm cautioning my client." He turned to Darryl. "You don't have to say anything more, understand? Yes, this says that you were in the car, but you don't have to explain why. Okay?"

A worried frown drew Darryl's eyebrows together. "So, what can I say?"

"I'd advise you to say nothing at this point. The police here have to prove beyond reasonable doubt that you murdered Huia. Not," he said firmly, "that you were just in the car, but that you actually committed the crime."

"I didn't kill her." He turned a beseeching look on Nyree. "I wouldn't. I loved Huia. She was the only one I could talk to."

"Darryl," McCraw cautioned again. "You don't have to say another word."

"But I didn't kill her. Can't I even say that?"

Nyree leaned in, sympathetic. "Then what did happen, Darryl? You took the car. You drove to Kelly's house. I'm right, aren't I?"

Darryl squirmed in his seat.

"I'm advising you not to say another word, Darryl. Anything you say from now on can be used as evidence against you." McCraw levelled a steely eye on Nyree. "I think I'd like to talk to my client in private."

But Darryl was already shaking his head. "No. I don't need to. Okay, I drove up to River Falls…"

"Darryl, this isn't a good idea. Let's just sit down somewhere quiet and discuss a course of action."

"I didn't kill her," he shouted at McCraw. He turned to Nyree. "I mean, I don't even know where she died." He gave it a second, then his brow furrowed. "Where was she actually murdered?"

"I'm sorry, Darryl, I can't tell you that."

"Do you *have* a primary scene?" McCraw switched a questioning gaze from Nyree to Callaghan and back. Seemed he'd been around the block enough times to pick up on the unsaid.

Callaghan spoke up. "We're still processing evidence. Until the final results come back, we can't confirm that."

"So, you can't even tell me where she died?" This from Darryl.

Callaghan ignored it. "Darryl, we've found your phone."

A look of total confusion. "What phone?"

"The one you lost. Do you want to see it?"

"It's not my phone."

Callaghan drew a plastic bag from his briefcase and placed it on the table between them.

"You don't have to confirm or deny it," McCraw said.

Darryl leaned in, sneering. "I just told you, that's not my phone."

"Well, you said you'd lost your phone. And it just so happens, the only calls on this phone have been made to and from Huia's phone, to Brodie Skinner's phone—"

"Why the hell would I call Brodie Skinner?"

"And it's done a location search on Huia's phone. That's some coincidence, wouldn't you say?"

"If he says it's not his phone, it's not his phone. Don't keep badgering him about it," McCraw chipped in. "Don't say anything else about the phone, Darryl. The burden of proof is on them."

Nyree switched gears. "Why did you drive up to River Falls?" She let it hang for a moment. "Darryl, we need to find out who murdered Huia. If it wasn't you, we need to know exactly what went on so we can rule you out."

He cut a desperate look to McCraw who opened his mouth to speak, then realized his words were falling on deaf ears.

"Okay. So, I went around to Mum and Dad's on Wednesday…"

A deep sigh from his lawyer who sat back in defeat.

Nyree urged him on, saying, "Go on."

"They were going apeshit. Like, Dad was yelling at Mum—which he never does. And she was crying and yelling and swearing. And like, she *never* uses swear words."

"So, they were really upset about something?"

A nod.

"And did they tell you what they were upset about?"

"Huia had come over the Saturday night before. You know, just a visit. And they'd had an argument."

"What kind of argument?"

A quick shrug. "I dunno. Ever since Huia moved in with Kelly, she'd changed. Like, she was getting smart. Talking back to Mum. Mum told her she was getting too full of herself and she'd get cut back down to size again, and that would serve her right. Then she called her a whore and Huia stormed out."

Nyree's eyebrows shot up. "She called her a whore because she was pregnant?"

Darryl nodded. "She went mental. She said she'd just be another statistic. Another useless single mother with her hand out. But Huia said she wouldn't. She said she'd be like Kelly, that she'd work every day and bring up the baby herself. She told her mum she didn't need them and she left in a huge huff."

"And what did your parents do after that?"

"They moaned about it. Said she was just an ungrateful brat and that she was always trying to get attention. Which wasn't true." The soulful look in Darryl's eyes almost broke Nyree's heart. "She was really miserable at home. When she moved in with Kelly, it was like she'd turned into a different person, y'know? It was like, for the first time in her life, she was…" He searched for the word, then said, "happy. I mean, really happy."

"And you were happy for her."

"Hell, yes. She'd had a shit of a time. At home, at school. Everywhere. She was a good person. She didn't deserve that."

Callaghan leaned forward this time. "So, what happened on Wednesday? What changed?"

"Apparently, Mum called Huia." He bit down hard on his lip.

"And what did she say?"

"She'd just found out Rawiri was selling the house. She went batshit. Called Huia all kinds of names."

Exactly what Nyree had guessed.

"And then what happened?"

Darryl crossed his arms tightly, nibbling on his thumbnail, eyes jumping from one to the other as he considered his response. "This was…I dunno…maybe just after one? Anyway, Dad had come home for lunch. Mum told him about it and he went ballistic. I mean, he just hit the roof. Next thing, the two of them are yelling. Dad said he was going to kill her." He shook his head at the memory.

"And you were there?"

A nod.

"He actually said that? That he was going to kill her?"

"Darryl, I'm serious," McCraw said. "Don't say another word."

Darryl's eyes flew open. He jerked forward. "He didn't mean he was actually going to kill her. I mean, he wouldn't."

"Okay, so what did he do, then?"

The Adam's apple in Darryl's throat bobbed as he swallowed. "He went out, got in his car, and drove off."

"Did he say where he was going?"

A brief silence followed. Then he said, "I think that was obvious."

CHAPTER 48

Peter Coburn's feet were sticking out from beneath a late model Honda Accord when Callaghan entered the workshop. It looked for all the world as though the car had landed on him from a height. Callaghan had seen that happen to a would-be home mechanic, once. Or at least, he'd been first on the scene shortly after. The very thought of it now made his blood run cold.

The auto shop was a small backstreet affair tucked between a Chinese takeaway joint and a laundromat on the outskirts of Whangārei. Cinderblock walls covered in old posters, and last year's calendar, a dirty reception desk set with a phone and grease-smeared order pads.

"Mr. Coburn?"

With the sound of creeper-board wheels on concrete, Peter Coburn slid out from under the car, his oil-blotched face screwed up as he blinked up into the light.

"Who wants to know?"

"Police, Mr. Coburn." Callaghan showed his ID and gave the place a quick once-over. Three cars sat with the bonnets up, awaiting attention. No one else around.

"I wonder if we could talk for a moment."

Coburn got to his feet, ripped a couple of paper towels from a nearby dispenser, and roughly wiped his hands. "What it about?"

As if he didn't know.

"I believe you made a trip to River Falls on Wednesday afternoon to visit your daughter."

He froze in place. "Who told you that?"

"Your son, Darryl. He said you'd driven up there, and he'd followed in Philip Wright's blue Holden Commodore."

Coburn's shoulders slumped. "Bloody little idiot. What else did he say?"

"Well, we'd like your perspective on it, if that's okay."

He angled his head, regarding Callaghan with a skeptical eye. "You think I murdered Huia?"

"We'd just like to know what happened." Callaghan gave it a beat, then added, "We could do this down at the station."

"I sent a lawyer to represent Darryl. What the hell's he doing?"

"He was present. However, Darryl chose to give us a statement, and we need to verify the facts."

"Stupid bugger. I told him to keep his gob shut." He looked away, angry, then dropped his head. "Okay, yeah, I drove up there. I wanted to go and see Huia. See what the hell was going on."

"And what was going on?"

He ran a tongue over dry lips before answering. "Rawiri Cooper owns a half share in the house we live in. He wanted to sell it so he could look after Huia."

"And that was a problem." A statement from Callaghan.

Clearly uncomfortable now, he shifted his weight, kept wiping his hands. "It was."

"In what way?"

A flash of fury crossed his face. "It's our *home*. We've lived there for eighteen years. And all of a sudden, Huia gets herself up the duff, and it's us that has to pay." He threw the wadded-up paper towels aside, gave it a second, trying to stifle the rage. "We've got mortgages on that place. We asked Rawiri years ago if we could buy him out, but nah, he wouldn't have a bar of it. He liked having the control over us. Next thing, he's selling it out from under us to keep Huia. I mean, it wasn't like he needed the money. He's loaded. Did he tell you that? Did he tell you what he owns?"

Callaghan said nothing, just let him rant on.

"He doesn't just own the house. He's got a gas station, the land the local supermarket's on, as well as a whole bunch of residential properties," Coburn said, counting them off on his oily fingers. "And that's before you count his interests in Māori land. The guy's rolling in it. So…" He nodded around the workshop before coming back to Callaghan. "I wanted to know why the hell he decides to sell our place and leave us on the street. Why can't he pick something else to sell?"

"So, why go to Huia? She's not the one selling the property."

A cynical snort burst from Coburn's lips. "Rawiri Cooper wouldn't give us the time of day, the bastard. He's holding it over us because he's Annette's ex. It's like he's waited for this day. Now he can really stick it to us."

"By selling the house?"

"Why else?"

"So, you got in your car and drove up to River Falls. And what did Huia have to say about this?"

He crossed his arms over his chest, defiant. "Dunno. She wasn't there. I knocked on the door, but no one answered. So, I left again."

"And what time was this?"

A shrug. "I dunno." He pressed a finger and thumb to his eyes. "Maybe four-fifteen? Four-thirty? I dunno."

"Did you know at this time that Darryl had stolen Philip Wright's car to follow you?"

A long intake of breath was accompanied by a frustrated roll of the eyes to the grimy ceiling. "Not then. It wasn't till I was going back through town that I saw him. He passed me going like a bat out of hell, so I turned around and followed. I lost him just outside River Falls but I guessed where he was going. He was just coming out of Kelly's street when I flagged him down."

"And what happened next?"

"I told him he was a bloody idiot. I told him that he couldn't have taken a more recognizable car if he tried." He made a derisive noise shook his head. "I said, 'You want to get done for auto theft? You're going the right way about it.' Up here for thinking, right?" He tapped himself on the temple.

THE WATER'S DEAD

"So, what happened then?"

"We ditched the car and drove back."

"And you went straight home?"

A long, hard stare. "Where else would we have gone?"

CHAPTER 49

"It's total bullshit...sorry, Ma'am," Callaghan said. But the frustration remained. "They've gotten together to corroborate each other's stories. They drive up there, no Huia, so they just drive home? What do they take us for? Surely, they'd go looking for her."

Nyree hadn't spoken since they'd left the interview. Caught in her own thoughts. Running scenarios through her mind. Then it hit her. "There's no dog."

"They don't have to have a dog. The only ones who saw the dog are the tourists. And that was down at Mason's Rock where they found her. Or maybe it was just a local out walking their dog."

"If the dog owner was up where the tourists said he was, there's no way he wouldn't see Huia. And what about the absence of blood in the car?"

"Philip Wright's blue Holden? There doesn't have to be. They've got two cars. Peter Coburn's a mechanic. He's got his choice of cars. What if he took a completely different car up to River Falls? That's the car we should be looking for."

"But why kill her?"

"You didn't see Peter Coburn's face when he was talking about Rawiri Cooper selling the house out from under them. The Coburns have got mortgages they'll never pay off. He's furious with Rawiri, even more furious with Huia. She gets pregnant and now they're losing their home. And let's face it, Peter's never been the perfect father to her. Those cigarette burns didn't get on Huia's legs all by themselves. He's been abusing her for years."

"Run it through for me," she said.

Callaghan perched at an angle on the incident room desk, the timeline plastered with photographs just to his left. He pointed to the photographs of Annette and Peter Coburn.

"Huia visits Annette and Peter on the Saturday before. Tells them she's pregnant. They're furious...or at least Annette is. It's too much for her. She's religious—"

"Where did that come from?" Nyree interrupted.

"Willis. He said there were religious pictures all down the hallway."

Nyree made a face. "I never got a religious fanatic vibe from her. But anyway..." she waved him on.

"Annette gets onto Peter. He's been abusing her for years and now the kid he never wanted—Huia—is selling them down the creek."

"So, who told them? It wasn't Huia."

"River Falls is a small town, and not far from Whangārei. Someone could have sent the message out."

Nyree placed the pen she was holding on the desk. "Did anyone ask them who told them?"

Callaghan thought back. "I'm sure Willis would have."

"But you're not sure. Check his transcripts." He made a note of it.

"No, wait." Callaghan framed his hands. "Okay, we're not sure who told the Coburns they were about to lose their house, but on Wednesday afternoon, Peter Coburn comes home. He's driving a car he's been working on, okay?"

She nodded, let him have that one.

"Annette tells him they're losing the house, that Rawiri's selling it out from under them. They're broke. They've got nowhere to go. And they both know Rawiri Cooper won't speak to them, so he jumps in the car and goes straight to see Huia."

Nyree added the obvious. "And Darryl Coburn steals Philip Wright's car and follows." She frowned. "Why not take his own car? Has anyone asked him that?"

"He didn't have enough gas, apparently. And he was too broke to pay for any."

Nyree tipped her head. "Okay."

"So, Peter Coburn drives to Huia's. He calls her on Annette's phone—"

"Why not his phone?"

Callaghan spread his hands and shook his head. "Who knows. Maybe his was dead. Or maybe Darryl's got it. He's lost his phone, so maybe he uses his mother's to call Huia and warn her Coburn's on his way to see her."

An even more doubtful look for Nyree.

"Anyway, Darryl tells Huia he'd like to meet her somewhere."

"Like the hut?" Nyree asked, pointing out the obvious flaw in Callaghan's theory.

"Okay," he conceded. "So, he doesn't meet her there. Maybe he goes to Huia's, forces her and Lily into the car. Remember, the witness across the street is off down the road delivering the dog to the neighbor and saw Philip Wright's blue Holden."

"But she didn't see anyone being forced into it."

"She only glanced across the road. Could have happened while she was at the neighbor's. Or what if Peter had already taken them?"

This time, Nyree drew a breath and dug her teeth into one side of her lip. "This contains a lot of maybes."

"Like I said, bear with me. So, what if Peter has already wrestled them into the car by the time the neighbor sees them. But as he's driving out, he recognizes Darryl driving Philip Wright's blue Holden. He calls him—"

"On his phone?"

"Correct. The phone records show there was one call made from Peter's phone to Annette's around that time."

"And while Peter's chatting to Darryl, Huia and Lily are happily sitting in the car with him?"

"Okay, he doesn't wrestle them into the car. He tells them he's…I dunno… he's taking them to lunch. Or dinner, or whatever. But they go willingly."

Conceding the point for the moment, but feeling even less convinced, Nyree sighed deeply. "Go on."

"But instead of the lovely dinner, he drives them up to Rawiri's hut."

"Why there?"

"Why not? Where else is he going to take them? He can't take them home. It's the only place he knows that's quiet enough to convince Huia to talk to Rawiri—with whatever means he intends," he added, eyebrows raised at the suggestion.

"This is a lot of trouble over a house. I mean, killing your stepdaughter and her unborn baby? C'mon."

"It's a lot of money. The Coburns are in some heavy debt with no way out now. With nowhere to live, they're never going to get a rental. They're on the streets."

Nyree had seen people do worse for less, so she let it go.

"Okay, go on."

"Huia refuses. Says they got what they deserved…or whatever. He's been abusing her for years. She's finally got one over him. Peter's furious. He grabs the first thing he sees—which is a tool of some kind—whacks her with it. Next thing, she's dead. He calls Darryl—"

"There's no coverage."

"There is out on the road."

"You're saying he kills her, then calmly walks out onto the main road, what? Five hundred meters away, and calls Darryl?"

"Correct."

"But there's only one phone call to Annette's phone from Peter's."

Callaghan searched the room while he thought. Then came back to her. "So, he doesn't call Darryl. He puts Huia in the borrowed car—"

"Why change her clothes? Where'd he get the home-made top from?"

"Maybe it was…in Huia's bag. I don't know. Maybe the top she had on was too covered in blood. He dumps her clothes in the rubbish bin and forgets about them. Then, on his way back through town, he spots Philip Wright's car. He immediately knows that it's Darryl."

Nyree lifted her eyebrows in doubt.

"Coincidences do happen."

"I know, but I don't like the timing," Nyree said. "Go on."

"Darryl's been driving around looking for them. Soon as Peter sees him, he flags him down, tells him what happened. Maybe to get a little empathy, he makes up a line about how Huia taunted him, said how much she hated the whole family and that she was glad they were out on the streets."

"From everything I've heard about Huia, I doubt she'd do that. She wasn't vindictive. She was easy-going. Even Darryl said that."

"I'm speculating here. Just bear with me." He waited until she waved him on. "So, the two of them take her body to Mason's Rock. It's the only place they know they can get rid of it successfully. And remember, this is just before the tourists get there. Then they ditch Philip Wright's car at the parking lot, and go home."

"What about Huia's car? How does that end up out at Inlet Road in the ditch?"

"Maybe Peter drove it out there and Darryl followed."

"That's unlikely. Where's he going to leave his car?"

"Okay." Callaghan nodded, rethinking the scenario. Desperate to make things fit. "Alright, so they go back to Kelly's place, leave Peter's car while they pick up Huia's, and drive it out there. Then they both push it over the bank."

"Why would they do that? They don't have to. And it's introducing evidence where they didn't have to." She was already shaking her head. "It just doesn't work. And where's Lily while all this is going on. What's she supposed to be doing?"

Callaghan lifted a sorrowful gaze on her. Said nothing. He didn't have to. The implication hung in the air like the Sword of Damocles.

And Nyree's heart broke into a million pieces all over again.

CHAPTER 50

Bowman already felt like she always got all the tedious jobs. But since the cock-up with the identity of Kiri Perrett at the pharmacy, she felt like she was going to get more. How dumb could she be? Why simply take the word of the pharmacist?

Then again, if the girl who'd picked up Lily Holmes's insulin wasn't Kiri Perrett, who was she?

She parked in the same slot that she and Henare had parked earlier that morning and got out. Cars came and went. Across the street the markets were abuzz, traffic slowing while cars edged their way into the already full park. Who knew where they all came from?

The gas station doors slid apart as Bowman entered. She stood just inside the entrance for a moment and looked around. Over at the counter was the kid, Jeff—the one that Danny Yelavich had called over to fill in while he showed them the video footage. No sign of Yelavich. Or Kiri Perrett.

Jeff looked up as she crossed to the counter. Pimply skin, curly brown hair, probably a high school student making a few bucks for uni.

"Hi, is Danny Yelavich around?"

"He's just gone down the road for a coffee. He'll be back soon."

Bowman cast a look back at the coffee maker behind her.

Jeff's eyes followed. "That coffee's shit," he said. "Danny only likes the stuff in town."

"Right." Bowman nodded.

"How well do you know Kiri Perrett?"

"Only from working here. Why? What's she done?"

"She hasn't done anything to my knowledge." Bowman gave him a brief smile. "When was the last time you saw her?"

Jeff rolled his eyes to the ceiling and made a face. "Um, last week sometime? Excuse me," he said as a customer, maybe early fifties wearing a plaid shirt, elbowed his way in to the counter, credit card ready.

Farmer, Bowman figured.

"Which pump?" Jeff asked.

"Number four. You looking for Kiri Perrett?" the guy asked Bowman.

"Do you know her?"

Jeff rang up the sale and the guy lent all his attention to placing his card on the terminal, waiting for it to beep, then putting it back into his pocket. He turned his full attention on Bowman. "Not really. She went to school with my youngest. Is this to do with Lily Holmes's abduction? I heard she was the one who picked up the prescription in the pharmacy."

"Weee...haven't confirmed anything yet," Bowman replied, wondering how the hell he knew this already. She was opening her mouth to continue when Jeff ducked his head and indicated toward the front window.

"Here's Danny now."

Sure enough, a dusty grey Ford Falcon cut through the forecourt and disappeared down the side of the building.

"Thanks," Bowman said and went headed for the front door. She followed a concreted path down the side of the building and came up behind the car, just as Danny Yelavich was opening the rear passenger's door and a big, black and tan dog jumped out.

CHAPTER 51

"That's why your car door was open the other day?" Bowman said.

They were sitting in the tiny office at the rear of the gas station. The minute Danny Yelavich had seen Bowman his eyes flashed panic and he busied himself tying up the dog, filling a water bowl from the outside tap, patting the dog as it settled next to the truck. Head down, his demeanor that of a condemned man. Finally, he wiped his hands down the thighs of his jeans and met her gaze.

The guy was guilty of something. Every movement, every look confirmed it. As if he'd been caught out for something terrible. Bowman didn't know what. She'd have to tread carefully. Let him take the lead.

She'd followed him back inside the gas station and into the office. Now he was leaning heavily on the tiny lunch table, one arm placed across the surface between them like a barrier, the other propping up his head. When she sat down opposite, he straightened, looking anywhere but at her.

"You want coffee?" He gestured to the machine in back of the store.

"I'm good."

He nodded.

But where to go from here.

The dog fit. The timing fit. After all, while they'd seen Kiri Perrett and Jeff, the young gas station attendant, on the video footage on the evening of the murder, there had been no sign of Yelavich. Question one: Did he kill Huia Coburn? Question two: Why would he?

She decided to take a punt. "Tell me what happened."

The corners of his mouth went down to signal doubt. "What? About Kiri? I don't know anything. I don't know where she is, if that's what you're asking."

Bowman tipped her head. "Y'know, this is a really small town. People talk."

Concentrating on a pen he was rolling between his fingers and thumbs, he shrugged it away. Suddenly, he dropped the pen, wiped his hands on his jeans, and leaned back. "I don't listen to gossip. I've got better things to do."

"I've worked in small towns. News goes through like a wildfire. Something happens and the next minute, everyone knows." She smiled. "It's incredible."

"I guess."

"And yet, when my colleague and I came in earlier, you didn't ask what it was about?"

"It's none of my business."

"Did you know why we were looking for Brodie Skinner?"

"I guess."

"But you didn't ask why?"

He pressed both hands between his knees. "Like I said, it's none of my business." Suddenly animated, he sucked in a breath and went to get up. "Listen, I have to get back to work."

"Sit down."

A brief hesitation, then he sat.

Bowman tried again. "Why don't you tell me what happened?"

He slumped back in the chair, legs wide, and laced both hands over the top of his head. "Nothing happened. I don't know what you're talking about."

She adjusted her position, leaned on her elbows, speaking calmly, tone loaded with empathy. "Do you know what the worst thing is?"

He dropped his hands into his lap and shook his head, eyes down. When she let the silence lie, he finally looked up.

"The worst—and I've heard this so many times," she said, and locked her fingers under her chin, "is having something so dreadful to live with, and not having anyone you can tell."

She sensed his knee jump under the table. He shifted position. "I don't have anything like that."

"How do you know Huia?" Another punt. After all, everyone knew just about everyone.

"She came in here. Lots of people come in here."

"To get gas?"

"Well, yeah. Why else?"

"When was the last time she came in to get gas?"

His mouth opened and closed. "I dunno. I can't be expected to know the last time every person in town came in to get gas, can I?"

"But you knew her car?"

"Well…yeah."

"A green Corolla. A scrape on the driver's door."

"I never noticed."

"She was in that day, wasn't she?"

Tears welled in his eyes. He dashed them aside and folded his arms tightly across his chest. Features taut. Mouth set in a thin line. Holding an emotional tidal wave in. "I didn't kill her." He dashed a finger under his nose.

Bowman waited. Let him stew. Then said, "Let's go down the station and you can tell me exactly what happened."

"I can't. I've got this place to run."

"Let me call the owner and have him come and take over. Who's the owner?"

The ache in his expression lingered. But he remained silent.

"Danny?" Bowman leaned a little closer, feeling pain radiate from every pore of his body, from every ounce of his being. "Who's the owner?"

"Rawiri Cooper. My stepdad."

CHAPTER 52

Nyree was on the warpath. Striding down the corridor towards Interview One, throwing accusations over her shoulder at Callaghan who was trotting along behind like a scolded dog. "Why didn't we pick up Huia's car at the gas station earlier in the day?"

"The officers tasked with canvassing all the gas stations were only covering that two-hour period."

"And what about the fact that Rawiri owns the gas station. And that his son runs it?"

"He's the stepson. They had different names. We had no reason—"

"A right cock-up." She paused at the closed door, took a deep breath to calm herself, then went inside.

Danny Yelavich looked up from where he sat nibbling his thumbnail, expression forlorn, chair pulled up to the table like a school kid awaiting punishment.

"Hello, Danny. I'm DI Nyree Bradshaw. This is DS Callaghan." She motioned Callaghan to a seat and they both positioned themselves opposite Yelavich. "Detective Bowman tells us you saw Huia on the day she was killed."

He gulped air and nodded.

"Do you want to tell us about that?"

A half shrug. "There's nothing to tell. She came in for gas." If he was going for the innocence act again, he had another think coming.

"Tell me, how do you know Huia?"

THE WATER'S DEAD

His face suddenly crumpled in pain. After a couple of hiccupping breaths, he said, "I guess everyone knows everyone in River Falls."

Nyree's eyebrows went up. Questioning.

"And…she's my sister…well, my stepsister. Or she was," he added bitterly. He dropped his head into his hands.

"And Rawiri Cooper is your stepfather?"

A tiny nod.

"Why don't we start at the beginning?" she said. "We know you've been sleeping at Rawiri's hut just north of Lightning Falls."

His gaze lifted. The look of surprise morphed slowly into resolution. "I live there."

"You can't rent anywhere else?" This from Callaghan who clearly couldn't understand it.

"It's complicated." When all he got were questioning stares, he added, "I owe money. I'm paying off debts."

"Who to?"

He shook his head slowly, regret burning. "No one. Just a deal that went wrong."

"A drug deal?"

He dropped his gaze to study his fingers. "No."

Nyree and Callaghan shared a knowing look. When he noticed, he said, "Look, I'm not dealing, if that's what you think."

"That's not what we're here for."

He dug his lower teeth into his lip and nodded.

"So, you needed the job and somewhere cheap to live to get these deals paid off?" Nyree asked.

"It's bloody hard up around here. There's no decent paying jobs. You can't get anywhere."

"I know. It's tough." She gave it a beat, then said, "Why didn't you ask your stepdad for a loan?"

Danny Yelavich snorted disgust and actually rolled his eyes. "I went to him. I told him if I didn't pay this money back fast, they were going to kill me. I mean, seriously, literally kill me."

"Who was going to kill you?" Callaghan chipped in.

He waved a dismissive hand. "Just…these guys."

"Gangs?"

This time, a deep breath of resignation. Nyree waited, let the silence hang. He looked toward the window, slowly shook his head. "You cannot get away from those bastards. They're evil. The old man knows that. When I went to him, told him, you know what he said? 'I'm not giving you money to give to a bunch of thugs. You owe it, you pay it.' I told him, I said, 'They'll kill me.' You know what he said? He said if they didn't, he would. That's whānau for you. That's family, right? Someone threatens to kill you, my so-called old man couldn't give a shit. The old lady's just as bad. She couldn't give a shit, either."

"So, what did you do?"

"The job came up at the gas station. Rawiri told me I could have it. Big deal. What these bastards say I owe them, it'll take me a lifetime to pay off. They said I could pay in installments. Installments, bullshit." A bitter burst of laughter. "By the time I pay what they say I owe each week, I've got nothing left. I told the old man. He said I could live in the hut."

"So, what happened then?"

Danny dropped his gaze to his lap where he clutched his hands. "I'm just keeping my head above water, y'know? Then Huia comes in, tells me she's preggers and that Dad's selling up a whole bunch of stuff to help her."

"When was this?" Nyree asked.

"Last Wednesday morning. At the garage." Tears welled. He cut a look back to the window, blinking hard.

"And you were angry?" Callaghan said.

"No! I wasn't angry. Not with her. Yeah sure, I was pissed at the old man. I mean, why help Huia and not me? But at the end of the day, it wasn't going to affect me. She'd said he was selling Annette's place to help her, and that I'd be okay." His gaze crossed from Nyree to Callaghan. "Well, she didn't know my sitch, did she? And even if the old man had sold the gas station, I wouldn't have blamed her. Just because he wanted to help her and not me. I mean, I'm not his flesh and blood, am I?"

Nyree softened her voice. "Why don't you walk us through the day?"

"What? Last Wednesday?" Danny Yelavich cut a beseeching look from Nyree to Callaghan and back. As if that was something he dreaded revisiting. Then he swallowed hard. "Okay, umm. I was here. Kiri had just come in to work. She was almost half an hour late. She's always bloody late. So, ah…I was over at the counter, and I see Huia's car pull in. She pumps gas into her car, like twenty bucks' worth or something. She's always broke…" He gave it a sobering moment. "…or she was. Anyway, she comes in looking all excited. I go, 'You're looking happy.' And she says, 'Yeah, guess what.'

"Then she tells me she's preggers, and Dad's over the moon. And like, I was, too."

He didn't sound it.

"Did she tell you when she'd told him?"

"She'd known a few days. Apparently, she'd gone back down to Whangārei and told the Bitch Squad…"

Nyree's eyebrows shot up. "The what?"

"The Bitch Squad. Annette and bloody Peter. Some parents. They only kept Huia around because Annette was getting parental payments from the old man. Course, when she left home, Annette went apeshit because the payments stopped. What a saint," he muttered.

Nyree glanced across at Callaghan, ensuring that despite the recording, he was making notes, then encouraged Danny on with a nod.

"Yeah, so, she's at the gas station. And I said, 'Can I catch up with you?' And she goes, 'What about?'" He hesitated.

Callaghan looked up. "What did you want to see her about?"

"Well…I thought maybe I could borrow some cash off her. Y'know, just to take the heat off me for a while."

"Okay."

"So, she said, yeah, we could meet. I mean, we got on okay, y'know?" He shifted uncomfortably in his seat, his shoulders visibly tensing up.

"Where did you agree to meet?"

"At the hut."

"What time did you ask to meet her?"

"I said after work. Like, around four." He nodded, then clamped his lower lip between his teeth before going on. "So, when I got up there, she was already there. I didn't know she was bringing the kid."

Nyree jumped straight in. "The kid? You mean Lily Holmes?"

"Yeah. So, I get out of the car. She's got the kid down at the pond there, looking at the ducks. I asked her to come inside, but she said, no, she didn't have much time. Anyway, I asked her if she could help me out, and she said she'd do what she could. I was..." He blinked back tears. "...so grateful, you know? She was a good person. Even the old man wouldn't help me out. But she would. So, I said, 'Look, I'll go and call Rawiri. Tell him what you said, tell him to call you, right?' Cos, he wouldn't believe shit from me."

He waited for Nyree and Callaghan to mumble acknowledgement, then licked his lips and went on. "So, I walked back to the main road. There's no coverage out at the hut. And it's quite a walk back. And I couldn't get a signal for a while. So, I tried to call Dad and his phone was busy. Like, I tried for ages. But I still couldn't get through."

"Okay," Nyree said. Already the story was beginning to sound sketchy. But she wanted to see where he was going with it.

"I went back, and..." Pain twisted his features into a tight mask. He sat forward, eyes squeezed shut against whatever image was going through his head. "I dunno...I dunno what happened. She was dead."

A stunned silence followed. Then Nyree said, "And you knew she was dead?"

His terror-stricken gaze lifted to Nyree, then dropped. A single nod.

"And where was Lily?"

He shook his head. "I dunno."

"Did you look for her?"

His haunted look came up, and solidified.

"I want to talk to a lawyer," Danny said.

CHAPTER 53

Nyree told Danny Yelavich he hadn't been arrested. She told him that he didn't need a lawyer until such time as that had happened, and that if he told them exactly what had transpired at the hut that Wednesday afternoon, they could find Lily and return her to her mother.

She also told him that situation could change.

Almost at once, Danny had broken down, tears streaming, face pressed into his hands. Amid a series of ragged breaths, shoulders heaving, he'd said he wasn't saying anything more until he'd spoken to a lawyer. As if he hadn't heard a word she'd said.

Callaghan and Nyree had reluctantly left him with a hot cup of tea and a uniformed officer while they headed back to Nyree's office.

"This close," Callaghan told Nyree, measuring a fraction of an inch between finger and thumb. "We should have pressed him."

"And what? Had him come up with even more lies? Let him stew a minute. He's racked with guilt. He's seen something he can't live with. He'll break."

They walked in silence for a moment.

Frustration boiled in Callaghan's voice. "You can't tell me that he just steps away for two minutes, comes back, and surprise, surprise, Huia's dead and Lily's vanished."

"How long is the walk back down to the main road?"

Callaghan made a face while he considered it. "Five minutes? Six at a dawdle."

"It's not long."

"Not long enough for someone to randomly turn up and kill Huia for no apparent reason, change her out of her clothes, wrap them in plastic bags, and take off with Lily."

Just as they passed the front desk, the desk sergeant called out. "Excuse me, Ma'am. Message came in for you about five minutes ago."

"What is it?" She took the note, opened it. It read:

ID from motorist driving north, said he picked up a hitchhiker last Wednesday—female answering to the description of Kiri Perrett just north of Whangārei, and dropped her just out of River Falls.

"Where is he?"

"In Whangārei. They're keeping him in Interview Three till someone can get there. He said he's got deliveries to make and he can't wait long."

"Bugger his deliveries. Get on the phone, call Hicks. Tell him to get in there and talk to him." She immediately turned to Callaghan. "Get whatever photos we have of Kiri and the girl from the pharmacy to Hicks so he's got them in front of him. Then double check the garments she was wearing last time she was seen. I want an absolute, positive ID before I do anything else."

"Yes, Ma'am."

The desk sergeant told her that Danny Yelavich's lawyer wouldn't be available for another half hour. Evidently, he'd called Rawiri Cooper, who had rallied support in the form of Eru Carter, a well-known local solicitor connected with some of New Zealand's top barristers. It seemed Rawiri expected the worst.

Back at her office, Nyree had just sat and fished out her desk calendar, checking the timeline, when Callaghan came in. "Did you get hold of Hicks?"

"He's on his way to speak to the van driver now."

"Well, that's another piece of the puzzle in place. But if it's Kiri Perrett, why would she be down in Whangārei? Did anybody ask?"

"Her mother said she's got family there."

"Have we had any other sightings of her?"

"None," Callaghan replied grimly.

"And what did m'laddo in there say about her when he was asked?" she said, referring to Danny Yelavich.

"Maintains he hasn't seen her since last week."

"Oh, does he now? I can see where this is going. He's going to say that Kiri appeared from nowhere, ostensibly traveling up from Whangārei at the perfect moment to murder Huia—"

"—for, as you said, no obvious reason."

"Then disappear."

"Which is bullshit," Callaghan told her. "Even if he's going for the 'Kiri-did-it' angle, how could he not see her?"

She did a slow headshake, one corner of her mouth tucked back. "I get the feeling he's telling us the truth about meeting Huia, though. But why does Kiri turn up at all? She didn't know Huia. She worked with Danny. What couldn't wait that she had to hitch up from Whangārei to see him? And the search tracking Huia was on Darryl's phone which was found under the waterfall bridge. Unless…" She blinked up at the thought.

"Unless…?"

"Unless that wasn't Darryl's phone. Could it be Kiri's?"

Callaghan looked doubtful. "We checked the number. It's definitely not hers. And the lost phone had recently registered on the cell site covering a small area around Coburn's house."

Nyree cupped her hands over her nose and mouth, squeezed her eyes shut. "For crying out friggin' loud."

She looked up suddenly. "Fingerprints. On the phone."

He heaved out a sigh. "None. Wiped clean." He gave her a second. "Look, it's plain and simple. Yelavich met her, asked Huia to loan him some of the cash from the house sale, she said no, so he grabbed the first thing to hand and whacked her. Next thing, she's dead. He moves the body so's not to be connected with her."

"Any blood found in his car?"

A grim expression. "Would there need to be?"

Nyree dug her teeth into her lower lip. "But why tell us he met with her? He could have lied through his teeth." She frowned deeply. "He's visibly shaken. He saw her die, and he can't shake that image. It's haunting him. And, yes, I think he moved her. Get Christine to cross-check his DNA with anything found on Huia's body, or the clothes in the trash. I think he changed her clothes and shifted her to get her away from the hut."

"To break the connection with himself."

"Or someone he knows." She checked her watch. "So, where's that bloody solicitor?"

CHAPTER 54

Hicks had just sat down to dinner when his phone pinged, signaling an incoming message. His wife, Jillian, who had just carried a heavy-lidded casserole dish to the table, preparing to serve up, gave him a long-suffering look and halted in her tracks. "Oh, you are kidding me."

"Let me see what they want." He called straight through to Whangārei Central, only to be told that a gentleman by the name of Gary Sound had driven a young woman answering to the description of Kiri Perrett to just outside River Falls on the day of Huia Coburn's murder. Now, Mr. Sound was now sitting in Interview Three, awaiting Hicks's presence.

"I'll be right there," he'd said, slipping a sideways glance to note Jillian's expression shift from exasperation to irritation. He scooted the chair back and got up. "Sorry, love. Duty calls."

"Not sorry enough."

He leaned in to kiss her on the cheek as she dropped the casserole dish onto the table with a clunk, but she jerked away. He persisted, as he always did, pecked her warm pink cheek, then gave her a wink as he grabbed a bread roll from the table and headed for the door.

"What time will you be back?" she called after him.

"Dunno. Shouldn't be long," he called back, which was what he always said. They both knew it was a lie.

Sure enough, Gary Sound was sitting in Interview Three with a cup of tea. A slim man in his early forties, black-framed glasses that made him look a little nerdy, pale blue shirt with the company logo on the left lapel. The second Hicks entered, Sound checked his watch and tsked.

"They said you'd be here half an hour ago," he complained. "I've got deliveries to make."

"I'm sorry to have kept you." Hicks sat opposite the guy and opened the file he'd been given on his way in, ignoring the attitude. With his pen out, and now at the ready, he confirmed the guy's name and details, then started. "Gary, I believe you picked up a young woman just north of Whangārei."

"That's what I told the woman on the phone. She told me to come in and see you. I don't know why. I don't know what else I can tell you."

"We really appreciate your help. If I show you some photographs, do you think you could identify the young woman?"

"Well, I can try. I was driving. Had my eyes on the road most of the time. Why? What's happened?" Realization lit up his features. A mask of horror. "She hasn't said I touched her or anything, did she? I didn't lay one finger on her. I swear, she got into the car—" he protested.

Hicks threw up one hand. "—Whoa, whoa, it's okay."

He remained insistent. "I never pick up hitchhikers. I only picked her up because someone bad might have."

"It's all right. We're not accusing you of anything. We just want to know about the girl."

Sound gave it some air, then nodded.

Hicks slipped the photographs he'd been emailed from the file, twisted them on the table and pushed them towards him. Sound pulled them in front of him, frowned deeply, and leaned in to study them. Then made a face.

"Do you recognize her?"

"Dunno. Could be that one." He tapped the hazy image lifted from the pharmacy security feed.

"You mean this one looks like her, or this *is* her?"

"Well, I'm just saying it looks like her. She had longish dark brown hair, brown eyes…I think. Picture isn't that clear, is it?" He shrugged. "Are all these pictures of the same kid?"

Hicks said nothing, just set the photo aside and let him return to the remaining images.

"Um ... " One side of his mouth tweaked back. He pushed two photos aside. "Not those ones. She was younger than that. Could be this one." He jabbed the second photo in the line-up. In fact, all remaining photographs were of Kiri Perrett, all supplied by her mother.

"What was she dressed in?"

"Well, not a school uniform," he said with a chuckle, tapping a nail on the high school photograph. Noting Hicks's lack of amusement, Sound sucked air through his teeth and scratched his scalp. "Ah, lemme think: jeans, one of those puffer jackets with a hood. You know the ones, with the fake fur around the edge. She had the hood up when I picked her up. It was raining. So, I didn't see much of her face."

"And you picked her up on the side of the road?"

"That's right."

"Whereabouts, exactly?"

"Just north of Kamo. Maybe a hundred meters past the turnoff. I had the feeling she'd just got there."

"What gave you that idea?"

"I dunno. Hitchhikers, I guess. You see them when you drive for a living. They start off all hopeful and smiling. After a while and no rides, they start looking pissed off."

"Do you remember what time this was?"

Gary Sound squinted down at the table in thought. After a moment, he drew a breath. "Lemme think. It was late afternoon. I'd just done the Whangārei run, so..." He rocked his head side to side in silent debate. "I reckon it was about five? Maybe half past?"

"Can you be any more precise?"

His lip jutted until he finally shook his head. "Nah, sorry. All I know was I had two more deliveries. I don't remember looking at the time."

A note of disappointment hung in Hicks's response. "Okay. Did the girl have anything with her? Like a pack, or a bag or anything?"

"Oh, yeah. She had a backpack. Like, a little blue one. I told her to stick it in the back seat but she said it was fine."

Hicks scribbled notes as he spoke. "So, how big was this backpack?"

"Like I said, just a little one. Like one you take on day trips. She sat there hugging it on her lap. I'd forgotten about that," he muttered.

"And did you notice what she had on her feet? Like, boots, sneakers…?"

Sound gave it a long moment. "Nah. Didn't notice." He squinted at the memory. "Sneakers, I think."

"And did she tell you her name?"

"Never asked."

"What did you talk about?"

Again, Gary Sound frowned while he retrieved the memories. "Um, I asked where she was going, and she said she just needed to get this point on the main highway. Said I could just drop her off anywhere near there. She was pretty quiet. I asked if she always hitchhikes. Like, it's dangerous, right? 'Specially for a young girl like her. But she said she always does it."

"Right." Hicks made a note of it. "Did she tell you where she'd been?"

"I'd have said if she did."

"Did she say if she was meeting anyone?"

"No, but she kept checking her phone, like she was expecting a call or something."

"Do you remember what kind of phone it was?"

"Nope. Just that it was in a blue case."

According to the reports, two of the phones relevant to the inquiry had blue cases: the kiwifruit-stealing tourist, Gabby, had a blue case with a daisy on the front; and the phone found by the kid under the Lightning Falls lookout also had a blue cover. That one had black marker pen letters smeared down the spine.

Hicks asked, "Do you remember if it had anything on the case?"

"Didn't notice. Like I said, I was driving. But she was glued to it. You know what these kids are like."

"I do. Got two of my own." Hicks smiled. Then produced a map. "Could you see what she had on the screen?"

"Nope. Like I said, eyes on the road."

Hicks nodded. Then swiveled the map towards him. "Can you point out on here where you let her out?"

Sound checked his watch and huffed, but pulled the map in and studied it. "Um…right here." He touched a fingernail to the main highway leading north.

"Is that exactly where you let her out?"

"Yeah. See this little line here? It's an unsealed lane leading into God knows where. I remember asking her if she really wanted to be dropped off there, and she said, yes. Like she was a bit pissed I'd even care. It's in the middle of nowhere. But I remember when I took off, I checked back in the rear-view mirror and I saw her cross the street and head into that lane." He shrugged. "I guessed someone she knew lived down there."

"Thank you, Mr. Sound." Hicks gathered up all the photographs and refolded the map.

"Is that it?" Having made such a big deal out of coming in, now Sound looked reluctant to leave.

"That's all we need, thank you. If you remember anything else, give me a call." Hicks handed him a business card.

Sound read it, then tucked it into his pocket and left.

That's when the desk sergeant leaned in through the doorway.

"Just got a message in from Comms. You've got orders to get over to Coburn's place. Apparently, they've got a delegation down there from River Falls all set to mete out their own justice."

"Rawiri Cooper?"

"I guess you'll find out. D.I. Bradshaw said she'll meet you there."

"Tell her I'm on my way," said Hicks.

CHAPTER 55

Far from the riot Nyree expected, the street right outside Peter and Annette Coburn's house was clear of all but a scrappy gaggle of reporters ready to capture anything that moved, two uniforms keeping the garden entrance clear, and a handful of nosy neighbors.

Out of her car, she tossed her palms skyward as Hicks approached. "So, where's this vigilante mob out for brutal justice?"

Hicks directed his gaze to where a few of the reporters were now looking their way and preparing to make their way over. "Not exactly sure. I got a message to say a 111 call went out from this address, and I was told to meet you here."

"Comms say who it was?"

"Nope. Caller didn't leave a name." His gaze crossed to the Coburns' driveway. "No sign of Peter Coburn's car, and we're still holding Darryl. Doesn't leave a lot in the way of suspects, does it?"

Behind them, neighbors stood at darkened windows, starring out. Curtains twitched at the houses across the street.

"Right." Nyree walked quickly toward the gate and the officer on guard let her through before the press could stop her. "Any sign of anyone inside?" she asked him.

"Knocked at the door but no-one answered, Ma'am. Lights were on a while back, but nothing since."

"Thanks."

At the top of the stairs, Nyree checked back into the street. All eyes on her. Reporters in front, neighbors now edging forward. An expectant air hung over them like a thundercloud. Nyree turned away from them and knocked on the mullioned glass panel and peered in. The distorted view of the Coburns' hallway showed no movement. So, she knocked again.

"Annette? It's Detective Inspector Nyree Bradshaw. Can you open the door, please?"

A shadow passed at the end of the hallway.

"Annette, can you open up? I'm here regarding the call you made to the Emergency Services. I want to make sure you're okay."

A faint call was the response. "Tell them to go away." It sounded as if she was at the rear of the house.

After another quick look back, Nyree put her head to the door, calling. "I have two officers keeping anyone from entering the property. They'll be served with a trespass notice if they step foot over the line." This time, a quick glance back and a nod to ensure Hicks passed the word on. As she knocked again, she could hear him shouting out the warning.

"Annette, let me see what I can do to help," she called. Then felt a dull thud of guilt that while she'd offered all the help she could to Kelly Holmes, she hadn't actually made the same offer to Annette Coburn. After all, she was also a mother who had lost a child. Instead, she'd viewed her as a suspect. Had she done that because her gut had told her the woman was guilty? Or because of the signs of abuse on her daughter's body? Something she could not come to terms with, regardless of the circumstances.

At last, the distorted outline of a form approached the door.

"Who's with you?" Annette called. The tension in her voice was palpable.

"Just me. I won't let anyone else in, okay?"

The lock clicked and the door cracked an inch. Annette peeked out, her head moving left then right so she could view the area behind Nyree. Then she widened it enough for Nyree to enter, and slammed it closed the moment she was inside.

She looked thinner, greyer, since Nyree first met her. Deep worry lines had developed between her eyes—or maybe they'd been there all along but weren't as noticeable. Dark bags beneath her eyes shadowed her face. To add to her dreary appearance, she wore lint-speckled black track pants that were almost through at the knees, and a badly pilled green jersey that showed streaks of grease down the front. As if suddenly realizing the state of herself, Annette dropped her gaze, and folded her arms defensively across her chest.

"What are you doing about them out there?"

Nyree followed the tipping of her head in the direction of the door.

"I've told the reporters to—"

"Not just them. *Them*." Annette's voice rose to a shriek on the final word. She jabbed a finger toward the front of the house. "We've got all kinds of scum going up and down the street in their cars. They slow down outside our house, take a good look, like they're threatening us, and then they drive off again. We're the *victims* here. I've lost my daughter. I've lost my only grandchild. And now we're being harassed in our own home. I want you to do something."

Nyree showed her both palms. "Okay, I totally understand how stressed you might be. Have you got any idea who's doing this?"

Annette's hands went heavenward. "Oh, God, use your imagination. You're the police. Aren't you supposed to protect the public?" Tears sprang in her eyes. "Well?"

"Look…let me see if I can get a female officer to drop by."

Her mouth dropped open. "*Drop by*? I'm not asking you to send someone out for a quick visit. I need someone to protect us around the clock. I want you to find whoever's doing this, and arrest them. This is harassment! We're victims and we're being treated like we're the guilty ones."

To the left was a small sewing room, the one Hicks had mentioned. Above it, the Savior stared out with an aching expression. Below, among the strips and scraps of discarded fabric, Nyree's eye picked out a small piece of familiar cloth. "Do you mind if I…?" She pointed.

"Why? What have we done now?"

But Nyree was already bending to pluck pieces of cloth from the pile, checking them, searching those below that of the homemade top Huia had been found wearing.

Annette stepped forward. "Excuse me!"

"I'm sorry. Did you make Huia's clothes? Tops or anything?"

"Sometimes. What's that got to do with anything?"

"You were shown the homemade top Huia was wearing when she was found, weren't you?"

Realization dawned in Annette's eyes. "You think I killed Huia?"

"I'm not saying you did."

"I want you to leave now." Annette marched to the front door and opened it.

"I'm sorry Annette, I want to find out who murdered your daughter as much as you do."

Her upper lip curled in distaste. "Well, you won't find them here."

CHAPTER 56

It was only day three and the team looked exhausted. Shoulders drooping, eyes reddened from worry and lack of sleep. Hicks sat round-shouldered, elbows on the desk with knuckles clenched beneath his chin, studying the timeline at the front of the room. Callaghan, perched on the corner of the adjacent desk, finger and thumb pressed to bleary eyes as he stifled a yawn. He looked up, arched his back and sucked in a breath. Bowman sat next to him, scraping the remaining nail polish from her thumbnail, eyes red, blonde hair messily raked back behind her ears.

Only Henare looked composed and fresh in his crisp white shirt, blue tie and immaculate suit. No one knew how he did it. He seemed to thrive on the stress of the job.

Behind Nyree, the door opened and Terry McFarlane shouldered his way into the room. As if there by special invitation. Nyree's hackles rose at the sight of him. Despite her words, here he was back again. She eyed him as he made his way to the nearest seat where Bowman shifted aside, her expression cool, as if repelled by his presence.

As McFarlane settled, straightening his suit jacket around him, his gaze crossed briefly to Henare, who met it with the ghost of a smile on his lips.

No love lost between the two. Nyree knew that. Whatever was going on now, she didn't have time for it. As for Terry McFarlane, she'd had enough of his shenanigans. To hell with what Nolan thought of him, she was sick of feeling intimidated by the man. It was time to stamp her authority on the situation. She'd get the briefing over, then give him the bollocking of a lifetime—let him know who was running this investigation.

She strode to the front of the room. "Are we all here?"

"Yes, Ma'am," came a mumbled chorus.

"Then this is where we're at." She turned to the board. "Darryl Coburn was released an hour ago. I'm assuming he's gone back to his flat. We've got a mass of evidence pointing directly at him at this stage, but suspicion has switched away from him and onto Danny Yelavich, Rawiri Cooper's stepson. And, as it transpires, Huia Coburn's step-brother." She turned back to the room. "According to Yelavich, he arranged to meet Huia at the hut on Rawiri Cooper's property, where he's been living after finding himself on the wrong end of a dodgy drug deal. Which fits. There were only three lots of tire treads at the hut. Danny Yelavich's, Huia's, and ours."

"Any idea who this deal was with?" asked Bowman.

"He's keeping that to himself at the moment. Says his connections are far scarier than us."

"That would indicate meth." This from Hicks who was now rocking on the back legs of his chair, arms folded. "And he wouldn't be the first to find those blokes scarier than us." A few nods of agreement around the room.

Bowman leaned forward to chip in with her two-cents'-worth, speaking to her fellow officers rather than Nyree. "Could this whole mess have gang connections? I heard there's an undercover operation going on up north. There's been talk about fishing vessels coming in and dumping off the coast. The packages get picked up by locals and go straight down to the Auckland market."

To which others added their opinions, which set the whole room abuzz, so Nyree raised a hand for quiet.

"Okay, guys. We can speculate about the whys and wherefores till the cows come home. We've got our own case to wrap up." She turned back to the board. "We've currently got Danny Yelavich taking up cell space in Whangārei while we sort out his story. He's sticking to his original statement that Huia drove out to Rawiri's hut with Lily in tow and asked if she'd help him out financially."

"That was nice of her," said Bowman.

"However," Nyree continued, "she told him that she'd have to talk to Rawiri first." She pointed at the map. "So, around about here, he goes off down the road to get coverage for the conversation, and leaves Huia and Lily looking at the ducks on the pond."

"How could this picture go wrong?" Hicks muttered cynically.

Nyree shrugged. "The point is, Yelavich says they drove up there. He says Huia knew the place. But here's where his story goes haywire. He tells us he met her, left her a few minutes, then came back to find her dead, and Lily missing. If he killed her, he'd naturally deny all knowledge. But I get the feeling he saw her die, and he's not about to tell us who did it."

"So, what…? He's more scared of whoever the killer was than us?" Bowman asked the room.

"Gang members?" Hicks ventured again. "He's already said he's more scared of them than us."

Nyree tucked one side of her mouth back, doubtful. "I think there'd be more phone numbers to be accounted for. As for the so-called phone call he made, there are no missed calls to Rawiri Cooper's phone, and no calls made from Danny's phone at that time. So that's rubbish."

"So, what do you think happened, Ma'am?"

"He admits meeting Huia. Plus, there are fresh tire marks matching Huia's car, which indicates she probably drove there. Danny says she had Lily with her. I think Huia and Danny have had an altercation and he's hit her with the first thing he can get his hands on, which was the grubber we found wrapped in plastic alongside the clothes."

Hicks raised a hand. "Did he have anything to say about why he changed her top? I mean, that's a pretty callous act for anyone who's just murdered someone."

"And why leave the clothes there? He had to know they'd be found." asked Bowman.

"Stupidity? He forgot?" someone else asked.

"He's made no further comment," Nyree replied.

This time, Henare spoke up. "What about Kiri Perrett? What's her role in all this?"

Nyree pressed her lips together and turned back to the board. Two photographs: one showing a young woman smiling out at them from one frame, her expression open and happy, dark brown hair tied into braids. Next to it, was the frame lifted from the pharmacy footage. In this one, her brown hair was loose around her shoulders, the hood of her jacket shadowing her face. "We have no idea. Gary Sound couldn't positively identify her. We've put out an alert, and her photograph is being broadcast on all TV channels. The sooner we find her, the better."

Hicks raised a hand. "Is Yelavich implying that Kiri hitchhiked all the way up from Whangārei, only to happen on Huia feeding the ducks at the exact moment he was down the road trying to call his dad? Bit of a bloody coincidence, if you ask me."

"Unless she was hiding in the bushes, watching," added Bowman.

"That's a possibility. The phone found under the bridge had tracked Huia to that location so it's entirely possible. But was that Kiri?" She moved to a large map of the area pinned to the adjacent wall, and pointed. "We know the phone registered on cell sites in the range of Coburn's house in the days proceeding. Why would Kiri be in that area? We have nothing to indicate she had any connection with the Coburns. We don't even have any connection between her and Huia, other than seeing her in the gas station."

"Still could have been Darryl Coburn, couldn't it? He and his father both drove up there," said Bowman.

"Kelly's neighbor ID'd the Holden Commodore," Hicks added with a shrug.

"He's not out of the picture. Neither is Peter Coburn. But if the girl is Kiri Perrett, what's she got to do with all this?" Nyree asked. "And why is she picking up an emergency script for Lily?" She stepped back from the board, studying the faces staring back at her from the photographs, and frowned. "There's something we're missing. Hicks, I want you to get back to Whangārei. I want lists of Huia's friends, contacts, any family members still sitting outside the picture. Clarkson, I want the same information on Kiri Perrett. And not just that she worked at the local gas station. Check out where she went to school, what groups she belongs to. There's a connection we've missed."

"Yes, Ma'am."

"Bowman, recheck all the phone calls. Make sure nothing's been missed."

Bowman sank a little more in her seat, clearly feeling the sting of the Kiri Perrett ID fiasco. "Yes, Ma'am."

"Henare…" Nyree called. He lifted his gaze from his notepad. "Go back up to the marae and find out who Kiri associated with. Talk to anyone who knows her. Find out where she'd have gone if she was in trouble."

"Yes, Ma'am."

A buzz of tension hung in the air as they noted down their tasks. Off to the side, Terry McFarlane straightened in his seat, casting a quizzical sneer over the team. "Is there something we're not saying here? Or has no one thought of it?" he asked, hands spread.

The room fell into silence.

Nyree, who had just closed down her laptop, looked up. "Explain?"

McFarlane frowned deeply as if it were obvious. "The elephant in the room."

The penny dropped. She knew exactly what he was about to say. "I think we've covered all our bases, Terry."

"Oh, come on! I can't be the only one who's noticed that you've interrogated every suspect within sixty miles of the crime scene…except the one person who could easily have done it."

Irritation crackled down her spine like an electric current. "We already have a number of suspects, but thank you for your input."

He looked around, his expression indicating he can't have been the only one thinking it. Others refused to meet his gaze, but shot wary glances up at Nyree. They'd obviously wondered the same thing.

McFarlane sat back. "So, you're actually ruling out the one person who perfectly fits the frame. The one person you haven't even interviewed. The one person closest to her," he said.

Bowman was the one to ask. "Who's that?"

"Isn't it obvious?" he asked, and looked around the room. "Kelly Holmes."

CHAPTER 57

"That young woman has suffered enough. I'm not putting her through the third degree just to satisfy your suspicions. *Suspicions*," she added, cutting him off before he could butt in, "that are completely unfounded."

Belligerent. Smug grin on his fat face. She knew he didn't like her; had no respect for her. She didn't care. She didn't have to prove anything to him. He was here to do *one* job. And it wasn't hers.

She squared up a stack of pages and stuffed the file into her briefcase. "I want you in my office in ten minutes. I want a report on how close are you to bringing in Sean Clemmons." She snapped her briefcase shut.

He deliberately ignored her, jabbed a finger in her direction. "Whose word have you got that Kelly Holmes went and met her friends? Have you asked that question?"

"I have questioned Kelly Holmes sufficiently to satisfy myself that she is out of the picture."

"Really? What if she killed the kid before she even left the house? What if Huia got home from her boyfriend's place to find the kid dead and the mother wondering what the hell to do? She could have killed both of them."

A second current of anger zinged down Nyree's spine. "There was no blood found at Kelly Holmes's place. And this isn't your case."

"I'm just asking, has that been investigated? After all, a little kiddie like that, one good whack over the head…or what about strangulation? There's no blood to find. And that wouldn't be unheard of. Young mothers under pressure. They lash out." He put the theory to the team who shared sheepish looks among themselves, but didn't dismiss the theory. "And what if she didn't kill Huia there? What if, instead of meeting her friends, she went along with them up to Rawiri Cooper's hut? After all, her DNA was found in Huia's car, wasn't it?"

Nyree wanted to hit him. Swing her briefcase around, smack him in the side of the head. Her cheeks burned red as she tamped down her anger. "It was obvious she'd have been in the car at some point. And besides, Huia went up there to meet up with Danny Yelavich to talk about the sale of the gas station."

He lifted both palms. "What if he helped bury the kid?"

Nyree knew she shouldn't respond, but she could see signs of doubt forming in the faces of the team—a tiny nod here, a mouth shrug there.

"So, you're saying that Huia comes home, finds Lily dead, and suggests they go for a meet with Danny who's happy to help bury her? That's absolute rubbish."

She walked to the door but he called after her.

"Okay, but what if Huia comes home, sees the kid's dead, and sympathizes with the mother. Says she understands. Tells her, 'Yeah, of course mothers get over-stressed. These things happen.'"

Nyree held her tongue. Just glowered at him, nostrils flared.

So, he went on.

"So, she says they can bury the kid together—that no one needs to know. All Kelly needs to do is act like the kid is missing. Or maybe that's Kelly's plan. And Huia goes along with it. After all, she's all the family she's got now." He searched the room for support.

"I can see that happening," Hicks chipped in. Which wasn't surprising. How often had he seen it? "Kelly Holmes was under a huge amount of financial pressure. I've seen it happen before. Like Terry said, mother suddenly snaps, lashes out at the child. And the emotional overload would ring true. Guilt would drive that."

That was the last straw. "Kelly Holmes is the victim here," Nyree said. "And why would she kill Huia?"

"Okay, so maybe she didn't." This from Bowman who shrugged at the possibility. "Maybe Danny Yelavich did kill her. Maybe Kelly killed Lily and Danny saw this as a way to get rid of Huia, save the gas station and his job. And Kelly's hardly going to tell anyone, is she? She's just killed her own child, who's probably now buried somewhere up by the hut."

"This is ridiculous."

"And she'd be under even more pressure when the payments stopped," Callaghan threw in.

Nyree shuddered, as if she'd been hit by a brick. "What payments? What are you talking about?"

"When I checked the bank accounts, I noticed there were regular payments going from Huia's account into Kelly's. Those payments stopped a few weeks back. Huia had stopped paying board. I'm just saying, that would have put Kelly under even more pressure."

"Why wasn't this in your report?" Nyree directed a glare at Callaghan.

"I put it in the notes. I assumed you'd seen it," Callaghan said mildly.

Shock was setting in. Nyree could feel the floor shifting beneath her feet, knocking her off balance. Could she have gotten this whole investigation wrong? Could she have been comforting the guilty party all this time? Confusion and indecision blurred her brain. What was it Nolan had said?

... *Terry's a damn good cop. He's got good instincts. Trust him.*

Had she missed something? Gotten too close to Kelly Holmes?

"I want those payments traced. I want to know exactly what dates they went through, who stopped them, when, and why. Hicks, get onto forensics and follow up the clothing found at the hut. Find any scrap of DNA, anything to link anyone to the scene, or to Kelly's house. Bowman," she hesitated, as if searching for a task. "Just...get all the photos that were taken out at that hut, go through them with a fine-toothed comb, get them enlarged, and pin them all up here."

Bowman dropped her shoulders and sighed. Another crap desk job. Was she ever going to live down that ID screw-up?

"Callaghan...?" He looked up, eyebrows raised. "Get onto Christine. See if she's come up with anything else we can use. Well?" she barked at the room.

"You've all got your orders. On with it."

The sound of scraping chairs and rustling paper broke the icy atmosphere.

As she opened the door, she cast a pained look back across the team. How many of them believed Kelly Holmes could have murdered her own child? Or Huia? Over the back, she noted the smirk Henare cast McFarlane, who immediately got up from his seat, mouth set disapprovingly before he turned and approached her.

"Ahh, Nyree, can I have a word?"

Nyree shot a glance back at Henare. The amusement hadn't left him. "What about?"

McFarlane followed her gaze back to the grinning Henare. "It's confidential."

Good. This would give her the opportunity to put him in his place. "In my office," she said, and walked out.

Nyree was already behind her desk and checking her emails by the time McFarlane appeared at the door.

"Come in." The annoyance in her voice echoed. Why it took him so long to get there, she had no idea. She gestured him to the seat opposite.

He sank into it, hands on his thighs, elbows out, like an old man. "Right. I ah…" He stroked his chin.

"Before you start," she cut in angrily, "you do not walk into my briefing room and divert the course of my investigation. Do you hear me?"

He drew an irritated breath and let his eyes drift to the window. "I was simply pointing out—"

"No! You do not point out anything. This is not your investigation. You do not have all the facts. We have carried out a thorough, and intensive investigation, and we have solid evidence leading to a suspect. And that suspect is not Kelly Holmes."

"From what I've heard, you seem to have evidence pointing to several suspects," he threw in. "So, which one is it?"

Her cheeks flashed hot. She wanted to reach over and slap him. "This investigation has nothing to do with you. You have been seconded to this office to find Sean Clemmons."

Another wave of irritation. "I already know that."

"Then how's that going? Hm? Because while you're full of theories on my investigation, I've heard nothing from you in terms of results."

His steely gaze met hers. "I'm working on it."

"How hard can it be to find a complete prat like Sean Clemmons? He's not exactly a criminal mastermind, is he? What the hell is going on? You're a seasoned detective. He's running rings around you."

"I already said, I'm working on it."

"So, tell me what you've got." She tipped her head, waiting.

"You'll get it in my report."

Their gazes locked. "I want that report on my desk in fifteen minutes."

"Yes, Ma'am."

"Now. What did you need to see me about?"

For the longest moment, he sat staring at her. No hint of expression on his face. Her words had obviously stung.

He broke the silence, saying, "It doesn't matter."

Perhaps she would have pressed him. Perhaps he'd already gotten her point. That she was in charge. Either way, the meeting was cut short by a knock on the door.

"Yes?"

The door opened and Callaghan leaned in. "Ma'am, we've had a call-in from a woman in Whangārei."

"Saying what?"

He shot McFarlane a glance. "That someone left a message for her to contact you. She says she could have information about Huia's murder."

CHAPTER 58

Denise Dalgleish was in Interview Three when Nyree and Callaghan arrived. Probably in her early forties, Denise wore a bright red roll-neck jersey over jeans, black boots, and her mousy brown hair caught up in a knot at the back of her head. A black raincoat dotted from an earlier shower hung over the back of the adjacent chair. She turned as Nyree entered. Bright blue eyes, face glowing, white rims under her eyes where sunglasses had protected the skin. She shifted around in her seat in greeting.

"Miss Dalgleish? I'm Detective Inspector Nyree Bradshaw, this is DS Callaghan." Nyree offered a hand which Denise took briefly, then settled back in her chair. "I believe you have some information that might help us."

Both she and Callaghan took their seats opposite her.

"Well, I hope so. I just got back from Australia yesterday and heard about Huia. I was one of her teachers down in Whangārei High. What happened?" She frowned deeply, clearly shocked.

"Her body was found last Wednesday. She'd been attacked."

"Any idea who would do that?"

Callaghan chipped in, saying, "That's what we're hoping you might be able to help us with."

"Right," she said, and gave a small headshake. As if the very idea was overwhelming. "I'll tell you what I can."

Nyree led in. "Let's start with how well you knew Huia."

"I was her form teacher for three years. She was dyslexic. Hid it well, but then," she said with a small shoulder shrug, "don't they all?"

"How well did she read?"

"I had her from year nine to year twelve. She had the reading level of a six-year-old when I first got her. I put her into remedial classes, but half the time she didn't show up."

"Have you any idea why? I mean, surely she'd want to learn."

"She was dreadfully bullied at school. I mean, you always get these types at schools, but having learning disabilities makes these kids perfect targets. Huia simply didn't want to be there."

"Was there nothing the school could do?" Nyree asked.

"At the time, we did what we could, but obviously, it wasn't enough."

"Was she happy at home?" Nyree asked, although she already guessed the answer.

Denise looked despairingly from Nyree to Callaghan. "Quite frankly, Annette Coburn was…well, how can I put this kindly? She wasn't coping. It was a second marriage and I think they were struggling financially. Huia needed love, companionship, emotional support. All the things kids need at that age. More, when you have a learning disability. I got the feeling she wasn't getting any help at home.

"I went to see Annette at one point, trying to iron it all out. She said that the school had failed her, that Huia wouldn't be back, and she all but threw me out. I couldn't exactly blame her. We did let Huia down."

"Did Huia make any friends? Anyone she could talk to?"

"There was one girl—Crystal. They became very close. But, of course, because of her relationship with Huia, that made Crystal a prime target as well. Most kids would take off, but this girl was very dependent on Huia."

The reference rang a bell, but Nyree asked, "This girl—Crystal…? Can you remember her other name?"

"Better than that," Denise said and lifted a shopping bag from the floor next to her feet. "I brought her yearbook. I thought you might like to see it."

Nyree gave Callaghan a hopeful look. It was more than they'd expected. "Absolutely."

Denise opened the book, flipping pages as she spoke. "Her name was

Crystal Robson. I met her mother a couple of times. She had a kind of hippy…Bohemian air about her." She stopped on a class photograph and tapped a nail on a girl in the bottom row. "Here we go. This is Huia." A sullen-looking girl, brown hair with ragged-cut bangs, her soulful gaze was focused off to the left. "And this," she said, moving to indicate a second girl in the top row. "This is Crystal."

The image showed a petite girl with long brown hair tied in pigtails that hung over each shoulder. Her gaze, in turn, was dull, long past caring, even in such a small image.

Nyree ran her finger along the names at the foot of the photograph. "Crystal Robson. Isn't that the name of the family directly across the street from the Coburns?"

"That'll be them," said Denise. "Tell the truth, I'm surprised they're still there. Annette hated them with such a passion, everyone knew about it."

"You mean everyone at the school?"

"Everyone everywhere. The whole street knew how she felt. She made life very difficult for them. Called the police on them, made threats, told anyone who'd stop and listen how evil they were. She tried to lay charges at one point. Had the police come out, but they couldn't make anything stick."

This time, Callaghan spoke. "How do you think that affected the relationship between the girls?"

Denise made an agonized face. "Like I said, I think for Huia, it was just companionship. She was very fond of Crystal, but for Crystal, it was different. She clung to Huia as if her life depended on it."

"Obsessively?" Callaghan suggested and looked to Nyree.

Denise gave a little shrug. "I suppose. So, maybe Annette was right. Maybe she saw what we didn't. Didn't excuse her reaction, though."

An icy fist had found its way into the pit of Nyree's stomach. Something in Denise's words had rung a distant bell but she couldn't place it. She placed a hand on the yearbook. "Do you remember the names of the kids who bullied them?"

"Better still, I can show you." Denise twisted the yearbook towards her, turned a couple of pages, and pressed a finger to a class photo. "Brodie Skinner and Danny Yelavich. A right pair of scallywags."

Nyree gazed down at the image and sure enough, there was Danny Yelavich, two along from Brodie Skinner.

"Do you mind if I hang on to this?"

"Absolutely. If you think it'll help."

"It could very well," Nyree replied.

"Just one thing," Denise said as they rose from the table. "Not so long ago, Crystal Robson committed suicide. I believe that was just after Huia moved up to River Falls."

CHAPTER 59

"So, where does that leave us?" Callaghan had one hand on the steering wheel, elbow resting on the window sill. A short drive back to the Coburns' street. But enough time to run over what they'd learned.

Nyree frowned down at the image in front of her. "That poor woman. I wonder if anyone knew Crystal was suicidal." She checked the yearbook, flipping pages to the one marked by the teacher. "She's tiny. There's no way she could have fought back against the likes of Yelavich and Skinner. I doubt Danny even knew Huia was his stepsister then."

Callaghan had his eyes pinned to the road, obviously not listening. "That's the problem with bullying—if you're on the wrong side of it, there's not many who'll stand up for you. Family or not."

"You know what I think? I don't think this was about Huia being lured unknowingly into some trap. She was a young woman growing into herself. And I think she was out to get those little bastards for everything they put her and Crystal through. She was just waiting for her moment. Soon as it cropped up, she'd see Danny Yelavich and Brodie Skinner pay for everything they put them through." She slammed the book closed and turned a glare on the passing streets. "And I say, bloody good on her."

"Plus, she was planning on dumping Skinner. Maybe she'd got something on him. Maybe he found out. He would not be happy. So, that would put him further into the frame. Mind if I grab something to eat? I'm starving."

"No, go ahead."

They stopped at a local bakery and while he was gone, Nyree found the image again, frowning down on it. "You poor little buggers," she muttered sadly. "You didn't stand a chance, did you?"

Callaghan got back into the car with a pre-packaged sandwich that Nyree eyed, wishing she'd gotten one.

"What'd you get?"

He lifted the corner. "Corned beef and pickle."

Her stomach gurgled at the aroma, but she returned her attention to the yearbook on her knee. "Crystal's suicide is what triggered Huia. That's why she suddenly found her strength."

Still munching, he tipped his head briefly. "And I think you're right. I think Crystal genuinely loved her. Five years is a long time for a schoolgirl crush. You heard the teacher—she was obsessed with Huia. Next thing, the love of her life moves away, she's got a boyfriend, and worse yet, she's pregnant." He took another bite, wiped his mouth on the accompanying serviette and spoke through the mouthful. "How many times have we seen that end well?"

"And no one to turn to. Certainly, neither of the mothers." Nyree cut a look to where he'd dropped a glob of pickle down his front. "You finished?"

He stopped mid-chew. "Ah, yeah."

"Let's see what Crystal's mother has to say, shall we?"

Seeming a little miffed at the interruption, he noisily sucked pickle from his thumb, rewrapped the remains of the sandwich, and reached across to tuck it into the glovebox. Then he hit the ignition and pulled out.

Fifteen minutes later, they pulled up in front of the Robson's house. Callaghan reached across, grabbed the sandwich out, took a quick bite, then returned it to the glovebox.

Noting her look, he said, "What? I'm starving."

She ducked her head towards it. "You want to finish it?"

"Yeah, nah, I'm good."

While Callaghan wiped off his hands, brushed the crumbs from his shirt, and dabbed at the pickle mark, Nyree switched a look across to the Coburn's house. No cars in the driveway, but a twitch of the front curtains confirmed someone was home.

"Doesn't miss a thing, does she?"

He leaned to follow her gaze. "Who? Annette?"

"Hm."

They both got out of the car and walked up the path leading to the Robson's house. An older villa style house built in the early 1900's with the gabled iron roof and covered front porch. Time and years of neglect had eaten away at the charm, leaving it weather-worn and paint-chipped. From up on the wooden front porch, Nyree checked back across the street while Callaghan knocked. No other signs of life at the Coburns'. Nyree had no doubt Annette was glued to the other side of the window.

After Callaghan had knocked a couple of times with no response, Nyree returned to the path and leaned to check down the side of the house. Sure enough, a beaten-up Honda sat at the end of the driveway.

"Car's there," she told Callaghan as she re-joined him at the door.

This time, he drove his finger into the bell-press next to the door, and leaned on it. Inside a jarring buzz spooled out, filling the space behind the door. A minute later, a figure appeared through the glass. They watched her approach and the door opened, framing a woman in her late forties/early fifties, long brown hair wound into a mound of dreads at the back of her head, smoker's lines around her lips, two deep frown-lines etched into her forehead, jeans, crumpled plaid shirt, bare feet. She scowled out at them.

"Yes?" she asked in a husky voice.

"Mrs. Robson?"

The woman's eyes shifted from Callaghan to Nyree and back. "It's Miz. And who wants to know?"

Both Nyree and Callaghan produced their ID's.

"I'm DS Callaghan, this is DI Bradshaw from Whangārei CIB. I wonder if we might have a chat?"

The frown deepened. She folded her arms and shifted her weight onto one hip. "What's it about this time? I told the other girl everything I know."

"We're investigating a recent homicide—"

"I know what you're investigating," she cut in. "I'm asking what it's got to do with me."

"May we come in?" Nyree asked gently.

After a second of indecision, she cut a glance to the Coburns' house across the street, then stepped back. "Yeah. Sure."

She held the door as they entered, peered out and closed it behind them. Despite the age difference, the house seemed to mirror that of the Coburns'. A long hallway led down the center of the house to the kitchen at the back, rooms branching off left and right.

"Is this about Annette Coburn? What's she saying now?" Nic Robson asked, speaking as she led them down the hallway.

"We're following up on your earlier statement," Nyree replied, cutting glances into rooms as they passed. At the end of the hallway stood a large kitchen/dining room. Nic Robson gestured to three chairs set around the dining table on which sat a sewing machine and some kind of garment in the making, silver pins and tissue pattern cut-outs scattered. Next to it sat an ashtray packed with cigarette butts. Scraps of fabric and thread littered the floor and table.

"You sew?" Nyree asked.

"Gotta make the mortgage payments somehow." Nic Robson pushed the garment aside and snatched up a pack of cigarettes. "You mind?"

"No, go ahead."

She savagely tugged out a cigarette, flicked a lighter to the end, and drew deeply, speaking through a cloud of smoke as she pushed the pack aside. "So, what do you want to know?" She blew the remaining smoke high into the air and crossed her legs.

Nyree softened her tone. "I was sorry to hear about your daughter."

Nic Robson froze briefly, then took another savage puff on her cigarette, avoiding eye contact as she sucked in sharply, then blew the smoke skyward again. "Is that why you're here?"

Still dreadfully brittle around the edges, Nyree figured. She had to step gently. "Can you tell us about your daughter's relationship with Huia Coburn?"

Nic rocked her head back and held her gaze to the ceiling. "Ah, Jesus, not this again."

"Not what again?"

"That bitch cannot let it go, can she?"

"Who are we talking about here?"

Jabbing a finger in the direction of the Coburns, she said, "Them over there. For a so-called Christian, Annette Coburn's a complete bloody cow. What's she said now?"

"You don't get on?"

A cynical snort as she tapped ash from the cigarette. "What do you think?"

"And why's that?"

"She tried to make out Crystal and Huia had a gay relationship."

"Was that true?"

The side of her fist came down on the table. "No! And even if it was, what's it got to do with Annette Coburn?"

Nyree reached over, covered Nic Robson's hand with hers. "I'm so sorry. I know this is hard to talk about. I know what it's like to lose a child. I won't ask any more than we have to."

Tears suddenly pooled in Nic's lower lids. She swallowed hard, and brushed them away. "God, I miss her. **She** drove me nuts, but…" Tears spilled over and raced down her cheeks. "…I'd do anything to have her back."

"I know."

Nic pressed her lips together so hard they turned white. Blinking to the ceiling to stave off further tears, she gave one hard sniff. "Sorry. It's just…"

"You don't have to apologize." She gave her a second, then said, "I wonder if you'd take a look at this yearbook and tell me if you recognize the kids that bullied them?"

"You mean someone'll do something about them after all this time?"

"I'll try." A shrug. "Can't offer you more than that."

Nic moved in her chair. "Crystal was traumatized at school. She was in counselling for years. I thought … "

"It's okay. I don't want to upset you any more than I already have. Just take a quick look and we'll leave you alone." Nyree lifted her briefcase, snapped open the clasps and took out the yearbook. She leafed through the pages until she found the school photograph Denise Dalgleish had marked.

"This is her and Huia, right?" Turning the book to face Nic, she tapped a finger on one, then the other.

Nic visibly paled at the sight of her daughter. "Yeah, that's them."

"Do you recognize any of the kids who were bullying her?" Nyree turned the two pages.

For the longest moment, Nic stared at the photo while a silent debate seemed to go on in her mind. As if even acknowledging her daughter's past tormentors might set into motion more of the loss she'd already experienced. Finally, she reached over and jabbed a finger on a figure in the image. Nyree leaned in to see a boy in the back row—shorter than most of his classmates, close-cut ginger hair, over-confident sneer.

"Brodie Skinner," Nyree confirmed. "And he bullied them both?"

"He was one of them. The little bastards."

"And the other?"

She stabbed a finger on the image. "Danny Yelavich, the little shit."

"Tell me, if Brodie Skinner was such a bully; if he made life so hard for them, how would Huia end in a relationship with him?"

Nyree already had a pretty good idea. But she wanted Nic Robson's take on it.

Hatred welled in her eyes, darkened her expression. "I have no idea. I wanted to strangle the little buggers."

"Did Crystal tell you what they did?"

"Yeah. Tripped them up in hallways, hit them, spat in their lunches, made up names and laughed at them in front of all the other kids. Next thing, the whole bloody school's doing it." Anger hung heavy in her features as the memories came back. "Kids that were supposed to be their friends gave them the silent treatment; others said they didn't want to touch them in case they caught something. Sounds stupid, but that stuff hurts," she added, perhaps from her own experience.

"And what did you do?"

Nic Robson turned look on Nyree, her tone suddenly light, cynical. "I went to see the teacher. I told her they were getting bullied, and she said she'd *see what she could do*. Which was friggin' nothing. Next thing we know,

Annette across the street starts up with her shit. Some mother she was. Talked about us like we're the lowest of the low. And yet, one night I had Huia stay over because she'd gotten home late, and Annette—wonderful Christian that she is—had thrown a blanket out on the porch so Huia could sleep out there. Mid-winter, it was. Bloody freezing outside. Jesus! If anyone deserved to get murdered it's her."

A stony silence gripped the room.

Then Nic said, "Sorry. Bad choice of words." She slipped another cigarette from the pack and lit up, sucking in sharply, holding it for a moment before expelling it into the air.

"Go on."

Nic massaged her forehead, then tapped the ash off her cigarette. "Danny approached them, asked if they wanted to go to a party." Another drag on the cigarette.

Nyree said nothing. Just waited.

"Huia told Crystal that if they went, maybe they could talk to these boys, make them stop."

"And did they?"

"Crystal told me she didn't want to go. But Huia said she was going, and where Huia went, Crystal went."

"So, where did they meet?"

"At Brodie Skinner's place. His parents were away. Crystal said when they got there, everything was going okay. They were actually having fun. Then Brodie stubbed his cigarette out on Huia's leg. When they got home, I put some salve on it. She didn't want her mother seeing it, poor kid. Then the other one grabbed Crystal. She said nothing happened, but I never believed her. I think he raped her." Nic turned a scathing eye on Nyree. "I'd kill him if I got half a chance. I know you're a cop, but I would."

"Which one was that? Brodie? Danny?"

"No. It was the other kid. I don't even know what he was doing there. He was always in trouble with the police. I heard he ended up in prison. Too good for him, if you ask me," she added sourly.

The comment sent an icy flash of recognition through Nyree as another piece of the puzzle clicked into place. Another clue as to what had happened the day Huia died. Already, she had his face squared up in her mind, could see the evidence forming. But she had to be sure, had to know.

"Who, Nic? Who was this boy?"

Nic Robson's lip curled on the name. "Sean Clemmons."

Frowning, Nyree pulled the yearbook onto her lap, flipping pages, searching face after face: *A rogue's gallery,* Terry McFarlane had said. He wasn't wrong. Several known offenders jumped out at her, their youth belying their crimes to come. She knew every one of them by name, by reputation. Each repeatedly through the justice system since this photograph. Each now with rap sheet as long as your arm.

In Huia's class photo was Brodie Skinner, ginger hair close-cropped, arrogant look on his face, the smug sneer that made her skin crawl. Two pages over, Danny Yelavich, hair already in dreads, eyes dull, features unreadable, he stared into space looking already lost. She left Danny and was searching along the rows of faces when one leaped out of the page at her—Tony, her son, her beautiful boy. The sudden sight of him gripped her chest.

She froze, pulled in a shuddering breath as she placed one gentle finger on the image as the memories flooded. His first day of school. Muddied shorts and skinned knees. That messy crop of unruly curls. Now, seeing him standing amid the rows of kids in this yearbook, she couldn't help but wonder where the time had gone; what she could have done. She cursed herself for forgetting this was his year; his life already slipping away out of her grasp.

Pulling herself out of the moment, pushing back all those emotions, and folding a protective layer around them, she twisted the yearbook to Nic and pointed. "Is this him? Is this the boy who you think raped Crystal?"

Nic glared down at the book, her features forming a mask of hatred. An emphatic nod this time.

As if the identification of Crystal's attacker had lifted an enormous burden, Nic's shoulders slumped and her head went down.

For Nyree, the seed of suspicion that had begun no more than a few hours early, now sprang fresh.

Sean Clemmons being arrested by the police. *The photos Annette had sent.* The more she thought about it, the more convinced she was. But she had to tread carefully. He was cunning. He thought he'd gotten away with it. One hint her suspicions were correct, the tables would turn.

"I'm so sorry for your loss, but thank you. You've been really helpful." Nyree got up, snatched up the yearbook, and indicated for Callaghan to follow.

Nic Robertson looked up hopefully. "So, you think it was him? That kid? You think he killed Huia?"

"We're still conducting our investigation. Take care of yourself. And thank you."

And they'd left with a barrage of questions in their wake.

Back in the car, Nyree was on the phone, issuing orders, directing officers as the rugged pastures sped past her window. "Callaghan and I are on our way there now. We're about five minutes away. I want the Armed Offenders Squad and Paramedics on alert. Get a negotiator up here. I don't know if they've got Lily there or not, but we can't take any risks. Get Hicks to hunt down Sean Clemmons's girlfriend, or anyone close to her. See what else we're dealing with." She hung up, dialed again.

Between calls, Callaghan spoke up. "You really think it's him?"

"I've got a pretty good idea what happened. I need proof."

"How did you make the connection?"

She lowered the phone, looked up, blinded to the passing scenery. "Bloody Sean Clemmons. He's been in the picture since school. Him and all the rest of his nasty little gang."

Callaghan frowned. "But why would Sean Clemmons kill Huia? I don't get it."

"This was never about Huia. I think she was literally in the wrong place at the wrong time. She was out to get them for all that bullying. She just got in the way. Remember Danny Yelavich said he had a deal gone wrong? That's what this is about."

Callaghan clicked. "So, Danny owed money to Sean Clemmons."

"Correct." Nyree hit the send button. "And there's more to this than we've been led to believe. I'll fill you in when we get back. But first, let's find Lily Holmes."

CHAPTER 60

After giving Nolan a brief update on the phone, Nyree looked up, scanned the surrounding countryside whizzing by, and told him, "We're almost there now."

Nolan sounded pensive. "Nyree, if they've got Lily, we need a negotiator out there."

"I've got him on standby. Let me get out there and check out the lay of the land. If Sean's out there, we'll back off and wait until the Armed Offenders Squad and the negotiator arrives. Call in an ambulance. If Lily's here, she'll need one." She hung up and immediately dialed McFarlane, noting they'd entered a narrow lane on the outskirts of Kamo. "Stop here," she told Callaghan, who pulled in at the side of the road.

The instant the line opened she cut McFarlane off before he could speak. "Where's Sean Clemmons?"

"Um, I gave you my report…"

"I know what was in the report. Where is he?"

A moment's silence. "Sorry, I'm not with you."

"Don't give me that crap, Terry. Sean Clemmons has been linked to Huia and Danny Yelavich. If he's involved, he could have Lily."

"Shit."

"Shit's only half of it. Now, where is he?"

"Where are you now?" he asked.

"I'm a hundred meters from Sean Clemmons's girlfriend's house in Kamo."

THE WATER'S DEAD

"Wait!"

"Wait? Why would I wait? Tell me what the hell is going on, Terry."

For the longest time, all she could hear was his breath down the line.

"Terry…!"

"Let me go out there."

"I'm already here. Every minute that passes, that child is closer to death. That's if she isn't already dead, now talk to me."

"Let me talk to him."

"I can bloody talk to him," Nyree barked, then realized she was in no state to be negotiating for the life of a child. She modified her tone. "Terry, talk to me. What do I need to know?"

"Look—I was trying to tell you."

"Tell me what?"

She let the silence spool out, exchanged a glance with Callaghan, then put her cell on speakerphone.

Terry took a breath, heaved it out. "Sean Clemmons is a major connection to a widespread drug importation racket."

"So, he's one of your informants."

"Correct."

Exactly what she'd suspected. "And that's why you haven't brought him in."

"Correct again."

That explained the tension between McFarlane and Henare. Henare obviously knew something. But in this job, throwing a senior officer under the bus wasn't done. Not without absolute proof.

"This is unforgivable, Terry."

"Listen to me, we've spent eight months nailing these bastards down. You cannot arrest Sean now."

A blast of boiling fury flashed through her. She stabbed the air as she spoke. "Don't tell me what I can and can't do. This is my case, Terry, and I intend to make absolutely sure that child's life takes precedence."

"I'm sorry, Nyree, I'm going to have to take this to Nolan."

"You do that, I'll see your arse fry." Next to her, Callaghan flinched. "You could be the difference between whether a six-year-old child lives or dies. You want that on your conscience?"

No response.

"Get me everything you have to date on Sean Clemmons and his cronies. I want to know exactly what I'm dealing with."

On the other end of the phone, Terry McFarlane was still calculating his position. "Wait. Just hear me out. We can both get what we want."

"Just get that information to me right now." Before he could respond, she hung up.

Callaghan ducked to regard the run-down wreck of a house at the address on file. Cream, weather-stained fibrolite cladding, rusting iron roof, six panel glass front door in which five panes had been broken and replaced with cardboard, rusted letterbox leaning against a wilting chain-link fence. The tinkle of a windchime hanging next to the door only lent it a deeper sense of despair.

It also looked deserted.

"You sure this is it?" he asked.

"According to the report Terry submitted, it's a rental in the name of Sherilyn Grant."

"The girlfriend."

"Who could live here? I wouldn't put a dog in there."

Callaghan's eyebrows shot up. "You been north lately?"

He was right. Poverty in the Far North had grown into a living thing. It radiated hopelessness across wrecked lives for miles. Nyree undid her seatbelt.

"Look." She pointed to where they could just see the rear end of a silver Mitzi parked out back of the property.

"Clemmons's?"

"That's the vehicle we've got on record for him."

Nyree unclasped her seatbelt and opened the door.

Callaghan's jaw dropped. "What are you doing? You're not going in, are you?" He snapped off his seatbelt. "I'll go."

"You watch my back. Better yet," she said as she eyed the place, "get around back. Cover the rear of the house."

With a deep breath, she walked calmly through the front gate of the property, up the front steps to the door, peeking in the side window as she did, then knocked.

No response. Just the lonesome tinkle of the windchime. Callaghan watched on from the footpath. He shrugged, so she knocked again.

After a moment, she moved back, searching left and right across the front of the house. A front window partially covered by a dirty grey net curtain stood low enough to look into, so she stepped into the overgrown garden strip beneath it, and cupped her hands to the glass. In the gloom she could just make out the shape of a battered couch, overturned coffee table, TV on its side on the floor. Between were newspapers, overturned bottles and ashtrays that had probably been on the coffee table…

…a shape…

…a body.

She turned and urgently signaled Callaghan from the car. "There's someone on the floor. Quick, get inside."

They met at the front door where she tried the handle—locked, so she drove her elbow through one of the cardboard patches, reached around and twisted the lock. The instant the door fell open, she dashed in.

Sherilyn Grant was beaten and bloody, long brown hair matted, eye just beginning to swell. As Nyree knelt beside her, the girl groaned, twisted around and attempted to get up. Her left wrist was bent at a horrifying angle.

"Just stay still. You're okay. There's an ambulance on the way." Nyree lifted her phone, dialed 111, and gave a short assessment and the address. "Hurry," she added, although she knew it was a waste of words. They'd get there as soon as they could.

Behind her, Callaghan went from room to room, checking, and calling, "Clear," at each one.

Nyree gently placed her hand on the girl's shoulder. "Sherilyn, where's Sean?"

"Leave me alone." She knocked Nyree's hand aside.

"Has he got Lily?"

"I don't know where she is." She curled over, cradling the broken wrist, and began to cry.

After opening and closing cupboards and doors, Callaghan made for the back door. Just as he opened it, the sound of a car roared into life.

"Oy!" Callaghan yelled, as a car engine leaped into life, a glimpse of silver flashing past a broken window and down the side of the house. Nyree raced to the front door just in time to see the Mitsubishi slide around Callaghan's car and barrel off down the driveway.

CHAPTER 61

Callaghan ran from around the back of the house, mouth bunched in rage. He raised both arms, dropped them. "The bugger was in the car. Didn't even see him."

"Get after him."

They both raced back to Callaghan's car. He hit the starter and swung it in such a tight circle, the back of the car spun out in the mud before Callaghan wrestled it back into control. Nyree scrambled to lock her seat belt and clung to it as the car bucked and rolled on the uneven ground, while Callaghan twisted the wheel this way and that as they sped around corners, scrubby branches scraping the doors and grass and twigs tearing along the underside of the car like wire brushes.

A flash of taillights through the scrub. Nyree pointed. "There he is!"

Callaghan didn't have to be told. He jammed his foot to the floor and the car hit a mound of hard earth that hammered the floor and sent them skyward. They dropped back into their seats with a bang and Callahan spun the wheel as the tires slid across layers of sodden grass. Up ahead, a spray of mud hit them as the Mitzi hit bounced through puddles, firing back stones that hit the car like bullets, ricocheting off the mud-streaked windshield and pinging off the bonnet. Suddenly, the Mitzi lost traction, skidding sideways. Then the scream of the engine as it left the ground, the crash of metal as it landed, and the car took off again. All they could see was a shield of dirt and a spray of mud, visibility down to a few feet, but Callaghan kept his foot down, swerving left and right as the lane twisted and turned in front of them.

One hand on the dash, teeth cracking together painfully on every bump, Nyree grabbed the radio receiver, called it in.

"We're headed north on…where the hell are we?" she asked Callaghan.

"West of Kamo…" He checked the GPS. "…Stott's hill."

"Stott's Hill," she relayed. "Get the chopper over here. Follow him. He could have Lily Holmes in the car with him."

They tore down the loose gravel road in a hail of stones. Every now and then they caught a splash of red tail lights as the car up ahead slowed just enough to twist around another bend and take off. Callaghan slalomed after, leaning the car this way and that. They were almost bumper to bumper when the Mitzi threw a left, down another dirt lane and Callaghan overshot the bend.

"Go back, go back," Nyree yelled.

Callaghan stamped on the brake, then slammed the car into reverse and they both pitched forward as the car shot back. When a burst of rain hammered down on the windscreen, Callaghan put the wipers on full, and hit the gas. The engine whined and the rear wheels spun in the sludge, but the instant they found grip, the car lurched forward but they'd lost sight of the Mitzi.

"Where the hell's he going?" Nyree lifted her phone, checked her own GPS. "There's nothing there. No road, nothing…" They careened along through gorse and straggly bushes until the surrounding growth parted and they burst into a wide-open vista, the angry green of the Tasman Sea beyond. Up ahead the Mitzi bounced and heaved over clods of earth and mounds of tussock.

"Keep going!" Nyree ordered and waved Callaghan on. Ahead, a gash in the ground opened up. The edge of a ridge, the Mitzi headed straight for it.

"What the…shit! Stop! There's a drop in front. Stop, stop, stop!"

Callaghan hit the brake and skidded to a stop while the Mitzi continued on, bucking through the field until the front of the car dropped over the edge and all they saw was the underside and the rear wheels as it dived out of sight.

"What's he doing?"

Nyree ripped off her seatbelt, opened the door and leaped out. At the edge of the gully, she paused. The car had skewed sideways on the way down, rolled once, and bounced back onto its wheels, the roof crushed leaving a trail of broken glass behind. Nyree scrambled down the bank, slipping on weather-dried grass, shimmying down on tiny stones that slid out from under her. Stumbling downwards, hand snatching at tussock and footholds, she was halfway down when a clod of earth gave way and she tumbled. Rolling over and over, arms flaying, she came to a halt at the bottom with a rock buried in her left buttock, a clod of earth jabbing her in the ribs, and a Californian thistle in her face.

A wave of shock and pain radiated from her core and ran to every extremity.

"Are you okay?" This from Callaghan who was sliding down the bank, arms spread for balance like a snowboarder.

She sat up, brushed herself down. "I'm alright. Go see if she's in the car. Hurry!"

Nyree pulled herself upright while momentum propelled Callaghan on down to where he slammed into the wrecked car, both hands slapping the bonnet as he came to a stop. She hurried over while he pulled open doors and leaned inside.

"Where the hell is he?" Callaghan demanded as he scanned the area around them.

She joined him, scrabbling along the side of the car, peering inside. "What? Where is he? Where'd he go?"

She tore open the back door and leaned in, desperately searching the back seat and floor while Callaghan peered back up to the top of the ridge, then back into the footwell of the car. "Jumped out in the bush, the bastard. He's determined, I'll give him that much. Look at this." He pointed.

Nyree peered over the seat to where the accelerator was pressed to the floor with a hunting pack.

"Oh, for crying … " She backed out of the car and went straight to the rear of the car. "Flick the boot, will you? If she's in there, I'll bloody kill him."

He leaned inside, found the lever and the boot sprang open.

Nyree hurried to the rear of the car, lifted the boot and searched. Then heaved out a sigh of relief.

"She's not here."

"She wasn't in the house."

"So, where the hell is she?"

"He can't have gotten far. Let's go."

CHAPTER 62

They'd found Sean Clemmons bloodied and limping in the direction of the main road. Evidently, he'd miscalculated his speed at the final corner and leaped from the car, hitting a tree stump on the side of the track. The momentum had flung him sideways and down into a gulley where he'd sprained his wrist and twisted his knee.

Now, after the twenty-five-minute trip to the Whangārei Police station and some preliminary medical treatment, he was sitting in Interview One with Nyree and Callaghan opposite. He'd been told Brodie Skinner had been picked up and was now being questioned in River Falls by Hicks, and that Henare and Bowman were seated in River Falls opposite Danny Yelavich, pummeling him with questions.

What he hadn't been told was that Sherilyn Grant sat opposite Willis in the very next room, or that all detectives were on the same page and comparing stories. Or that a set of photographs lifted from Huia's phone not only shone a light on the abuse she'd suffered at Brodie Skinner's hands, but also told the story of a young woman in an abusive relationship fighting back.

Images that had ignited a fire in Nyree's belly—a fire of rage. Not just for Huia, but for so many others.

Clasping her hands tightly together on the table to keep them from trembling, she began. "Sean, why don't you save all of us some time and tell us where Lily Holmes is."

For the umpteenth time, Clemmons's bored gaze slid across to the window, then back. "I already told you, I don't know."

Nyree wanted to reach across the table and throttle him. The truth about who had murdered Huia, who had little Lily Holmes, and where she was being kept, were a mere heartbeat away. At last, she could bring that child back to her mother, where she should be.

Dead or alive.

Next to her, Callaghan flipped open the file in front of him. "We know that the girl picking up a prescription for Lily Holmes in the River Falls Pharmacy on Friday 17th, was Sherilyn Grant. Now, why would she do that?"

Clemmons made a mock show of ignorance. "How would I know? Go ask her."

"We did. Let me see here…" She made a show over flicking over pages in her file. Nothing there, but it looked good. "Sherilyn says you told her to. Just like you told her to hitchhike up to Rawiri's cabin and help take Lily back to your place. Am I right?"

"Well, if she hitchhiked up there, how'd she get home?" A smug grin.

Nyree leaned a little closer to him. "Good question. I think Danny took you all back to Sean's place, along with Lily Holmes. And when Sherilyn realized there wasn't enough insulin, you made her go to the pharmacy and pick up another prescription."

"And how'm I supposed to have got there without a car?" Another smug grin.

That threw her. She'd just been fishing—she hadn't covered that angle.

"I think someone took you there. How close am I, Sean? Pretty well spot on, I'd say, wouldn't you?" A tiny smile. Just to show him she wasn't rattled, to lead him to believe she knew more than he thought.

Ignoring the defiant sneer, Nyree flicked to another page on the report and leaned in, chin rested on her clasped hands. "What was it that Huia did, Sean? What could someone like her have done that justified killing her?"

Callaghan chipped in, saying, "It'd have to be something big. Did she threaten to expose who was running your drug empire? Is that it?"

Clemmons snorted. "Tell me what drugs you found on me to support that. Oh, yeah, that's right. You found a big, fat nothing, that's what." He tapped the table. "If you wanna know who killed Huia Coburn, go ask Danny Yelavich. I'm not going down for something that arsehole did."

On the table between them, Nyree's phone rang: Bowman.

"Sorry to bother you, Ma'am, but I've just sent you a few of the photos. It's just that while I was printing them out and enlarging them, I came across a couple of things you might find interesting."

"Tell me." She turned away, waving Callaghan on with the interview as she listened.

Bowman gave her the condensed version. Then said, "Check photo numbers three and four."

Nyree flicked through her email, came to the photos and opened up photograph three.

"Got it," she said, excusing herself while she stepped out of the room, leaving Callaghan to continue with the interrogation. Once in the hallway, she spread two fingers on the screen to enlarge the image.

"Is that Terry McFarlane arresting Brodie Skinner?"

"Yep. He was working with the Drug Squad down in Whangārei five years back."

"Good work, Bowman," she said, "And what's the other thing you found?"

"Well, if you look carefully on photograph four, the coveralls Sean is wearing have a logo here on the left pocket."

In photo four, she found that smart-arse little rat, smug look on his face. Him and Skinner. Both in their teens. Both criminals in the making.

Again, Nyree enlarged the image. The image was pixelated and unreadable, but sure enough, there was the logo. "And...?"

"It's a logo used by a spare parts outfit that used to operate just north of Hikurangi."

"Are you saying he worked there?"

"Part time. It's closed down now, and the place is vacant. But I tracked down the owners, and called them. They said he worked there for about four weeks until they caught him stealing car parts, so they sacked him. Well, no surprises there. So, anyway, they shut up shop about a year ago, but they keep an eye on the place, you know, burglars, druggies, whatever. Anyway, security footage picked up him and some other bloke hanging round there a couple of days ago."

That tingle of excitement reignited down Nyree's spine. "Is that so?"

"Well, I'm just wondering, like, if he still had access to the yard—you know, kept a key or something, he could have taken Lily there. I mean, it's a long shot—"

"Good work, Bowman," Nyree cut her off. "Well done. Text me the address of this yard, and get onto the owner. Tell him to meet me there and let me in. Then tell them I want a copy of that footage." She checked her watch, and located her car keys. "Callaghan's in Interview One with Clemmons. Soon as he's out, tell him where I am."

"Are you going there now, Ma'am?"

Nyree was already headed for the car. "Yep. Get on the phone for backup and the negotiator. Then get an ambulance straight over there. If Lily's there we're going to need them. Good work, Bowman, bloody good work."

A burst of pride resounded in Bowman's reply. "Thank you, Ma'am," she said.

But Nyree had already hung up.

CHAPTER 63

Two minutes down State Highway One, the radio crackled into life—backup was on the way. What were their orders?

"Tell them to remain out of sight until I say," Nyree said. "I want to see the lay of the land before we go busting in there. I need to know *a*, if she's there. And *b,* if she's alive."

Siren wailing, lights flashing, she wove through traffic, down side streets, cutting to the opposite side of the road and back as traffic pulled over, and the openings allowed. Eight hundred meters to her destination, she cut the siren, slowed until she was right outside, and stopped, searching up and down the street.

No other units in sight.

"Bloody typical," she muttered, cutting the ignition and twisting in her seat to scan the entire area. Furious, she got out and ran a calloused eye over the ten-foot chain-link fence enclosing the yard. Twenty meters or so beyond, she could see a run-down office with a sign pointing to the reception area at the front. She paused at two steel-framed gates anchored together by a chain and padlocked. When she rattled them, two Rottweilers burst from the office porch and headed for her, deep-throated barking, drool flying, and threw themselves at the fence, huge paws rattling the wire, all hot breath and fangs, so Nyree jumped back.

They lunged and leapt at the fence over and over, all teeth and noise.

"Shut up!"

Dammit. Even if she could get in there, the dogs would eat her alive.

She checked the street again. Still no one.

"Bugger it!"

Was this even worth it? After all, it was a long shot.

Muttering curses, she hesitated for second, trying to decide who to stand down first, when her eye lit on something midway between her and the office and she stopped in her tracks. A mound of dirty grey fabric spewing tiny puffs of stuffing had been abandoned in a puddle. Easy to disregard in the surrounding filth and debris. But still fully recognizable from the photos.

Bun-Buns.

"Bloody hell. Where the hell is everyone?" she demanded of the empty street.

With one eye on the dogs and a hand on her pounding heart, Nyree moved position at the fence and leaned in. "Hello! Lily, sweetheart, can you hear me?"

Again, the dogs raced along to meet her, leaping at the wire, barking and snarling, so she stepped back, pulse racing in her ears as she rescanned the empty street. "Oh, come off it."

Lily Holmes could be in there, her little life draining away while Nyree stood there helpless.

"To hell with this," she growled and turned for the car. She'd just opened the boot, searching for something to remove the chain, when a single marked police unit pulled in.

She dashed over as a uniformed PC got out, spotted the dogs and faltered.

Nyree didn't have time for sissies. "Get your bolt cutters over here and open this gate. C'mon, c'mon." She waved him on, then marched back to the entrance.

"Um, shouldn't we should wait for Animal Control?"

She paused at the gate and jabbed a finger at the chain. "Just get the cutters here, and get this chain off. If that child is in there, we don't have time to wait."

He opened the boot, came back with the cutters. As he positioned the cutters on the chain, one of the dogs leapt at him and he took a rapid step back. "Jesus! You'd never make it to the door, Ma'am."

"Just get on with it!"

With the dogs hurling themselves at him and rattling the wire, he stepped forward again, positioned the bolt-cutters, strained at the effort.

"You want me to do it?" She stuck out a hand.

He gave her an acid glance, and renewed his efforts. The bolt cutters snapped together and the chain fell loose. In relief, the cop hauled out the chain, loosening it from the gate while holding it closed. "I'll go." It clearly wasn't his first choice.

"I'll go. You wait here for backup." She stepped across him, grabbed the gate, breath heaving in her chest, sweat flashing on her brow, but ready.

"They'll kill you before you get one foot over the threshold."

She tsked, looked around. "Wait here."

She raced back to the car, ripped open the door, yanked open the glovebox, and came back unwrapping Callaghan's half-eaten sandwich which she thrust it into his hand. "Here, see if you can lure them away with this while I duck in."

He dropped a horrified look to the mangled sandwich, then lifted it on her. "They'll wolf this back in two seconds flat."

"Just get on with it, will you!" She pointed. "Well, go on!"

"Oy!" he shouted at the dogs. "Look here. Yum, yum." He threw a crust over the fence and one of the dogs leapt on it, scoffing it down. Now, both dogs stood tall, all attention on the cop.

"Go, go. Take them down the fence."

He moved along, shaking the sandwich, both dogs following, mesmerized.

The instant the gate was cleared, Nyree hauled it open and rushed inside, making straight for the office as two more units pulled in. At the top of the steps, she twisted the handle, shoved her shoulder to the door. "Bugger it. It's locked! Bring the ram!"

At the far end of the yard, the two dogs turned, beady, black eyes locked on her.

"Well, hurry up!"

Both leapt into life, bounding towards her. She gasped, swiveled her head, eyes squeezed shut. Waiting for the attack. Waiting for death. Then heard a voice.

"Oy, there!"

Back pressed to the door, heart banging, she slit her eyes open and peeked out to see the dogs had stopped short. Both stood rigid, ears pricked, as a short, barrel-chested guy in tan shirt and pants sauntered into the yard, calling them.

"Come 'ere, ya big dummies," he called as the dogs bounded over to him.

The cop next to her said, "That's Artie Taylor, Ma'am. Animal Control."

"About ruddy time." Head spinning, pulse racing, Nyree knocked on the office door. "Lily? Can you hear me, sweetheart? Don't be afraid, I've come to take you home to your mummy." She glanced back as a burly officer with a lattice-work of tattoos down each arm hurried up the steps and stood with the ram, poised. "Listen, darling," she called, face close to the door, "there's going to be a big noise, but don't be afraid. You're safe now."

No response from inside, so she turned to the officer and nodded. "Go, go, go."

The cop hoisted the ram, drew it back, and swung it into the door with a deadening thunk. The wood next to the handle splintered exposing the lock mechanism, so he gave it a thump with his fist and the door wobbled open.

"Ma'am." He stepped back.

Shouldering her way past him, she fell inside. The air was thick and musty, black tarpaulins covering the windows. She turned on the spot, searching the room while the officer ripped one of the covers down. Light flooded the dingy office with a wash of dust motes. A grimy desk, a couple of broken chairs, pile of junk.

No Lily.

"Lily? Where are you, sweetheart?" Desperate now, she made for a door leading to the bathroom and shoved it open. From a mound of filthy blankets on the floor next to the sink, she could see a child's hand. She dashed across and threw back the blankets to find little Lily Holmes, face ashen, soft red hair streaked with sweat, but breathing.

"She's unconscious. Where the hell are the paramedics?" she yelled, just as two cops behind her parted and a couple of ambulance officers dressed in green squeezed in carrying a canvas bag and angled in beside her.

"She's diabetic. Check her breathing. Check her blood pressure," Nyree insisted, hovering over them while they worked. Then realized she was in the way and they knew exactly what to do.

She stepped back, hugging herself in the doorway while they checked Lily's vitals, lifted her eyelids and peered in, took her temperature.

"Let's get a line in. She's badly dehydrated."

"Is she alright? Is she going to be okay?" Nyree was pressing them with the same questions a mother would. But she had to know.

"We'll get a better idea once we get her back to the hospital."

"Be careful with her." Nyree tsked at herself. As if they'd be anything else. With her brow crumpled, features tight with worry, she followed as they loaded her gently onto a gurney and trundled into the back of the vehicle which had reversed as close to the office as they could.

Exhaustion and relief prickled in her veins as Nyree watched the ambulance rumble out of the yard, turn right, and vanish in the direction of Whangārei hospital. As soon as it was gone, she straightened with renewed energy and drew in a deep breath. She had a job to finish.

The man who murdered Huia Coburn and dumped Lily here was pictured on that CCTV footage. Now she knew exactly who that man was.

"Wait till I get my hands on him," she growled to herself and she stormed back to the car. "He'll rot in prison, if I've got anything to do with it."

CHAPTER 64

Back in Whangārei, an ashen-faced Danny accepted the requested glass of water before continuing.

Henare let him take a gulp and put the glass down before picking up the questioning again. "So, first you said you didn't know who murdered Huia."

"Yeah, I know."

Henare checked his notes. "And now you're saying Sean did it."

He nodded. "Yeah, I just…he's a friggin' psycho. He'll kill me if he finds out I blabbed."

"How did Sean get to the hut?"

The blank expression told Henare the mental wheels were slipping on a bedrock of lies. Then he snapped to and said, "I took him with me."

"And then the two of you took Huia to the river. Is that correct? And you're sure this time?"

"I wanted to leave her somewhere she'd be found. You know, she was my stepsister. I didn't want her just left there for ages with nobody finding her. But Sean dragged her into the river. It was flooding and she went in and disappeared. Then we took the dog, split up, and went to find Lily."

"And did you find her?"

A thoughtful look, then a quick nod. "Sean picked her up down by the waterfall."

"Did she see who murdered Huia?"

"Don't think so. She kept asking for her."

"What happened next?"

"We went back to the hut and cleaned up. It was…" Paling visibly at the sickening memory, Danny took a deep, shuddering breath, studied his nails for a moment. "I just…I didn't know what to do." His chin crumpled, then continued. "Sean took her tee-shirt and jacket off. He made me help him put a tee-shirt on her—so he could carry her without getting…y'know." His voice trailed away, then he bit hard into his lip and sent a horror-ridden look to the ceiling. With a hiccupping gulp, he brought his focus back to the table. "Then he called up Sherilyn. She said she didn't have the car, he did."

"I thought you took Sean up there."

"Yeah, he'd left his car in town. I picked him up. So, then Sean drove Huia's car out to Inlet Road, and we pushed it over the bank."

Henare's eyebrows went up. "And then you all took Lily back to Sean's."

"That's it."

A hint of truth threaded throughout. The rest was utter rubbish. They both knew it. So, Henare flicked back through the notes and started again.

Next door, Sherilyn Grant's right hand had been plastered. She sat with her eyes swollen, nose streaming. Hicks handed her a box of tissues. She ripped several out and savagely wiped her nose and eyes, then sat staring into the bunched-up wad in her hand.

"Do you want to talk about it?" asked Hicks.

Her mouth tightened as she shook her head.

"How long have you known Sean?"

A hiccupping swallow. "Since school."

"You were in the same class?"

Another headshake. "He was a couple of years ahead of me."

"You moved in with him pretty much straight after you left school, though, didn't you? Did he look after you?"

A shrug. She sniffed hard and let her eyes lift to a point between them as the memories seemed to come.

"A guy like that. I guess he would've had money. Everything you needed… somewhere safe to live, plenty of drugs and booze.?" Hicks smiled. "Well," he tipped his head. "That's what your mum said."

Hicks had met her mother. Sat down at what passed as the kitchen table in the dirt-poor suburb of the tiny town she'd moved to after she'd been evicted from her last place. He'd met her meth-dead eyes straight on, and knew exactly why her daughter had left home at the age of sixteen.

"And seriously, after meeting her, I can see Sean's attraction."

A steely gaze met his.

Hicks took a deep, calm breath. "Listen, I know you didn't have anything to do with Huia Coburn's death. I mean, why would you?" No reply, so he went on. "Did Sean have anything to do with her death?"

Another hard swallow. This time, tears welled.

"It was the other guy. I'd only seen him around, but Sean knew him."

"And he's the one that beat you up and took Lily?"

Her eyes came up to meet his. Tears burst from her lower lids to run down her cheeks. She shook her head slowly as her gaze returned to the table. Her face crumpled. "I didn't know what to do. I thought she was going to die. I kept telling Sean to call an ambulance, but this guy turned up and grabbed her and took off."

"Did he take her to hospital?"

"I don't know where he took her."

"Looks like you did your best to help Lily."

Sherilyn sucked in a breath, studied the plaster cast on her arm.

"Lily's just a little girl who's gotten mixed up in this. She's got a mum who's worried sick about her. Sherilyn…tell me everything you know."

Again, her face crumpled. The words were just behind her teeth.

Hicks reached out a hand, covered hers. "You can tell me."

So, she did.

CHAPTER 65

"Still doesn't tell us much," Callaghan complained to Nyree after watching the interview online. "Doesn't know who, doesn't know where."

Not if you asked Nyree. It backed up exactly what she thought. They were sitting in the incident room in River Falls, staring at the board, lines radiating between the suspects. All the overly-enlarged photographs Bowman had pinned up surrounding them.

Callaghan ducked his head at them. "She didn't half do a job on getting them blown up."

"Yeah, well don't knock her. She picked up that logo on Sean's overalls." She got up and walked the periphery of the room in frustration. "There's still something we've missed. There has to be evidence."

"Do we have enough to charge Clemmons?"

She gave it some thought. "I've got too many questions. Why leave Lily at the abandoned car yard? He had to know we'd track her to Sherilyn's."

"Not necessarily. Perhaps he planned to pick her up later, take her to the hospital."

Her eyes widened. "That's a generous assumption."

"Look, Sean Clemmons and Skinner were up to their necks in drugs. They probably owed money. And I'll tell you what, I wouldn't want to owe money to those gangs up north. You wouldn't last five minutes." The corners of his mouth went down at the thought. "What if Huia got mixed up in that somehow? Ended up with the gangs putting out a hit on her. She went looking for Skinner, wound up in the wrong place at the wrong time."

"We'd have found it." She paused in front of the photo taken out front of the hut, eyes narrowed, and tapped it. "That's weird. Look at this."

Callaghan also studied it. "What is it?"

"The car tires here. What do you see?"

He moved a little closer and tapped the picture. "Well, the arrow forensics stuck there indicates it's our pool car tires, and those are Huia's tires."

"Exactly. This is Huia's tire mark, right? And, this one is the pool car."

His eyes shifted back and forth, from one tread mark to the other. He frowned as the implication sank in. "They've marked them wrong."

"I don't think so. Huia's tire track crosses over the station pool car's. And the only way that could happen…"

His eyes met hers. "Is if the pool car was there before Huia." He made a face. "So, what are you saying. That it's a cop? From River Falls? No way."

"It's a cop, alright. But not just any cop. I'll bet you anything you like Terry McFarlane took that pool car, and was up at that hut on the day Huia died."

His face blanched. A deadpan expression as though she was barking mad and he'd only just picked it up.

"It's him! Every scrap of evidence points to him. Sherilyn says she didn't know who he was. Like hell, she doesn't. She's terrified of him. She knows exactly what would happen if she fingered him as the one who beat her up and took Lily."

"Listen, I know there's some tension going on between you, but—"

She cut him off. "Terry McFarlane fits all the criteria. He's the one Huia was meeting at the hut. She called him, told him she could prove beyond a shadow of a doubt that Brodie Skinner and Sean Clemmons were up to their necks in high profit drug deals. He's the one Huia took all her evidence to because she remembered him from her schooldays. That's why she printed out all those photographs. She knew McFarlane, thought he was the only one she could trust."

Callaghan butted in, saying, "Anyone in the station could have taken that car."

"Who else had any reason to be there?"

He jabbed a finger at the photograph. "It's a fraction of crossover. There could be any number of reasons for that. A trick of the light. It's rained like hell up there…"

"Oh, rain my foot," she sneered. "That photo is from further down the track, under the trees. How's rain going to shift car tracks?"

"There'll be some explanation. Wouldn't forensics have picked it up? And why would Huia go to all this trouble to drop her own boyfriend into it?"

"Because she wanted payback. That's what this is about. She wasn't the timid kid getting bullied anymore. She'd grown up, found her confidence. And she wanted to see those ratbags put away for what they did to Crystal. Her best friend commits suicide because of these little toe-rags, and what better way to pay them back than calling up the cop who put them away the first time? So, she calls him. That's who she was calling on the day she died. That's whose phone was found under the bridge—"

"Oh, come on, Ma'am. Even if it's true, a cop like Terry wouldn't make such a stupid mistake."

"Maybe, maybe not. But why do you think the suspects have changed from one day to the next? I'll tell you why—Terry McFarlane's been leading us around by the nose, framing Clemmons or Skinner, or whoever he could." She pointed off into the distance. "However that phone got down under that bridge, it fits. Huia demands this cop arrests both Clemmons and Skinner. But, oh no…" She crossed to the photos of McFarlane with Clemmons, jabbed a finger on the image. "Terry McFarlane can't do that. That would bust open his Operation Whatever-it-is he's working on up north. Sean's the key to his great undercover drug bust and he can't have that happen. Jesus!" she said and turned to Callaghan. "*It was him*. He's the one who got Sean out early. Don't you see it?"

Callaghan perched on the edge of the desk, arms crossed, head slowly going side to side in denial.

Ignoring him, she continued on. "McFarlane's been working this big operation for eight months. Eight bloody months. This would be his Rockstar moment—Terry McFarlane, the big hero." She framed the words in the air.

"All he's got standing in his way is this one girl, and she's about to bring his whole operation crashing down around him."

Callaghan lifted his head, still deadpan. "Listen, Terry goes off-script sometimes. We all know that. But murder? Kidnapping? C'mon. And how could he get Sean Clemmons out of prison?"

"He knows the system like the back of his hand. He's pulled strings, made sure his favorite informant is out there, mixing it up with all the gangs, bringing all that intel back to him. Next thing, Huia calls him up, demands he arrest them both…"

"Based on what? Her word?"

For a second, Nyree paused with her eyes narrowed at the images on the board, scenarios spinning through her brain. Brodie Skinner. Sean Clemmons. That gallery of rogues. "She's got proof. She wasn't stupid. She wouldn't call him up unless she's got absolute proof."

He tossed both hands in the air. "We didn't find any proof. We checked her room at Kelly's, her room at Annette's. We just about pulled the marae and the Māori community apart. There was nothing."

Nyree wasn't listening. Connections crashed through her mind, one after the other. "You're right. Go see the desk sergeant out front and find out who took that car out before we had it, and what days. Then get onto Christine. Find out what the hell was on that piece of paper in Huia's pocket. After that, track down bloody Terry McFarlane and get him into my office. And hurry."

CHAPTER 66

It just so happened that Callaghan clocked Terry McFarlane pulling into the police station lot as he got to the front desk. McFarlane skipped up the steps, stopped when he saw the look on Callaghan's face. Callaghan passed on Nyree's request to see him. When pressed Callaghan denied all knowledge of the reason, and got out as soon as he could. So, five minutes later, McFarlane appeared in Nyree's doorway with a quick knock, and peered in.

"You wanted to see me?"

She did a double-take. "Jeez, that was quick."

"I just got in."

She leaned around to check the hallway behind him, and fumbled the files on her desk. She wasn't ready. Didn't matter. "Close the door."

He gave it a look, switched his attention to her, then gingerly shut it. "This is all very serious. What's it about?"

"Sit down, Terry." She pulled herself together, closed down her laptop and moved it aside. "When was the last time you took the pool car out?"

He gave her a puzzled frown. "I don't use the pool car. What's this about?"

"Where were you last Wednesday?"

He blinked at her. Then the slimy smile formed. "What? You think I murdered Huia Coburn?"

"I'm simply asking the question."

His demeanor cooled. "If you're doing what I think you're doing, I'd back off pretty bloody quick if I was you."

"Well, if I've got this so wrong, why don't you tell me exactly where you were and what happened."

McFarlane's head jerked back. As if he didn't know. "When what happened?"

Nyree slammed a hand down on the desk, causing everything on it to jump. "Let's cut the bullshit, Terry. You were there—"

"—I what?"

"I'm giving you one chance to tell me what happened."

His features morphed into a look of disbelief. "You're off your nut."

"Did Huia call you? Demanding that you arrest Skinner? Or Clemmons? Or both."

"I don't believe this."

"Did Huia call you!"

He leaned hard in, fist pounding the desk, face flushed with anger. "No!"

Calm now, she sat back, adrenaline prickling her veins. "You called her on the burner phone we found under the bridge…remember? Blue cover, smudge down the back? And you knew exactly where she was. Because you carried out a Where's My Phone search for her."

"Oh, Jesus, change the record, Nyree."

"According to the report we got from forensics, that phone was clean. Not a whisker on it. Except for the battery." She let him squirm for a second. "It had a partial thumb print. Not enough to run through the database, but enough to make a match."

He swiped a knuckle under his nose, then folded his arms and chuckled without humor. "And you think it's mine?"

"You told her you needed proof. You couldn't arrest Skinner unless you had solid evidence. And that's what she gave you. But that evidence didn't just finger Skinner, did it? Huia unwittingly had something that pulled you into the picture. What did you do with that evidence, Terry? Burn it?"

McFarlane rocked his head back. "Oh, come on…"

"You took the pool car up to Rawiri's hut—"

"I just said I didn't use the pool car." His patience was thinning.

On a roll now, she continued on. "You told her to bring all the evidence. But nobody else had *so* much to lose, did they? Come on, explain. Where were you last Wednesday?" Before he could answer, the phone on her desk rang. An internal call. She glanced at it, considered ignoring it, then snatched it up. "What is it?"

"Callaghan here, Ma'am. I've got the schedule of officers who've taken the pool car in the past week. Terry's name isn't anywhere on it."

'Terry's name.' Like they were old friends. She knew Callaghan's allegiance to him; knew how Callaghan admired him. Just like the rest. The chill of betrayal gripped her as she hung up. Across the desk, McFarlane had obviously heard because he angled his head ever so slightly, that smartarse grin tugging back one side of his mouth.

"Well, I believe this little chat is over." He slapped both hands on his thighs and got up.

Nyree glared up at him. "Don't get too comfortable. I know it was you and I'll prove it."

He tipped his head. "Good luck with that, Nyree." Just as he opened the door, he turned back. "This is a tough job. I know that as much as anyone. You used to be a good cop. But ever since that kid of yours—"

"Don't you dare!" Flames burst in her gut. "You do not bring my son into this."

"You're finished, Nyree. You just don't know it yet."

Cheeks burning, blood coursing hatred through her veins, she jabbed a finger at him. "You do what you want. I know you murdered that innocent girl and her unborn baby, you put a child's life at risk, and you framed Danny Yelavich and Sean Clemmons for it. And God help me, I won't sleep till I see you pay for it."

"Get some counselling, Nyree. You should have had it years ago."

And he walked out leaving her gulping like a beached fish.

Nyree settled slowly back in her chair. All the blood that had rushed to her face quietly receded leaving her head swimming. What a bloody mess. He goaded her and she fell for it.

Of course, he'd run straight to Nolan. Nolan thought the sun shone out of McFarlane's arse.

And if she wasn't mortified enough at her own behavior, now, she realized with a dawning sense of dread, she'd probably just destroyed her own career.

CHAPTER 67

The pale blue hospital ward walls were bright with pictures of owls and trains, Disney cartoons and television characters. Nyree asked at the nurse's station and was directed three doors down to the room.

When she got there, she placed a hand on the handle, peered through the glass window in the door, and hesitated. Inside, she could see Kelly Holmes sitting at her daughter's bedside, reading her a story. The little girl lay wide-eyed, listening to her mother. Nyree didn't want to disturb them. She was about to abandon the visit and quietly leave, when Kelly glanced up, smiled, and waved her in.

"Nyree! Sorry, I mean, Inspector Bradshaw!" She beamed as Nyree pushed open the door and peered in.

"Nyree's fine." She returned a broad smile, found herself choking up at the sight of the child looking so well—the child she'd thrown everything into finding. That sweet little face looking up at her.

Kelly indicated a chair. "Come on in. Lily would love to see you again. She wasn't exactly herself when you saw her the last time, were you, baby?"

Nyree braced herself as Kelly angled a second seat into position at the bedside. "I know you're busy. It's so nice of you to come and see us." She grabbed Nyree's hand and drew her across to the bed where the bright, pink-cheeked, auburn-haired child looked up and smiled. "Baby, this is the lady who brought you home to Mummy."

"Hello, Lily. I won't disturb you."

"No, please," Kelly begged. "I've told her all about you, how hard you worked to find her. Haven't I, Sweetie?"

"Are you a police lady?" Lily asked. "My friend Brian says the police help people when they're in trouble."

Nyree felt a bubble of warmth well up from somewhere deep down. Something she needed. Especially now. "Yes, they do. And I'm very pleased to meet you at last, Lily. I can see your mum is reading you a story, so I won't keep her."

"You're leaving already? You only just…" Kelly's face flushed as she shook it away. "Sorry, you're probably incredibly busy, and here's me trying to make you stay longer. But it was really nice of you to come."

Nyree hesitated. "When you've got a sec, I need to have a quick chat with you."

"Well," she glanced back at Lily, "what about now?"

"Oh. Um…" She cast a worried look at the child.

"Come and sit down. Lily and I would love some company, wouldn't we sweetie?"

Nyree pulled her mouth into a wide, fake smile, and sat.

"What did you want to talk about?"

Wrinkling her nose, Nyree widened the smile. "It's nothing."

"Have they caught him?"

"Well, not quite."

Kelly's smile faded and her brow furrowed. "But you must know who did it. I mean, you've been working night and day on it. You know where Lily was."

"Well, that's the thing: I may need to talk to Lily when she's better."

"I've already asked her. She said she doesn't know anything."

"Are you sure? She didn't see anyone, see…anything?" Nyree asked cautiously.

Lily's smile had also faded and now her pale eyebrows had risen in the middle with worry.

"I don't want her upset. Please don't ask her anything just yet. When the other cop came in asking questions, I told him the same."

Nyree blinked. "Other cop? What other cop?"

"Um...McDonald...something like that?"

"McFarlane?"

"That's him. He was so nice. He said he'd been on the case and wanted to know how Lily was. But I told him the same thing—that she couldn't tell us anything at all. The doctors think she's traumatized. Any memory of it has totally gone. Which is a blessing." She stroked her daughter's hair back from her face, smiling down at her.

"Well, wasn't that nice of Detective McFarlane to come and see you? When was this, by the way?"

"Not long after she got here." Kelly pressed both hands between her knees. "So, what happens now? Do you keep looking for whoever did this?"

"We certainly do."

"How long do you search for?" The question came tentatively. As if Kelly didn't really want the answer.

"Until we have enough proof to charge him. We'll get him, Kelly. Don't worry about that." Easing herself out of the chair, she was suddenly aware of the wave of exhaustion washing through her. "I'd better run along and let you get back to your story."

"Thank you for coming."

"I'm just relieved to see you back together again," Nyree told her. "And I wouldn't have missed the chance to meet you, Lily. But I do have to go." She made a show of checking her watch. "Oh, look at the time. I have someone else I need to see."

With one last forced smile, she left without looking back.

She wasn't lying. She really did have someone to see. She should have done it sooner. She'd put it off, hoping some new evidence would turn up. When it hadn't, she'd called him; asked if she could meet.

All she was praying for was that Terry McFarlane hadn't beaten her to it.

CHAPTER 68

Her meeting with Nolan was scheduled for two o'clock. Three hours away.

Punishing her. Like a kid sent to the principal. And more than enough time for McFarlane to draw up a good defense plan. He probably called Nolan up the second he left her office; told him she was off her nut, that she should be sectioned.

Dammit, why was she even going there? As soon as she packed up her things, she'd put in for retirement. Should have long ago.

By the time she pulled into River Falls police station, the fury had abated and she'd resigned herself to her fate. In the adjacent parking slot, she noted the River Falls unmarked pool car and her muscles tensed.

Forcing herself to calm, she plucked her key from the ignition and got out.

Let it go. Just get your stuff and go home.

Inside, the desk sergeant was chatting to one of the uniforms. He gave Nyree a cool nod. "Ma'am."

"Any messages?"

"Let me check."

Next to her the uniform was filling out a form. She watched for a second, frowning. "What's that?"

Sergeant Berry came back with a couple of Post-it notes and handed them to her. "Pool car log, Ma'am."

Her mouth fell open. "You get the officer to fill out the log themselves?"

"I transcribe it into the system, Ma'am." Defensive now, he snatched back the clipboard while the officer next to her gave her a snotty look and headed out.

"So, if Terry McFarlane forgot to fill out your form, it wouldn't get logged. Is that what you're saying?"

"Well, I wouldn't know. I wasn't here until Thursday."

"But that means..."

Let it go. It's not your fight.

"Forget it." She made a dismissive noise at the absurdity, snatched up her messages and marched back to her office.

Halfway down the hallway, she squeezed past two uniforms who'd just exited the Incident Room carrying cardboard cartons.

"What's all this?" Nyree leaned in to see what the cartons contained.

"Evidence, Ma'am. We were told to box it up and send it back to Whangārei."

Inside the box she spotted a kid's coloring book in a plastic bag, the name Aroha scrawled on the cover.

Frowning, Nyree snatched it up before they moved on. "Aroha? Who's Aroha? Where's this come from?"

"Collected evidence from the Māori community up by the marae, Ma'am. That's one of the books they brought back. Apparently, one of the kids there was helping Huia Coburn to read and write."

"This Aroha?" She tapped the name on the book.

"Yes, Ma'am." The cop hesitated, suddenly guilt-stricken. "Well, there's nothing in them. Every page was searched. They're just kids' writing lessons."

"Right. Kids' writing lessons."

That meant Rawiri wasn't the only one spending time with Huia. Nyree dropped the book back into the box and headed straight to the car. No one had mentioned these books. No one had mentioned a kid named Aroha helping Huia. And knowing girls, if Aroha had been friendly enough to help Huia, what else would she do?

She hit the ignition, ignoring the accusing look on the cop's face in the car next to her, and swerved out of the lot, headed for the marae.

CHAPTER 69

No phones on the marae meant Nyree couldn't call ahead. Instead, she'd driven straight to the front door and asked to see Aroha—whoever she was.

Nyree waited, pacing while they located the girl. The instant Nyree saw her, she remembered. She was the child who'd interrupted Henare's first meeting with Kingi Hanson. She remembered him talking about it.

Possibly ten, eleven? Big brown eyes, a blush of pink coloring her milk chocolate cheeks, feet bare despite the inclement weather.

Smiling, Nyree bent to speak to her. "Hello, Aroha. You don't know me. I came here a few days ago asking about Huia."

Aroha cast a timid look back to her grandfather, who gave a small nod of encouragement.

"Huia was my friend." On hearing her own voice, Aroha pressed closer to the old man and clung even more tightly to his hand.

"Do you know why I'm asking? I'm a detective with the police, and I'm trying to find the person who hurt Huia." She drew out her ID, held it up so the girl could see it.

Another quick glance up at Hanson who responded with smile of encouragement and a squeeze of the hand.

"Mummy said Huia's with God now."

"That's right. And you were such a good friend, you were helping her to read and write, weren't you?" When the child simply blinked at her, Nyree added, "I saw your lesson books. That was very kind of you."

THE WATER'S DEAD

"Huia couldn't read. She asked me to help her."

"You were a very good friend." Nyree gave it a beat, let the child's nervousness abate a little more, then continued. "Did Huia ask you to do anything else for her?" At the flash of guilt in the child's eyes, Nyree said, "Like keeping anything for her?"

Aroha checked with Hanson again, then leaned forward, hand cupped to her mouth whispering, "I hid it. It was a secret."

"Do you know what I think? I think Huia would understand if you showed me. Do you think you could do that?"

Indecision crinkled her brow. For the longest time, Aroha searched middle ground as she weighed up Nyree's request. Then she looked up. "I helped her write in her diary. And I hid it."

Nyree's eyebrows shot up and her heart flipped. "Her diary?"

Aroha's brown curls bounced with a nod. "And she had all these photos and bits of paper she printed out. She couldn't read them so she asked me to read them for her." Now she'd found her voice, the nervousness receded.

No wonder the team dismissed Aroha. She would have been far too timid to speak.

"Can you show me the pieces of paper and photos she brought to you?"

She pointed back. "They're in my room." Another guilty glance up at Hanson, who said,

"It's okay. Just tell the truth."

Dropping his hand now, Aroha led Nyree to a small green, fibrolite house where she raced to a tiny room in back. Plain wood walls, nothing in the way of décor, Aroha's room consisted of a wire-wove bed with a patchwork coverlet, hand crocheted wool mat on the floor, and a small wooden dresser on which a hand knitted doll was slumped.

With her confidence growing by the second now, Aroha dropped to her knees to reach under her bed. Angling around, she lugged out a wooden box, perhaps a foot square. Nyree dropped to her knees, the box between them, hope blossoming in her breast like two kids finding a treasure trove.

Aroha held the box on her lap, both hands clamped over the lid while she regarded Nyree. "When the policemen came, I hid it in the gully cos Huia

301

told me not to show anyone."

Kneeling opposite the child, Nyree placed a reassuring hand on hers. "I promise you, this will help me find the person who hurt Huia. She would understand."

After considering Nyree's words for a moment, Aroha lifted the lid from the box and set it aside. Inside were layers of papers, printed emails, handwritten letters, print-outs of photographs. Nyree immediately recognized some of the photographs as being ones that Annette had sent through.

Aroha reached in, lifted a small book, and clutched it to her chest for a moment, considering her actions seriously, before offering it across to Nyree.

"And this is her diary?"

"I did the writing. Huia told me what to say."

Nyree opened the diary, flicking through pages of childish script until she hit the previous Tuesday, the day before Huia died.

Written in large, wobbly whorls, the entry read, *I called Mikfarlin again...*

Aroha pointed to the line. "I was going to put 'policeman', but Huia said to write his name." Flicking to an earlier page the writing was an almost entirely illegible. Unless you knew what you were reading. Heart sinking, she returned to the previous page.

...Meeting at Danny's at 4:30. I told him what Brodie was doing he said he'll see...

It could be argued that this was nothing more than a child's story. McFarlane's name was incorrectly spelled, and it wasn't even in Huia's hand. Setting the diary aside, Nyree turned her focus to the emails, letters and notes, probably taken from Brodie Skinner's house, probably in his handwriting. Then more printouts of photos, grainy but clearly showing Clemmons, Skinner, all taken from a distance—perhaps the next room.

Huia had taken huge risks to get these. It was far more than Nyree could have hoped for. But still nothing to connect McFarlane directly to her murder. Nyree flicked through the diary from beginning to end, and a card fluttered to the floor.

She picked it up, turned it. Didn't matter, she already knew exactly what it was. A business card with the name DS Terrance McFarlane on the front.

When she flipped it, a handwritten phone number on the back—the same number as the phone found under the bridge.

Tamping down her excitement, she said, "I know this is a big ask, but would you mind if I take this box back to my station with me? I'll be careful with it. I promise"

Aroha dug her teeth into her lower lip for a moment, then nodded.

"Thank you. Thank you so much."

Nyree got up and went for the car. Now she had to figure out how to handle this.

CHAPTER 70

Back in Whangārei, Nyree's head buzzed making connection on connection as she headed for her office. The minute she could put everything together, she'd go and see Nolan—finally prove who murdered Huia Coburn.

So transfixed was she, that as she hurried down the hallway to her office, she didn't notice Henare step out of Interview One until he called her back. Frustration prickling, she spun around. "Yes, what?"

"Could you spare a sec, Ma'am?"

Desperate to get to the computer, brow deeply furrowed, she paused. "I'm in a bit of a panic. Is it urgent?"

He tossed a quick glance back into Interview One, then closed the door. "Could be. I've been running a second interview with Sherilyn Grant."

"Come on, then." She tipped her head in the direction she was going and walked on. "So, what's Sherilyn got to say for herself?" She shouldered her door open, dumped the box on the desk, flicked on her laptop and sat. Then looked up.

"Well, come on. Spit it out."

"Sherilyn says that Sean Clemmons and Danny Yelavich took the body to the river and dumped her."

"Oh, yes, same hymn sheet."

Henare moved gingerly into her office. "She says they weren't the only two."

That sat her up. "So, who else was there?"

"She didn't know who he was. Older guy, suit but no tie, grey hair…"

The tiniest of smiles touched her lips. "Yeah. Terry bloody McFarlane. Is she saying he killed her?"

He jutted a lip, shrugged. "She doesn't know."

"Yeah, not much good, is it?"

"But according to Sean, he says he went up there with *a friend*."

"Of course. His mate Terry. Go on."

"The way she heard it, when Huia turned up it all went off. Sean and McFarlane yelling, Lily crying," he said, waving a hand. "Next minute, Huia wades in, yelling at McFarlane to arrest the bloody lot of them."

"Correct. And that's when she realized he wasn't there to help her—he was there to help himself. He wanted to get his grubby hands on the evidence she had. But this is all hearsay. So, what does she say happened next?"

"Terry told Huia and Lily to wait in the hut—"

"Shoved them in there, more like."

"—told them to just calm down while they worked out what they had to do next. When they opened the hut back up, Lily was gone."

"And they left them shut up in that hole while they came up with a plan." Nyree's blood began to boil all over again. The trauma that child must have gone through. As for Huia, she'd spent years battling to find her strength, to make herself heard. And when she did, she'd reached out for help, to Terry McFarlane—the only cop she knew. "So, who found her? McFarlane?"

"Nope. He told Sean and Danny to go. They went off with Skinner's dog—"

"Skinner's dog. God, the poor kid must have been terrified."

"They found her down by the waterfall. When they took her back to the hut, Huia was dead. Sean called up Sherilyn, got her to hitchhike up and look after Lily. Then Terry took them home."

The image hit Nyree like a brick. She didn't want to know, but had to ask. "Did Lily see Huia…y'know, afterwards?"

"I don't think so. Sean told Sherilyn she was covered over with her jacket when they got back."

"Small mercies." Nyree felt a wash of relief. "Trouble is, this is still hearsay, and it's Sherilyn's word against a cop. That's where it all falls short."

"Lily...?" he asked tentatively.

A quick headshake. "Too traumatized. Her mother won't let her speak about it."

He bunched his mouth, nodding. "Well, there is something else I found."

She waited. "Go on."

"You know that bit of paper that was in Huia's pocket?"

Her heart fell. She'd hoped for something new. "The ink was too washed out to read."

"I know. So, I called a mate down in forensics. He said the paper was a particular brand—high quality stuff. Very thin, but strong. Fine lines. It's all in the report."

Her pulse picked up a notch. "But...?"

"It had a particular tear pattern down the edge. Like a map of Bream Bay."

She opened her hands in confusion.

"The thing is..." He leaned to one side, plucked a notebook from his pocket. "I...um...found this. It's Terry McFarlane's."

Hope flooded like new rain. "Go on..."

"Well, I turned to the date Huia died, and..." He opened the notebook, swiveled it on the desk towards her. "That page is torn out."

CHAPTER 71

The issue was how to track him down. No way was McFarlane going to face up to Nyree again. First thing he'd do was go into defensive mode; pick up all the evidence, destroy what he could, discredit her. Hadn't he been doing that from the start?

Sitting across from her, Joe Henare called him and pressed the speakerphone button.

From the second he picked up, McFarlane sounded cagey.

"What is it?"

Henare's response sounded flat. "Yeah, gidday. Ah, listen, I wonder if I can have a quick word."

"What about?"

"Where are you?"

The long silence that followed was broken by the distant tinkle of a windchime. "Let me talk to Nyree."

Of course, he knew. She drew a nervous breath, folded one hand over the other on her desktop and leaned to speak. "I'm here, Terry. Where are you?"

The cogs of his mind must have been spinning. "What have you got?"

"Enough."

He let out a scathing snort. "Yeah, sure."

"Let's meet up and talk this out."

White noise hissing down the line and the occasional tinkle of the windchime, as if he was turning on the spot, scanning the landscape while his options formed and reformed in his mind. Then he came back. "It didn't happen the way you think."

"Then tell me what did happen. Let's see what we can do."

A resigned chuckle. "Yeah, that's right. We'll sort it. Everything'll be hunky dory."

"Talk me through it, Terry."

Another long silence. Nyree could just about see him, standing there massaging his forehead while those options diminished.

"I shoved her ... okay, I shoved her hard. She went backwards. Just went over. Flat on her back. Next thing, there's this look on her face. You know that look?"

Nyree said nothing. Just let him talk.

A shuddering breath down the line. "I couldn't fucking believe it. The thing was on the ground behind her. I didn't even see it. I mean, who leaves a fucking grubber there? Just dumped in the grass." A heavy sigh echoed down the line and into the room. "I...I panicked."

Henare scribbled something in his notebook, swiveled it towards her—*Bullshit! Face bruising.*

Nyree nodded agreement. "It was an accident, Terry. You should have come straight in."

"Don't give me that *it'll all be okay* bullshit. It's manslaughter. You know it. I know it." An audible swallow. "I'm not going to prison, Nyree. I'm not."

"It may not come to that," she began, but he'd already hung up.

Henare's face had paled. "What do we do, Ma'am?"

"We go pick him up, that's what." She plucked her keys from the desk and rounded her desk.

"I'll get an APB out on his car."

"Forget it. I know exactly where he is, but he won't be there long. Come with me."

"I'll follow," he said.

They jumped in their respective cars. She hit the ignition, stamped her foot on the gas and shot backwards, screeched to a halt, then bulleted out of the park. As soon as she hit the main street, she hit the gas. Siren blaring, lights blazing, swinging around traffic, blasting the horn when the traffic up ahead failed to move fast enough. The address was still in the GPS but she kept her eyes riveted to the road ahead, foot pressed flat to the floor until the entrance to the dirt road loomed into view.

Slowing, she checked back and forth, then swerved into the lane. Behind her, Henare was nowhere to be seen. Didn't matter. He'd catch up.

Cutting the lights and siren, she eased the car over the next two k's, bumping over potholes, stones clacking on the underside of the car. As she approached Sherilyn Grant's house, she slowed and gently rounded the last bend, then jerked the wheel as a dark grey Honda lurched out in front of her, swinging hard around her.

"You bastard!"

She slammed a foot on the brake and threw the car into reverse so hard Nyree felt the seatbelt cut in and her head jerk forward. When the rear of the car hit the scrub behind, she smashed the car into drive and tore after him.

Where the hell was Henare?

One hand white-knuckling the wheel, steering this way and that, Nyree picked up her phone and dialed. Three rings; four. "C'mon, pick up, pick up."

At the end of the lane, the Honda loomed into view momentarily, then swung out onto the main road with a squeal of tires, and took off. Nyree tossed the phone onto the passenger's seat, shot a quick glance to her right, checking for traffic, then spun the wheel and followed.

Screaming past traffic, weaving between cars, she snatched up her phone and dialed again. "Come on, pick up, pick up, Terry."

Traffic parted as she flew past. Up ahead, McFarlane, fifty meters ahead. Suddenly, the Honda spun left, the back end sliding out before he got control and took off again.

"Where the hell are you going?"

The GPS indicated a dead-end lane, so she slowed the car, indicated and turned after him. Dread oozed through Nyree's veins like an oil slick. "Where are you going, Terry?"

With her mind reeling, she kept a steady hand on the wheel, eyes glued to the car ahead.

She cruised after him for some while, the dirt lane rocking and rolling beneath, until the brush either side gave way to an open vista of deep, blue ocean just beyond a scrubby outlook area surrounded by a solid, white painted barrier.

McFarlane was already out of his car. Seemingly oblivious to the arrival of a second car, he stood looking out over the immense view of sky meeting sea; of seabirds wheeling carelessly overhead; of the crash of the sea on rocks far below while the chill breeze swirled.

Nyree got out of the car. Waited.

No sign of Henare. Only the sound of the sea and the birds and the wind.

Without turning, McFarlane spoke. "You know, this is the New Zealand I grew up in. White beaches you could spend the whole day on and never see another soul. Long golden summers, soft winters. Good people. That was all I wanted." He tipped his head back, eyes closed, letting the memories wash over him. Then he turned, an aching sadness in his expression. "I wanted to make everything the way it used to be. You know? Easy days when you didn't have to worry where the kids were. No one prowling the internet trying to get them hooked on drugs, or raping them, killing them. Innocent kids." His features puckered, eyes squeezed shut as he did a slow headshake. "I wanted to make a difference. I wanted to make it good again." An all-consuming ache bled into his voice.

Nyree could only shrug, helpless. "That's why we all do it, Terry."

He drew a long, slow breath, and turned to regard the distant horizon again. Blue meeting blue. Gulls flying free. The Tasman Sea air riffling his hair. "Have you even noticed the poverty around here? I mean, seriously noticed it?"

"Of course, I have."

His head was already shaking. "I really don't think so. You're privileged. You're one of the blessed; good job, rich—"

"*Rich?* On my salary? Give me a break."

"Look around." He gestured widely at the surrounding area. "Did you see Sherilyn Grant's place? It's a dump. I wouldn't put my worst enemy in a place like that. And you know what?"

"We're all doing our best, Terry."

"That's a bloody mansion compared to what some families up here live in."

"I can't do anything about that."

He chuckled again. This time with real humor. His head dropped, finger and thumb pressed to his eyes. He lifted his gaze, regarding her. "You're unbelievable." A sad shake of the head. "You uphold the law. You're the big I Am. But you don't give a flying fuck about the people; what they're living with. The bloody disasters unfolding day after day after day."

"That's not my job, Terry. This is my job. This is what I do." She gave him a minute. "Come back with me. Let's sit down. See what we can sort out."

He snorted. "That won't take long." He moved to the barrier, sat on the upper board and sat watching her.

Nyree sucked in a hard breath. "Terry, don't." One hand up, she moved slowly forward. "Come back with me. We'll work it out."

He stood gazing far out to sea for a moment. Then turned, looked her straight in the eye. "You are so naïve."

Behind her, the sound of a car, gravel under tires, stones clacking. It rounded the last bend and stopped—Henare.

Nyree felt her shoulders relax, felt a sense of calm flood. Neither of them spoke as Henare pulled the car to a halt, and got out. Tucked his keys into his pocket as he regarded them both.

"So, what's happening."

"We're taking you in," she told McFarlane. "Joe?" She waved Henare over.

He stood firm. She turned to wave him on. He was staring at her. Stock still. Just staring.

"Well, come on!" She gestured toward McFarlane.

Their eyes met and a silent message ran between them.

"Sorry, Ma'am."

"Sorry Ma'am wha...?" A wave of pinpricks ran over her skin as the light dawned. Seeing it now, clicking that last piece into place, she tipped her head slowly back, eyes closed and turned on the spot. "You are bloody kidding me."

"Nope." McFarlane slowly rose to his feet. "Joe here's been working with me up north. See, I told you. I will not let you fuck this up. People need us."

"Why, Joe?" she demanded. "You're a good cop. You're going to throw it all away after this…arsehole?"

"It's about the people. My people."

Suddenly, the words hit her. "Your people…? What…?" Then the second wave hit. "Oh, for crying out loud. You're not working to bring the drug traffickers in." Not a question. A statement. "You're working *with* them."

"There's no money up here."

"Oh, *of course*. This is all purely altruistic. All out of the goodness of your hearts. Nothing in it for Terry McFarlane." She threw out her hands. "And what about the addicts?" She stabbed a finger back down the road. "What about those poor bastards at the other end—those whose lives are ruined by this shit?"

McFarlane spread his hands. "Oh, you mean those poor, entitled arseholes down in Auckland with more money than they know what to do with. Those poor sods driving Mercs and eating out down at the Viaduct every night? You mean those poor people?"

"The product doesn't stay here in the north," Henare said. "Just the money."

"And this is all to help them? What a pair of holy crusaders you two turned out to be. Jesus." It was as though Nyree's entire world had flipped. As if she'd suddenly woken up to some parallel universe. Nothing seemed real. Everything she'd believed had actually been hanging on the edge of a lie— Henare's edgy relationship with McFarlane; the interference in her investigation. All blocking her. All because at least one of these two knew exactly how and why Huia Coburn died; knew exactly where Lily Holmes was every minute of the investigation.

Two innocents: collateral damage. Nothing more.

Silence spooled out for the longest time. There was one more question. They all knew it. She didn't want to ask. She had to. "So, what happens now?"

CHAPTER 72

McFarlane took a long slow breath. "Well, it's a shame. You came up here, trumped up charges, yelling all your accusations. Henare was here. You witnessed it, didn't you, mate."

He looked guilt stricken, but said, "Was terrible." He dropped his gaze.

McFarlane picked it up. "See? Totally unhinged. Nothing we could do."

Nyree's blood froze in her veins.

McFarlane continued as though he was already recounting the story to Nolan. "We tried to stop you, Nyree. But you were completely off your gourd. Nolan knew that. Jesus, everyone knew it." He bunched his mouth, a slow shake of the head.

"You cannot hope to get away with this. There's evidence."

"Not anymore."

"Unfortunately, Huia's diary disappeared straight after you found it," he told her mildly. "Joe here made sure of that, didn't you, mate."

Henare said nothing. He clearly wasn't there by choice.

"What's he got on you, Joe? Let's work it out."

But McFarlane carried on. "That diary would have told a totally different story. And we couldn't have that, could we?"

"Jesus." The word slipped her lips. The extent of how much they'd tidied up after themselves came wave after wave.

Heart in her mouth, adrenaline pumping, Nyree spun around and made a dash for the car. In that same instant, Henare flashed across, cutting her off.

His vice-like grip clamped down on her arm and in a single move, he whirled her around, swinging her into a bear hug. Arms pinned, breath squeezed out of her, she fought and wrestled against him, kicking and grunting as he held her. He lifted her, feet coming off the ground as McFarlane opened the boot.

"Well, come on!"

She felt Henare take a deep breath, and she went over, the hard edge of the boot scraping her thigh, head hitting the thin boot carpet with a thud, hands pressing her back as the lid of the boot came down and darkness enveloped her.

Outside she could hear angry voices, then car doors opening and closing as the suspension took their weight. Already her fingers were searching for the catch, hunting for release as the stink of tires and dirt and rubber enveloped her. The engine started. Her only hope was to get out. Once they opened the boot, she'd never overpower them. All the way, she yelled and screamed, hammered on the metal lid as she bumped and rocked in the dark. Back over the stony road until they eventually swerved back onto the main road and the hum of the tires on blacktop picked up.

They wound over roads, up hills and down valleys. No point yelling and wasting her breath. Who was going to stop a cop? Who would believe her over them? So, she lay quiet, mind racing, fingers searching until they came to the metal bar pressed into her shin—a wheel wrench.

Finally, the car cornered, bumped over stony ground, then came to a stop. Nyree writhed, twisting around, working the wrench up into her hands. Then she lay ready, like a spring.

The instant the boot opened and Henare leaned to grab her, she swiped out with the wheel wrench, but he blocked it, pulling it from her grasp.

"Oy, we'll have none of that." This from McFarlane. "Just get out."

She emerged into the light to find herself at Rawiri's hut—the very scene of Huia Coburn's death.

"What's this? Poetic justice?"

McFarlane stuck his hands on his hips and looked around. The semi-circle of dense, ragged bush surrounding them, the oily surface of the pond, the silence. "This scene's been gone over, well and truly. Ground's soft, easy digging. You're going to vanish, Nyree. I wish it hadn't come to this, but like I said, I'm not going away."

"They'll find me." Although she didn't feel so sure. He was right. This area would eventually be forgotten. "And who's going to take the hit? Who have you got lined up to go down for Huia's murder?"

"Well, Danny Yelavich is doing pretty well for that at the moment. What do you reckon, Hens?"

She watched them for a second. McFarlane so cocky. Henare, not so much. Head down, biting his lip.

"Joe. You can get out of this. You were coerced by a senior officer."

He said nothing.

She stepped back, stepped back. Then spun around and ran.

Through the bushes, footsteps behind her, branches raking her face, feet pounding, heart thumping. She didn't look back. She could hear Henare—right behind her. Twigs snapped as she leapt over fallen logs and dived under heavy branches. She ducked and dived, felt another vice-like grip grab her shoulder just as she broke into a clearing and her senses caught up.

Right in front of her the gaping wound of Mason's Rock, water flooding over the edge. And twenty mourners with the kaumatua, all gaping at her.

CHAPTER 73

Henry Patton was on the desk when she arrived. Once again, he looked up and smiled.

"Back again already?"

"Sucker for punishment," she said and looked around. Dingy as ever. How do you build a brand-new prison facility, paint it with light, bright colors, stick in all the latest amenities, and still have it feel this miserable?

He cleared the paperwork, then pressed the button on the wall. The heavy grid door slid across and Nyree stepped inside.

"Just as well you called ahead," Henry said. "He was just off for a walkabout."

"Inside, I guess."

Henry chuckled. "Oh, we don't let them out. We wouldn't see them again." Henry slid a cardkey down the door slot.

Moving through the same security procedures, the same metal detectors, the same rigors as every other time, Nyree held her heart in her mouth.

What would his reaction be? Would he even see her?

A surly prison officer accompanied her into the visitation room where she sat at the same table as the last time she was here. It wasn't until she'd placed her purse on the floor and clasped her hands on the tabletop that she realized how badly her hands were shaking. She had just taken a deep, calming breath when the door opened and Tony appeared, cuffed hand and foot, a guard at his side.

Nyree jumped to her feet, suddenly lost for words.

He sauntered across and sat opposite her. "I heard McFarlane topped himself."

"News travels fast." She lowered herself onto the chair.

Dimples formed on his cheeks when he smiled. She'd forgotten them. Those same dimples she kissed when he was a child. That smile could light a fire in her heart. All those years lost. "The jungle drums. What else are you gonna do in here?" He leaned back, head tipped, regarded her. "He was a bastard. No one's going to miss him."

She frowned as the memory of the man came to her. A man literally on the edge. "I certainly won't."

"Word has it he was planning to have Sean take the fall."

"That's what it looks like. I wondered why Sean would do something as stupid as terrifying Emere Grady while I was there, then vandalizing my house."

"Good old McFarlane," Tony said with a grin. "He really goes the extra mile."

They sat silent for a moment, then Tony said, "What about the other bloke?"

"Henare? He'll go down. Turned out, he'd let a couple of deals go through. Guys he knew. McFarlane found out, and that was it. McFarlane held it over him. Shame," she added. "He was a good cop."

Tony's mouth twisted in thought. Just the way it did when he was six. That image snatched her breath away. "I remember your first day of school."

The grin dropped. "You wouldn't remember my last day of school."

Guilt washed through her. She dropped her gaze. Then lifted it. "I can't change the past. Only the future. And that's down to you."

His eyes stayed on her. Not moving. "Do you remember what I said last time you were here?"

"You told me not to come back."

"But you're still here."

"And so are you," she said, eyebrows raised in question.

"I've got my reasons."

"Which are?"

"You'll find out." He gave it a second, then said, "And what about you? Why are you here?"

Every nerve jangled. For a brief second, she found herself fighting back the impending tears. She pushed them aside, calming herself.

"You're my son, Tony. I've been a shit mum in the past. I know that. But I'll *always* love you. No matter what. And I'll always come back. I will never give up on you. Not ever. For better or worse, I'm afraid you're stuck with me."

For the longest moment, his dark stare bored into her. Motionless. Then he drew in a deep breath and heaved out a weary sigh. "Then I guess I'll be seeing you again."

A smile formed on the edge of her mouth. "You better believe it," she said.

THE END

Other titles by Catherine

The Elizabeth McClaine Thriller Series
    The Candidate's Daughter
    Child of the State
    A Stolen Woman

Standalone Titles
    Last Seen Leaving
    The Contestant
    Dropping Dead in Delby Rish

Acknowledgements

There was a point in time where this novel became universally known among my friends as "This bloody book", and if it weren't for the love, support, and a certain amount of nagging by some very important and influential people in my life, it never would have been finished.

First and foremost, Dale Bell. Dale was a neighbor whom I barely knew before asking her to board with me while she built her new house. With her, she brought two dogs, a range of dietary requirements her daughter described as being, "Like feeding a toddler," an actual belly-laugh-a-day, and more encouragement and love than I could ever have dreamed of.

Andrea Scott, whose advice on forensic procedure and how a dead body presents in situ both grossed me out and intrigued me at the same time. Her guidance also gave me the chance to add authenticity to this book.

To my dear friend and fellow writer, Jill Nojack. Jill volunteered to be my first reader and first proof reader. Her kind words were so encouraging, she's the reason I kept going.

To all my early readers, including Margaret Chettleburgh, Margaret Matthews, and many others, whose eagle eyes for typos prevented the book from reading like an English to Russian language lesson.

To my publicist, Karen McKenzie of Lighthouse PR, whose experience, contacts, knowledge of the industry, and incredible gift for quelling the nerves was amazing.

To Nationwide books for their fabulous support in getting this book into stores.

And last, but certainly not least, to all my readers – both long-time followers, and new, I thank you. I'm humbled by your willingness to take in my words and come along for the ride with me.

That's why I write.

Catherine

One Last Thing

Thank you for buying and reading my work. Writing a book is a long and lonely process, so when I send a new story out there, I love to hear from my readers.

The next page will give you an opportunity to share your thoughts about this book with other readers, as well as with your friends on Facebook and Twitter. If you enjoyed the read, I'd be honored if you'd take a moment to spread the word. On digital, you'll find most of the message already set up, so it should only take a moment. (If you really loved it, a review on your favorite book retailer or Goodreads—even one line to let others know what you thought of the book—would be appreciated more than you know)

Catherine.